**Lauren McCrossan** was a City lawyer who could not swim when she met her professional surfer husband, Gabe. She is now a full-time author and magazine journalist who surfs her way around the world. Her favourite surf destinations are Hawaii, Ireland and south-west France. Her least favourite is the reef that nearly killed Lauren and left her with a Harry Potter scar to remember it by. Lauren's second novel, *Angel on Air*, was longlisted for the Romantic Novel of the Year Award 2003. Her first novel, *Serve Cool*, is also available from Time Warner.

'Warm and wonderfully witty. A good story either brings a smile to your face or a lump to your throat and preferably both, and *Water Wings* does just that. It's funny and moving and the characters stayed in my mind long after I'd finished reading' Jane Wenham-Jones

'Very funny. Very heart-warming' Carole Matthews

'Sharp, hilarious and poignant, *Water Wings* is the sort of book long hot baths are made for' Imogen Edward-Jones

'Perfect escapism' *OK!*

'A funny, pacey take on temptation' *Cosmopolitan*

Also by Lauren McCrossan

*Serve Cool*
*Angel on Air*

# Water
# Wings

LAUREN McCROSSAN

**time**warner
paperbacks

A *Time Warner* Paperback

First published in Great Britain as a paperback original in 2005
by Time Warner Paperbacks

A CIP catalogue record for this book
is available from the British Library.

ISBN 0 7515 3583 4

Typeset in Berkeley by M Rules
Printed and bound in Great Britain by Clays Ltd, St Ives plc

Time Warner Paperbacks
An imprint of
Time Warner Book Group UK
Brettenham House
Lancaster Place
London WC2E 7EN

www.twbg.co.uk

*This story is for*
*Frances Tighe-Fitzgerald, a truly*
*beautiful person who always loved the ocean.*
*And*
*My favourite surfer, Gabriel*

# Acknowledgements

Thank you so much to all the people out there who buy, read, sell, review and promote my books. Without all of you, of course, my fictional world would have no purpose. I hope you enjoy the ride . . .

A huge thanks as always to my mum, dad and brothers for everything you do. Also to my unique family of McCrossans, McCaffertys, Whites, Higgins and Grattans, and all my close friends who give me endless support.

Thank you to my fab agent Jonathan Lloyd, a genuine diamond among *fugazzis*; to all the Curtis Brown crew, especially Keirsten Clark (good luck!); to my editors Tara Lawrence and Jo Coen for your help and guidance; to Sarah Rustin and all at Time Warner.

I could not have written *Water Wings* and stayed sane throughout the process without the particular help of a few people I would especially like to mention. A big thank you, even bigger hugs and a mini *shaka* to:

Gabe – who made me write, made me surf and made me who I am today. xx

Darcey – our little surfer girl who has enough character to fill a thousand books.

Debbie – my sister for ever who always makes me giggle.

Rob and Vicki – fantastic friends, surfers and Olympians. You are pure gold.

The Fitzgeralds – my second family in Bundoran who make me feel like I have come home. Thanks especially to Richard and my brilliant advisor Maíre.

The rest of my Irish surf crew – including Matt Britton at Tyrconnell Cottages, John Macarthy, Dave Blount, Adam 'nae bother te ya' Wilson and Handsome Frank. Also Joel Conroy and Mick Doyle – the coolest 'media darlings' in town.

Mandy and Neale (aka Mr and Mrs Haynes!), Madeline and Buzz – life would not be the same without you guys.

Michaela – your personality always inspires me. Love to Molly and baby Gabriel.

Kelly – my treasured friend with wonderful wit. Maybe one day you'll be able to surf like me!

All my surfing buddies – especially those at Quiksilver, Roxy, Na Pali, Carve, Surf Europe and Surfgirl.

*Mahalo* and Love always
xx Lauren

# Water Wings

# CHAPTER ONE

# *Butterfly*

'Your character doesn't have motivation. You're a feckin' chicken nugget. Sorry to disappoint you, Miss Armstrong, but this isn't Hollywood and you're definitely no Nicole bloody Kidman. Now do you think you could just get out there and be a breaded savoury snack or do you need me to give you some character motivation? As in my boot up your arse.'

'Bloody cheek,' I mutter, grabbing my Captain Chicken bag and tripping over my giant orange claws to make a hasty exit. 'He doesn't know raw talent when he sees it. I'm an actress, I'm too good for this stuff.'

I ignore the jeers from passing young truants as I make my way along Dublin's busiest shopping zone, Grafton Street, while trying to blend into the background. Not an easy task considering I am a three-foot-wide chicken nugget with a barbecue-dip hat, chicken-claw feet and a built-in Captain Chicken soundtrack playing at full volume from speakers concealed somewhere about my giant person.

How did it come to this? At what point did my status change from up-and-coming-actress-partaking-of-stopgap-jobs-to-get-by to stopgap-job-full-time-loser-pretending-to-be-up-and-coming-actress? I am thirty-one and ten days old. I have been dreaming of seeing my name in lights for as long as I can remember. Thus far my greatest achievement is playing a rollerblading granny in a dentures advert and teaching drama to disinterested kids in schools in order to get my Equity card.

My school careers officer always told me I had unrealistic goals. Mind you, he also recommended nursing or childcare to ninety-five per cent of the girls in my year. The other five per cent he assumed would be pregnant before careers became an option so he didn't waste his time. Very progressive education. Perhaps I should have listened to my parents. The academically brilliant Georgina and Frank Armstrong. My father, a successful barrister, smiled knowingly every time I mentioned 'the acting lark', as he likes to call it, which he also combined with a fatherly expression of derision and sympathy. My mother always presumed my dream would be to follow her into the numerically baffling world of accountancy. My younger brother Ed and I were even expected to enjoy 'challenging' ourselves with Mensa brainteaser books and Pythagoras puzzles. No chance of a family game of Hungry Hippos in our house on Christmas Day. Ed, now a barrister with a swotty barrister girlfriend called Tania, excelled at figuring out how old A is if B is four times as old as C and D were a week ago last Tuesday, while I tended to conclude 'Who the hell cares?' or often 'How the fuck am I supposed to know?' I was an artist, not a mathematician. Nevertheless, Mum stoically resisted my pleas to be sent to stage school, insisting that I 'Leave the dreadful *Fame* rubbish to the Americans' and adding, 'Anyway, legwarmers make your ankles look chubby.' That is my problem. I have been mentally scarred by my brainiac family. (Humour me; I need to lay the blame for my failure somewhere.)

I rub my orange gloves together to warm my hands against the stinging February chill and exhale heavily. The sound reverberates around the inside of my costume and comes back at my eardrums in the form of a chorus of sighs.

2

Oh come on, Milly, I scold myself, it's not that bad, and besides, at least no one will recognise you in this get-up.

'Fuck me!' yells a voice from the other side of the street. 'If it isn't Milly Armstrong.'

*I want to die.*

Turning my head, as much as I can turn it independently of the ton of padding around my shoulders, I glance nervously towards the voice. As if I need a positive identification. I could never forget the voice of the man I loved. Love. Now under normal circumstances, bumping into an ex-boyfriend I still hold a torch for would be bad news. Bumping into an ex-boyfriend whom I still hold an entire avenue of streetlights for while dressed as a chicken nugget is like seeing Kate Adie running breathlessly into your town wearing a flak jacket. You just know something disastrous is about to occur.

I blush under the several inches of yellow face paint as the beautiful Dan Clancy strides towards me; I silently wish I had worn some lip-gloss. Although what that could possibly add to my current attire I am at pains to know. My eyes lock on to the figure emerging from the crowds of shoppers and refuse to budge, my heart melting in a totally non-feminist fashion with every step he takes.

Dan Clancy is over six foot tall, slim yet hunky, and has a simply perfect face framed by relaxed rich-chocolate curls. Those mild hazel eyes, that soft mouth, the black wool overcoat over a crisp white shirt and grey trousers . . . I hold my breath. The whole package is a fabulous advert for the male species. In fact, Dan Clancy is so perfect I swear God must have put in overtime on this one creation. Lisa Stansfield may have been 'All Woman', but Dan Clancy is 'All Man and Some'. He is also one of those men touched by the wand of the pretty fairy but only just enough to make him crazily gorgeous without appearing effeminate or childish. Add to that the fact that my ex-boyfriend is now Ireland's brightest acting star and he is nothing short of stunning. He was my

3

first Irish love. My only Irish love. I love him still. I can't help myself.

So, you may wonder, why did I let this one slip through the net? In truth, fuck knows. I have asked myself the same question for the last year, ten days and two hours. (Sad.) Some people assume he dumped me, but of course that's not true. I simply agreed to a . . . how shall I put this? To a more 'spacious' relationship in order to give our 'art' room to breathe. Dan's career subsequently blasted into aerobic overdrive while mine spluttered and gasped for air. I knew I should have handcuffed him to my bed and never let him go. In fact, the way he looks today, that could still be an option.

I realise Dan is staring at me, his familiar lopsided smile playing on his distinctly suckable lips and a look of sympathy in his doe-like eyes.

*Don't pity me, please, just take me home and ravish me.*

'How's it going, Milly?' Dan asks, his breath visible in the air between us.

*How do you think? Look at the state of me, for heaven's sake.*

'Fine, marvellous, great, just great,' I stutter. 'Dan, what a lovely surprise, I haven't seen you for, ooh, yonks.'

*Why right now then, oh cruel fate?*

'I know, Milly, I'm sorry,' he says, stepping close enough that I can inhale his aroma – 212 Men with a hint of irresistible pheromones. 'I've been so busy with work, you know. Castings, meetings, trips to the States, the usual stuff.'

I nod knowingly, as if my life is also dogged by the same trauma of success.

'Sam has me in mind for a big project, so I'm back and forth to Hollywood every five minutes.'

'Sam?' I whimper.

'Sam Mendes,' Dan replies nonchalantly, as if referring to the local corner-shop owner. 'He's a great guy.'

*Of course he is.*

I smile with gritted teeth as I visualise a chasm opening between us. Dan and I are living in different worlds. Only a year ago we were two inseparable aspiring actors practising scripts together in bed, the pages crumpled by our pre-reading frantic sex. Now Dan has entered the Hollywood set and here I am flogging poor-quality deep-fried poultry to impolite shoppers to pay off my overdraft. As we lapse into an uncomfortable silence, my mouth becomes dry. My tongue, which not so long ago would have merrily licked chocolate body paint off this man's most intimate parts, retracts to the back of my throat, embarrassed by my situation. What can I say to him? We have nothing in common any more. Dan's awareness of conversational etiquette unfortunately fills the silence.

'So, Milly,' he begins, his Irish lilt disguised by a thick Shakespearean drawl, 'tell me what you've been up to.'

*Do I have to?*

I hop from one giant claw to the other and stare at the pavement.

*Dear God, if you were ever planning to send an earthquake rippling through Ireland, now would be a very good time.*

'Well,' I cough, 'I'm, you know, doing this and that and the other and, um, various acting jobs here and there and, ooh, let me see . . .'

Dan reaches out a long-fingered tanned hand to touch my bare forearm and looks at me with what could be empathy, sympathy or simple condescension. I squirm, blushing from the arm upwards under his touch.

'And, er, I still go to lots of castings just like in the good old days and my agent, Gerald, well he is so positive that some day soon I will get that one big break and . . .'

I cringe at my own desperate tone. Why do dreams seem so good until you have to put them into words? Who am I trying to kid, Dan or myself?

'Anyway,' I sniff, avoiding his piercing gaze, 'in between I do these promotional jobs just to make sure I am financially secure, prepare for the future, you know. Some of them are really brilliant anyway. Only last week I got paid seventy euros to hand out free samples of a new alcopop in a pub in Temple Bar for the night. Easy money.'

My voice cracks and runs out of steam like an ancient train engine on its last ascent to the scrapyard. Which, incidentally, is infinitely more glamorous than I feel at this moment. Why can't I bump into ex-boyfriends (this one in particular) when I'm looking like an unflustered goddess of a magical world? Why do they always crop up when I'm having an ugly day or a bad hair day or a bad everything day? When I am looking like a desperado who hasn't got over him yet. Why? Because I *am* a desperado who hasn't got over him yet, and I just know the truth is written all over my face paint.

'You're looking great, Mimi,' Dan whispers to my down-turned head.

I gasp at his use of the pet name he once gave me.

'Still a size eight under all that padding?'

'Hmm, mmm,' I nod, sucking in my size-ten-in-some-shops-size-twelve-in-most stomach. 'And I'm still five foot seven . . .'

'In two-inch heels.'

Dan finishes my sentence for me with a companionable smile so warm it acts like Superglue on the pieces of my broken heart, sticking them firmly together as my eyes lock on his. I smile back while trying to silence the thoughts in my head. Suddenly the words I intended to keep private drop into my lungs and are forced out of my mouth before I can control them.

'I've missed you, Dan,' I say so loud that it makes me jump.

'You too,' Dan replies, this time with sincerity.

*YES!*

'We must meet up for a coffee some time,' he adds to my flushed face.

I nod my barbecue-dip hat enthusiastically and wrinkle my nose against the cold breeze that rattles down Grafton

Street. A chiffon scarf blows past in the wind and comes to rest on Dan's shoulder, nestling into his neck. I cannot tear my eyes away from his and my lips are in spasm from their desire to kiss him. So much for women's lib.

'Coffee would be lovely, Dan,' I breathe in my best seductive tone. 'How about right now?'

'Wight now?' squeaks a voice so shrill it could shatter glass. 'Ooh, we couldn't possibwy do coffee wight now, Pumpkin, we've got a kazillion things to do, and anyway, you naughty boy, Mr Coffee is bad for Pumpkin's kidney widneys, isn't he?'

I stare open-mouthed at the talking object on Dan's shoulder and emit an audible gasp when I realise that the long yellow scarf attached to his arm is in fact a very blonde, very tall, very *very* thin woman. I peer at the creature while it nuzzles into Dan's neck as if it belongs there, assuring myself that it is human. I conclude that the pillow-like blowjob lips give it away, not to mention the two perfect grapefruits stuck to its chest where its boobs should be.

'Forgive me,' Dan interrupts before my bewildered stare develops into a wide-eyed gape. 'This is Roma.'

It bloody well would be, wouldn't it? Trust him to have a girlfriend named after a jar of pasta sauce.

*Girlfriend.* My brain has already plucked the word from its dictionary and is swinging it behind my eyes before Dan has even uttered it. I quickly clamp my lips together to conceal the sounds of desperation that are crashing around in my chest. Hold on, maybe she's not his girlfriend. I mean, he has been flirting with me for the last ten minutes, but then again he is Dan Clancy, the natural-born flirt. Perhaps they are just really good friends. Why then is she kissing his neck like that, and where the hell does she think she is putting her left hand? All right, so maybe she is his girlfriend, but maybe Dan has just realised he still loves me. Yes, that's it, that scenario I can work with.

'So, Pumpkin,' Roma tweets, offering a small collection of

insect bones for me to shake hands with, 'are you going to introduce me to your wittle fwiend?'

I feel like a hamster being tormented in a pet shop.

'Roma, this is Milly,' Dan smiles stiffly, 'my . . . an old . . . an old friend of mine.'

Now there is a lot wrong with that sentence, 'old' and 'friend' being two words I find myself disagreeing with. 'This is Milly, the love of my life' would have been more acceptable, I think.

Roma raises an eyebrow and purses her inflatable mouth until her face is almost entirely obscured by her lips.

'Milly,' she repeats, although it sounds more like Miwwy. 'What a sweet costume. What are you?'

*What am I? Do the Captain Chicken tasty nugget soundtrack, the smelly pile of nugget samples and the distinctly nuggety appearance of my attire not give you a clue?*

'I'm duck pâté in a biscuit crumb,' I reply drily.

To which Roma nods her head excitedly like a plastic dog in the back window of a Ford Capri. Not that I am prone to making stereotypical assumptions about people, but by the way Roma is clinging to Dan's arm I assume that her head is so full of air her minuscule body will take off if she ever lets go.

'Try one, they're really yummy,' I say, thrusting the box of greasy nuggets in Roma's face. (My attempt to assist gravity in keeping the skinny cow on the ground.)

'Ooh, no no, I couldn't, Miwwy. This body is meat fwee, gwuten fwee and fat fwee, isn't it, Pumpkin?'

'You don't say, Roma, well that is a surprise,' I scowl, while suppressing the urge to shove every nugget I've got left down her emaciated excuse for a throat.

How can Dan love this thing? She may be a woman on the inside, but just look at the outside; it's a skeleton with silicon implants. And what is with all the 'Pumpkin' shit? Dan Clancy is not the 'Pumpkin' sort, and besides, if he had to be any sort of vegetable at all, it would be a much more sleek and sexy one, like a . . . like a . . .

8

I sniff and dejectedly tap my claw, stuck for the appropriate vegetable to represent this god of a man. Jesus, my life becomes sadder by the second.

'Right then,' Dan coughs uncomfortably when it is clear that our conversational triangle is losing its shape, 'we had better be off. Roma's got a shoot.'

*By that I assume you mean fashion rather than bang bang. Shame.*

'And I have some people to see.'

The emphasis on the word 'people' makes it clear that Dan moves in circles where his 'people' meet their 'people' and blah-de-blah. I am embarrassed by my own normality (abnormal costume aside).

'Ooh yes, I have got a wovely wittle shoot and we wouldn't want to intewwupt your, um, darwing wittle job,' Roma giggles, denting my pride beyond recognition.

'Work? Oh, what this? Ha ha,' I laugh too loudly. 'Oh, I don't really see this as work. It's more of a research thing for me as an actress, and besides, the boss is a real gem. Fab to work for, really good fun. He idolises me, you know, because I'm in *the business*.' My fingers make quotation marks in the air.

'Hey there yourself. I am not paying you to stand around and gab on to your pals, Miss Armstrong,' booms the voice of my boss, who appears from behind me carrying a cup of takeaway coffee in one hand and my chicken nugget sample refills in the other. 'Jaysus Christ, they beg me for the feckin' work and then they can't be arsed to give out a few wee pieces of chicken. You pretend actresses are the worst so you are, all high and mighty and up yerselves even though you've never been on telly in yer lives. Now do some bloody work before I have to fire your chicken nugget arse.'

'Ha ha, what a joker,' I snort unattractively as Dan's left eyebrow reaches his hairline and Roma throws me a look of utter disdain.

*I lost. I lost to a dumb-blonde pasta-sauce-named girl.*

Four air-kisses later, Dan and Roma turn on their designer heels and float off down the street to continue living their wonderful life. Even from a distance they exude an aura of confidence, success and wealth. Women gape when they recognise Dan Clancy, the screen stud who sets many hearts a-fluttering. Jealous expressions follow Roma, the woman playing the role most women would die for. Tears blur my eyes as I watch them leave. I could have been her, that should have been me, I wail silently. Give or take a full body transplant and frontal lobotomy.

'Right. That. Is. It,' I mutter under my breath while my heart weeps in pain. 'That is it. Milly Armstrong, you are better than her. You are better than all this.' I lift my chin determinedly. 'My life is going to change from this moment on. I want a piece of what they are having. I want a piece of success. I want a piece of him.'

'Hey, ya gobshite, I want a piece of that bloody chicken,' shouts a runny-nosed boy, who whacks me in the stomach and tries to grab as many nuggets as his dirty fingers can carry. 'Give it me now or I'll get me feckin' da on ya.'

I tip the box of poultry over his head and strut off down the street. I may be a chicken nugget but now I am a chicken nugget with a mission.

# CHAPTER TWO

## *The Tide Turns*

'I have never been so humiliated in my life,' I sigh, trudging sorrowfully into the flat and hurling myself on to the sofa.

'Don't be daft. I bet you have,' my best friend and flatmate Fiona smirks, looking up at me from her cross-legged position on the floor. 'Why, what's going on, like?'

'Two words. Dan. Clancy.'

Fi wrinkles her freckled button nose.

'Ah, shite, that name's always trouble.'

'Oh, and two more words. Chicken nugget suit.'

'That's three words, but what about it? Dan Clancy was never in a chicken nugget suit?'

'No.'

My cheeks flame redder than Fi's sleek chin-length hair at the far too recent memory.

'I was the one . . . Look, it doesn't matter, it was just a job.' I flap my hand and pat the expanse of cream leather sofa beside me. 'Come and sit here and give me some sympathy and I might just describe the whole sorry episode in all its gory detail.'

'I'm bloody trying, but' – she clamps her tongue between her teeth and struggles to extricate herself from a tangled lotus position – 'I'm feckin' stuck. Jaysus, that's the last time I take that doctor's advice. Relaxing? Like shite it is. This yoga is

11

bad for your health. Give us a hand, will you, Milly? Preferably before my feet disappear up me arse. Thanks a million.'

I grab chocolate, crisps and cold beers from the kitchen (a varied if not nutritious diet), change into comforting fluffy pyjamas and snuggle on the sofa next to Fi. The perfect recipe for a girls' night in. We flick on the television, which is so huge I feel like a Borrower compared to the giants on the screen. If furnishing our flat had been reliant on my budget, we would probably be sitting on inflatable chairs trying to convince ourselves that playing charades is a fun way to spend an evening. In fact, we wouldn't have the flat at all, at least not this spacious, high-ceilinged Georgian one in Ballsbridge, a trendy residential area of Dublin. Fortunately money is no object to Fi; the advantage I suppose of having very rich, although absent, parents. I resisted entering the realm of the penniless sponger for as long as I could, but Fi continually insisted I would be doing her a favour if we moved in together. My funny, sweet and loyal friend has suffered from depression for years and according to her my friendship is 'better than any Prozac'. I suspect she is just being kind. On the other hand, if it is true, I should bottle myself and make a fortune.

'So what did you get up to while I was out making a prat of myself?' I ask before drowning my sorrows in cold, refreshing Corona.

Fi shrugs and bites her tongue while she thinks.

'Ah, you know, like, I just fell in love with the fella of my dreams until he buggered off in his plane to ride some girl with a dodgy perm.'

'Exactly how many times have you watched *Top Gun* in the last month, Fi? You're going to burn a hole in the DVD.'

'I've got two,' Fi giggles casually, 'I rotate. But come here now, did you see I went shopping?'

I munch on a chocolate finger and glance around our

living room. If minimalist is the style of the era then we are definitely maximalist. Higgledy-piggledy piles of DVDs and videos largely of the chick-flick and light-hearted comedy variety surround the enormous television/cinema screen. The wall to our left is totally concealed by bookshelves that are stocked to bursting with brightly coloured novels (Fi refuses to purchase any book with a less than cheerful cover). The leather corner sofa occupies the only free floor space, the rest being filled by yoga mats, a gym ball (used once), several pairs of shoes, countless crumpled magazines and the products of some of Fi's latest hobbies. Fi's energy for time-filling pursuits astounds me. She used to have very little motivation for anything, but since she found the right medication, that has all changed. The problem is, Fi doesn't know where to channel her precious new commodity. Recent hobbies have included wonky pottery making, mosaic-ing every inanimate object she can lay her hands on, badge making, and shopping for useless household paraphernalia. I peer at the nearest windowsill and frown.

'Oh, you bought a . . . thing. What is that?'

Fi springs up from the sofa and negotiates the minefield of floor junk to plug in today's purchase. The object immediately lights up and begins to wiggle while playing a strangled ukulele melody.

'Wow,' I grimace, stifling a giggle, 'it's a . . . a noisy lamp that has fits.'

'It's a hula dancing lamp,' Fi announces proudly. 'I found it in one of those vintage shops in Camden Street. Don't you think it's grand?'

'Er, well, it's definitely different.'

'Look, the grass skirt swishes and everything. It plays five tunes over and over again.'

'Lovely. Ukulele entertainment twenty-four/seven, just what I've always wanted. Fi,' I snort as the wiggling hula-girl base goes into overdrive, 'you really should get out more.'

Fi bounces back towards the sofa and whacks me playfully with a cushion.

'I did get out and that's what I found.'

'All right then, stay in and get yourself a boyfriend.'

'What?' Fi laughs through a mouthful of Maltesers. 'Now what would I want one of those useless feckers for? Men are nothing but trouble.'

'Not all of them,' I sniff.

'Ah, now there you go doing that again.'

'Doing what?'

Fi clasps her hands under her pointy little chin and flutters her eyelashes comically.

'Going all dreamy-eyed over that gobshite Dan Clancy.'

'I am not,' I retort, avoiding the mischievous look in Fi's eyes, 'and anyway, he's not a gobshite, he's just . . . he's just gorgeous.'

'Aye right, and he knows it too. I tell you, Milly, he's an egotistical arsehole so he is. Always has been, always will be. You can't see it because you're under that spell of his, but Dan Clancy doesn't know how to treat a woman. He can't love anyone but himself, that boy. And anyhow, if you ask me he has had far too much influence in your life.' Fi pauses while attempting to fit three chocolate fingers in her mouth at once. 'That fella thinks he can just swan in after not calling you for months and act all horny and handsome to keep you gagging for it while he's off playing the field. And he's after dumping you to feck off and be a great success. The man's a feckin' flirt with no morals. It's not on, like.'

I pause as my mind stumbles somewhere around the horny and handsome bit.

'He didn't dump me,' I pout eventually, 'we broke up mutually.'

'Aye right, whatever,' Fi sighs, raising her eyes to the ceiling. 'Well, I reckon you should show him, so you should.'

'Show him what?'

I stab angrily at the television remote control, searching for anything to take my mind off my aching heart and the image of Roma the perfectly plastic girl nuzzling into my man's soft, warm, tanned neck.

'Show him what you can be without him, the ignorant bollix.'

I flick through the channels and shrug.

'Yeah, Fi, I've got a very shiny future with Captain Chicken that will make him positively green with envy. Besides, even if I did have something to show Dan Clancy he wouldn't be looking. Not when you consider the gluttonous supply of eye candy queuing up at his door.'

At the mention of candy, Fi stuffs another eye-watering mouthful of chocolate into her small mouth. Honestly, if my best friend doesn't suddenly balloon when she hits thirty there is no justice in this world. She puts it down to nervous energy, which could be right. Her mind races faster than the Ferrari team, often confusing itself in the process. Some would say Fi demonstrates a certain ditziness, but I think that is underestimating her. Besides, her tendency to lack concentration is endearing and her overworked brain obviously uses the energy meant for her hips. So there is a lot to be said for ditziness.

'Dumph be fkin shap,' Fi mumbles, sending particles of chocolate spittle flying across the sofa.

'In English please?'

'I said' – Fi swallows and grins – 'don't be a feckin' sap. All you need to do is get the job at your audition tomorrow, make a film, get famous and Bob's your bloody Monkhouse.'

She flings her arms wide in a flourishing finish.

'Lovely idea, Miss O'Reilly, but I haven't got an audition tomorrow.'

'Sure you have. Your man called earlier. Jaysus, what's his name now? Didn't I tell you?'

I slowly lower the remote control in time with my sinking stomach.

'No, Fi, you didn't tell me. Who exactly called earlier?'

The words stick to the roof of my mouth like crunchy peanut butter. Fi pokes her tongue between her teeth and peers at the ceiling as if for inspiration. OK, the lack of concentration can be endearing, but it can also be a bit annoying at times. At times like this time right now.

'Ah now, what do you call your man?'

I bite hard on a handful of Pringles.

'You know, the one with the voice so deep you could drill oil with it. Dead posh, like. Sounds like he's got a moustache.'

'Gerald?' I frown. 'My acting agent, you mean?'

'Aye, that's the one. Sure, you've got an audition, you know, for some film thing tomorrow. Somewhere in Dublin. He said it's about the beach, so you have to look er . . . what did he say now? Beachy or some shite. I wrote it down next to the phone.'

Throwing myself off the sofa, I stumble towards the telephone and dive for the notepad that contains more scribbles than a Pollock painting.

'Shit, shit, shit,' I hiss as I try to make sense of Fi's hasty notes. 'I've got a reading for an Irish film. It's funded by the Film Board and they want me to try for the lead. Jesus, Fi, I wish you'd said earlier.' I glance at the enormous ticking clock on the sitting room wall. 'It's too late to call Gerald now and I'm not ready and there's no way I'm going to be ready for tomorrow morning at such short notice, and . . . and . . .'

Fi reaches out and yanks me back down on to the sofa.

'Now don't be going all hyperwhatsit. It's only an audition, like, and sure you've done millions of the things.'

'But this is a biggy, Fi,' I wail, 'and this could be the one, my one big break. I decided today after seeing Dan with that girl that I was going to go for it, to change my life, and now this pops up out of the blue. This could have been what I've been waiting for, but it's too late, I'm not ready.'

'Ah now, of course you're ready, Milly, you're a professional.'

'A professional what? Chicken nugget girl? I'm a dreamer, Fi. They want people who look like Roma; they're the ones who make it. They're the ones who end up with people like Dan. I'm just a promo girl with impossible dreams.'

'You are not,' Fi begins softly, wrapping her tiny arm protectively around my shoulders. 'You're the best.'

I sigh and fiddle with the buttons on the remote control.

'Thanks, Fi, you're a great mate, you know, but I'm not the best, I'm not getting anywhere. Seeing Dan today has made me realise how much he has moved on and I haven't. I'm just treading water, trying not to drown.'

'Now for tonight's movie premiere on TV3,' the television voice-over man interrupts loudly, 'the brilliant and irresistible Dan Clancy in *Last Year's Love*.'

'OH FUCK OFF!' Fi shouts, hurling a cushion at the television.

I gaze at Dan's chiselled features on the screen and wince.

'You can show him, Milly,' Fi says determinedly. 'You can get this role and stick two fingers up at him and his Barbie Doll sidekick.'

*You can get this role and get rid of his Barbie Doll sidekick*, my mind plots silently. *You can win him back.*

I turn to Fi and bite my bottom lip.

'Do you really think I can do it?' I whisper.

'Too right I do,' Fi replies confidently, 'and don't you go thinking I'm gonna let you give up on this now. I want at least one bloody starry premiere out of our friendship.'

I laugh and allow myself to be dragged off the sofa by my excitable friend.

'Come on now, no buts, we are gonna get you looking beachy if it takes all feckin' night, and we are gonna show that Dan Clancy what you are made of. Now that skin of yours is too peachy white, so we'll smother you up to the eyeballs in fake tan, and I've got some Sun-In left over from my Bon Jovi era somewhere, so I have.'

I clasp my shoulder-length sleek brown hair protectively and grimace.

'Today Milly Armstrong, tomorrow Pamela Anderson,' Fi hoots, punching the air. 'We're gonna make you famous.'

'God help me,' I giggle, and trip out of the room towards my fate.

# CHAPTER THREE

## *Making a Splash*

*Sun-In?* This morning I awoke with a mop of hair so bleached and straw-like I look as if I accidentally strayed too close to Mars. Either that or Wurzel Gummidge slipped into my room in the middle of the night and replaced my head with one of his spare ones. As for the fake tan . . . Imagine if you will a satsuma with a blotchiness problem and you've just about got it. After staring dumbstruck at the mirror for a good forty minutes, I do the best I can with a jar of exfoliating body wash that succeeds in scraping several years' worth of skin cells away and leaves my face looking fresh to say the least, if a little too small for my neck. I then apply the juice of two lemons to further reduce my satsuma qualities; a tip I picked up somewhere in the realms of daytime TV. A great idea in theory perhaps, but let me make a suggestion. Seriously astringent lemon juice on raw-rubbed skin is probably about as painful as applying hydrochloric acid to recent burns. Beachy they wanted, painfully rosy-cheeked and ragged they have got. I knew I shouldn't have listened to Fi, especially when she was on a chocolate sugar high. Did I really let her slap shiny gold nail polish all over my far-too-expensive-yet-necessary acrylic nails? I must have been mad.

My image disaster is not helped by the fact that today Ireland is doing its stereotypical best to reassure any stray

February tourists that yes it does rain here. In droves, whatever droves are. Bloody pissing it down would be a more apt description. Of course, being (I like to think) a young trendy, I do not possess an umbrella. For no matter how the brolly makers try to jazz them up with denim-look fabric and glittery bits, umbrellas will never escape that subset of fashion that also includes pac-a-macs and granny headscarves. Consequently, in an attempt to stay young, I have to get wet instead. Which is probably an even worse idea than Fi's Sun-In.

The auditions are being held at Dublin's wonderfully historical university, Trinity College. Jumping off the bus near College Green, I leg it through the horizontal sheets of rain, dodging muddy puddles and even muddier students on bikes as I go, before slipping through the entrance to the college grounds. Realising that I am in danger of arriving at the audition with perspiring armpits wetter than my bedraggled-dog-with-head-out-of-car-window hair, I force myself to walk the final short distance to the audition room. Following the 'Auditions This Way' signs past grand stone buildings and groups of students, I am somewhat calmed by the learned atmosphere within the grounds. In fact, whenever I stray into the hallowed portals of Trinity College I am always comforted by the thought that great men and women have studied and strived to develop their talents right here in this very university. I bet these walls have seen some action. TCD was founded in the late sixteenth century and old alumni include legendary writers Samuel Beckett and Oscar Wilde. It is hard to imagine such talent arising from the groups of modern-day students sheltering in the various doorways and corners of the grounds. They are all here – the ones with unwashed hair, goatees and Tibetan tie-dye 'year out' trousers; the glammed-up, perma-tanned cheerleader chicks with no American football teams to cheer; the depressed-looking Gothic ones with black nails and even blacker moods; the geeky computer nerds with compulsory thick-rimmed glasses; the serious ones who rush along talking to themselves with armfuls of books; and the hundreds of nondescript normal ones in various shades of denim who probably make up the 2:2 brigade of which I would be part, but who could equally as likely become the future Nobel prize winners. So much possibility, so many bright futures ahead. Please let some of it rub off on me today at least.

I skip across the cobbled quadrangle, which I remember well from my days with Dan Clancy, yet another of TCD's esteemed alumni. He had finished his drama course by the time we met but we would often spend lazy afternoons strolling through the grounds or sitting on the grass practising scripts for our auditions. Dan was determined that one day he would return to his university as a successful actor, thus achieving the great heights predicted for him by his tutors. Apparently, he set the drama department alight with his portrayal of McMurphy in *One Flew Over the Cuckoo's Nest* and was named by his fellow students as the most likely to succeed. Rumour has it that he also set the knickers of many a female member of the drama department alight (not literally, of course) with his portrayal of Dan Clancy the irrepressible gigolo. Not while I was with him, of course. Well, unless you believe everything Fi says, which I don't . . . or don't like to. Anyway, now is not the time to dwell on the whys and wherefores of Dan Clancy, especially as only one set of double doors lies between me and the first leading role of my career.

Taking one last deep breath of talented university air, I reach out a shaky hand for the door handle. My mobile phone beeps suddenly and insistently, making me drop my bag as my nerves are already on edge. I step back from the door and delve for the phone among lip-glosses, books, scripts and lucky charms. *Message received*, it informs me merrily. Let me guess, this was all a big joke and I haven't really got an audition at all, collect the chicken nugget suit and do not pass Go. I peer at the name beside the little envelope symbol and almost wet myself with excitement. *Danmob*, it informs me teasingly (I resisted the urge to add incriminating nicknames to my phone list). I press the select button, hold my breath and read on.

*Hey babe, sooo gr8 2 c u yesterday. U r the cutest chicken nugget ever. Want 2 c u again soon for that coffee?! xx your man Dan*

I chew my lip to prevent the emission of girly squeals and re-read the message twice more. *Coffee?!* What does *coffee?!* mean? Surely the *?!* suggests more than one spoon of Nescafé, two of sugar, doesn't it? Not to mention the *babe, cutest* and *your man* parts. Are they just not a written testament to how irresistible this man found me to be yesterday? I bloomin' well think so.

'HA!' I shout, bouncing around in a semi-circle until my back is to the audition room door. 'This is meant to be. He wants me, I want him and we're both going to be famous actors.' I punch the air victoriously. 'Up yours, Roma you stick girl. Dan Clancy wants a real woman with wobbly bits and boobs and quite right too, ha ha, skinny bitch!'

'Uh hum, Miss Armstrong?' questions a hesitant voice behind me.

I spin around and fix a crazed smile to my suddenly dry lips when I see a woman standing in the doorway dressed entirely in white and so skinny she would occupy less airspace than Casper the friendly ghost. Jesus Christ, what planet do these women come from?

'Miss Amelia Armstrong?' the vision in white repeats with an expression so stern I am reminded of Miss Hannigan in the *Annie* orphanage.

'Um, yes,' I croak, 'that's me.'

'Oh,' she replies with obvious disappointment. 'The director will see you now.' Adding over her shoulder, 'Wobbly bits and all.'

*Sarcastic old witch.*

'Thank you,' I beam sweetly, reaching out for the door that she releases to spring back in my orange and red face.

I grit my teeth, muster all the confidence I can find, flick back my straw fringe and enter the audition room. This is it. May the Force of Dan Clancy be with me.

'Ring, damn you!' I hiss sharply at my mobile phone that sits silently on the café table beside my fourth cup of cappuccino.

If I consume any more coffee I risk walking out of here with a chocolate-topped frothy head. I am also well aware that the caffeine is doing little to calm my nerves. I have developed shakes upon the shakes I already had when I stumbled out of the audition room three hours ago, bleary-eyed and with a brain like dreary grey Play-Doh.

The day consisted of an exhausting six hours of read-throughs, improvisation and screen tests just for the female role. Unusually for such projects, the director Matthew (just 'Matthew' – I think he was going for the single-name Madonna thing) was determined to have his leading lady cast within the day. After the twenty-fifth time that Matthew informed us how the leading man was a 'very very exciting' prospect, I began to realise where his priorities lay (and very likely where his body would like to lie too).

'He's a darling, an absolute darling. If we land him this film could shoot through the roof, pif pof POOF!' Matthew squealed dramatically, at which point maturity escaped me and I dissolved into a giggling mess.

Anyway, like the reality popstar shows (only thankfully without the need for me to succumb to the total humiliation of trying to be Britney Spears when I am clearly not), our numbers dwindled as the unchosen few were sent home with harsh calls of 'Next!' By the end of the day only two of us remained – myself and a girl called Bliss. She swore it was her real name, but then people like Bliss always do. Bliss was HUGE. I would like to say in a Roseanne Barr kind of way, but actually she was huge in that sleek, Amazonian, I-could-be-a-supermodel-but-I-can't-really-be-arsed kind of way.

With legs and a neck so long she should rightly have been a giraffe, combined with porcelain skin, cushion-like collagen lips, hair as black as Guinness and the ice-cool confidence that only a girl called Bliss could possibly possess. Next to her I felt like the short, slightly scruffy girl someone like Bliss would choose to befriend at school to make herself look even more beautiful. The beautiful people always have one – the uglier, fatter, less trendy friend. Make that the uglier, fatter, less trendy friend with radioactive orange skin and bleach-destroyed hair.

Why then, you might ask, am I bothering to wait for the phone call from Gerald, my agent, to let me know whether I got the job? The phone call that is taking so long to materialise that I am beginning to suspect Gerald has run off to the Midwest to learn the ancient art of American Indian smoke signals before delivering the news. Well, I may not be Bliss-ful in one sense but I do have a certain amount of self-belief. I *can* act and I *do* have talent, and today feels like a lucky day. Just take the text message from Dan as I was about to enter the room; now that was perfect timing. So, you never know. A girl must have confidence in herself after all.

Oh, and there was one other minor factor that may push the decision my way . . . a matter of a little white lie during our final interviews. A little white lie that just kind of slipped out the way they do. I'm sure it's not a problem, though, and besides, we all have to push the boundaries a little to get what we want. Don't we? A squirming feeling in my coffee-flooded stomach urges me to call Fi for advice. Was lying to the director a bad thing or doesn't everyone fake his or her CV just a little? I grab the phone, scurry towards the ladies' room and dial the flat.

'You told him what?' Fi laughs hysterically until her laughter erupts into an uncontrollable coughing fit. 'Ah now, Milly, that was a mighty porkie pie that one. Sure you must be more of a fruit loop than I am.'

'You're not a fruit loop,' I respond naturally, 'and actually

24

neither am I, thank you very much you cheeky cow. I was just trying to secure the role.'

'Sure it's better than spreading your legs on the casting couch.'

'He wouldn't have been interested, believe me.'

'So what exactly did you tell him?'

I suck in my cheeks and make a popping sound with my mouth.

'Um, well, just what I told you really.'

Fi remains silent, waiting for me to incriminate myself further.

'I just kind of said that I could swim.'

'And?'

'And surf.'

'And?'

'All right, and that I've been surfing since the age of three and I am a natural water baby.'

I hear Fi's nostrils erupt into the receiver.

'Ya big eejit, Milly,' she laughs uproariously. 'The last time we went swimming you wouldn't get out of the baby pool.'

'It was warmer,' I mumble moodily, hoping that Fi can't sense how much I am blushing. 'Anyway, I'm sure it's no big deal. This was my one big chance, and besides, they have stuntwomen for the action scenes in these kinds of movies. When I found out it was about a surfer girl in Ireland I had to lie, and Matthew won't be expecting me to hurl myself into the Irish Sea and hang ten or whatever it is these surfers do.'

'Aye, but Matthew won't be expecting you to have the capacity to sink in a small puddle either.'

'I'm not that bad a swimmer, I just have a slight fear, that's all.'

'Since you nearly drowned, you mean.' Fi's tone turns more serious. 'Honestly, Milly, are you sure this is a good idea?'

I run my tongue along my lips, which have become suddenly parched.

'Thanks for your concern, Fi, but I haven't even got the role yet, and even if I do, I've got a good feeling in my stomach about this.'

'Ah, that'll be a bit of diarrhoea from all that caffeine you've been drinking.'

'Thank you, that's delightful. Now bugger off so that I can wait for this call.'

'OK now, good luck, Milly. Shamrocks and leprechauns and the luck of the Irish and all that shite. I'll be thinking about you, and be sure to let me know as soon as you know.'

'I will, I will,' I say above the flapping butterflies in my gut. 'Now shoo and let me get back to my pacing up and down.'

'Cheerio now.'

I grip the mobile tightly in my right hand and stare at myself in the toilet wall mirror, smoothing out the wrinkles on my forehead with my left (did I ever not have those?). The mirror clouds with the condensation from my sighs. Have you ever wanted something so badly that you feel as if you will die if you don't get it? Granted, I know in the logical part of my brain that I won't simply drop dead if I don't get this part, but there will definitely be a prolonged period of mourning.

'Please let me get it,' I pray to the ceiling just as an old woman creaks her way through the door of the toilets.

'Pardon, dear?'

'Oh, nothing, I'm just . . .' *Talking to myself?* 'Nothing.'

I blush at my first signs of madness and slip quickly into the nearest cubicle. Of course, as soon as I settle on the cold seat and relax my bowels, the mobile I have been begging to ring for the last aeon bursts into song. Sod's Law, isn't it? Here I am sitting on the toilet with an old woman tinkling away in the cubicle next door while *Gerald Agent* flashes urgently on the mobile's screen. Leaving me with a dilemma. Do I risk missing the call and quickly continue with my, er . . . business? Or do I answer the call and talk to my agent

26

to the accompanying sound of running water? In my world, telephones and toilets do not make a comfortable combination. Oh why did I drink all those diuretic coffees?

'Hello?' I cringe as my pelvic floor muscles clench in a reflex action. (Good practice for childbirth, apparently.)

'Amelia? Gerald. Are you sitting down?'

'Um . . . yes,' I reply, glancing down at the rim of the toilet seat.

Gerald's manner of speech is firm and to the point, as it has always been since I first signed with his agency as a newcomer to Dublin five years ago. (I figured there would be fewer actors in Ireland so the competition would be less, and I was keen to extricate myself from the prying eyes of my disapproving family.) I suspect Gerald, who has been an agent for twenty years since moving to Dublin from London, likes me to think that he is constantly rushed off his feet with hot-shot deals and therefore that he can spare little time for small talk. I have my doubts. If all his clients are as sought after in the business as I am, then he must have plenty of free time on his hands to drink whiskey, have extended lunch breaks, practise his abrupt manner, pick his nose and do whatever it is agents like Gerald do in a day.

A rasping smoker's cough blasts my ear before Gerald continues with a wheeze.

'Right, well either the planets are in alignment or we are witnessing a miracle, because I received a call from the film company and it appears' – my heart almost stops beating – 'they want you, Amelia.'

'WHAT?' I squeal, completely losing my cool. 'They what? Oh wow, oh my God, that's brilliant, that's just . . . oh, that's amazing.'

'Yes, isn't it,' Gerald replies drily. 'Congratulations, darling. About bloody time.'

'Thank you,' I gasp, choosing to ignore the latter three words. My head feels as if it is spinning like the freaky girl in *The Exorcist*. They want me. *They* want *me*! This is it. This is the moment I have been waiting for my whole life. If I were in a film now they would be playing 'This Is My Moment' by Martine McCutcheon while I danced ecstatically around the room. What am I saying, *if* I were in a film? I *am* going to be in a film. As the leading lady. I want to scream, I want to jump up and down but my knickers being around my ankles somewhat restricts the chance for impromptu celebrations. This fact and Gerald's throaty voice bring me suddenly back to reality.

'I'm sorry, Gerald, I missed that. What was your concern?' I ask, simultaneously grabbing the tail end of his sentence and the melamine cubicle wall for support.

'I said, Amelia, I was a little concerned when the director explained that their main reason for choosing you was that you are a natural water woman. Now correct me if I am mistaken here, but are you not so terrified of water that you had to turn down that advert for Dolphin bathrooms?'

I silently chew my lip.

'And given that you are about as near to being a water baby as I am to signing Robert De Niro to my books, I must admit to being rather surprised to hear that you have been surfing since you were two years old.'

'Three years old,' I correct him before I can stop myself.

'Oh, really? Well, I must say that came as a bolt out of the big blue yonder to me, darling, and here was I thinking you had no hidden talents.'

I don't think that was a compliment.

'Of course, the director said you looked like a surf chick, what with your' – Gerald clears his throat – 'sun-bleached hair and all-over tanned skin.'

His sentence ends on a questioning upstroke.

'Now goodness only knows what you have been up to since we last met but I do hope you realise that this project has a small budget and can't afford stuntwomen and the like, so the whole film rests on the fact that the leading lady can swim and surf better than Flipper.'

28

'Does it?' My voice cracks.

'Oh yes. It does.'

My pelvic floor muscles are now so tightly clenched that I have almost reverted to being a virgin.

'Obviously I am delighted for you, Amelia,' Gerald continues darkly, 'but I do need a little reassurance that when filming starts in July you will be ready.'

I nod stiffly. Not the greatest way of communicating on the telephone, I know, but I have been gripped by a sudden feeling of panic. July? That is only four months away. How can I learn to swim properly and surf and rehearse the whole script in four months? Four years wouldn't be long enough to prepare me to give myself up to the mercy of the ocean. Or to the deep end of a swimming pool for that matter. It can't be that essential to the plot, can it?

'In short,' Gerald adds sternly, 'if you haven't turned yourself into a female Duncan Goodhew by the end of June, darling, you will be out on your ear faster than you can say, "I'm a desperate liar".'

Seemingly it can.

'So I leave you with this piece of advice. Buy some of those inflatable water wings, get in that swimming pool, start doggy paddling and buy yourself a surfboard. Our reputations are on the line here, Amelia. Do not mess this up.'

'I won't, Gerald, don't worry,' I manage to say before the line goes dead.

No, don't worry, worry is not an option; full-blown panic is much more appropriate. Oh, Milly, what have you gone and done this time?

'I hate to say I told you so,' Fi shrugs while struggling to open a bottle of extravagant champagne (her treat).

'Why do people say that when they clearly love being able to say "I told you so"?' I grumble, ducking as Fi turns the ready-to-explode bottle in my direction like a loaded sub-machine-gun.

'Ah now, don't be going getting all feisty on me. I only told you to get beachy. I didn't tell you to pass yourself off as half woman, half fish.'

'Give me that before you take my eye out, would you?'

I grab the bottle and gently ease out the cork. The golden bubbles erupt into our awaiting slender pink flutes.

'I don't know why we're celebrating,' I sigh, half-heartedly clinking my glass against Fi's. 'As soon as they find out I'm scared of the water they'll dump me for Miss Bliss anyway.'

Fi places her glass on the kitchen worktop and pulls herself up on to the granite surface beside me.

'Not necessarily now,' she winks, tapping her nose and fixing her eyes on mine with a conspiratorial expression.

'Oh, and how do you figure that one out, Miss O'Marple?'

'Because,' Fi smirks, her blanched teeth glistening under the kitchen spotlight, 'after we spoke the second time, I had a wild good idea.'

'And that is supposed to make me feel better, is it?'

I point an orange-stained finger to the distressed bleached strands on my head where my glossy dark hair once was.

Fi flaps her hands excitedly as if trying to take flight from the work surface, which she probably could, considering how little she weighs.

'Sure it's a better idea than that one. I admit the Sun-In might have been a bit much but it kinda suits ya with your tan and all.'

I raise my eyebrows and say nothing.

Fi continues confidently. 'Well now, while you were out becoming a famous actress yourself, I made a big decision. There I was trying to keep myself busy making that shite' – we both glance silently at the roughly painted plaster-of-Paris gnome on the kitchen table – 'and you know I thought, Milly, what the feck am I doing? Jaysus, I haven't even got a garden and I'm not yet thirty and I'm making feckin' gnomes.'

I silently agree. Fi gulps her champagne, wrinkles her

nose when the bubbles hit and then carries on enthusiastically.

'You know I thought just because I've been labelled with this depression thing it doesn't mean I have to act like an eejit. Millions of great, successful, intelligent people have depression and they still get on. I might have up and down days but I can at least try to make more ups than downs. And what you said about the hula lamp and about getting out more' – I twiddle my fingers guiltily – 'you were right, Milly. I've got money, I've got the best friend in the world, but I just sit in here wasting my time. It's no wonder I can't quite beat it. But I want to. So . . .'

I sip my champagne pensively.

'So I decided I have the motivation now to improve myself. To help myself and basically change my life.'

'Wow,' I say when Fi finishes with a rosy-cheeked flourish, 'that's great, Fi, but are you sure? I mean, that sounds like a pretty big call and you've never been that big on change. Trying a different loaf of bread for you is like parting from a dear friend.'

'Don't mock me now, Milly,' Fi giggles. 'I'm on a roll here, so just roll with me, hey?'

'Sorry. Roll away.'

My friend's determined decision is great, but what this has got to do with my inability to walk on water I have absolutely no idea. Knowing Fi, probably nothing at all.

'Well now, to start with I decided I need a change of scenery. Otherwise I'm just gonna end up being one of those foxtrot fannies with no focus at all. Ladies who lunch,' she explains in response to my confused frown. 'Except I don't even do that, like. So what happened was, I had the TV on while I was painting the gnome and there was this travel show on, which was set in County Donegal, you know over on the west coast. It was so gorgeous and I thought I'd like to go there again some time. And then I thought, what's stopping me going there now?'

I sip and listen as my friend continues, her eyes sparkling.

'Sure it's only a few hours away and it would be such a change. I've got all the time in the world *and* I've got family there. Ma, Da and I used to go there for our holidays all the time when Sean and I were little and I loved it. My Ma's sister Mary Heggarty lives there, and my cousins. Isn't that grand?'

'Great,' I smile. 'So you're saying you want to go on holiday?'

'Yeah, but a long holiday for, like, four months. It'll be so cool; you and me heading west like Thelma and Louise. If we meet Brad Pitt I'm having him, OK?'

'But, Fi, I can't just bugger off to County Donegal for four months. I've got to prepare for this part from now until July. That's why we're drinking this champagne. Remember?'

Of course I remember, which is why it was such a good idea. You see, I remembered after we talked on the phone that my cousin was into all that surfing business.'

'In Ireland?'

'Yeah, and guess what, he still does it. I called my Auntie Mary tonight and Cormac, we all call him Mac, is only the lifeguard on the beach out there and he teaches surfing to kids too. Sure, he was a bit of a bollix when we were young but apparently he grew up all right so. Isn't that perfect, Milly? Mac can teach you to surf and I can see my family that I haven't seen for feckin' ages. It'll be great craic, so you have to say you'll come. It's all sorted anyhow.'

'What's all sorted? You lost me somewhere around the foxtrot fannies,' I reply, blowing my hair off my face in exasperation.

I've got a focus for Fiona O'Reilly – professional riddle writer.

'Surfing lessons in County Donegal with Mac as our teacher. We go on Monday.'

'Yeah, right,' I snort, sending champagne bubbles shooting up the back of my nostrils. 'You can't go surfing in Donegal.'

'Don't be daft, 'course you can. There's a feckin' ocean there. What more do you want?'

'Uh, how about warm water, a palm-tree-lined beach, tanned surfers with six-packs and a distinct lack of penguins? Come on, Fi, you don't really expect me to go surfing on the west coast of Ireland in March, do you? I'll freeze my tits off.'

'I already have!' Fi giggles, clasping her hands to her chest, which is admittedly less developed than Africa.

'Well mine are important to me,' I laugh. 'I've got women like Bliss to compete with, and besides, I can't afford to go on holiday for four months.'

'It's research and I'm paying, so it's no bother at all. I'll just have a cut of your millions when you're famous, like. I'm serious now, Milly, we can do this, it'll be fantastic and you'll be helping me too. Sure we can get you surfing like . . . whatever a famous surfer calls himself, in no time. Besides, you don't get penguins in Donegal, ya gobshite.'

'It's probably too cold for them. Can't we go to Hawaii or somewhere? We could re-enact that *Blue Crush* film.'

'No, I'm scared of flying.'

Fi hops down from the worktop and pulls her tiny suede hipsters up to meet her jaggedy hipbones.

'Since when have you been scared of flying?'

'Since men with beards started blowing the feckers up. Now so, that's settled then,' she calls over her shoulder as she heads out of the kitchen towards the bathroom. 'County Donegal here we come. It'll be grand, Milly, we're girls with a mission.'

'Mission?' I grunt to myself when my excitable friend is out of earshot. 'Death wish more like.'

One thing I can safely say is that there is no way I am going surfing in the Atlantic Ocean, especially the bit smacking its icy self against the cliffs of Donegal, whether my career depends on it or not. In fact, I would rather peel my own skin off with my teeth. Sorry, Fi, but it is just not going to happen.

# CHAPTER FOUR

# *Wild Blue Yonder*

By Saturday lunchtime my ear has already been bent by Fi's constant pestering. I resist telling her that 'suffering for my art', as she puts it, should not necessarily involve my own death under a twenty-foot wave while wearing an unflattering rubber suit. Just imagine the post-mortem pictures, for heaven's sake.

My persistently ringing telephone is my only escape from Fi's nagging and I instantly recognise the fake Yankee Doodle accent of my promotions work agent, Truly Scrumptious (of which she is neither), the source of my chicken nugget fiasco.

'Job for you, honey,' Truly informs me brightly. 'Running a coffee shop at a business fair and demonstrating the latest in cappuccino/latte whisks while you do so. Do you think you could manage that?'

*I have an English degree from Southampton University*, I want to shout. *I'm sure I have the mental capacity to whisk up a few friggin' lattes.*

'That sounds fine,' I mutter through tightly gritted teeth. 'When does the job start?'

'Monday afternoon, hon, but Monday morning you will be required to complete a course on the hand whisk's functions with Julius, the latte coordinator, before they can let you loose with one.'

*Golly, won't the world just be my big, shiny oyster once Julius presents me with my HND in manual whisking?*

'And dress skimpy,' Truly adds firmly. 'The skimpier the better for this client.'

In the thirty seconds that follow, I mentally weigh up my options for Monday morning:

a) I remain in my safe promo world and whisk coffees while wearing hotpants for less money than Roma would open her eyes for, never mind get out of bed. A risk-free option, admittedly, but five more years of this escapade will not get me to where I want to be.

b) I take a risk and embark on Fi's crazy plan, which may lead to my untimely death in the icy waters of Donegal but which could also prepare me for the greatest role of my life.

Am I a chicken? (Other than when I am paid to be, that is.)

'I'm sorry, Truly,' I answer with an audible waver in my voice, 'but I won't be able to take that job or any other job for the foreseeable future. You see, er, I won't be available. I have an acting job.'

'Really?' Her tone fails to conceal her surprise.

'Yes, really. I leave for a research trip first thing Monday morning, in fact.'

'Do you now?' Fi laughs when I shakily replace the receiver.

'Don't get carried away,' I reply before she begins cartwheeling victoriously around the room. 'I need time to think about this.'

That time proves to be a single minute before my mobile rings a second time.

'You answer it,' I plead with Fi, who spins on her heel and swiftly heads towards the kitchen.

'I can't, I'm having confidence problems answering the telephone today,' she lies with a mischievous wink. 'It's my depression, you know.'

I shake my head and laugh at the way Fi mocks her own condition, and then I reach for the phone.

'Hello, Amelia, darling, it's only me,' my mother begins with enough just-ringing-to-see-how-you-are perkiness to let me know there is an ulterior motive behind the call.

'Hi, guys,' I reply, knowing full well that my father will be present on the second extension line.

My parents always speak to me on the phone at the same time because my mother's accountant brain tells her this will halve the length of the telephone calls and therefore halve the bill. The common-sense part of my brain tells me that the muddled simultaneous conversations and repetition that inevitably occurs ultimately result in the calls being twice the length they would be if we did away with the multiple extension game and just behaved like normal human beings.

'Top o' the mornin' to ya, ha ha,' my father quips in an Irish accent worthy of a (bad) Hollywood movie, from his position on line two.

My father, Frank Armstrong, loves to indulge in these supposed Irish colloquialisms despite my having explained on numerous occasions that Ireland is not all *Ballykissangel* on a large scale. It is a multi-cultural, multi-accented and, believe it or not, modern nation. Nevertheless, in the minds of Frank and Georgina Armstrong (and most American tourists in search of their 'roots'), all Irish people live in either a castle or a tumbledown hand-built stone cottage, milk their own cows, listen to Daniel O'Donnell, travel to the shops by lame donkey and share their medieval village life with an abundance of leprechauns and fairies (or should I say 'faeries').

'So, pudding,' Dad snorts, 'how are the leprechauns?'

See what I mean?

'They're fine, Dad. We were out with a few last night as it happens. Drinking Guinness, playing the tin whistle, eating potatoes and betting on the donkey races. The usual really.'

'Marvellous, marvellous, and how is the rain?'

'Wet,' I reply, peering out of the window at the crisp February sunshine splitting the clouds.

'And,' he coughs, 'the acting lark?'

There you have it, the sliding scale of important issues as interpreted by my father – 1) Leprechauns, 2) Rain, 3) My Career. Oh, he must be so proud. Dawn begins to break somewhere inside my head and I realise I do actually have a chance to make my father and mother proud of me and it certainly is not by taking a course in coffee whisks with a man called Julius. What am I thinking? How can I reject Fi's kind offer of help in exchange for the crummy working life everybody knows I have been leading since I arrived in Dublin seeking my fame and fortune? My stomach churns nervously. What if I can pull this off? Would my family take me seriously then? Would people look at me and say, 'I want to be just like Milly Armstrong, she knew what she wanted and she didn't stop until she got it'? I tingle with excitement while I summon up the courage to answer my father's question.

'Actually, Dad, I do have something quite awesome in the pipeline. You won't believe it, but only yesterday I . . .'

'I'm sorry, we are a bit rushed, dear; I'm scooting off to the chiropodist for my bunions. Honestly, Frank, stop asking irrelevant questions,' my mother interrupts impatiently, causing my pride to run for cover.

'We just wanted to call to give you the wonderful news,' my mother continues, trundling over my own news with a conversational steamroller.

'Oh?' I feign enthusiasm.

'Yes, you will never guess. Go on, have a guess, darling.'

'Um, Ed has been made Prime Minister and granted the key to the kingdom for having his own personal sun shining out of his ar—'

'Ooh, jealous,' interrupts another female voice.

'Jesus, how many bloody people are on this line? I feel like I'm on a conference call with an Old Trafford capacity crowd.'

'It's Tania, darling, and don't swear,' Mum scolds quietly. 'One never hears Ed swearing like a railway worker.'

'?' is all I can say.

*Where does she get these phrases?*

'That's because I'm perfect,' Ed laughs, joining the throng.

I told you these calls are complicated.

'And in the red corner,' I groan. 'It's just the five of us then, how intimate.'

So the 'discussion' races on, with hardly a sentence completed before someone else butts in. Including bloody Tania, who is not even technically family and consequently should not be allowed to indulge in our ridiculous inter-family pursuits. The call follows so many tangents in such a short space of time that a graph of our topics of conversation would look like an aerial-view sketch of Spaghetti Junction.

'Anyway, Eddie, tell your sister your news,' Mum says. 'I have to leave the chops out to thaw before we go, and your father isn't supposed to be spending too much time on the phone.'

'Why not?' I cut in, imagining that the accountant of the family has placed money-saving phone call restrictions on the man of the house. 'Has he been gossiping with his friends too much and not getting his homework done?'

'Don't be silly, darling,' my mother replies without humour. 'It's this stress thing. He is supposed to be out walking and the like, not cooped up indoors straining his brain with telephone waves.'

'Oh,' I frown, 'what stress thing?'

'Georgina, don't go making a fuss now. It's nothing, Amelia,' my father pipes up.

'Are you sure, Dad?'

39

My father huffs and puffs and deflects my genuine concern.

'Of course I'm sure, pudding. It was just a bit of high blood pressure, that's all. Not bloody surprising after the fortnight I have had in court, fighting over the custody of a racehorse in front of a wholly nonsensical bunch of magistrates who are more lame than the bloody horse.'

'Right,' I sigh, losing sight of the direction of this conversation.

'Come on now, Edward, spill the beans, lad,' my father continues hurriedly.

To save you the trouble of listening to my brother's huge ego in full flow, I will paraphrase the beans that are subsequently spilled. Apparently Ed has landed a huge case at work and will be representing a very famous client in what will undoubtedly become infamous litigation. He will be the one being interviewed daily for BBC News outside the Royal Courts of Justice. He will be the one whose career will blast into orbit and beyond if he wins, which of course, knowing Ed as I do, he will. He will be the one to come out of it all in the end with a pay packet large enough to help Bono settle the national debt of a developing country. Which will then provide a deposit for the mansion he and swotty Tania are planning to buy, in which no doubt they will raise their nauseous offspring. Ed also delights in pointing out the irony of the fact that, try as I might to achieve fame on television, he will be doing just that without having to spend years slogging his guts out for an Equity card. An example of sibling rivalry at its finest. Not that I am jealous. Oh all right, of course I am jealous, but I'm not about to let Ed know that. Besides, he doesn't know that I have just landed a film role and that come Monday I will be on a train to Donegal to begin my research. Well, what do you know? My decision is made.

'What time do we get to Donegal then?' I shout over the clickety-clack of the rickety orange train.

40

I say clickety-clack, but imagine if you will four thousand primary school children simultaneously shouting 'clickety-clack' at the top of their ear-piercing voices and you will probably still be underestimating the decibel levels of this train. In fact, I am beginning to wonder whether this retro boneshaker will ever actually get us to our destination with our bodies intact. On the other hand, from the look of it, I guess it has been making this journey successfully for the last forty years. I just pray that today is not the day it chooses to disintegrate en route.

'Ah, would you look, a cow!' Fi squeals, pressing her city-dweller nose up against the train window. 'And there, look look, it's a big hedge!'

Fi has been in a heightened state of bubbliness since we loaded our bags into the taxi just after lunchtime and wove precariously through the city traffic to Connolly station for the 1.35 train. Granted, I find it hard to get excited over a big hedge, but I definitely have stirrings of anticipation in my belly. For a start, I have, I am ashamed to admit, never visited the reportedly breathtaking west coast of Ireland in the five years I have lived in the Republic. Secondly, Fi's ability to be thrilled by the simplest little adventure in life is somewhat catching. I love to see the sparkle in her eyes on days like these when the lingering shadows lighten in her mind, letting her heart beat contentedly. Thirdly, I really feel as if this is the first gutsy, positive step I have taken in my life for a long while. Of course, I may bottle the challenge when faced with a ravaging ocean, but at least I have crawled out from under my rock to have a go at making my own luck. Meeting Dan did me a favour. This is, as they say, the first day of the rest of my life. It is just a shame we couldn't have found a more glamorous way to travel; the ancient upholstery in this train is making me feel decidedly grubby. Anyone for a stale crisp? I think I have plenty embedded in my backside.

'We're almost there, so we are, Milly,' says Fi, clapping her hands and peering through the smeared windowpane. 'Would you look at the view, it's mighty so it is.'

I brush the window free from grime and look outside expecting to see more of the Irish city life I have grown accustomed to.

'Bloody hell, Fi,' I gasp, 'it's . . . it's gorgeous.'

Honestly. It truly, truly is. Gorgeous. In just three hours, the tightly packed houses and busy streets of the city have been magically whisked away and replaced with fields so green that they appear to have been over-enthusiastically painted by a child who has just discovered primary colours. There are stone cottages and flowers and flocks of birds that swoop up from the hedges as we pass, disappearing into the sky that is a wash of blues, oranges and rosy-cheeked pinks. Rising out of fields so level that they appear to have been smoothed down with a giant iron are huge flat-topped hills, mountains even, standing boldly in the distance. The mountains are purple in this light, topped by the little fluffy clouds that someone sang about in the eighties. Now I am not usually the sort of girl who dreams of escaping to the solitude of the countryside. I'm a city girl, just like Fi. I like shops and bars and bustle and . . . shops. But for a few minutes, I am speechless. We may no longer be near to the learned realm of Trinity College with its Samuel Beckett and Oscar Wilde but we are now in W.B. Yeats country. Poetryville. And I may not be a poet, but I am suddenly inspired. I no longer feel like Milly Armstrong on holiday with her bored-with-routine best mate; I am an actress researching her latest role. I am like Nicole Kidman, going rural to create her character in *Far and Away* (only probably on a slightly smaller budget).

As we step off the train in County Sligo, a half-hour drive from our final destination in County Donegal, and wheel our cases towards the red-brick ticket hall, the fresh Atlantic breeze begins to blow away the worries woven like cobwebs in my head. *Whoosh*. The chasm between Dan's life and mine, my own doubts and those projected on me by my family in my ability, the fact that I lied to land my role, the ever-niggling worry about money and the ludicrously small size of Dan's girlfriend's hips. Not to mention the fact that if I don't metamorphose into the Little Mermaid by July, my career will be well and truly sunk. Despite all that, the further we walk, the better I feel and I am quickly beginning to suspect that this is the best idea Fiona O'Reilly has had since I met her.

'There he is!' Fi shouts, running ahead of me towards a shiny new-looking four-wheel-drive parked outside the station entrance. 'My cousin Cormac,' she calls back to me. 'Jaysus, Mac, look at you!'

Look at him? Too right I am looking at him. In fact, my eyes have hopped out of their sockets and scampered across the forecourt to get a better view. He is tall enough but not huge, I would guess on the six-foot mark. His shoulders are noticeably broad, like the frame of a swimmer, and he has weathered, character-rich skin. Like a juicy, meaty rump steak just begging me to take a bite. This man has all the evident Celtic traits – unruly chocolate-brown hair with auburn lights, freckles still visible through his tan, green eyes shining like cat's eyes on the side of a motorway and an accent that is thick but easy on the ear. I walk slowly towards him and concentrate on keeping my tongue inside my mouth. As I approach, a gust of wind catches my hair and blows it wildly around my head. Suddenly I experience the strangest sensation as the constant niggling problem occupying space in my head – Dan Clancy – is also whipped out of my mind and into the air. At least for a second or two.

'Hello there, I'm Mac. How's it goin'?' he says politely, reaching out his hand.

'Fine thanks,' I try to say but it comes out as a squeaky
'Fine thanks.'

I place my comparatively tiny hand in his and meek
shake it, attempting to fix my eyes confidently on his face
I do so. However, before I know what is happening, my l

43

eye involuntarily shuts in a wink so obvious that I could be in a *Carry On* film.

'Shit!' I yelp, jumping backwards and furiously rubbing my eye. 'It was the wind. I wasn't winking, you know, it was the wind.'

'Yeah, right, ya gobshite,' Fi honks loudly. 'The wind my arse.'

Mac grabs my case, positively hurls it into the back of the car and makes a rapid escape to the driver's door.

*Nice one, Milly, now he thinks you're gagging for it.*

'Right then,' Fi giggles, flicking her thumb towards the back seat, 'get in, we've got some waves to catch. Oh, and don't forget your fanny, hey, I think you dropped it out there in the car park.'

*Subtle, Fiona, very subtle.*

# CHAPTER FIVE

# *Up Shit Creek Without a Paddle*

Mac and I don't hit it off. To begin with, I put this down to shyness on his part, as I am largely, make that *totally*, ignored by our delightfully hunky chauffeur. In fact it soon becomes obvious that Mac would rather we were crushed from behind by a runaway ten-ton truck than risk making eye contact with me in the rear-view mirror when checking the road behind. My attempts at conversation also blow out of the open window without the slightest grunt of acknowledgement. I conclude that either he is too overwhelmed by my beauty or (as is admittedly more likely) he is trying to work out why the passenger in the back of his car has a face more marmaladey than David Dickinson.

I eventually give up trying to converse with Mac and Fi, allowing them a moment to catch up on family matters. Well, I say a moment, but by the time they have discussed Colleen's engagement to Barry, cousin Emmett's forthcoming wedding, how many sprogs Siobhan, Sinead, Moira, Marie and Marian have dropped in the last two years, the houses Adam, Brendan, Malachi, Joseph and Johnny have built or plan to build, not to mention the whys, wherefores and what-they're-up-to's of hundreds of first, second and third cousins, I begin to suspect that either the Heggartys are devout Catholics who favour only the rhythm method of contraception, or that Fi descends from the human equivalent of rabbits. It is just selfish having that many relatives. What's wrong with the good old British extended family of three distant cousins and two mad aunts whom you never have any contact with beyond a cheap card at Christmas and the division of their posthumous assets? Much more the Armstrong style. On the other hand, this is the closest Fi has to immediate family and I can tell from the look on her face that she already feels part of something special. I let them chat, only jumping in when they both (infrequently) pause for breath at the same time.

'Are Catholics allowed to use the Pill here now?' I ask as my brain continues to dwell on the epidemic of offspring in this family I am hearing about. 'Do you know, Mac? Are you Catholic?'

Mac suddenly acknowledges my existence by throwing a narrow-eyed stare towards the back seat via the rear-view mirror. This first moment of genuine eye contact would have sent Ian Paisley crying for his mummy. I squirm in my seat but force a smile.

'Why do you ask?' he replies coldly. 'What difference does religion make?'

'Erm, I'm just interested, I suppose,' I cough. 'You know, trying to educate myself.'

'Next you'll be wanting to know if my dad was in the IRA and if I've ever made a bomb,' he growls without a hint of sarcasm.

I swallow and fiddle with my hair to hide my embarrassment.

'No, I was just making conversation actually.'

'Then next time make it a decent one, for feck's sake.'

My skin sizzles as a reaction to his acidic words and I feel my cheeks burning. I see a label being stapled to my forehead in Mac's darkening imagination. Milly Armstrong, fluffy-headed English intruder with about as much grasp of social and political affairs as most women have of the offside

46

rule. I am at once embarrassed and furious. Who does this country boy think he is? How dare he ridicule me? Not that I care what Mac Heggarty thinks of me. Not even a little bit. I stick out my bottom lip and scowl at the passing trees. Why did I let Fi talk me into this?

'Here you are, the cottage,' says Mac as, ten minutes of silence on my part later, he hurls the jeep into a ninety-degree turn down a ridiculously narrow driveway, causing me to breathe in.

'Ah, look it, Milly, it's lovely,' Fi enthuses, leaping out of the car and swinging her arms wide, 'and just as I remember it from years ago.'

I don't doubt that, I think, as my eyes look beyond the cosmetic coat of exterior paint to the suspiciously crumbly brickwork. The 'cottage', as Mac so quaintly describes it, is an old and fragile two-storey town house built so close to the water's edge that I wonder how the foundations can possibly withstand even the smallest storm.

'The ocean comes right up to the sea defence at the back wall at high tide,' Mac informs us while I tilt my head to look down the side of the house. 'But you're all right unless the waves get massive, then you just have to be sure to close the windows at the back.'

'Grand,' Fi nods, accepting the keys that are clumped together on a bit of frayed orange rope. 'This is gonna be mighty isn't it, Milly?'

I try to smile but my cheek muscles spasm nervously.

'The town's just that way,' says Mac, dumping my suitcase precariously close to my big toe, 'and my folks are still up at the big house, Fi, so give them a shout if you need any-thing, hey? Ma will be expecting you.'

Fi beams and pulls Mac into a hug. I instantly reject the hug idea, consider a handshake and eventually decide on a weak wave as Mac spins the car around and careers out on to the main road.

'Well now, isn't this grand?' says Fi, struggling with the

lock of the glossy blue door. 'It looks like the gingerbread house in "Red Riding Hood".'

'"Hansel and Gretel", you mean.'

'That's the cookie. So nice of Auntie Mary to offer it us though, Milly, don't you think?'

I have to admit that from the outside it is almost appealing, the woodwork painted in bright canary yellow and the bricks coated in thick pink paint. It has the outward appearance of a giant pink frosted cake but there is a definite whiff of oldness about the whole row of five houses sprouting from the left side of our cottage. The front yard is little more than a communal car park but I can already picture the ocean views from our back windows, the thought of which causes my spirits to rise. Aware of Fi's genuine excitement about returning to her childhood holiday location, I try to think positively that this is our fresh start, despite my initial reservations about my angry bulldog of a surf teacher. At least we have a cute little house to stay in alone together during our adventure. I peer over Fi's shoulder when she opens the door to catch a glimpse of the interior of the cottage.

'What's it like?' I ask anxiously. 'Is it modern or chintzy florals?'

'Ehm, I dunno. It's too dark like.'

Fi moves her hand along the wall to locate a light switch.

'Ta daa!' She flings her arms in the air like a ringmaster introducing his prize circus act and then slowly lowers them as our eyes adjust to the orange light and focus on the cottage's entrance hall.

'I see what you mean about gingerbread,' I croak after a moment of awestruck silence. 'It's very . . . *brown*.'

Brown is an understatement. The wallpaper is dark brown, dotted indiscriminately with what appear to be drab, dead orangey-brown flowers. The skirting boards are brown, the doorframe is brown, the single lampshade is brown and the carpet tiles are a chequerboard of dark brown and occasionally

(I never thought I would be pleased to see it) beige. I am aware that both of us are holding our breath as Fi steps inside and places her hand on the brown door ahead and gently pushes it open.

'Is it brown?' I ask meekly before following Fi into the living room.

Imagine, if you will, immersing yourself entirely in a giant bottle of HP sauce, only without the pleasant taste. Everything is dark brown and musty. In fact, if it were any darker it would be a cave.

'Call the CIA, I think I've found Osama Bin Laden's hangout,' I cough, steadying myself against the sixties wallpaper and promptly becoming entangled in a cobweb of disconcerting thickness.

Fi clears her throat and tiptoes into the centre of the room. She looks out of place in her lemon-yellow trousers, cream jacket and favourite pink glittery runners.

'Watch out for dead people,' I snort, following her gingerly towards the smeared holes masquerading as windows at the other side of the room.

'Ah now, it's not that bad,' Fi replies shakily. She sticks out her tongue as she struggles to open the window. 'It's got a fierce bit of character.'

'Character? Jesus Christ, Fi, if I met this character in the street on a dark night I'd run for my life. It's fierce all right. In fact, it's positively terrifying.'

I perch timidly on the arm of a deep-green (most probably, although I can't quite make out the exact colour in this light) sofa, screwing up my face when a cloud of dust escapes from the threadbare upholstery and shoots up my nostrils.

'Sure, it might be a wee bit dusty,' says Fi, flapping a tiny hand in front of her face, 'but it'll be fine after a clean so it will.'

'A clean of industrial proportions perhaps. If there was a market for antique dust and bad smells, your aunt and uncle would be millionaires by now.'

Fi smiles and plonks herself beside me on the arm of the sofa. There is a loud crack before the arm breaks off and we are deposited with a thump on the (brown) shagpile carpet.

'Jaysus,' Fi howls, rubbing her bony bum and sniggering loudly, 'this is a gas, isn't it?'

I pull her to her feet and lean back against the window, exhaling deeply.

'Yes, very funny,' I reply drily. 'So now you've had your joke, can we go and stay somewhere that doesn't smell of dead people?'

'You're obsessed with dead people, ya mad eejit, and no, we can't go anywhere else because I'd upset Auntie Mary and Uncle Podraig.'

*So what?* I want to scream. *I don't give a shite about Mary and bloody Podraig and I certainly don't want to stay in their crap little house that they haven't been arsed to clean for the last three decades. Let's run while we've got the chance.*

I want to shout it. I want to grab Fi by the wrist and drag her to the nearest hotel. On the train, this all seemed like a bit of an adventure, but now we are here, I am not so sure. The house, the moody surf instructor, and the task we are taking on; it is all becoming a grim reality and I am gripped by stage fright.

'Look it, Milly, the ocean's right there in our back garden. How mighty is that?' says Fi, tilting her head to look at me quizzically.

I morosely rub the cuff of my jumper sleeve against the pane of glass and peer out at the lines of frothy whitewater that are hurling themselves against the rocks at the bottom of the cottage's back wall.

'It looks cold,' I say with a shiver.

'It probably is feckin' cold,' Fi giggles, 'and we'll be finding that out tomorrow, so we will.'

I feel my chest automatically tighten.

'Tomorrow? Give me a break; I'm not going out there, out in that stuff, right out in that sea tomorrow!'

'Sure you are, Milly, that's why we're here. We aren't here for a break like, you said this is research.'

'I know.'

I shuffle my feet and open my eyes wide as another wave smashes against the wall with surprising force.

'I just need a bit of time to get used to it.'

'Ah well, you've got four months for that.'

My heart thuds wearily against my ribcage. Four months is a long time. How can I stay in this hovel for four months? Sixteen weeks. One hundred and twelve days. One hundred and twelve times twenty-four hours. Lots and lots of minutes. Hundreds and thousands of seconds. (Where's Carol Vorderman when you need her?) In other words, a hell of a long time. I have been kidding myself. I had visions of surfing a tropical-looking ocean amongst leaping dolphins while gentle waves guide me to the shore. That is how it looks in the movies, after all. I can't go out there in that vicious boiling pot of frothing grey water. It would be a death wish. One that is very likely to come true.

'I'm sorry, Fi, but I can't do it,' I whisper.

'Can't do what?'

She touches my rigid arm as I cling desperately to the rotting window frame.

'This. This whole palaver. I was imagining it was going to be easy but it's not, it's impossible, Fi, and I'm sorry I brought you all this way under false pretences, but I can't do it.' My voice steadily increases in volume as my anxiousness takes hold. 'I can't stay in this scary cave of a house; I don't want to be in this weird little town. It's pretty enough but that ocean just looks . . . eugh. Surfing is for tough girls and macho men like your cousin and I am absolutely not going to get into a wetsuit and prat about making a fool of myself just to give him a laugh.' I can feel myself getting carried away. 'Mac has got a bigger ego than Michael bloody Flatley and he doesn't like me. I don't like him either so why would he want to teach me to surf? Anyway, I'm sorry, but

51

there's every chance he could be a terrorist the way he reacted to a religious question. You don't know him well, Fi, how do we know that the moment your back is turned he won't have his foot on my head trying to "accidentally" drown me, hmm? My life is worth more than that, Fi, and right now coming clean with the director of this film and explaining that I am a hopeless liar is infinitely more preferable than getting in THAT ocean with THAT up-his-own-arse cousin of yours.'

'Ah now, that's a shame,' says a deep voice from the door-way, "cos I just came to tell you I'd meet you in the morning to get some wetsuits for our lesson tomorrow.'

I turn my head and shoulders stiffly to identify Mac's bulky silhouette on the far side of the room. I am aware that my mouth is open but I am incapable of further movement or speech.

'Got to run though,' Mac says coldly, his green eyes burning into me like heat-seeking missiles, 'got to get back up my own arse.'

'Welcome to Donegal, Milly,' Fi tuts as her cousin disappears silently out of the door, 'ya feckin' gobshite.'

# CHAPTER SIX

## *Rivers of Grease*

I sleep well despite a nutrition-free dinner of crisps and fizzy drinks left over from the train journey. Fi sleeps intermittently, as she always does. Her mind tends to become a whirling dervish of issues as soon as her head hits the pillow, so she often gets up several times a night to read, write, do aerobics or whatever it takes to exhaust her brain and convince it that night-time is for sleeping. Regular lack of log-like sleep would turn me into a moody cow, but Fi is used to it and still manages to function.

I open my eyes and sit up to see that the morning has dawned unexpectedly bright, considering the amount of dread its arrival instils in me. Rays of sun ease their way through the yellowed net curtain and fall on to our twin beds, gradually warming my icy toes and encouraging me to greet the day's arrival. Yesterday may have been a fresh start, but today is so fresh I feel as if my nostrils have been dry-cleaned. Fi and I discussed my reservations after Mac's hasty departure and I have to admit to feeling embarrassed at myself. I am a grown-up, and leaving my familiar surroundings should not get me so ruffled. Life is about adventure after all, and Fi almost has me convinced that we can do this, and that it could even (dare I say it) be fun.

I pull on a thigh-length cream wool jumper and black

trousers, yank on my cosy khaki Ugg boots and tramp downstairs to where Fi is nervously inspecting the limescale-encrusted kettle.

'How about we find a café for brekkie?' I ask, grimacing at the tannin-stained mugs Fi has retrieved from one of the brown cupboards.

'I think that's a grand idea,' says Fi, scurrying off to the hallway to find her pink runners. 'There used to be a fantastic one up in the old church building that did some mighty buns and cakes back when I was a cub.'

'Well as long as they've baked some fresh ones since, that sounds fine by me,' I giggle, following her out of the front door and into the nose-tingling March air.

The houses look even brighter in the early-morning sunlight and I inadvertently allow a spring to enter my step as I trip along the alleyway at the side of the house, down to the ocean behind. A green metal railing runs along the sea wall that is just a matter of four or five feet from the back windows of our house (which we have nicknamed Pooh Corner due to its sheer *brown-ness*). I lean on the railing, close my eyes and breathe in the sea air. It is true; everything smells so much better in the countryside.

'Jaysus, will you look at those waves!' Fi hoots, nudging me and pointing out towards the ocean. 'They're feckin' massive feckers.'

'Bloody hell,' I gasp, opening my eyes to ogle the giant peaks of water rising up in the distance like an oceanic mountain range, 'they're huge. People don't go surfing out there, do they?'

A shiver runs down my spine like a torrent of ice-cold seawater rushing down the back of my neck.

*Tell me they don't. Please tell me I won't have to.*

'Well it looks like they do, hey,' Fi replies, moving her arm around to point towards the rocky cliff to our right, 'because there's our Mac and one of his mates with their boards and wetsuits looking like right proper surfer dudes too. Come on, Milly, let's catch them up and you can apologise for yesterday.'

'Ooh, sounds fab,' I grumble, and grudgingly follow her along the sea wall path towards the two men.

We reach Mac and his friend just as they step out of the water on to the slick, black rocks where I had expected golden sand to be. Both are wearing wetsuits and are carrying their boards tucked neatly under one arm, clearly at ease with the task. Whereas Mac's friend's wetsuit seems to accentuate his thin body and angular joints, Mac's stretches across his muscular frame like the smooth coat of a black stallion. His strong, broad shoulders taper into a surprisingly slim waist before the neoprene of the wetsuit stretches outwards again to cover his firm long legs. When he flicks his hair back from his face, sending droplets of water flying around him like a watery halo, I feel myself blush and quickly glance at Fiona. Her mouth is open like the entrance to the Channel Tunnel as her eyes observe the two men. I smile. Her cousin is undoubtedly stunning and could almost look like a superhero in that rubber suit. If he weren't such a moody git, that is. Superheroes can't be 'super' depending on their mood; it just wouldn't work.

'Right, now you can apologise,' Fi whispers.

I groan inwardly and watch as Mac approaches, trying to think of the right words to say that won't make me completely lose face. How can I put it?

*I'm sorry I called you a terrorist and potential murderer. I am really a very nice, open-minded person and I am sure you are too, so can we be friends and you can just promise not to drown me?*

I squirm. This is not going to be easy. I decide to begin with an icebreaker to lighten the mood.

'Been surfing then?' I say with a cheek-splitting smile.

'No, I've been out picking feckin' potatoes in my bloody wetsuit. What does it look like I've been doing, hey?' Mac grunts in response.

I momentarily wonder whether it is possible to swallow your own head whole, and then silently skulk along behind Fi, Mac and his friend in the direction of the town.

As far as I can see, the town is little more than a glorified village. It consists primarily of a single long street, inventively named 'Main Street'. Smaller roads run off Main Street like veins from an artery but these are little more than passageways leading towards the mountains to the east and the seafront to the west. Main Street is crammed with an abundance of tacky shamrock-covered memorabilia shops for the tourists and long-standing, traditional and slightly dirty-looking pubs for the locals. Newspaper shops selling everything from magazines to illuminated crucifixes, and quaint cafés dissect the monotony, while several neon-lit arcades stand out from the Olde Oirish norm like teenagers on a SAGA coach tour. There appear to be only two shops providing sartorial inspiration for the inhabitants of the town. The first and most fitting of these is Joyce's Fashion Emporium, a boutique still boasting shiny yellow paper in its windows to protect the hand-knitted creations within. The second shop is a far too modern and trendy surf shop that looks as out of place in Main Street as the arcades.

Surfboards and images of bikini-clad girls on sun-scorched beaches fill the windows. I pull my jacket tight around my neck as a blast of cold air whips up the street. I tilt my head at the life-size photo of the surf chick smiling as she exits the water in an itsy-bitsy bikini.

'Where does this surf shop think we are, California?' I giggle.

'This is Dave's family's surf shop,' Mac replies sourly, pointing towards his friend beside me.

I grimace at the slim blond man whom I now know to be Dave and mouth 'sorry', silently thanking the Lord that I didn't add the opinion that opening a surf shop in this god-forsaken town is nothing short of lunacy.

'Don't worry about it,' Dave shrugs with a friendly smile.

'Mac and I will just go in here and get decent. Why don't yous two girls go on away up to the café in the old church there and we'll join yous for breakfast in a minute or two? If you're hungry at all, that is?'

'Feckin' starving,' Fi enthuses, clutching her concave stomach. She smiles broadly at Dave, whose cheeks visibly redden despite being already rosy from the wind.

'See yous there,' Fi adds. 'Don't be long now.'

'*See yous there, don't be long now*,' I tweet mockingly as Fi gives Dave a flirty wink and skips off up the road. 'Do we have to have breakfast with them, Fi? I'm sorry but I can't help it, that cousin of yours makes me nervous.'

'Do we have to have breakfast with them, Dave?' I hear as Mac's distinctive voice carries on the wind from the surf shop doorway. 'That high-maintenance friend of my cousin's is doing my head in.'

'I can recommend the Full Irish,' Dave chirps when, one mug of cheap instant coffee later, they join us at our PVC-tablecloth-topped breakfast table.

'Aye, Bridget here makes a mighty soda bread to go with the best bacon in Donegal,' says Mac, wrapping a muscular arm around the shoulders of our middle-aged waitress.

Bridget blushes from her salt-and-pepper hair to the hem of her pale-green tabard and gazes up into Mac's emerald eyes.

'Away ye go now, Cormac Heggarty,' she giggles like a self-conscious schoolgirl, 'don't you be flirtin' with me or Mr McGonigle will be after ye.'

Mac laughs delightedly, revealing a comfortable smile I have not previously witnessed and a set of straight white teeth with a boyish gap between the front two.

'Ah, but the lady has a husband, so sure I'll just have to make do with the breakfast.'

I raise my eyebrows at the way Fi's cousin can turn on the playful charm to flirt when he chooses to.

'Typical surf instructor,' I whisper to Fi. 'Thinks he's bloody irresistible.'

'Oh and he is,' Dave replies quietly, his head appearing suddenly between my right shoulder and Fi's left. 'He's got the credentials to prove it.'

The breakfast arrives on plates large enough to land a helicopter on. I let Fi do most of the talking while I concentrate on trying to digest sausage, bacon, beans, black pudding, tinned button mushrooms, fried bread, soda bread and deep-fried potato cubes, all washed down with a river of lard and two more cups of chicory instant. Now, I like my food, but usually I would draw the line at a meal of dead animal, processed veg and carbohydrate shouting 'FAT BUM AND CELLULITE, FREE WITH EVERY MEAL!' with such glee. Today, however, something is making me want to finish every last fat calorie on this plate. That something is the knowing expression on Mac Heggarty's face as he watches me from across the table. That and the way he mockingly comments, 'Bet this isn't your usual style, hey, princess? Don't go smudging your lipstick with the grease now.'

All right, so Mac thinks he knows me now, does he? He has decided I am a high-maintenance prima donna with a posh Hampshire accent and aristocratic attitudes to match. Well, country boy, you may think you have got my number but I am a much more complex and, although I say so myself, fascinating creature than you may think. Not to mention stubborn. Which is why I am going to eat every last morsel of this disgustingly lardy breakfast even if it kills me (which is likely) or pushes me up to a size fourteen.

'Gorgeous,' says Fi, pushing her clean plate away and sitting back to rub her full stomach. 'I could eat that all again.'

'I'm sure you could,' Dave replies. His smiling eyes connect with Fi's across the plastic carnations on the table between them. 'I bet you'd still have a body like Kylie too.'

'Don't be an eejit, Dave,' Fi snorts, 'I haven't got a body like Kylie feckin' Minogue.' She kicks Dave's leg under the table.

'Aye, you have so.' Dave grins back and returns the jovial kick.

'No I haven't.' Kick, flirtatious slap of the hand.

'Yeah you have.' Kick, tickle of the wrist.

'I have not.' Kick, wink, squeeze of the fingers.

'You have s—'

'OK, can we cool it with the conversational ping-pong?' I snap, feeling distinctly uncomfortable sitting opposite Mac, in the presence of such blatant flirting. 'Yes, Fi, you do have a better arse than Kylie, and no, Dave, Fi does not have a boyfriend. OK? Is that all sorted? Now can we exit this greasy spoon and get on with the reason we came here, do you think?'

'Ooh look it, the drama queen reveals herself.'

I whip my head up to respond to Mac's comment but pause when I catch the expression of genuine amusement on his face. My sharp retort catches in my throat as Mac creases his lightly freckled nose and treats me to his second smile of the day. I gulp, look down at the empty plate and choke on a stray particle of black pudding gristle lingering in the back of my throat. Gross.

'Excuse me,' I cough and scurry off to the toilet.

'Sure it must have been sunny in Dublin this winter,' I hear Dave comment. 'She's got a fierce orange tan on herself.'

'It's fake,' Fi replies before I slam the toilet door shut and forcibly exhale.

'You've got a message,' Fi informs me on my return to the table several minutes and deep breaths later. She hands me my mobile. 'It's from dickhead. He wants to meet for' – she mimes inverted commas with her fingers – 'coffee.'

'Thank you for respecting my privacy.'

'No problem,' Fi shrugs in total innocence. 'Text back

and tell him from me he can shove his coffee up his thespian arse along with his giant ego and go somewhere else for a free ride.'

I avert my eyes from the curious gazes across the table and concentrate on reading Dan's text.

*Hi Mimi what u doin? Fancy a coffee and chat? Miss u call me xx Dan the man.*

'Wanker,' Fi grunts while my heart does a silent leap.

'Dan Clancy,' she adds in response to Mac and Dave's inquisitive looks.

'The actor?' Dave asks.

'The very same. These two' – Fi flicks her head in my direction – 'were an item for a while. Love's young dream apparently until Dan "the man" realised he couldn't love anyone but himself so he gave her the heave-ho on Valentine's Day last year, for feck's sake.'

'He never did?'

'No, he—' I begin.

'He totally did, Dave, and more to the point, that is our Milly's birthday.'

'No way, that's double shite.'

'The bastard.'

I blink, fold my arms and wait for Fi and Dave's exchange of tuts and shaken heads to run out of steam. They are already like a double act and we have only been here since five o'clock last night. I can feel Mac's eyes piercing through my burning left cheek. He says nothing.

'Have you quite finished discussing my personal life or would you like me to wait while all my dirty laundry is washed in public?'

Fi raises a finger to her lips and clicks her tongue.

'No, I think that's about it for now. Just getting these fellas up to date on things.'

'Very thoughtful, Fiona.'

'No problem at all.'

I sigh. 'So how about we stick to discussing this surfing

thing? I'm sure Dave and Mac aren't interested in the ins and outs of my love life.'

'Oh, I don't know, it's always nice for us country folk to hear about how the other half live.'

Mac is mocking me, I know, so I bite my lip and concentrate on the tablecloth.

'Right then, I suggest we head down to the surf shop and fix you maisies up with boards and wetsuits,' says Dave after a pregnant pause.

Fi leaps off her creaky chair and practically sprints for the door.

'Fantastic idea, Dave. Come on, Milly, this'll be great craic, so it will.'

'Hmm, skin-tight rubber suits to wear in public. I can't wait to squeeze myself into one of those,' I grunt, and stomp to the door.

I glance up at Mac, who holds the café door open for me, an unreadable smile playing on his lips.

'After you, Mrs Clancy.'

I flick my hair and march proudly past, just pausing to comment over my shoulder, 'And for your information, he did not dump me, we broke up mutually.'

'Ah but of course you did, Mrs Clancy,' Mac chuckles victoriously, 'of course you did.'

# CHAPTER SEVEN

## *Neoprene Nightmares*

Standing in the surf shop I feel as if I have stepped through the changing cubicle in a *Mr Benn* cartoon and been transported from west Ireland to the sunny shores of California. The turquoise wooden-slat surf shack walls are adorned with pictures of perma-tanned surf gods pulling off manoeuvres on smooth azure waves. In one corner stands a six-foot fake (yet rather impressive) palm tree which, combined with the fake hibiscus flowers, coconuts and Hawaiian print material throughout the shop, creates the myth that we are in some tropical paradise. Of course, one would only have to step out of the door in one of the skimpy surf-chick creations to realise that a below-freezing wind chill awaits those daring to bare their midriff. I pick up a pair of minute denim pedal pushers and marvel at the size of the waist. Fi may be able to get into them without the need for organ removal but I bet most girls with an appetite for carbohydrates and chocolate would have trouble getting them up past their knees. Just how small are the women in the surfing community? From the size of these clothes, I am surprised they don't get lost in the sand.

I give up trying to locate a size twelve among the Sindy doll clothes and turn my attention to the rear half of the shop where Mac and Dave are showing Fiona the surprisingly extensive range of surfboards and wetsuits. Surely that many people aren't mad enough to go surfing in Ireland, I wonder, just as Dave tells Fi that surfing is the fastest-growing sport in the country. Somehow I have my doubts. I suspect most people buying a wetsuit from this shop are simply preparing for an emergency flooding situation.

I walk the length of the back wall of the shop, running my fingers lightly along a row of glossy new surfboards. There are tall ones, short ones, fat, thin and pointy ones. Each price tag has a description of the board along with some numbers, which I guess to be the dimensions, scribbled by hand in marker pen. I squint at the label attached to a towering, sleek red board shaped like a pointed dart.

*Bushman Hawaiian big-wave gun*, it reads, $9'6'' \times 19'' \times 3''$.

*Small-wave high-performance Al Merrick shortboard*, the next label informs me, $6'1'' \times 18\frac{1}{4}'' \times 2\frac{1}{4}''$.

'Specialist small-wave Q-Stix Fish for summer fun,' I read aloud. 'What is that? Er, five feet and ten inches times um . . .'

'By nineteen by two and three eighths.' Dave finishes the sentence for me.

'What does all this mean, Dave?'

Dave gently taps the smooth edges of the smallest board.

'This, Milly, is one of the most important decisions a surfer has to make. What board to ride on a particular wave on a certain day.'

I scan the racks of boards and frown.

'But I thought they would all be much the same.'

'Far from it. See, if we sent you out on this little Fish here, you wouldn't have a hope in hell of catchin' anything. Apart from hypothermia before the rescue boat comes to get ya.'

Which is a cheering thought.

'Mac here would ride anything from a six-foot-two, seeing as he's a chunky fella' – Dave flexes his own biceps jovially – 'to this beauty of a nine-six here. Now that red one's a mighty board so it is for feckin' mighty surf. Like twenty-five-footers. If you're lucky, maisies, you might just see it in action with these winter and early spring swells.'

'I am not going anywhere near a twenty-five-foot wave thank you very much,' I shiver. 'Twenty-five centimetres will be big enough for me. Do you really go out when it's that big, Mac?'

Mac shrugs one shoulder and looks away without answering.

Huh, I knew he wouldn't be *that* brave. Perhaps in his ego-filled dreams, but not out in that ocean on one of these sticks of fibreglass. I smile victoriously and follow Dave as he looks at the rows of surfboards through his floppy blond fringe.

I keep my eyes on the 'Bushman Hawaiian big-wave gun', hoping my board will be just as attractive, if a touch smaller and easier to carry. I take a deep breath when I realise that there is in fact a whole world revolving around surfing that I know absolutely nothing about. There is the equipment, the lingo and so much information. I have only four months to assimilate it all, put it into practice and emerge as a dedicated water woman if I am going to keep this film role. Am I just naïve, I wonder, or stark raving bonkers?

'Well now, let's see,' says Dave, smoothing his hair behind his ears and fixing his twinkly hazel eyes on Fiona's petite figure, 'sure you're just a wee thing, Fiona, so this cute little mini-mal will be grand.'

Dave reaches into the racks of boards and pulls out a slab of highly polished moulded fibreglass decorated top to bottom with pink and red flowers.

'Wow, I love it; it's gorgeous, really bloody gorgeous!' Fi enthuses, clasping the board with both hands and pulling it towards her.

Dave grins proudly before bending his slim frame over a box of bits and pieces.

'I've even got a matching pink leash,' he says, emerging

from the box. 'Now you attach one end to the board and the other to your ankle, then hopefully we won't be losing either of yous. And here's a block of wax for the top, or as we call it the deck,' he smiles. 'That makes the board less slippy. Sure with all that you'll be surfing in no time at all.'

Fi gently rests the board on the floor, accepts the handful of goodies and beams.

'Thanks a million, Dave, I really love it. It's so beautiful with the flowers and the colours and, Jaysus, it's much too pretty to get wet like. Can Milly have one the same so as we can be surfing twins?'

Dave and Mac exchange quick glances that I fail to interpret and move their way down the rows of boards, stopping every once in a while to size me up with their eyes. I shuffle uncomfortably but, despite my initial reluctance about venturing into this world, I can't help but feel a thrill of anticipation. I just never realised how pretty sports equipment could be. These boards are stunning, so shiny and colourful, like individual works of art. Will I get the glossy Bushman gun or will mine be an Al Merrick high-performance whatsit? I grin proudly to myself, pleased that I am already mastering some of the terminology.

'Ah now, there's the one, that'll be perfect, Dave. Just what this city lady needs.'

I suck air through my teeth and step nervously forward to receive my prize from Mac. Even if it hasn't got pink *and* red flowers on it, just one or the other will do.

'Well you're a fair bit bigger than Fiona here,' Dave remarks. *Skinny git.*

'So Mac's probably right, this would be best for you, Milly.'

I feel my cheeks flush as Mac nods firmly and passes his choice of weapon to Dave, who then deposits into my outstretched arms what can only be described as a giant pockmarked blue and yellow sponge with neither pretty painted things, nor a glossy coat, nor anything remotely resembling an iota of style or desirability. It is nothing but a huge chunk of chunky polystyrene for chunky people to try and surf on. It is crap and I am gutted.

'But . . .' I whisper, trying not to sound ungrateful but aware that Mac is watching me, awaiting my reaction, 'but can't I possibly have a mini-mal thing like Fiona's? I mean, hers is so pretty and this is just, well, you know, a bit . . .'

*Crap?*

*Spongy?*

*Like a crap, giant sponge for crap, spongy people?*

'. . . a bit big,' I squeak, afraid that I might be about to cry.

'Yeah, but you need a bigger board than Fi 'cos you're a bigger person,' Mac replies with very little tact. 'A common mistake is starting to learn on one too small and you just won't get anywhere. It's not about the colours and flowers, you know, princess.'

'I know that,' I snap, 'and stop calling me princess.'

Mac sighs and lets go of the board, which I struggle to catch.

'Dave here knows best, so you'll just have to make do with this one, and if you want me to teach you then you'd better be ready to do as I say. I'm not taking you out there if you're going to argue with me and end up hurting yourself.'

I lower my eyes during Mac's frosty scolding and shift my feet uncomfortably on the wooden floor.

'OK?' he persists.

'OK,' I mumble moodily.

'Right then, so now that's sorted, how's about we get on and find some feckin' wetsuits. Dave?'

Dave nods at his friend and leads the way. I drag the board along, stumbling every time my hand slips from around its bulky middle.

'Don't wait for me,' I grumble to myself, 'just save me the crappiest wetsuit and really make my day.'

If there is someone you really don't like in life then my advice is to buy him or her a wetsuit and force him or her to wear it in public. This wetsuit is worse than my top ten list of bad things ever invented, all combined to make the baddest of bad things ever. Now I understand why surf-chick clothes are so small, because surf chicks also have to wear wetsuits, and these are, I now realise, the most unflattering item of clothing ever invented. Even worse than knee-length box-pleated skirts, and jumpsuits. Wetsuits leave absolutely nothing to the imagination. In fact, I would rather be standing in the middle of this shop dressed only in a PVC thong and nipple tassles, which gives you some idea of how bad it really is. At least then I would not have a thick layer of sweaty rubber adding bulk to the bulk I already have but had previously managed to conceal by dressing sensibly. Not only am I squashed into this wetsuit, though, my feet are also encased in black rubber booties, I have a pair of rubber gloves (not the Marigold type) cutting off the circulation in my hands and Dave insisted that I try on a rubber hood contraption to keep my ears warm in the water. The whole get-up is nothing short of ridiculous and I now feel like the Michelin Man's younger sister squeezed into a giant black condom. Fi, of course, hops up and down next to me in a black, red and pink ensemble, looking like a multicoloured stripe of low-fat liquorice and twice as tasty. Tell me, am I allowed to hate my best friend?

'OK, so we're after getting the boards, wetsuits, leashes, wax, and stuff. 'Fraid we can't do anything about the raw talent,' Dave chuckles.

At least that is what I think he says, although my hearing is somewhat impaired by a thick layer of neoprene.

'So what d'ya think, Mac, are these chicks ready for surfing?'

'Aye, I guess so,' Mac replies, eyeing my sweaty face wearily. 'You won't be needing the hood, that was just Dave messin' with you.'

*I would laugh if my face were not being squashed to a pulp by a rubber helmet that is tighter than my own skin.*

I try to remove the hood but feel as if in doing so I will also succeed in removing most of my head. I gesture with my rubber hands as best I can that I will need help to take it off but Mac somehow misinterprets this as *I love this gimp mask so much, I would like to keep it on for the rest of the day*.

'Now then, how about we go ahead and get in the water?'

*What? Now? Like right now? Absolutely no way, José.*

'Mighty!' Fi shrieks, grabbing her board and springing towards the shop doorway. 'Come on, Milly.'

'Mumph,' I reply as I try to peel the rubber hood from my mouth. 'Numph, wumphoo.'

I heave the polystyrene lump under my arm and frantically waddle after them like an overweight penguin.

'I'll take yous to the main beach in town,' says Mac. 'It's more sheltered round there than the reefs or the other beaches and the surf is smaller so.'

'STOP!' I shout when I find the superhero strength from within to rip the rubber balaclava off my head, 'Ow, fuck, I think I just pulled one of my ears off.'

Fi places her board on the floor and springs towards me. She softly clamps my cheeks between her hands and turns my head from side to side.

'Aye, they've gone a bit squashed tomato-ey like but you've still got the two ears. Now then, Milly, what's up with ya?'

I wrinkle my rubber-stretched face and wish that Mac and Dave would stop gawping at me long enough for me to throw my melodramatic hissy fit in peace.

'I don't, er . . . I can't, um . . . I don't believe I am available for an actual lesson today.'

Mac groans, Dave sniggers and Fi tilts her head to look at me.

'Why not, Milly?' she asks, one hand placed on her jutting right hipbone.

'Because . . .'

*Because I am one hundred and ten per cent fucking terrified of going anywhere near the sea and I am not comfortable with*

*your choice of surf instructor and I am very likely to lose my
world out of my bottom with nerves any minute now, which is
not a pleasant prospect in this outfit?*

'Because I have to do some other preparatory research
first. There is much more to acting than just getting on and
doing it.'

'Bollocks,' Mac tuts loud enough for me to overhear.

'But Milly, you're all set to go and surely there's no harm
in just starting like ya mean to go on and getting in there.
There's no time like the present.'

*Oh yes there is, David my friend, there is tomorrow or the
next day or next week or never. Much better than the present if
you ask me.*

I briefly glance over at Mac, expecting to see an expression of anger on his tanned face. Instead, however, I am
positive I see a look of disappointment flash across his eyes.
For a split second, I consider just explaining my fears to
this man. Telling him how scared I am of the water but that
I also want this job. That, with the right encouragement and
support, I really want to master this sport and rise to the
challenge. After all, Mac is a fully qualified lifeguard and
apparently a rather accomplished surfer so he must surely
possess some degree of approachability. Otherwise no one
would want to pay to attend his surf lessons or be rescued by
him and be forever indebted to the moody bastard. The
words *Help me, Mac, I am just a big scaredy-cat* tiptoe nervously to the tip of my tongue, but my pride, and the fact that
this man has shown me no kindness or given me any special
treatment so far, makes me push the confession back into my
throat and causes me to cough.

'You see, maybe I'm coming down with a cold.' I cough
again. 'Look, guys, thanks again for getting the board and
wetsuit sorted, they're, um, great and I will definitely be
taking lessons from you, Mac, and paying for them of
course, but just not today.'

Mac nods without smiling.

'It's not that I am putting it off or anything. I am just—'

'Putting it off,' Fi interrupts with a smirk.

I begin to retreat to the back of the shop before they can drag me out of the door and down to the beach.

'Look,' I call over my shoulder, 'we have got four months to do all this, so what's the rush?'

No response.

'Anyway, I must get on and do some research, make some important phone calls and stuff, so I'll just go ahead and get out of this wetsuit now if that's OK with you?'

Without awaiting their reply, I throw myself breathlessly into one of the changing cubicles.

By the way, I have also now discovered another reason why surf chicks are so petite. Because when on dry land, and especially during times of stress, these wetsuits heat up to bone-melting temperatures. Why bother with the boring old Atkins diet when you can wear one of these things for a couple of days and simply melt yourself down to a size six? Granted, you might look a bit ridiculous and you will probably start to smell, but surely that is a small price to pay for effective shrinkage?

If I thought getting into the wetsuit was hard, then getting out of it again requires the sort of contortionism that would make Houdini's eyes water. I struggle with the back zip that runs from the neck to my lower back, almost double-jointing both arms in the process. I am then supposed to be able to remove my entire body through a hole apparently smaller than the circumference of my head while the sweaty neoprene clings determinedly to my arms and legs. Finally, having stretched, pinged and yanked in every conceivable direction, my arms spring free, whacking the sides of the cubicle as they do so in celebration of their emancipation from their rubbery captor.

'Would ya be needin' a hand in there?' Dave asks with a chortle in response to my porcine grunts.

70

'Uh, n . . . no, uh, th . . . thanks,' I reply as calmly as possible, wincing as I push the wetsuit down towards my ankles, seemingly removing a layer of skin en route.

I am almost back to normal. That is, if you can call standing in an Irish high street shop in a pale-blue swimsuit two sizes too small, hence cutting off my circulation in rather essential parts, with one foot still entrapped in a heap of neoprene, *normal*. Not to mention the fact that my skin has turned a delightful patchwork of orange, pink and off-white where my fake tan has rubbed off in blotches. I scowl at my reflection in the cubicle mirror, which surely must be one of those disproportionately-podgy-reflection ones, and scrape my lank hair back behind my ears. I look more of a wreck than I feel, which is definitely saying something.

Taking a deep breath, I bend down and struggle to release my right foot from the ankle of the wetsuit. I pull, I push, and I stand on the suit with the other foot and yank my right leg upwards. I swear at it, I break two nails. Damn this fucking stupid invention. I heave, I sigh, I try one last-ditch attempt to pull my foot out of the impossibly small hole. My ankle pops out, I topple to one side and crash out of the cubicle, landing in a spectacular heap at the feet of Mac, Dave and several bemused customers. My cringingly tight swimming costume does little to cover my shame.

'Ah, poor lassie,' I hear one woman whisper loudly to another, 'she's got that vitiligo thing like your one Michael Jackson. Look it, her skin's all patchy.'

Dave laughs uproariously before reaching out a hand and helping me to my feet. Mac, whom I expected to rejoice in my embarrassment, looks away, either pretending not to notice or to save his eyes from the unpleasant sight. Blushing so much even my toenails turn red, I fight my way back into the cubicle and ensure my whole backside has followed me to safety.

What is wrong with me? Ever since I embarked on this clearly ill-fated plan, I have done nothing but make a total tit of myself. In fact, since meeting Dan on Grafton Street, my life has been thrown into disarray; some good, some bad, but all confusing. Seeing his face and body again made me remember why I love him. Talking to him and hearing about his life gave me the motivation (and perhaps the luck) to land the role in this film. Does it matter, though, that my success so far is based on the lie that I can surf? Is that why everything I do in front of my surf instructor makes me look like some sort of uncoordinated retard? Is it a surfy hippie karma thing that is making my life go a bit whoops-upside-your-head? I sniff and sadly pull on my warm clothes, glad to be back in a baggy, unrevealing silhouette. I sigh, suddenly craving the explosion of emotion and happiness I used to feel whenever Dan called me or whenever we were together. With Dan, I felt as if I could do anything and be whoever I wanted to be. I felt as if I could achieve as many goals as David Beckham and still set myself up for more. All right, I didn't actually achieve any of them at that time, but Dan made me feel as if I had the potential. We shared the dream, Dan and I. We fantasised about when we would eventually make it as actors. Now Dan is living the dream and, from the glow he radiated when we met the other day, the dream looks to be every bit as good as I imagined.

I stare at myself in the mirror and run my acrylic nails through my hair. I pull it into a tidy knot at the base of my neck then I lick my fingers and moisten the ends of my eyelashes to make them appear fuller. A dab of lip-gloss from the pocket of my trousers and I am ready. Ready to speak to Dan.

# CHAPTER EIGHT

## *Floods of Hormones*

I nearly hang up on the tenth (yes, I counted) ring when I hear a click followed by the dulcet tones of the only man who can make my spine tingle from the other side of the country.

'D.C.,' he says smoothly, sounding every bit the confident Hollywood film star.

'D.C. is it now?' I try to disguise the nervousness in my voice, feeling like a teenager who has psyched up all day to ring her favourite crush. 'Well hi there, D.C., this is A.A.'

'Oh, you would definitely be more than a double A, darling. If I remember rightly there was more than a handful to play with in your delightful breasts.'

A high-pitched giggle escapes from the back of my throat before I can stop it. I quickly glance around from my position on the sea wall to check that no one is witnessing me losing my cool. Not bad, I think, only ten seconds into the phone call and already Dan is in full flirt mode. He is, it seems, as reliable as he ever was. Fi used to say that his sexual innuendos were to cover up for his otherwise dull conversation. I, of course, disagree. Doesn't every girl enjoy a bit of flirting with the right man?

'So how are things?' I ask, hoping that I sound casual, yet sultry, with just a hint of irresistible sex bomb.

'Things are great, Mimi. I have had new offers by the dozen so it's a bit of a bind trawling through them all, you know, trying to sort out the good from the bad.'

'Hmm,' I squeak, already feeling out of my league, 'that is such a bind, isn't it?'

*Not that I would have the faintest idea.*

'What about you, Mimi, any news to report or shall we discuss it over dinner?'

I do, I admit, briefly consider hotfooting it back to Dublin on an oestrogen-fuelled mission, but even I can see that, having only arrived yesterday, that would make me rather sad. Oh, and Fi would kill me.

'I would love to do dinner, Dan, but I'm afraid I can't. Fi and I are over on the west coast in County Donegal for a few weeks.'

'A few weeks? Jesus Christ, was it a bet you lost or something? Or no, let me guess, this is another of your flatmate's wacky ideas. How is the fiery-haired midget by the way, still clinically mental?'

'Don't call her that, Dan,' I scold firmly. 'She is not mental.'

'You could have fooled me. That girl is hyperactive and completely unpredictable. Not to mention the fact that she doesn't like me. I mean, come on, Mimi, how screwed up is that?'

I frown, wishing Dan wouldn't say things that make him sound egotistical. Not that he is, you understand, he just has trouble phrasing things correctly sometimes.

'Fi has depression,' I carry on, ignoring his comments, 'you know that, Dan. It's a physical condition and it doesn't mean she is mental at all. You should show a little compassion.'

'Why? Because she feels a bit sad now and again? Life is hard for all of us, Milly, but we don't all go turning our moods into a vote for sympathy. If you ask me, she's just lazy.'

'I didn't ask you,' I reply, 'but you know there is much more to it than that. Fi has already had harder things to deal with in her life than most of us will ever have to face. Now don't be so facetious.'

I bite hard on my tongue. Despite my natural instinct to keep fighting my best friend's corner and to explain the reasons behind her illness and to rave about how brave Fi has become since the horrendous death of her only brother, Sean, I decide that now is not the time. I am well aware that, regardless of the prevalence of depression in our society these days, for many people the slightest mention of any mental illness still conjures up images of padded cells and rocking zombies in straitjackets. 'Pull yourself together,' people used to comment to Fi. 'What have you got to be depressed about?' Because her arm isn't in a cast and her illness isn't visible, many people just do not understand it. They think she's making it up. If they looked around them, they would probably realise that many of the people they know – the unlikely ones, the life-and-soul-of-the-party ones – are suffering in silence too.

This lack of understanding makes me angry, but then I suppose before I knew Fi I wouldn't have understood it myself. I was blissfully unaware. I also know that Dan has little time for Fi's problems because of the simple fact that she made her dislike of him so obvious. She is one girl who is definitely not a Dan Clancy fan, in his professional capacity or otherwise.

I take a deep breath. We are supposed to be indulging in some sizzlingly flirtatious phone time here, not getting all serious and heavy. I cradle my mobile between my right shoulder and ear and quickly reapply my lip-gloss. (I know there is no video link but it doesn't do to try and talk sexy with chapped lips.)

'So, as I was saying, Dan, we're over here for a few weeks in a . . . er, lovely little town just south of the border, right by the sea.'

'Why so long? Shouldn't you be back here in Dublin trying to find work? Pardon me for speaking my mind, Mimi honey, but you're not exactly going to stumble across the big time all the way over there in bog country.'

'That is where you are wrong, young Mr Clancy,' I declare proudly, 'because the fact is, I am here to research my role . . . my *leading* role in the next Irish film production tipped for the big time.'

'Oh yes?'

'Yes, yes, yes,' I laugh, 'isn't it great? I have a job, Dan, a real acting job, and I am just sooo excited about it. I just had to tell you, especially since we always used to fantasise about this happening. Do you remember, Dan? Sitting on St Stephen's Green, watching the world go by and planning what we would wear to our first premiere and what we would say in our first media interviews. Do you remember?'

'Of course I remember,' Dan replies in a strangely serious tone.

I cough. 'Well, of course, you are much further along than me in the business, you're living the dream, but maybe I am going to get there too. Wouldn't that be fabulous?'

There is a pause before Dan speaks again.

'Fabulous, Milly, it truly is fabulous. Such a shame I can't take you out to celebrate. The champagne, the slap-up meal, the slap of your inner thigh against my skin as you straddle me and make me explode.'

I gulp (no pun intended) and hurriedly cross my legs.

'Dan' – I clear my throat – 'don't.'

'Why? Am I making you horny?'

This is more than I expected. We broke up over a year ago now and have had almost no contact until that chance meeting a few days ago. If he still has feelings for me, then why the separation? Why can we not still be together?

'What about Roma?' I croak weakly while hormones shoot electric shocks through my tightly pressed-together thighs.

'Roma?' Dan repeats nonchalantly.

'Yes. Is she not your gi . . . your . . .'

'Milly Armstrong,' he laughs, 'why would I want to talk about her when I can be talking about you? Come on now, baby, tell me all your news. This is just so unbelievable and I want to know everything. Tell me all.'

So I do. I sit on the sea wall, merrily swinging my legs and gazing out at the waves breaking against the flat black rocks in the distance. All the time I push the telephone closer to my ear as if to push Dan's voice deeper inside my head. I want him inside me, deep inside me.

I tell Dan everything, from the message from Gerald about the audition, to my hurried preparation the night before and the subsequent image disasters. I tell him about getting his message just as I reached the audition room, which felt like a sign of good luck, and about competing with Bliss for the role. I even tell him about my little white lie and how it has led to me being marooned in Donegal for the best part of four months in order that I can carry my lie right through to fruition. The more I talk, the more excited and proud I feel. I embellish details here and there to impress my movie star ex-boyfriend. I tell him that Matthew, the director, was so impressed with me he was desperate for me to have the part, and that there is talk of the leading man being a big name to help to turn the film into a block-buster. I relay every detail to Dan, who listens intently. I leave nothing out.

'Well, well, well,' Dan whistles finally when I come to a breathless stop, 'it seems Milly Armstrong has got that big break at last. Watch out, you'll be competing with me for publicity before I know it.'

'Oh, I doubt that, Dan,' I giggle.

'Who would have thought it? Perhaps Hollywood is set to have an influx of Irish assets.'

I blush. 'Perhaps.'

'Well you just stay there and get stuck into that research,

baby doll. You won't be missing anything over here, I don't wonder. And,' he adds with an exaggerated sigh, 'I will take a rain check on that dinner date.'

'For now,' I reply softly.

'For now,' Dan repeats, his voice deep and velvety in my ear.

I end the call and clasp the phone to my chest, all at once feeling loved, supported and inspired by my connection with a man like Dan. There is no time for self-doubt here. If Dan were in this situation what would he do? He wouldn't sit around doubting himself, scared to try lest he should fail. No, Dan would just take the bull by the horny . . . excuse me, horns . . . and throw himself into the role of a lifetime. I have my dream to reach out for, and with Dan behind me and Fi by my side, there is no way I can fail.

# CHAPTER NINE

## *Water Features*

I succeed in delaying my first surfing lesson for the best part of five days. (I may be motivated but I am not a masochist.) Of course I invest my time constructively by researching as much as I can about surfing in general so that I am no longer a complete kook among the local surfer dudes. I buy surfing magazines from Dave's shop and read them from cover to cover. In actual fact, half of what I read I fail to understand, as the articles are littered with jargon and in-crowd cool-speak that I do not recognise as being part of the English language as I know it. I begin a note-book of slang words to ask Dave and Mac the meanings of ('kook' being one of them. It means a know-nothing dork or something along those lines, which is probably what I am to Mac and Dave). Cutbacks, floaters and barrels are, I discover, all manoeuvres performed by the surfer as he rides the face of the wave.

'Don't be going worrying about those so,' Mac kindly informs me. 'If we just get you standing up and going in a straight line it'll be a feckin' miracle.'

Charming.

Slang words such as 'gnarly' and 'stoked' are used, Dave tells me, in the context of 'Man, that wave was so *gnarly*, but I made it and I'm totally *stoked*' – which apparently means

'Golly, I thought that nasty big wave was going to pound me through to Timbuktu but it was tickety-boo in the end and I am jolly pleased with myself as it happens' (a rough translation).

'Aye, I have to admit you do hear surfers goin' on like that, but just don't overdo the dude shite or you'll end up soundin' like a stoned Californian hippie,' Dave adds by way of warning.

With some jargon tucked safely under my belt for a rainy day, I then curl up on the sofa with my best friend to look at the pictures in the glossy publications. Girls, if you have never flicked through a surfing magazine, do yourself a favour and settle yourself comfortably in a corner of W.H. Smith to check one out. Fi and I fall in love with each turn of the page.

'Ooh, check out that six-pack. Jaysus, you could use that as a magazine rack,' Fi giggles, pointing at one of the beach scene photographs.

'Six times world champion Kelly Slater,' I purr, running my finger down the muscular surfer's naked torso above his star-patterned board shorts. 'Hmm mmm, he can champion my world any day. Look at the man, Fi, he's totally edible.'

'Cute,' Fi sniggers, 'very cute, but that picture there freaks me out a bit like. How can he stay on the board upside down five feet in the feckin' sky?'

I turn the magazine upside down and shrug.

'Dunno, he must have sticky feet.'

Fi snorts. 'Just as long as he hasn't got sticky hands, that's OK by me.'

We ooh and aah and snigger like schoolgirls. We gaze at the images of tropical scenery and imagine going out surfing in nothing but a tiny bikini and our sleek, bronzed skin (I may need a body double for that dream). We gawp at the photographs of strong girls fearlessly charging monstrous waves before returning to the less daunting male images. I would hate to sound non-PC, but the glorious aesthetics of this sport certainly make for interesting research. Thank God I am not researching darts.

Fi and I then move on to surfing DVDs. On Dave's advice, we rent every cheesy Hollywood surfing production the Ballyshannon video store has in stock and supplement these with more soulful DVDs from the surf shop. Our selection consists of *Point Break* (of course), *Blue Crush* and *Blue Juice* (blue being a rather obvious theme here), *Big Wednesday*, *North Shore*, *Thicker Than Water* and *Litmus*. To help our research, Dave also very kindly gives us a loan of a widescreen TV and a DVD player. Pooh Corner does have a television of sorts, but our faux-mahogany antique set with manual channel dial was created before the need for three channel numbers, never mind the need to communicate with digital video technology. Besides, the firework display of sparks emitted from the back of the set every time we bravely switch it on has started to make me nervous. One spark on this highly flammable ancient foam-filled sofa and whoosh, a fireball would engulf us and every brown object in seconds.

Dave delivers the equipment at lunchtime on Wednesday and sets it all up in no time. He happily accepts the offer of coffee, biscuits and a place on the sofa next to Fi. He then seems to forget all about shop opening hours and settles in to watch *Big Wednesday* with us while giving a running commentary of every scene. I try to keep up.

'What did he say? "That's just the lemon next to the pie"? What does that mean in proper English?'

'It means Big Wednesday hasn't arrived yet, Milly. There are more monstrous waves yet to come.'

'Right. That's just the lemon . . .'

'Don't worry, you don't have to talk like that.'

'Thank God. I might have agreed to learn to surf but I don't want to sound like a total chump.'

By the time we have watched Keanu Reeves and Patrick Swayze playing it cool in *Point Break*, Dave and Fi are leaning on one another, sharing a bowl of sugar-coated popcorn and chattering animatedly during the slow bits. By our Friday-evening viewing of *Litmus*, which features the very waves just outside our cottage window, they have become a commentary double act and seem to share the same opinion of every scene. I don't mean to sound selfish, but I am starting to feel like a spare part in my own research project.

'Right now, who's for a bit of your one Catherine Zeta Jones Douglas Toomanynames in *Blue Juice*?' Dave asks.

'Not me,' I say with an exaggerated yawn. 'This surf movie marathon is tiring.'

Fi shrugs casually. 'Sure, Dave, why not? I'm not tired at all. I'm not a big sleeper anyhow.'

'She's nocturnal actually.'

Dave laughs and leaves his treasured position beside Fi to return the empty popcorn bowl to the kitchenette attached to the sitting room.

'Put the kettle back on while you're over there, Dave,' Fi yells over her shoulder.

'Put your knickers back on after he's had his wicked way with you,' I whisper into her ear before I scarper out of the door.

'Do you like him?' I ask Fi the next evening while we take a walk along the main beach to appreciate the crisp March sunset.

'Who?'

'Saddam Hussein, Fi, who do you think?'

Fi wrinkles her nose until her brain gets up to speed.

'Who, Dave? 'Course I like him. He's a lovely fella, so he is, and he knows so much about stuff like films. Not just those surfing films but like the ins and outs of how films are made and about the cameras and the directors and all that. Dave has this video camera himself that he likes to mess about with. I think films are his passion, which is mighty. It's great to have a passion, I think.'

Fi stops marching along the sand and pulls herself up on to a flat rock facing the sea. I pull myself up beside her.

'Aye so, I do like him, he's nice like.'

I turn my head to study Fi's profile.

'Nice?'

'Yeah, nice. Grand, lovely, a nice lad.'

'And that would be as far as it goes, would it, Fiona O'Reilly?'

'Sure it is, he's my cousin's best mate.'

'Your cousin's only mate by the looks of it. Anyway, what difference does that make? That doesn't make the two of you related so it wouldn't be a weirdy incestuous thing.'

Fi looks at her feet and taps her runners together to shake off the sand.

'I know that, Milly, but I'm just not ready for a relationship with someone. I need to sort myself out first' – she points to her head – 'in here like.'

'So how are you doing' – I playfully tap her head with my knuckle – 'in there?'

'Ah, not bad at all. I still have a long way to go. I can't seem to get over Sean's death. I can't forgive myself for it either, but that's something else entirely. And my dad doesn't add much to my trust in men, you know.'

I nod.

'But I was just after thinking today, in fact, that I don't think I've had a proper down day since we got here. Sure, I've had my moments in the dark in the middle of the night or when I've been walking through the town and remembered coming here with my folks and Sean, but they've only been moments. I haven't woken up feeling heavy since we left Dublin.'

By this I know my friend means 'heavy' in the sense of waking up with a heavy heart and the weight of the world on her shoulders. She could never mean heavy in the sense that most of us would relate to, with her being so petite. Mind you, I think Fi's version of heavy is worse than feeling a bit

83

too chubby for drainpipe hipsters. She has tried to describe the feeling to me on several occasions when I have pushed her to. She has explained how she can go to bed feeling carefree and on top of the world only to wake up the next morning (after she eventually gets to sleep) feeling automatically negative and for some reason not ready to face the day.

'Well I'm glad you feel more positive. Maybe it's the exercise giving you happy hormones.'

'Aye, that surfing is jam-packed with serotonin. Then again, so is chocolate, so I better not ignore that part of the medicine,' she grins.

I smile. 'I guess I can never really understand how it is for you. Not unless I could get in your head,' I say softly.

'Jaysus, you wouldn't want to be in this head, it's a feckin' mess so it is. Just one big chemical imbalance, but hey, it makes me more interesting.'

'It sure does.'

Of course, with or without the depression, Fi would probably still be as mad as a box of frogs. That is why I love her.

'I like it here, Milly,' Fi smiles as we watch the sun sink into the ocean, 'I like being with my cousins and I like having a change of scenery. It's just so gorgeous here, don't you think?'

'Who is?' I nudge her in the ribs.

'Ya big eejit, Milly. Ah look, is that a seal out there?'

My eyes follow the direction of her outstretched arm.

'No, I think it's just a log.'

'Shite. Can we pretend it's a seal though?'

'If you like,' I snigger, 'or how about a crocodile?'

'Jaysus, you don't get crocobloodydiles out there, do you?'

I grimace. 'I hope not, or else there is no way on earth I am ever getting in that water.'

'Speaking of which,' Fi pipes up before I can swallow my own fateful words, 'when *are* you going to get in that water?'

'Hmm?'

'You heard me, Milly. Water, wobbly waves, surfing, you. When are you going to put all this theoretical research into practice and actually get your hair wet?'

*Never?*

'Soon,' I sniff.

As the sun drops surprisingly quickly beneath the horizon, Fi hops off the rock and holds out a hand to help me down.

'Tomorrow,' she announces determinedly.

She turns on her heel and marches off along the beach towards home. Her voice carries to me on the cross-shore wind.

'Tomorrow you, Milly Armstrong, are going to get in the sea. Not just your toes, like, but all of you, even your precious hair.'

'But . . .' I whine, jogging to catch her up.

'No buts.'

Fi slips her arm through mine and smiles up at me, her red hair glinting against the reds and pinks of the sky.

'You can do this, I totally know you can, but maybe you're just after needing a wee push.'

'Or a big push. Off the edge of that big cliff up there.' I jerk my head towards the rocky headland above us. 'Don't make me do it yet, Fi, I'm not ready.'

'Don't be daft now, of course you're ready. Tomorrow it is and no arguments.'

I stick out my bottom lip. 'I thought you were my friend.'

'I am,' she grins, gripping my arm tight, 'but sometimes friends have to be cruel to be kind. Tomorrow it is. It'll be great craic, believe me.'

Her determined enthusiasm makes me nervous. The rapidly darkening sky makes me more nervous still. Dark means night and night means that day will come far too soon for my liking. Looming fast is my rendezvous with death-by-drowning.

# CHAPTER TEN

## *Ripples*

My first memory of going swimming is a family day out to Bournemouth beach when I was about six. It was one of those bank holidays in May when the sun peeks out from behind a thick blanket of cloud and immediately convinces the entire south of England to don their most hideous summer clothes (drawstring Bermuda shorts and pasty knees obligatory) and head en masse to the coast. I remember we spent the best part of the day in a traffic jam on the M3, sweating out most of our bodily fluids in the back of Dad's Rover while Montegos and Cortinas overheated all around us. When we finally reached the pebbly sand on the shores of Bournemouth and located our square metre of space between the encampments of windbreakers and giant cool boxes, we were ordered to strip down to our square Speedo swimming cozzies and hurl ourselves into the sea. This was done under the guise of being tremendous fun, but looking back, I think it was a way of cooling our raging temperatures and frayed nerves, Mum's and Dad's included.

My parents had never been the sort to think of sending us to swimming lessons to ensure our survival should we unwittingly tumble into a deep pond one day and not have the skills to save ourselves. Sport was not something we were trained in at an early age, yet somehow Ed and I were still expected to excel at any sporting pursuit we tried. That was just the way it was with Georgina and Frank Armstrong. My mother was naturally a great swimmer and tennis player and my father was a Cambridge Blue rower and rugby player. As far as they were concerned, we had sporting prowess in our genes. Of course, even at the age of three, Ed took to the water like a small otter. After several shaky steps to test the temperature, he took my father's hand and ventured in. Seconds later, they were positively frolicking in the small waves lurching on to the pebbly shore. Ed even put his head under *on purpose* and laughed when he was cartwheeled on to the beach by the shorebreak. Meanwhile, my mother decided to go for a short twenty-mile (or so it seemed) swim. Her lithe body, which is still lithe twenty-five years on (how we are related I just don't know), disappeared out towards the end of the pier. I was left alone, age six, at the edge of the water with nothing more buoyant than a navy-blue school regulation swimsuit to assist my first run-in with the ocean.

I wasn't a precious child. I liked climbing trees and splattering myself in muddy puddles as much as the next six-year-old, but even at that young age I could not understand how immersing oneself in what felt like an Arctic ice floe could be considered enjoyable. Everyone who took to the water that day in Bournemouth seemed to emerge either ghostly white or painfully blue and with enough sand in their sagging costumes to construct their own beach when they got home. In the water they shrieked and screamed, which to me sounded more like wails of misfortune than squeals of sheer delight. Nevertheless, after my father's umpteenth distracted call of encouragement I took the plunge. Timidly at first, my podgy knees literally cracking together with the mixture of cold and fear. I shuffled my feet along the pebbles, which grew smaller the further I ventured. The water washed up to my waist and I gasped just in time to swallow almost an entire wave in a single gulp. I remember how the salt stung my eyes and how the frothy whitewater rushed towards and all around me until I became disorientated. The screaming kids merged into one hysterical wail in my waterlogged ears. I rubbed my eyes and looked around for Ed and my father but I couldn't make them out among the hundreds of similarly white bodies in identical Speedo trunks. I called out, but every time I opened my mouth more water went in until I was coughing and spluttering and gasping for air. Then it happened. It looked like a multicoloured circus whale (should there be any whales in the circus) flying through the air with its mouth open. Only when it was upon me did I realise it was a family of neon-clad children hurtling out of control towards me on a giant green lilo, screaming with excitement as the wave catapulted them over my head and on to the beach. I went under, my little arms and legs flailing aimlessly like the unsuspecting victims in a *Jaws* movie. I tried to grasp on to anything solid but all I could feel was water. I whirled round and round in the froth, not knowing which way was up. Once I thought I saw the sky but then I lost it again as a giant foot landed on my head from someone up above me. I was running out of air, my head was spinning in time with my body. I tried to call out but swallowed more water. One final gasp and then everything went black.

I didn't *officially* drown. By that I mean I wasn't carried lifeless from the water by a David Hasselhoff lookalike who then pumped my chest until water spurted out of my mouth. However, I was dragged out of the five inches of water by a very nice ice-cream man from Bognor Regis who raced to my aid with his 'Teddy Bears' Picnic' jingle wailing like a siren. My father's face was the first one I recognised and all I remember of that is a flash of fear followed by guilt, followed by annoyance. Why did I have to go and do something selfish like drown myself while in his care and ruin the only day off he and my mother had taken together for months? As for my mother, she was concerned at first and fussed around me for a while, even taking me back to the ice-cream van ambulance for a 99 Flake with monkey-blood sauce *and* a Cornetto (the posh ice-cream of my childhood) as a thank-you to my friendly-faced saviour. However, once she realised I was not going to die and that she was not going to be arrested by Social Services for being a neglectful mother, she soon came to the conclusion that if I was going to be so attention-seeking every time we came to the beach then we would never do it again. We did, against my will I might add, but I never went in the sea again. Why couldn't I be a good, sensible swimmer like Ed? they wondered aloud. Why? Because Dad had kindly provided Ed with a pair of orange water wings while I was left to rely on my own ability to resist dangerous currents. I decided then that there was something weird about my body in the fact that it just didn't seem to want to float. Perhaps, I worried throughout my formative years, my skin was not waterproof.

This fear of the water and my tendency to sink continued all through my school years. Thankfully (in one sense) my primary school was too academically focused to bother with things like swimming lessons. Once I got to secondary school, I tried my best to swim widths of the grotty yellow-tiled pool, until I discovered around the age of thirteen that if a girl had her period, she could get out of the whole sorry débâcle by sitting out of the lesson and whispering 'P' to the teacher calling the register. I think Mrs Spooner began to get a little concerned when I appeared to have a period every week for three years, but she was too polite to delve into matters gynaecological. From that moment on, swimming was no longer a part of my life. After leaving school I had no need for swimming pools or aqua-aerobics. I wasn't planning to fall off a ferry or tumble into a river and I had about as much desire to go on a water sports holiday as I did to try nude base-jumping. I just didn't need to be able to swim. Until now.

'What d'you mean, you can't swim?' Mac scowls, his forehead wrinkling to a deep groove between his dark eyebrows. 'Do you mean you just don't like it?'

I clutch the foam board close to me and shiver like a wet chihuahua, my feet seeming to be superglued to the sand. I feel stupid, I want to cry, and I am about to wet myself if I don't get to a toilet soon. Mind you, Dave told Fiona that surfers wee in their wetsuits to keep warm, which is just . . . yuck . . . absolutely nooo way.

'It's not that she doesn't like it,' says Fi with a dramatic hand gesture, 'it's just that she can't. She nearly drowned once and it's turned into this huge pathological fear and, like, she almost has a panic attack in the bath!'

I can always rely on Fi to get things completely out of proportion.

'Jaysus, Mary and Joseph,' Mac groans. He raises his eyes heavenwards. 'You didn't tell me that about your one now, did you, Fiona?'

I look down at the cold wet sand while they discuss my shortcomings as if I am Fi's hard-of-hearing, totally incapable ward.

'It's not quite that bad actually,' I butt in eventually, 'but I did have a slight drowning experience when I was younger which has made me a bit, well, afraid. So perhaps I just need a bit of time and, er, understanding.'

'How young?' Mac asks.

'Pardon?'

'How young were you? When you "drowned".' He makes giant inverted comma signs in the air with his big fingers.

'Oh, um, I was about six. Yeah, it was on a day trip to—'

'Six! Jaysus Christ, that's feckin' years ago now. Surely you can't still be scared after thirty years, for God's sake.'

'It's twenty-five years actually,' I pout, 'and thank you so much for your compassion.'

'Look it, I don't mean to be a bastard.'

'You're making a pretty good job of it, though,' I grumble.

90

Mac's tone of voice softens a little. 'OK, come here now, I am sorry for your bad experience, but I don't want to go making you do things you don't want to do. It just won't work.'

'But she *has* to do it,' says Fi.

'Aye, maybe so, but she sure doesn't *want* to. I mean you've been here now a week tomorrow and we've only just got you to the water.'

Personally I don't see the problem with that, but I nod and quietly mumble, 'I was researching.'

Mac takes a deep breath and exhales very slowly. I avoid eye contact and silently wish for the beach to turn into quicksand and swallow up my wetsuit-clad body (which, I imagine, would give any beach a bad case of indigestion).

'To be honest with you, Milly, my reputation is on the line here.'

*Oh no, I am about to be thrown out of the class for being a crap pupil and I haven't even started yet.*

'I want to learn,' I say with as much sincerity as I can muster, 'but I just . . . it's just a bit . . .'

'Wet?' Fiona suggests when I pause.

'Dauntin'?' says Dave, who has kindly decided to increase the humiliation factor of this whole event by videoing my learn-to-surf fiasco.

I shrug and try to pretend there is not a camera lens invading my personal space.

'Don't tell me you're worried about breaking one of those fancy nails of yours,' says Mac, arching one eyebrow.

I dig my nails into the foam edges of the surfboard, feeling both stupid and embarrassed.

'No, of course I'm not.'

*Although they are rather pricey and they do look pretty good.*

'Right, so if you say you want to learn, why don't we just take it slowly but work up to getting you in that water? Otherwise I have a maggot's-arse chance of teaching you how to surf.'

I look from Mac to the rumbling ocean and wonder what a maggot's arse has got to do with anything. My attention turns to Fi, who is hopping about from one foot to the other to keep warm in the, shall we say, fresh sea breeze. Dave still has the video camera trained on my furrowed brow while his own eyes behind the lens flit back and forth between his shot and Fi's pert little bum in her neat-fitting wetsuit.

I inhale as if I am in a yoga class and count to ten while I summon the courage to face this challenge I created for myself. After all, I made this waterbed so I am the one who has to lie in it, and if I don't pull it off, the only role I will be accepting is coffee whisk girl, frothing with a smile. I count to twenty and grip the surfboard even tighter. I then count to thirty and beyond while the sound of breaking waves echoes in my head like approaching thunder. Damn, why am I such a scaredy-cat?

Mac rubs his palms together as if to warm them and then claps his hands. I jump.

'Sure, we can start on the beach today and go through the basics at least. Then we'll see about the water part, OK?'

'OK.' I smile thankfully.

'So lie your boards flat on the sand there and I'll teach you a bit about the paddling and jumping up.'

'Ooh, that's what they did in *Point Break*, I loved that bit, so I did,' Fi squeals. She throws herself down on top of her board and flails her arms around as if she is paddling out to sea.

Dave looks down at her outstretched body and gives a nervous cough, trying, I imagine, to erase the fantasy from his mind of his own body swapping places with that lucky slab of fibreglass beneath her.

'Come on now, Milly, put your board down and we can start.'

'OK, right, Mac, er, let's get this show on the road.'

'Let go of it then.'

'Hmm?'

'I said let go of the surfboard.'

'What?'

Mac moves close to me and begins to slowly peel my fingers from the edges of the board.

'Jaysus, that's an iron grip you've got there, so it is. You're after putting holes in the deck of the board there with those talons of yours. Sure, anyone would think you don't trust me.'

I release my grip and blink several times, my mind in a daze.

'I don't,' I hear myself reply with brutal honesty. 'Give me one good reason why I should.'

I am lying in Pooh Corner's chocolate-coloured bath (which makes the bubble bath look decidedly cappuccino) when Fi barges in waving my mobile phone.

'Milly Armstrong, stop soaping up that sexy fella will you, and talk to your ma.'

I leap out of the bath, wrap a towel around me and wag a scolding finger at my friend. Grabbing the phone, I brave the cottage's sub-zero room temperature and make a dash along the hall to the bedroom.

'Hi, Mum, how are you?' I shiver.

'Top o' the evenin' to ya, me Oirish colleen. How are the shamrocks a-growin'?'

'Oh, hi, Dad, I thought it was—'

'Hello, darling,' my mother pipes up on the extension line (of course). 'What was that about a soapy young man?'

Ears like a bat, my mother, when it suits her.

'Just one of Fi's witticisms, Mother, don't worry about it.'

'Well I am not the one who should be worried, Amelia; it's you who should be careful if you are getting up to those sorts of antics. Too many visitors trampling through the garden is certain to damage the flowers, if you know what I mean.'

After thirty-one years of my mother's strange phraseology, I unfortunately do know what she means.

'Mum, I am not having random sex with anybody, thank you very much. In fact, if you must know I am not having any—'

'I must not know, Amelia. There is no need to be so aggressive with the truth. Privacy is a virtue.'

'That's patience actually. And anyway, you were the one who brought up trampled flowers.'

My mother clears her throat and I can picture her primly crossing her slim legs in a pair of neatly tailored navy slacks.

'I am just trying to protect you. You're my little girl and you always will be.'

I groan inwardly.

'Your father and I do not want to receive a telephone call informing us that you have one of those nasty rashes' – she says the last word in a whisper – 'or that we are to have a grandchild fathered by a nameless native inbred gypsy.'

Good God, how do the older generation get away with talking like that?

'We are too old for that sort of shock.'

'You aren't old,' I tut. I feel suddenly protective of the two people at the end of the telephone line.

'Jolly good,' my father laughs, 'the grey hair, stiff bones and sagging skin must all be a figment of my imagination then. I am relieved, pudding.'

I smile as my father chuckles and then the chuckle becomes a chesty cough; the sort of cough that older people have, which culminates in an audible dislodgement of phlegm. Which is pleasant.

'Now then, can we move on from the women's business and get to the point of the telephone call?' he eventually adds.

'In a moment, Frank, in a moment. I am having a chat with my long-distance daughter. Now, where were we?'

I close my eyes and reach for the duvet to wrap myself up

in. I then settle myself in for the long haul. My mother is evidently under budget on the phone bill allowance this week and plans to use the excess up on me. What a treat.

'What's new in the world of the Armstrongs?' Fi chirps when I walk into the sitting room, rubbing my right ear, which is burning from over-use.

'Not much really.'

'Not much? But you were on that phone for feckin' ages. How can there be not much?'

I yawn and plonk myself down on the sofa. I know that Fi always likes to hear my family's news because she doesn't have an immediate family of her own, so, despite having no desire to regurgitate a frankly exhausting conversation, I give in.

'Well, Mum called to tell me that she bumped into an old boyfriend of mine in the bank in Southampton. He wears lovely suits apparently and, I quote, "He has done so well with that acne problem of his by turning vegan. He looks a little jaundiced but he has grown a super moustache."'

'Jaysus,' Fi grimaces, 'sounds nasty. So you've always had shite taste in men?'

'It was a very long time ago,' I reply, ignoring her jibe aimed at Dan Clancy. 'Anyway, my mother also wanted me to know that they won't have a spare room next time I go home to visit because they are turning it into a gym.'

'A gym? Bloody hell, that's a bit trendy, like. I didn't know your folks were fitness fanatics.'

'They're not really.' I pause to ponder. 'I mean, they were sporty at college and when we were younger. You know about my mum and her swimming ability. Lately, though, they have just been middle-aged workaholics.'

'A bit like me,' Fi giggles. She reaches out and pats my hand. 'Ah, but you should be proud of them, Milly, if they're starting to pump iron. It's grand, so it is.'

'I don't think my mother will be pumping much iron, she

just kept raving on about a sunbed she was planning to buy from Argos.'

'Right. Joining the ranks of the unrealistically tanned English people?'

'Exactly.'

'So what's the problem? Other than your ma planning to turn herself into a brown leather handbag, that is.'

I turn to look at Fi and try to frown but realise I am already frowning.

'What do you mean, what's the problem?'

'You look all like that' – Fi screws up her face – 'and you can't be that desperate to go and stay in your folks' spare room, so what are you after worrying about?'

'I don't know.' I shrug. 'I guess I just feel a bit worried about my dad.'

'Why?'

I pause, feeling suddenly guilty about talking this through with Fi, whose own family is so dysfunctional she doesn't even know what country her parents are living in. Or, indeed, if they are living at all.

'I don't need sheltering, Milly,' she says as if reading my innermost thoughts. 'Now tell me.'

I sigh. 'The thing is, the last time I spoke to them my father had high blood pressure due to stress. Now my mother is hinting that the stress is affecting his health even more.'

'Hinting?'

'Yes, well every time she tried to tell me the details, my father changed the subject, which tells me he is trying to hide something. He is a typical proud older man. Thinks he is invincible and doesn't like to show weakness to the women of the family. He also thinks he could teach most doctors a thing or two so he rarely listens to a word they have to say whenever he is forced into setting foot in a surgery. Anyway, it's probably nothing, and I don't want you to worry about it, Fi. I think I just felt a bit . . . a bit strange

96

when they were on the telephone and so far away, as if I was suddenly facing my parents' mortality.' My voice trails away.

'Hmm, well we all die, Milly,' Fi replies with a visible maturity that stems, I know, from the death of her brother.

She puts her arm around me and pulls me into a hug.

'Some die too soon,' she carries on, 'and to be honest, some hang around far too long, outstaying their welcome like.'

I laugh weakly.

'But I am sure your folks will be around to wind you up for a long while yet.'

'Unlike yours,' I say quietly.

'Ah well, parents, hey, nothing but feckin' trouble so they are,' Fi snorts. 'Now enough about that. Hows about we sneak off to Gallagher's Bar for a quick pint to spark ourselves up?'

I lick my lips.

'Ooh, I could go a Guinness right now.'

'Aye, me too, and after that surf lesson today, I reckon we deserve it.'

I hop off the sofa and wriggle the still damp towel higher up to cover my chest.

'Not that we actually made it as far as the water, Fi, thanks to yours truly, but I reckon prancing about on a public beach in that stupid suit for an hour is enough to warrant a pint or two. In fact, I might just have three or four to help erase the horrible image of myself from my mind.'

'Good idea,' Fi whoops, following me up the stairs, 'and you might want to be putting some clothes on or you'll be getting the steamin' old drunks all excited in that get-up.'

I slap her hand away from my bare thigh and rummage in a drawer for some clothes with minimal creases.

'Should we ask Mac and Dave, like?' Fi suggests casually.

I grin and raise my eyebrows. 'If you want.'

'Right then,' Fi whistles, 'I'll give them a call and sort it out. Ah now, this will be grand, so it will. I heard that Gallagher's is buzzing on a Sunday night, and there might even be a traditional music session on to entertain you English tourists.'

I slip into a tight black polo neck jumper and laugh.

'As if you are going there for the culture, Miss O'Reilly. I know what you're after, and it hasn't got anything to do with musical instruments.'

'Oh, I don't know,' she laughs, placing one hand on her hip and one finger comically against her lips, 'I might have a go at playing the flute.'

'Fiona!' I wheeze, almost falling over as I yank up my jeans.

'Don't worry, Milly,' Fi grins as she bounces happily on the bed, 'I won't go leaving you out. I'll see if I can find you a fiddle!'

# CHAPTER ELEVEN

## *Waterlogged*

The following Sunday we accept an invitation to dinner with Uncle Podraig (pronounced Porick) and Auntie Mary. Not that we have much choice, because I get the feeling that turning down an offer of dinner in this town is akin to calling the Pope an iron lung with rosary beads.

'They'll be so disappointed if you don't come,' I overhear Mac telling Fiona when he comes over to deliver the handwritten invitation at around six o'clock.

*We'll be so disappointed if you don't come*, reads the handwritten note.

'Ah, they'll be so dis—'

'Yes, Fiona, I get the sodding message,' I grumble, pushing my half-eaten bacon sandwich to one side and stomping up the stairs to get ready.

I spend the next half an hour dreading the evening that looms ahead of me like a smear test appointment. Socialising with other people's families is generally more awkward than socialising with one's own family, and believe me, that is saying something. The thought of spending an evening in the company of Fi's notoriously huge extended family, the members of which are all related to my complicated surfing instructor, fills me with dread. I have thus far succeeded in avoiding family reunions for a fortnight by filling my days with surf lessons, beach walks and research and my nights with eating, drinking, eating more and sleeping heavily. Basically I have left Fi to do the family duties alone but she was more than willing to get to know the Heggartys without my hindrance. Tonight, however, I have to face my discomfort and show some amount of appreciation to the family who have let me stay rent free in their ancient brown excuse for a cottage that could not be rented out to blind squatters if they tried.

When we arrive at the house, a short walk inland from Pooh Corner, I am pleasantly surprised by my first impression. The house nestles in the shelter of one of the tabletop mountains bordering the town and is surrounded by fields full of comfortably fat cattle. The building itself is a mishmash of architectural styles, clearly having been extended several times over the decades to accommodate the regular human reproduction within the Heggarty clan. Even before we press gingerly on the doorbell, I am expecting the house to be fairly full, because Fiona earlier explained that Mary and Podraig live here with Mac's sisters Kathleen and Colleen, along with Colleen's fiancé Barry (who, thanks to the strict rules of the Catholic Church, has a separate room with a single bed and, according to the same rules, isn't even permitted to masturbate, the poor sod) and Mac's brother Johnny. What I am not prepared for, however, is a scene more befitting Terminal Three at Heathrow airport in the height of summer during an air traffic control strike. Utter chaos.

The minute the door is opened by a strikingly beautiful young girl with eyes like polished jade, who is later introduced as Johnny's girlfriend Onya, we find ourselves in the midst of a rowdy game being played by five or six small children. They all look identical, with dark auburn hair and cute dustings of freckles across their noses. Some are wearing frilly dresses and the rest I assume to be boys. I am not quite certain of the rules of the game but it seems to involve

100

hitting each other over the head and screaming until they turn red in the face. We pick our way through the disinterested mob, tripping over the countless pairs of shoes and boots that litter the hallway. We follow Onya, who glides along with the grace of a woodland elf, her waist-length wheat-coloured hair swishing hypnotically from side to side. Onya silently directs us into an expansive sitting room, which is decorated in every eye-baffling floral print known to man. I have to hand it to Auntie Mary, when she chooses an interior decor theme, she really does run with it, no holds barred. There are so many clashing florals in here – on the sofas, chairs, walls, floors and pictures – that I am glad I don't suffer from hayfever.

I blink and try to find a familiar face in the football-match-sized crowd. Even Mac's intense scowl would do, just to give my face a rest from the wide plastic smile I have fixed to my lips. I feel like the new girl at school, standing in the middle of assembly while I am curiously surveyed like an alien life form. However, the newly descended silence in the room doesn't last long when a cheerful-faced woman with cheeks the colour of beetroot hustles from the kitchen in a cloud of cooking smells and lets out a shriek of delight that would wake the dead. She throws her arms in the air and races across the room towards us, smiling like a lottery winner as she tramples over yet more children. Auntie Mary, I presume.

As soon as I prise myself from the overwhelming bosom of Mary's floral apron, I am shepherded along by Uncle Podraig to meet the rest of the crowd. There is Colleen and Barry; Johnny and the lovely Onya; Kathleen; Siobhan, Sinead, their husbands Noel and Danny; their children a, b, c, d and e (I instantly forget their names; suffice to say they have auburn hair and freckles); Adam, Brendan, Malachi, Joseph; (can there possibly be others?); yet more children, f, g, h to k; the parish priest Father Ted (actually it's not, but I missed his real name); Moira, Marie and their husbands and

101

huge numbers of offspring; the family dog, Eric; three stray mongrels; eight kittens in a basket; a budgie with one foot; a baby in a Moses basket who doesn't seem to belong to anyone; and, would you believe it, the one and only Joyce from Joyce's Fashion Emporium, who is sporting a turquoise knitted skirt and cardigan ensemble from her own boutique. My head is spinning by the time I make it to the far side of the room, where I am deposited on to one of the sofas beside Colleen (or is it Siobhan?) and Onya, while Podraig races off to pour me a drink.

'What's the party in aid of?' I breathlessly ask Onya in a whisper.

She tilts her delicate head towards me and blinks.

'It's Sunday,' she replies softly before turning her gaze back to the room.

I needn't have worried about having anything to say to the Heggartys because it is not until two hours later that I manage to get a word in edgeways, and only then to confirm that I am in town for four months. The topics of conversation whizz around the room like a swarm of excitable flies, crossing over one another and occasionally colliding but almost impossible to follow. Everyone talks at the same time despite the fact that no one else appears to be listening. The volume in the room is similar to being at a boy-band gig at The Point in Dublin. (I'm guessing.) People laugh, heckle and shout. Father Ted starts to sing one song while Sinead and Siobhan impress with another in voices more melodic than the beautiful Corrs. I make eye contact with Uncle Podraig at one point and am immediately engaged in a one-way discussion, more of a soliloquy really, about Gaelic football, of which I have neither the slightest comprehension nor interest. My eye contact is locked in for a full twenty minutes until Mary interrupts the onslaught with a shouted 'Ah away wi' ya now, Podraig, you'd bore a glass eye to sleep so you would. Now leave the poor lassie be.' Only when the dinner is produced are the vocal cords in the room given a momentary rest while plates are filled and quickly emptied.

I sit at the giant farmhouse-style dinner table between Sinead (or Siobhan) and Malachi (I think) with Fiona and Adam (or it might be Brendan . . . oh, I give up) opposite. I can hardly see Fiona due to the mountain of food on my plate that would have come in very handy when Jesus was trying to feed the five thousand. (A holy thought I know, but there is a priest in the room and one conversation in three around the table seems to involve Jesus in some way.) I stare at my plate, which is piled to overflowing with what looks like three different kinds of meat, four types of potato, every vegetable known to man and a sea of gravy so deep I suddenly realise where the term 'gravy boat' originated. I am going to need one to have any chance of making it through this ocean of Bisto. Unfortunately, having worked up a hunger during this afternoon's surf lesson, I then satisfied it by wolfing down two packets of crisps, a KitKat and half a Jamaica Ginger Cake even before the doorstop bacon sandwich. I now have the appetite of a small gnat, but I silently force the food down out of sheer politeness. Several hundred mastications later, I lower my knife and fork and swallow the final mouthful, willing the gravy-sodden roast potato to make it as far as my stomach. I am so full, however, that there appears to be a gastronomic traffic jam as far up as my tonsils. I close my eyes and take deep meditative breaths. Now I know how it must feel to be six months pregnant.

'Ah now, well done, Milly, you've done a great job there,' says Auntie Mary, appearing suddenly by my side and whisking away my empty plate.

I breathe a sigh of relief.

'You must have been starved with the hunger after all that messin' about in the water you've been doing with our Mac, I hear, ya poor wee lassie.'

'Yes, I was.' I nod with embarrassment when the rest of

the table turn to look at me. 'But that was very tasty, thank you, Mrs Heggarty.'

'Now 'twas nothing too fancy,' Mary beams, 'and call me Mary. But you'll have a drop more?'

My stomach contracts in fear as Mary bustles towards the head of the table and begins to dig a giant ladle into a bowl of yet more potatoes.

'Er, no thank you,' I squeak. 'I'm absolutely full.'

'Don't be daft,' Mary tuts, turning her attention to a pile of sliced pork the size of a small piglet. 'You'll have some more meat, won't you? And some lovely cabbage.'

'No, really, Mary,' I protest, 'I really couldn't.'

'Go on now. Just a few more potatoes, and there's some gorgeous beef.'

'But—'

'Podraig, will you pass Milly the gravy?'

'Please—' I wail helplessly as Fiona lets out an amused snort across the table.

'No bother at all,' Mary chirps. 'I like a girl who enjoys her food, so I do.'

She places the plate down in front of me with a heavy thud. A roast potato rolls down the mountainside and lands on the floral tablecloth, a journey of several seconds.

'Eat up now,' says Mary heartily, slapping my back. 'There's apple crumble and custard for afters.'

Following another ten thousand calories of food, two Irish coffees and a hefty measure of neat whiskey, I am finally discharged from the table and manage to crawl as far as the sofa, incredibly without the weight-bearing assistance of an industrial crane. I collapse next to Fi and wrap my arms protectively around my stomach just in case my belly button gives way and I explode all over the sitting room.

'Jesus Christ, Fi,' I groan, 'if we eat like that until the end of June, the only film role I'll be getting will be as the whale in *Free Willy 4*. I feel like a giant beanbag.'

'Irish hospitality,' Fi giggles in response. 'Auntie Mary is famed for her wild good dinners, like, and apparently that wasn't even a big one.'

I splutter my disbelief and watch as Onya wafts past again as light as a feather despite the fact that she has just consumed more food than I usually eat in a week. She has to be bulimic.

I settle back on the sofa and wait for the army of guests to clatter into the room but only Mary, Podraig, Kathleen, Colleen, Barry, Johnny and Onya appear to be joining us. The others have either collapsed through overeating or else it is not considered impolite at Mary's house to eat and run. Not that running would be an option for me right now; I could not even manage a Weeble wobble. I am just drifting into a post-gluttony snooze while ten different conversations buzz around me when I hear the front door open and close and heavy footsteps enter the room.

'Hiya, Mac, how's the form?' asks Podraig as a dishevelled Mac appears and plonks himself down on a flowery armchair.

'Grand,' Mac replies, groaning slightly as he leans down to untie his boots. He nods his head at me and smiles stiffly before turning to Fi and giving her a familiar wink.

'Sorry I missed dinner, Ma, but I had admin to do after my surf lessons.'

'You're a good lad,' Mary beams proudly. 'I've kept you some warming in the oven. Now you just rest there and I'll fetch it for ya.'

I frown, watching Mac being fussed over, complimented and pampered as if we are witnessing the long-awaited return of the prodigal son. He's only been out doing a bit of poncing around on the beach, I think, not working a twenty-eight-hour shift down a mine, for God's sake.

Sitting here, I can see why Mac is often moody and stubborn. Spoiled children never like to be challenged or questioned. Thirty-something spoiled children still attached to their adoring mother's floral apron strings are even harder to please. For someone who has decided I am a high-maintenance city diva, he is doing a grand job of having his every whim catered for here in Mummy's house.

I sip my whiskey and watch as Mary fetches Mac's dinner while old Podraig carefully pours his son a drink and delivers it into his hand. I want to like Mac, you know. After all, he is the instructor upon whom I am pinning my hopes and dreams of stardom and I would be lying if I didn't say he is handsome. His unsettling, moody, macho temperament, however, prevents 'handsome' being translated into 'attractive', if you know what I mean. Nevertheless, I want Mac to like me. Largely because it is never a pleasant thing to receive a negative response when getting to know someone, but also because it would just make this process a whole lot easier. Basically, however, we are as chalky and cheesy as the White Cliffs of Dover and Cheddar Gorge. Mac is a homeboy who, I suspect, has never travelled further than Sligo railway station. He appears to enjoy being a big fish in a little pond and has no desire to be like Nemo and explore the rest of the ocean. He has few friends but has selected Dave to be his admiring sidekick. Mac doesn't need anyone else; his family and surf students give him all the ego-boosting he requires. I, on the other hand, left Southampton and my ever-critical family to head alone to Dublin and at least try to make an impact on the world. I took a risk in life. Mac is playing it safe. How can he criticise me? Perhaps I make him feel daunted by my get-up-and-go. Yes, that's it, he's jealous.

I choke back a mouthful of whiskey when Mac looks up sharply from his dinner and catches me staring at him. He stares back, a frown passing across his brow, before he flicks his unruly hair and his eyes dart back to his plate. I squirm deeper into my chair and avert my eyes. One thing is for sure, I note smugly, Mac Heggarty is no Dan Clancy and never will be. Dan is the sort of man I need, not some spoiled little country boy with a god complex.

'So, girls, how are yous enjoying the surfing?' asks Johnny, who has not spoken to us all evening except to ask for the gravy. I take it he and Onya are the quiet ones. Well, there has to be at least one. Fi turns her head towards me and nods. My cue to address the room.

'Oh, er, yes, it is really fab,' I say, my voice peculiarly having become more English than Camilla Parker-Bowles.

'Rayly farb,' sniggers fourteen-year-old Kathleen.

My cheeks start to burn and I look towards my feet.

'We've had lessons with Mac all week,' I carry on. 'Fourteen more weeks and hopefully I will be a surf chick.'

'That's if we ever manage to get you in the bloody water,' says Mac through a mouthful of food. 'I've never had to do so much beach instruction in my life.'

'Milly's fierce scared of the water,' Fi explains, causing my blush to spread to my ears. 'She nearly drowned once when she was a cub . . .'

I pray for one still-hungry dinner guest to eat me alive as Fi recounts the tale of my near-drowning incident for the umpteenth time and a smile spreads across Mac's lips. My embarrassment reaches my fingertips when the whole room erupts in gasps, 'Jaysus's and guffaws (largely from Kathleen).

'What a brave girl,' Podraig exclaims, 'taking on the perils of the ocean just to get a part in a TV show.'

'Aye,' Mac tuts, 'so brave she might get that posh hair-do of hers wet eventually.'

I self-consciously touch a hand to my hair that, admittedly, I lathered with half a bottle of intense conditioner when we got home from today's lesson regardless of the fact that it was only slightly damp from sea spray. I wouldn't exactly call it posh, though, I'm hardly investing in celebrity hair extensions every five minutes. What does he expect me to do, have it butchered at the local barber shop?

'I will get wet,' I retort firmly, 'and I did my best today actually. I tried so hard that I even broke three nails.'

Not the best argument to assert my derring-do personality, I know, but Mac's assumption that I'm scared of breaking a nail has been niggling at me for a week now. Speaking of which . . .

'There isn't a nail bar in town, is there?' I ask Onya in what I intend to be a whisper.

Mac laughs raucously, sending a potato missile flying across the room.

'Aye, sure,' he chortles, sharing a wink with Johnny, 'there's McGonigle's Hardware at the top of Main Street. You'll get a few nails in there.'

'Now don't be cruel to the girl, Mac,' says Mary, although she is laughing all the same. She turns back to me. 'So what is this TV show all about then, Milly? Will we get to see it?'

I ignore Mac's raised eyebrow and purse my lips together, preparing my response.

'It's a film based around the beach and a surfer. It's being made by a well-known production company. You might have heard of the director, he won an award for that arty movie last year, *The Way She Moves*.'

I pause to wait for their recognition but there is silence in the room and a sea of blank expressions. I press on.

'Well, anyway, he's a great director and he ran auditions in Dublin which my *agent*' – I say this with an important emphasis in order to impress, but there is not a single flicker of excitation – 'er, well, he put me forward for it. It was a long day of auditions and read-throughs but in the end I got the part. The leading lady, in fact.'

I don't expect a round of applause but a hint of 'ooh, didn't she do well' would be nice. Mac sniffs, Podraig nods his feigned interest and the others smile weakly.

'So what else have you been in?' Johnny asks, probably out of politeness.

'Oh, um.' I squirm in my seat and rack my brains for anything that doesn't involve dressing up as breaded poultry or advertising dentures. 'I've been in a few productions here

108

and there, but you know it is very difficult to get a break these days. I have got an Equity card, though.'

'But you have to be careful with those things,' Podraig tuts seriously. 'Fierce easy to build up lots of debt, and then what do you do? No, I don't touch credit cards meself. Much better to go out and get a proper job than live like that, so it is.'

I consider trying to explain what an Equity card is and how to aspiring actors it is like Willy Wonka's golden ticket, but I give up, my pride sufficiently flattened. Fiona pats my leg to indicate her support and rises to my defence.

'Milly has got fantastic potential, they say. And she's got like millions of contacts in the business. She's going to be a big star one day. Just like that Dan Clancy . . .'

My heart sinks as I know what is coming next.

'She even went out with him, like.'

Now this piece of news causes a stir in the room. Even the beautiful Onya eyes me with pleasant surprise, as if she has just realised I am in fact a woman, although obviously not as delicious as herself.

'Really?' she asks in her will'o-the-wisp-y little voice.

'Now there's a dish,' Colleen adds with a whistle.

'Feckin' gorgeous,' Kathleen approves.

'Don't curse, Kathleen,' says Mary. 'But Jaysus, he is a bloody mighty man himself.'

'So what's he like?' asks Colleen, a noticeable cherry flush on her cheeks.

'How long were you an item?' Onya breathes.

'Does he invite you to his premieres?' Johnny enquires.

'Has he got a big—'

'KATHLEEN!' Mary interrupts with spectacular timing.

Fiona giggles beside me. I pause while deciding which question to tackle first, if any of them. Do I really want a family whose members rabbit on more than Chas and Dave to know the ins and outs of my relationship with an international star? I doubt anything is kept private in this town, gossip being more exciting than the reality. Only the other day I heard the newsagent telling a group of customers that Joyce from Joyce's Fashion Emporium had changed her monthly magazine subscription from the *RTE Guide* to *Irish Tatler* and did that mean she was having an affair or simply getting hoi-polloi ideas above her station? I mean, for heaven's sake. No, I want to keep Dan all to myself, not have him speculated about over a wash and blue rinse in the local hairdressers.

I open my mouth to speak, but before I can form a suitable response, Mac moves his broad shoulders forwards, leans his forearms on his knees and says, 'So, Mrs Clancy, you never explained what it felt like when he dumped you on your birthday.'

My shoulders stiffen as every pair of inquisitive eyes in the room flits towards my astonished face.

'He never did?'

'The bastard.'

'When was that now?'

'No, it never was! Valentine's Day you say, Fiona?'

'The bastard.'

. . . and so it continues.

I wait for the commotion to die down, and glance across at Mac, who sits back in his chair, smugly observing my deep embarrassment.

'Ah yes, how the other half live, hey,' he comments with a smile. 'If only our lives here in town could be as fun as that, for sure.'

I curse him into my tumbler of strong whiskey while Fi attempts to jump to my defence but basically just succeeds in feeding the gossipmongers everything they need to keep my ears burning for a few weeks. What is it with this guy? Why does he derive so much pleasure from making me uncomfortable? Fair enough, we have nothing in common, but just because I will never be the mermaid to his merman, does that give him any justification for behaving like such an arse? We can't all be water babies. I am intelligent, friendly, down-to-earth and willing (if somewhat slow) to learn to surf. What more does he want? Whatever happened to the pupil being seduced by her horny instructor? Not that I would be interested, but a bit of effort on his part might be nice.

I feel the hairs on the back of my neck bristle as anger bubbles inside me and visibly heats my cheeks while the rest of the Heggartys discuss my misfortune at the hands of Ireland's darling.

'Well sure, he must have high standards now he's over in Hollywood.'

'Aye, you're right there, Ma, there must be shiteloads of slappers wantin' to get in his pants.'

'Don't curse so, Kathleen.'

'She's right though, Ma. It would take a special sort to bag that one now.'

'Right enough, Colleen, he is one of Ireland's finest himself.'

'Ah, but I'm more of a Colin Farrell girl meself. He's gorgeous.'

'What? But you told me you hated the fella.'

'Don't be daft, Barry, sure I'd boot you out of bed for himself any night of the week.'

'Well now, t'anks a million, Colleen ya tramp.'

'Now there, Barry, it's just the drink talking. Our Colleen wouldn't be doin' that, would ya now?'

'If I had the chance, Da, if I had the chance. Jaysus, give me the two of they, Dan and Colin, at once and I'd be a happy woman.'

I watch the alcohol-fuelled discussion escalate around me, tempers fraying and curses flowing, while I moodily gulp down my whiskey and surreptitiously refill my glass when no one is looking. Not only am I pissed off at Mac throwing my secrets into the ring to be torn apart by the lions, I am also pissed off at the general presumption that only someone like Cameron Diaz could be in with a chance of landing Dan Clancy for anything more than a one-night shag. Do they think I am not good enough for him? Yes. Don't they realise I am myself on the verge of becoming a screen starlet like Miss Diaz, only shorter and not so angular? No. Can I get a word in edgeways to defend myself? Fat chance. Why do Irish people talk so much? Gulp, eugh, this whiskey is strong.

'Any woman in their right mind wouldn't touch that Clancy fella with a bargepole,' Barry huffs, 'what with all the ridin' he'll be doin'. The man will have all sorts of itches and diseases.'

'Don't be an eejit, Barry,' scolds Johnny, the most sober of the men. 'Have some respect for Milly here, she's just after being dumped by the bastard.'

'It was last year actually!' I finally erupt when I spot a millisecond gap in the conversation. 'And I will have you know he did NOT dump me. OK? I already explained all this to Mac but he chose to misunderstand. It was a MUTUAL decision,' I splutter loudly. 'A mutual agreement between Dan and me to have time apart so that we could concentrate on our careers before we . . . you know, before we rushed into marriage and children and a life together. It was all very amicable and modern and we are still very close and he calls me *all* the time, quite frankly, so we will probably get back together,' I continue hurriedly, my words tripping over themselves to get out before the roof of the fantasy collapses on top of them. 'In fact we will *definitely* get back together just as soon as I have achieved the success that I deserve and Dan achieves his goals. OK? Anyway, Dan is totally championing me all the way. In fact, he was the one who recommended me for this role, and Matthew the director agreed with him as soon as I auditioned.' My pulse races as I continue. 'I mean, ha ha, why aim for just one Oscar in the family when we can have two? And he is truly wonderful and this film was all his idea,' I lie despite Fi's tuts of protest, my head spinning in a whiskey-fume tornado, 'and I AM going to be a huge success and then we WILL be together again and all I have to do is learn to surf if Mac would give me a bloody chance. But I WILL do it and I WILL go in the water and then everyone will see I can do it and Dan will admit he is head over heels in love with me and you can all stop mocking me and I will be the envy of every girl and yes, yes, Kathleen, if you must know, the answer to your question is YES. I have seen it, I have touched it, and I know for sure, one hundred per cent, that yes, Dan Clancy does have a very BIG PENIS!'.

I grit my teeth together in a huge crocodile smile and flash a victorious glance around the room. It is only when the red mist clears from my eyes that I realise every single one of them is staring at me incredulously, mouths ajar, as if I have just taken my head off and turned it inside out before their very eyes. Mac, for once, is speechless. Mary performs the sign of the cross repeatedly and mumbles a hasty prayer. Fiona sinks back into the sofa beside me and clears her throat over and over again. Only Kathleen is smiling triumphantly, because their guest has just shouted 'big penis' in front of her parents. What was I thinking? Where did my sanity go? I just said 'BIG PENIS' in a household of devout Catholics who have had a priest over for dinner. I close my eyes and pray for a bolt of lightning to fry my aching brain to a crisp.

Finally it is Uncle Podraig who eases himself out of his chair and creaks his aged self across the room. He walks towards me and gives me a condescending pat on the head as if I am an over-excited ten-year-old.

'Well now, that's grand,' he coughs in my ear. 'What a lovely story. Now, who's for a pint of whiskey? I could sure do with a stiff one.'

# CHAPTER TWELVE

## *Water Works*

To give credit to Fiona, she does not mention the incident again except to laugh about Podraig having said 'stiff one' just after I shouted 'big penis', which sent Kathleen into further hysterical convulsions. However I do occasionally catch Fi eyeing me suspiciously as if any minute I will again choose to display my loony qualities and be carted off to the Mentalist Motel. Over the next fortnight, Mac is suddenly 'indisposed' and unable to spare even five minutes from whatever it is lifeguards and surf instructors do to teach me how to float, never mind swim and surf. I am quite thankful to be spared the humiliation of facing Mac, who will undoubtedly have recounted the whole sorry outburst word for word to Dave and probably re-enacted it for Dave's video camera to preserve my shame for prosperity. I am beginning to draw the conclusion that this exercise has been a complete waste of time. I have now spent a month in this town and, other than my landlocked lessons, I am no closer to learning to surf than I was back in February. I will accept some responsibility for this, of course, but I am not the surf instructor here. Quite honestly, I doubt he even knows proper teaching methods. If I had my way, we would be out of here before you could say good riddance. The problem is, Fiona is so enjoying herself that I can't bring myself to ruin her experience of being in County Donegal with her newly acquainted relatives. I certainly gave it a good shot, mind you, but Fi and her family are still on speaking terms. She has taken to visiting Mary and Podraig every day and meeting her girl cousins for coffee and gossip in one of the local tearooms. They all have so much to say that this pastime usually takes up most of an afternoon. My friend has suddenly become a social butterfly, flitting from one Heggarty residence to another and invariably returning with some clingfilmed gastronomic offering or other, usually involving meat and potatoes.

Fi has also taken to spending a couple of evenings a week in Gallagher's Bar with Dave and Mac. Every time she goes out with 'the boys', as she likes to call them, we go through the same routine of Fi asking me to join them; me saying 'No thanks, I have stuff to do'; Fi replying that she feels guilty enjoying herself without me; me assuring her that I have urgent research to be getting on with and that I have no time to waste; Fi skipping out of the door to sup comforting pints of Guinness in front of a roaring peat fire; me slumping morosely onto the dusty old sofa to watch episodes of *Fair City* and *EastEnders*, while feeling hideously sorry for myself.

During the ceaselessly windy March days, I find plenty to keep me occupied. Just between you and me, I find myself indulging in cleaning, which is something I have to admit to never having been a fan of. Fortunately Fi has the sense to employ a cleaner in our Ballsbridge flat, thus keeping the delights of Toilet Ducks and loo brushes at arm's length. However, while I may not be a fan of cleaning, neither am I particularly fond of living in a house where the carpet tiles walk across the floor by themselves, thanks to the colonies of six- and eight-legged creatures living beneath them. Obviously I can't do much about the decor in Pooh Corner, other than gutting the place and investing in forty tins of white emulsion, but I can tackle the years of grime. At first

I curse inch-thick tidemarks on the bath and yell expletives at the limescale-encrusted taps. (One tip here – if anyone recommends you buy a chocolate-brown bathroom suite, just say NO.) I stretch three pairs of rubber gloves over one another before going into biological warfare with the inhabitants of the kitchen cupboards. I even buy a face mask from McGonigle's Hardware to assist with the hoovering. It is only when I catch myself singing 'Whistle While You Work' as I invest copious amounts of elbow grease in cleaning the windows that I realise with a start that I am actually quite enjoying myself. I may be turning into Hilda Ogden from *Coronation Street* but this 'cleaning lark', as my dad would undoubtedly call it, is strangely rewarding. We can even go to sleep at night now without checking under the bed for forty-year-old spiders with territorial issues.

When not masquerading as a scrubber, I take long walks along the cliff paths that meander up and down the coastline. When Fi joins me, we walk arm in arm, admiring the scenery and generally putting the world to rights while we comfortably chat. When I walk alone, I have time to think, my thoughts blown around my head by the fresh sea air. I daydream about eventually starting to film the project. About having my own trailer stocked full of munchies and posh toiletries and staffed by a team of top stylists employed to make me look a million dollars at all times. I push the surfing difficulties to the back of my mind and concentrate instead on the premieres, the interviews, the glamour and the fame. I can't wait. I want it all to happen now.

It is during one of these walks that reality smacks me square between the eyes when I happen to step close to a cliff edge in order to peer down at a rather mutant-looking seal in the water below. My head spins and I suddenly envisage myself tumbling down into the ocean out here in the middle of nowhere with only a deformed seal to save me from certain death. I realise then that if I fell/was pushed/was required by a salary-paying, no-messing film company to jump into that water, I would (bar some sort of miracle) most certainly drown. There is no way, all good intentions aside, that I could ever pull off a water-based stunt regardless of the importance to my career. It is at this point that I decide to take the matter into my own hands and teach myself the basics. Stuff Mac Heggarty, I don't need him or his video-obsessed sidekick. I am thirty-one years old, for goodness' sake, I can teach myself to swim. Of course I can. Once I have mastered the art of floating around in a few inches of water, how hard can surfing possibly be?

I prepare for my first trip to the local swimming pool as thoroughly as the Germans prepared to invade Poland. I shave every possible embarrassing hair and I exfoliate, buff and moisturise my skin to the texture of a teenager's (if only temporarily). I then practise taking deep breaths to ready my lungs for water-based exercise. However, the excessive inhalation combined with the nerves I have been trying to suppress all morning causes me to hyperventilate. I then almost suffocate when Fi tries to save me by sticking my head in a plastic carrier bag.

'Well Jaysus, I couldn't find a feckin' paper one,' she groans after I wrestle my head from her steely grip, 'and I thought this would do the job like.'

Remind me not to rely on my best friend if I happen to be drowning.

Despite Fi's apparent murder attempt, I agree to let her come with me to the pool as I do not relish the thought of making the dash from the changing room to the water on my own. Now it may seem odd that I am happy for my petite red-haired friend in her petite racy red swimsuit to accompany me (of the average body shape and ill-fitting suit) to a swimming pool, but there is method to my madness. By my calculations, ninety-nine per cent of the eyes in the pool will be concentrating on Fi for so long (either through admiration or jealousy) that by the time they have even acknowledged my presence, I will be safely hidden below the water level. But I will of course adopt the boobs-out, stomach-in, bum-up, legs-tightened-for-minimum-wobble swimsuit pose just in case.

Fi and I roll our costumes in two of Pooh Corner's brown and orange towels, pack enough toiletries for a week's holiday abroad and wrap up warm against the north wind that is howling over the country from Iceland. We hurry along the seafront so fast that we are out of breath by the time we reach the pool on the headland. It is housed in a strikingly modern glass and metal multicoloured structure that stands out from the town's old architecture like a lapdancer in a convent. I peer in one of the enormous windows that stretch the entire length of one wall and gasp when I realise the pool (and the bodies therein) is visible to any Tom, Dick or Dirty Harry who happens to be passing and fancies a gawp.

'Come on now, it's not like you know many people here, sure, and besides, Milly, you look grand in a swimsuit,' Fi reassures me.

'Yeah,' I grumble as she drags me through the turnstile, 'like a big, huge grand piano in need of some urgent restoration.'

'Ya big gobshite, Milly, you do not. Hello there, two for the big watery thing that represents everything my friend here sees as evil. Oh, and two of your sexiest swimming hats just to top off our look.'

The girl at the front desk grins at Fi as she hands over the skull-hugging Lycra swimming caps that are compulsory in public pools in Ireland. If any woman succeeds in looking anything close to attractive with one of these things on her head while wearing a swimming costume, I would love to meet her. On second thoughts, no I really would not. Especially not right at this moment.

I stand shivering in the damp changing cubicle as I am gripped by a sudden desperate fear of:

a) the semi-naked dash to the poolside;

b) the prospect of actually forcing myself to enter the water; and

c) the semi-naked dash back from the poolside;

which pretty much covers everything.

Fi bangs repeatedly on the door, trying to lure me out into the open with promises like 'I promise you won't know a soul', 'I promise you will look grand' and finally 'I promise to buy you that outfit you liked in Morgan in Sligo *and* lunch in Bistro Bianconi with *two* desserts!'

She got me. I am out of the cubicle like a shot and leap over the verruca-infested footbath leading to the poolside as if I have been fired out of a cannon.

'Which is the shallow end?' I whisper urgently to Fi.

'Let's see now . . . erm, d'you know, I haven't a clue. Right, well, ah look, it's down there, so it is.'

She points.

'Right there where Mac's standing.'

'Great, come on then, let's . . . What did you just say?'

My head spins around so fast I get whiplash in my neck muscles. I instantly recognise Mac's broad shoulders silhouetted against the windows.

'Quick, Fi, he's got his back to us,' I hiss. 'Let's make a run for it.'

'Has he not seen us? Mac, MAC, OVER HERE!'

Fi has no idea about discretion. Not to mention shame. She waves her arms wildly as if she is bringing a plane in to land. To be honest, if Mac hadn't spotted her, I wouldn't have rated his chances of saving someone lost at sea.

Mac waves back and strides towards us, while I act like Liz Hurley and contort my body into the most flattering pose I can muster in this get-up.

'Hey, girls, how's it goin'?' Mac kisses Fi on the cheek. 'I didn't know you were regulars in here now.'

'Oh yes, we come here all . . .' I begin.

119

'First time,' Fi grins. 'Milly is totally shiteing herself so she is.'

See what I mean about that discretion?

Mac smiles down at me and I just know he is remembering that the last time we saw each other I shouted 'BIG PENIS' at his parents.

'So you're off for a swim then, Mrs Clancy?'

I think back to the day we met on the seafront, a month ago now.

'No, actually,' I pout, 'I'm going to pick potatoes in my swimming costume. What does it bloody look like I'm doing?'

Mac's jaw drops and his forehead creases, sending his eyebrows skywards. He then does something that I don't expect. Mac surprises me. He surprises me by throwing his head back and laughing out loud.

'Good one,' he chuckles, his green eyes sparkling under the glaring lights above the pool. 'You got me there so you did, Milly.'

I squirm as I realise a smile is spreading its way across my face from one ear to the other, framed by an instant blush. I made him laugh. I made him laugh and he said my name in such a familiar way. I ruffle my feathers with pride. Until, that is, the realisation dawns that my feathers actually consist of a scrap of Lycra, a desperately unflattering swimming cap and an expanse of white flesh. The smile disappears and I mutter something incomprehensible even to myself before shuffling off towards the shallow end. For once, the prospect of immersing myself neck-deep in water is not so bad. I say a silent prayer, grasp the railings of the shallow end stairs and lower myself into the pool. Which, I might add, is colder than a bath left to stagnate for a week in a draughty house. And they wonder why we prefer drinking pints in a cosy pub to partaking in public exercise!

'This swimming business is not too bad, you know, Fi. I feel quite relaxed, in fact.'

'You haven't lifted your feet off the bottom yet, ya big eejit. I wouldn't exactly call hanging on to this wall and yacking for an hour in the shallow end *swimming* like.'

I squeeze my eyes shut as a young boy flies past my head and dive-bombs into the water.

'Ah well, at least you got your hair wet,' Fi snorts.

I laugh and wipe the stinging water from my eyes just in time to see a crocodile of young children being led into the pool for a lesson.

'Oh my God, let's get out of here, Fi, before that lot start pissing in the pool.'

We haul ourselves out of the water and I fiddle with the bum of my costume, which appears to be aiming to touch the back of my knees.

'Well that was grand, Milly. I'll just have a wee word with Dave before we go.'

'Dave?' I shriek.

I turn my back to the windows and nervously glance around the pool.

'You're taking the piss, right?'

'No I'm not, sure, he's over there, look it.'

*Do I have to?*

'Look, Milly, over there. Did I not mention it?'

'No you bloody well did not, Fiona. Jesus Christ!' I leap behind the nearest pillar as my frantic eyes focus on Dave, focusing on me with his bloody video camera. 'Shit, Fi, who else did you invite along for an ogle, the local news crew? And what the hell does he think he is doing filming us in our swimming costumes? Is the man an idiot or just a certified perv?'

Fi shrugs nonchalantly and waves at Dave, who smiles back delightedly.

'He's filming your progress, Milly, he's doing you a favour.'

'A *favour*? I'll do him a favour in a minute. I'll shove that camera right where he will never be able to use it for porno purposes ever again.'

'Ah now, don't be like that, Dave's a mate. Come on, give him a wave.'

'I will not give him a wave, I'll give him a smack in the gob. Bloody hell, I am so embarrassed I could die.'

I shield my face and make a run for the changing room. I fiddle with the locker key, grab my damp, creased clothes and stomp into a cubicle. I plonk myself down on the wooden bench and hold my head in my hands. I hear Fi hopping up and down outside the door.

'It's all right, Milly, come on now, don't be a drama queen.'

'I *am* a drama queen,' I reply moodily. 'It's my job.'

'I know, but . . . oh, I was only trying to help like. I thought a record of all your hard work would be fantastic for you to keep.'

'Why?' I sniff. 'Why would I want a record of all this crap, Fi? This is just one big humiliation process, and as far as I can see I have so far achieved precisely fuck-all.' I sigh and wipe chloriney tears from my eyes. 'Oh, this is daft. I'm not a movie star. I can't parade around in front of the camera in my pants. This is useless, Fi. I think I should just jack it all in and go home.'

'Don't do that, Milly,' Fi pleads as my mobile begins to ring in the pile of clothes beside me.

'Hello?' I answer morosely. 'Who is it?'

'Amelia? Gerald,' my agent barks. 'Just checking up on how the research is going out there in the Wild West. Have they got you walking on water yet?'

I grimace and balance the mobile between my right ear and shoulder while I struggle to wrap a towel around myself. Gerald always calls at such inopportune moments.

'GERALD, HI!' I reply overenthusiastically. 'Er yes, Gerald, there are no problems at all, none, not a one. I've, um, just been doing a bit of training at the pool as a matter of fact. Fifty lengths, all under water, no problems at all, everything is hunky double dory.'

*Am I overdoing the reassurance? Do people always lie to their agent as much as I do?*

I hear Fi snort outside the door.

'Marvellous,' Gerald wheezes into the receiver, before taking a gulp of what I instinctively know to be single malt. 'That's what I want to hear. This film role is big, Amelia. Big for you and big for me. We . . . *you* can't go messing this up, do you hear?'

I nod silently into the phone and wrap my top teeth around my bottom lip.

'So no bullshit.' He is always one for the straight talk approach. 'I want you in that water twenty-five hours a day until you grow gills. If you're not surfing like a Hawaiian by now you should be. Comprende?'

Another silent nod.

'Good, glad we understand each other. I will be in touch, Amelia. Have a nice day.'

I stare at the phone when the line goes dead and consider walking back to the poolside and dropping it in the deep end. That way Gerald wouldn't be able to get in touch. Then I wouldn't have to explain how I am no nearer to being a surf chick than I am to appearing on the cover of *Vogue*. But then . . . I won't get this role and I won't be a film star. I'll go back to Captain Chicken duties or being a coffee whisk demonstrator and my parents will be right. I grit my teeth and pause to think.

'Are you OK in there, Milly? Don't want you passing out after all that underwater work, like,' Fi sniggers.

I slowly open the door, and I can't help but laugh when I see the amused expression on my best friend's face.

'Oh, Fi, this is all such a mess, isn't it? Now Gerald thinks I am an Olympic swimmer in the making.'

Fi holds up the towel while I get changed.

'Maybe you could be. I can see you in one of those fancy full-length costumes they wear now. Maybe you have this hidden talent that has just never been nurtured.'

'Well, it's very well hidden.'

I groan as I drop a sock in a puddle of water on the cold tiled floor. Fresh tears threaten to burst out of my eyes but I quickly blink them away. Fi tilts her head and looks at me thoughtfully.

'Look, Milly, we are intelligent women, right?'

I nod half-heartedly. Fi carries on.

'OK, so I might be a bit loopy, and you might tell more lies than an American President, but you can't deny we're resourceful, right?'

A firmer nod this time.

'So if anyone can pull this off, sure the two of us can. We've got each other, we've got Mac and Dave, we've got three months, shiteloads of spirit and a whole feckin' ocean of waves out there for you to practise on, right?'

Fi sticks out her pointy little chin and smiles confidently.

'So I say we don't give up, we face this thing, we take it on and we have fun while we're doing it, right?'

'Right,' I reply shakily.

'Grand.' Fi pulls me into a hug. 'Milly, we are gonna put all the daftness behind us and start again. And I know exactly what we are going to do.'

# CHAPTER THIRTEEN

# *Water Under the Bridge*

We find Mac on the main beach. Here the waves always seem to be smaller, gently lapping the shore and cooling the paws of many an over-walked dog. Mac is in the middle of giving a surf lesson, so we keep our distance at first and perch on the low wall that runs along the back of the beach, separating it from a children's park and the rustiest collection of aged rides ever to label itself as a fairground. Fi buys two polystyrene cups of watery hot chocolate from the beach café (otherwise described as a yellowing old caravan stocking traditional seaside fare of choc-ices and the like).

'You're at the bloody seaside now, you'll eat the ice-cream and you'll bloody well enjoy it too!' I imagine parents screaming at their frostbitten offspring.

Mac stands tall in the centre of a group of about thirty children aged, I would estimate, between thirteen and fourteen. He has changed his clothes since we met at the pool, exchanging loose jeans and a hooded top for his figure-skimming wetsuit. His hair curls every which way and moves wildly in the onshore breeze, clearly dry and thus suggesting that he has not yet been in the water himself. The children, however, charge in and out of the sea like a flock of small birds diving into a birdbath to refresh themselves. They are watched by Mac and two other men, neither of whom is wearing a wetsuit. From their uniform beige chinos and slightly weary expressions as they observe the mêlée of excited children, I take them to be teachers in charge of a school day out. Enjoying being let out of the confines of the institution for the day but bemoaning the fact that they have to spend this rare free time with their boisterous pupils. Mac, on the other hand, surprises me with the undivided attention he is giving the group. Unaware that Fi and I are watching, he displays a kind of patience and encouragement I have not witnessed from him before. He is clearly enjoying himself as he stands on the shoreline doling out orders, cheering successfully caught waves and running to the rescue of the uncoordinated. He bends on his haunches to be at the same level as the smaller members of the class, nodding and smiling as they breathlessly recount their tales of adventure on the high seas. Perhaps the fact that I haven't yet explored the low seas never mind any high ones has something to do with Mac's impatient and unimpressed attitude towards me. He pats some of his pupils on the back and exchanges manly handshakes with those more advanced through puberty. In return, every pupil eyes him adoringly, boys and girls alike. They vie for Mac's attention, waving at him frantically on the rare occasion that they do get both feet on the board for more than a second.

'Mac, look at me!'

'Did ya see me, Mac, did ya?'

'Hey Mac, I'm surfin' like you so I am!'

Their high-pitched effervescence reaches me on the wind and I am surprised to find myself laughing along with Mac.

'Isn't he just grand at what he does?' Fi marvels proudly. 'Look it, those wains think he's God, so they do.'

I nod slowly and reflect on how these children seem to adore Mac, when the only side of him I have so far been acquainted with is a rather harsh, sarcastic one with little time for strangers. Other than this morning at the pool, I have rarely even seen him smile. Between you and me, I think we may have inadvertently stumbled across Mac's soft side. It could just be the grim cup of hot chocolate, but (and this is also between you and me) this soft side seems to be having the strangest effect on my stomach. As for the hard parts of Mac Heggarty, I am not even going to dwell on those.

I shake my head back to reality and gulp my drink too fast, scalding the tip of my tongue. What am I thinking? This is the man who has done nothing but mock me since I arrived. The man who snapped at me when I asked a simple question about religion, who thinks I act like a princess though falls very short of treating me like one, and who has about as much faith in my ability to learn to surf as my parents have in my acting career. Concentrate. This is not the time to be developing some poxy instructor crush, like every single girl who has ever gone skiing in the history of white-toothed ski instructors. This is the time to be focusing on my blossoming career and on the chance I have been praying for during every crap job I have ever been obliged to undertake. I am on a mission and this instructor is going to help me achieve it. End of story.

I have to hand it to him, though, he wears that neoprene well.

Fi nudges me with her sharp elbow and flicks her head towards the beach.

'Away ye go then, Milly, let's get this party started.'

'What do you mean, away I go? Go where?'

'There, ya big eejit. Over there to my cousin. Or did you not notice the rubber-coated hunk of a man in the middle of all those wee cubs?'

Fi winks at me mischievously. I shrug and concentrate on the undissolved remains of cheap cocoa powder at the bottom of the cup.

'I can't just go over there, Fi.'

'Why not?' she squawks. 'Did you leave your legs back at the swimming pool?'

'No, it's just, well, he looks very busy and I don't want to interrupt.'

'Sure it's only a feckin' surf lesson for a few kids. He won't mind at all like.'

'Only a "feckin' surf lesson"? Fi, what happens if I distract Mac and while we are chatting a young child in his care is washed away by a freak wave and drowns and Mac is held responsible and he goes to prison and loses everything and his reputation is in tatters and . . .'

'Jaysus Christ, girl, you're full of shite at times.'

She pushes me forcefully off the wall.

'Now quit making excuses and get yourself over there. All you have to do is be a bit remorseful for being his crappiest pupil ever, say you want to try again and butter him up until he gives you another lesson. Oh, and you know, maybe throw in a sorry, like, for cursing in front of his ma.'

'Thanks, Fi,' I grumble to myself as I start to make my way slowly down the beach, 'you always make things sound so simple.'

I pick my way through the scattered mounds of seaweed and stumble every second step on concealed piles of pebbles. I try to compose myself by going over a well-structured conversation in my head, but as I near Mac and the rabble of young surfers my mind keeps reverting back to two thoughts: *Am I really his crappiest pupil ever?* and *How would Mac look if I buttered him up? Literally.*

I start to sweat although a wind cold enough to be Eskimo air-conditioning is stinging my chlorinated skin. My hand subconsciously delves into my pocket for my lip-gloss and I begin to apply a smooth layer to my lips before I realise what I am doing.

'Hey, would you look at that lady,' shouts one of the children, whose wetsuit is so large it hangs in wrinkles around his knees. 'She's puttin' on lipstick fer ya, Mac.'

'Is she, me arse!' squeals another.

'I tell ya, she is. She must fancy Mac, hey. She wants to kiss him on the lips.'

'Na, she wants to *ride* him.'

'RIDE HIM!' they hoot, gyrating their hips like mini Tom Joneses. 'That lady wants to RIDE ya, Mac.'

I shove the lip-gloss hurriedly back in my pocket and consider pretending to just be casually passing and to not have noticed the only other people in a two-mile radius, but I grit my teeth and carry on. I cannot be intimidated by a group of mouthy adolescents who probably still need bedtime stories. I am an adult, for goodness' sake . . . A thoroughly intimidated one.

'Patrick O'Connell, don't be so bold,' scolds the younger of the two teachers, who obviously senses my discomfort, although I see a smile flash across his lips.

'Richard Fitzgerald, if you say ride one more time, I swear I will roast you,' warns the other.

Mac, meanwhile, chuckles to himself and slowly raises one eyebrow so high that by the time we come face to face it has all but disappeared under his hairline. He says nothing by way of greeting but instead silently watches me squirm.

'Hello again,' I say as casually as possible. 'I wondered if I could perhaps have a quiet chat.'

'Chat away.' Mac shrugs, folding his arms protectively across that broad chest of his.

I make sharp movements with my head, trying to indicate that I would like to chat out of earshot of the thirty giggly children who are currently making faces at me behind Mac's back.

'She wants ya on yer own, Mac.' Patrick O'Connell whistles snidely.

'Oooooooh,' coo the rest of the group in unison.

Damn, this is really not helping matters. I persevere.

'Can I just have a moment?'

'For a *ride*,' adds Richard Fitzgerald in a half-whisper.

'I can't leave the cubs here,' Mac replies with another nonchalant shrug. 'I'm in charge so you'll have to say whatever it is you have to say in front of them. Just don't swear the way you did at my ma's house. Innocent ears are listening.'

All right, smartarse, there was no need for that. Besides, this little lot look about as innocent as Winona Ryder doing her shopping at Saks, and if that O'Bloody Connell one doesn't stop making that gesture with his tongue I am going to have to have words with his teacher.

'Right,' I reply, raising my chin proudly. 'OK then. Um, I just wanted to say . . .' – I clear my throat several times in quick succession – 'how was your swim at the pool?'

'Er, I didn't go swimming, actually. I was just organising some training for the new lifeguards there.'

'Lovely, and so how did that go?'

'What? The organising?'

'Yes, the organising.'

Mac frowns. 'It was grand, yeah. No problems at all.'

'Great,' I smile, twiddling my thumbs, 'that's good to know.'

'Yeah.'

'Yeah, yep, great.'

I sniff and look down at my feet, which, I realise, are starting to sink into the wet sand.

'So, um, how was your swim there?' Mac asks after an uneasy pause.

'Great thanks.'

'You went in the water?'

'Yes. It was, er . . . great.'

'Great.'

'Righto,' I say.

The 'o' floats out on the wind for several uncomfortable seconds. I swing my arms and click my tongue against the roof of my mouth.

'So I'll be off then and leave you to it, shall I?'

'But, Milly . . .'

'I'll just get going then.' I jerk my thumb back up the beach in Fi's direction.

'Milly . . .'

'OK then, Mac, bye now.'

'Milly!'

Mac's firm tone stops me in my tracks. I turn to look up at him, squinting as the sun pokes through the clouds.

'Look it, that lady's winkin' at him!' one of the kids sniggers.

I blink hurriedly.

'So what was it you actually wanted to talk to me about, Milly?'

I press my lips together.

'Nothing. OK, well there was a little something, but it can wait if you're too busy.'

'I am busy,' Mac replies, nodding towards the sniggering children huddled in a group behind him, 'but not too busy that I can't hear what you have to say. You've interrupted us already so you may as well. Go on, Milly, I don't bite.'

I clamp my teeth together as Pat O'Connell remarks, 'But I bet she'd like you to, hey!'

'All right, well I wanted to talk to you . . .' I begin. 'But I'd just like to say, just so you know, that I wouldn't.'

'Wouldn't what?'

'I wouldn't want, you know,' I whisper, jerking my head towards the O'Connell boy.

Mac scowls in confusion. 'No, I'm sorry, I don't know.'

'I'm saying I wouldn't want you to BITE ME,' I say so loudly the words echo off the cliffs and bounce back at us at double the volume, which causes the children to collapse into a heap of hysteria.

There is no getting away from it; I deal with these delicate situations with the skill of a UN negotiator.

'Well Holy God, I am glad we cleared that up so,' Mac sniggers. 'Biting is off the menu.'

'She's quare in the head,' one of the children remarks.

'Who said that?' one of the beige teachers yawns.

I finally pull myself together and get to the point without further embarrassment.

'I wanted to talk to you about surf lessons, Mac.'

'See, sham, I told ya she wants Mac to teach her how to *ride*,' the Fitzgerald boy cackles.

I underestimated the power of young minds.

'I am warning you, Richard Fitzgerald,' his teacher says wearily.

'So am I, you little shi—'

'What about the surf lessons, Milly?' Mac interrupts tactfully.

I step closer and whisper, 'What are you doing here with these little *darlings* anyway? You're not a schoolteacher, are you?'

Mac shrugs, and I notice his cheeks colour at this question.

'No, it's just a programme we do with the kids, a cross-border integration scheme to mix the North and the South of Ireland through surfing and other sports. It's grand really.'

'So you're in charge, are you?' I ask with genuine interest.

'Aye, well only the surfing bits. It's dead rewarding, you know. It kinda helps break down some of the barriers these cubs have learned to build between themselves because of religion and where they're from, you know. Sure, I'm not saving the world but it all helps, I think. Besides, even if I'm just teaching them to be safe in the water then that's a good thing. They might save one of their mates' lives one day, and that's a gift in itself so.'

I pause for a second before I speak again, totally taken aback by this sincerity that I haven't witnessed before and by the fact that Mac just let out a whole stream of conversation directed at me, which is a first. The cross-border scheme sounds like a marvellous idea and Mac is clearly the driving force behind it. His modesty warms me to him and I let a smile touch my glossed lips. Mac smiles back and I see the look in his eyes soften for a second before a cloud passes over the sun and his steely expression returns.

'Right, so what about these surf lessons?'

I see the wall between us slide back into place.

I sigh. 'Look, Mac, the thing is, I know we kind of got off on the wrong foot here and' – I take a deep breath – 'I know you think I'm some precious city girl from England who doesn't know the arse end of a surfboard from the . . . from the other end of it, but I'm really not like that. And I'm sorry about, you know, calling you a terrorist because I can see you are far from it. Not that I ever really thought you were. I was just being silly and freaking out a bit and, no, I can't see you in a balaclava, ha ha. Not with a face like . . .'

My voice trails off. Damn, this honesty is catching.

'With a face like what?'

'Pardon me?'

'With a face like a total dish,' one of the schoolgirls remarks in a high-pitched giggle.

'A face like Michael Flatley?' Mac asks.

He raises an eyebrow and gives me a lopsided smile, much like Dan does, only . . . different somehow.

I cough and nervously jangle some change in my pocket.

'Oh yes, sorry about the Michael Flatley ego comment too. And about suspecting you might want to drown me and for slagging off Pooh . . . er, the cottage. And for saying big pee-you-know-what in front of your parents, and basically, Mac, for throwing your offer of help back in your face at every opportunity and for perhaps acting a bit diva-ish now and again.' I stop and screw up my face in thought. 'Actually, come to think of it, I have been behaving like a total tit, haven't I?'

'She said "TIT",' snorts the O'Connell boy, amusing his friends immensely.

'Jaysus, this is better than a filum,' says another.

'Or reality TV,' I hear someone laugh, but I am beyond caring what they think. Let them enjoy it.

'I am sorry, Mac. I guess I really haven't been your ideal pupil. Maybe Fi was right and I am the crappiest one ever.'

Two white teeth emerge to bite his bottom lip but Mac says nothing, watching me in what appears to be a mixture of sincerity and bemusement.

'The thing is, I haven't been myself since I arrived because I have got so mixed up in this whole film thing. I have told lie after lie until I don't know what's true any more, and if I fail, my parents will be right and I will be a loser at the age of thirty-one. You have to understand that I do really want to learn to surf because I really really want . . . no, I *need* this job more than anything, but the truth is' – I take a very deep breath of eye-watering fresh air – 'the truth is I am scared.'

'Scared of failing?' Mac asks softly.

'Mainly scared of dying actually. Dying with a lungful of salt water at the murky bottom of the ocean.'

'Ah, Milly, I don't plan on letting you drown. Saving people is my job.'

'I know,' I reply. I feel stupid and vulnerable right now. 'I know that, but although you might think I am a confident city chick who thinks she knows everything, I am in fact a total scaredy-cat. A completely petrified one hundred per cent scaredy-cat. I am such a wimp, Mac, that I didn't even move from clinging to the wall of the shallowest part of the shallow end of the pool this morning after I saw you.'

'Jaysus, aren't girls shite?' Fitzgerald groans.

'You probably don't realise what it feels like to be scared, Mac,' I whimper, 'with you being so tough and macho and all that.'

Mac bites his lip again and my eyes fix on the cute gap

between his middle teeth. He tilts his head on one side and stares at me for what feels like several minutes but is probably only a couple of seconds.

'You think I'm macho?'

'Er, well, macho in the sense that, well, you can be quite domineering.'

He shakes his head, his hair falling loosely around his ears.

'You have no idea, Milly. I have been scared. Many times in fact, but one time in particular. I have even cried once or twice.'

'Have you?'

'Ah, for feck's sake,' Fitzgerald groans again.

'FITZGERALD, get over here NOW!' shouts the teacher.

'Well,' Mac sighs, oblivious to the cheeky-faced dark-haired boy being dragged away by his left ear, 'I admire your honesty, Milly.'

'And I yours.'

We pause, but not uncomfortably. I am aware of a sudden connection between us but I am not quite sure how to handle it. Is this the first glimmer of a proper friendship?

Mac reaches out a hand. I glance at it briefly and then accept it. His palm is warm, his fingers so large that they envelop my hand entirely. I shiver as a vibration runs up my arm, stopping somewhere near the part of my brain that acknowledges how good the touch of a man feels. By that I mean just *a* man, of course, not *this* man in particular. He doesn't make me feel the way Dan makes me feel, but it is still nice to recognise the warm feeling of friendship.

'OK, you're on. I'll teach you to surf, Milly, but you have to do what I say and no more of the fartin'-about-like-a-princess shite.'

I nod and concentrate on stopping my hand sweating in his grasp. Is it just me or has the weather turned hot all of a sudden?

'And we might have to actually get in the water at some point to make the mission a total success, you know.'

'Yes, Mac, I do realise that.'

Mac nods his head and smiles. 'Right then, sure, there's no time like the present.'

'I beg your pardon?'

Mac drops my hand and claps his own together. The children, who by now have dissolved into a chaotic playground scrum, scramble around for their surfboards and charge off towards the waves.

'Hows about you give me a hand with these cubs and their surf lesson?'

'Oh what, you mean like right now kind of thing?' I grimace.

'Aye, right now.'

'Oh, well I would love to really,' I lie, 'but I should get back to Fi. She's waiting for me over there and we have some stuff to do.'

'Stuff?' Mac knits his brow questioningly.

'Yes, just stuff but important stuff and I have kept her waiting. So I had better be off. I would rather start with a one-to-one anyway, to be honest.'

*Because these confident teenagers scare me half to death.*

Mac places a firm hand on my shoulder. I feel my muscles twitch.

'Sure there's plenty of time for a one-to-one.'

My muscles start to spasm.

'But Fi is waiting over . . .'

I turn my head and blanch when I realise my ever-supportive best friend has scarpered, the sneaky cow.

'No excuses left, Milly?' Mac smiles when I turn back.

'I guess not. All right then, you got me.'

'Grand, so let's get started, shall we?'

Mac walks off towards the shoreline like the Pied Piper with his group of little drowned rats in tow. He stops to add, 'I know you don't trust me, but I actually have a hunch that you might just enjoy surfing.'

*I doubt it*, I think to myself as I gingerly follow him to the water's edge. Nevertheless, I have got a new reputation to create as a non-precious, non-princessy, up-for-anything, gung-ho surf chick, so, hey, I'm willing to give it a go.

Just as long as I don't have to get my hair wet.

## CHAPTER FOURTEEN

# *Paddle, Forrest, Paddle!*

I help Mac with his cross-border integration scheme all week. I learn surfing technique just listening to Mac's instructions to the children and I make mental notes of the important points while pretending to my young friends that I know it all already. Of course, being an unqualified surf instructor and a qualified waterphobe, Mac does not bestow upon me a serious position of responsibility, which is sensible. I simply assist. I assist the girls in getting in and out of their wetsuits with the least amount of pubescent embarrassment. I assist Mac in keeping an eye on the groups of ten in the water at one time. I assist in the after-surf beach football games by putting out the goalposts and keeping score (but not by demonstrating my hideously girly ball-control skills). I even assist young Emily Malloy from Ballyshannon in setting up her first date with Adam Wilson from Portrush. I am proud to be doing my own bit for cross-border integration. While doing all that, I find myself laughing and chatting comfortably with Mac and I revel in the joy on the face of each child when they finally stand up and ride a wave. God, I aspire to be like them!

I also make progress in my relationship with the ocean. On Monday I stand as close to the edge as I can without getting my shoes wet. By Wednesday, I am in bare feet (in Ireland in March, I must add for extra Brownie points) and I wade in as far as my mid-calves. By the end of Thursday, I am so enthralled by watching our tiniest, most timid pupil finally catching a wave that I forget to watch the sea and am soaked right up to my waist. I get wet and I don't mind. I am immersed in all the fun. Mac, however, does find my unplanned drenching hugely entertaining.

Now it is Friday. Friday 1 April, no less. The day when fools come out to play and to do foolish things in the name of fun. I really suspect this might not be the best day to be attempting to do the thing I have been dreading since all this began. However, I have committed myself to the cause and I cannot let the children down. Don't ask me why, but I also feel as though I want to prove myself to Mac. I guess over the last week we have finally become friends and I would like him to respect me, at least for trying. He respects every kid who gives surfing a go no matter how successful they are, and he instils in them the importance of supporting each other as friends. Today, I am going to need more support than Jordan's breasts if I am ever going to pull this off.

I stand on the shore and stare at the mass of water before me, feeling my knees knock together with fear through the rubber of my wetsuit. Mac is definitely speaking because I can see his lips move but his voice is drowned out (bad choice of words) by the constant rumble and interspersed crashes that come with infinite gallons of frothy water picking up speed as they travel across the globe to hurtle themselves against a few metres of sand. The waves are small (or so Mac says), just one to two feet apparently, although whoever's feet he used to measure them must wear extremely large shoes. The conditions have been described as very favourable but I am not convinced. From where I stand, if one of these buggers lands on my head, I will be instantly crushed and reduced to plankton before Mac has even had a chance to throw me a life buoy. I am terrified, frightened, petrified, quaking and every other word synonymous with the feeling manifested by a locked jaw, jelly legs and rather unsightly upper lip perspiration.

'Right then, did everyone get that?' says Mac, surveying the group of shivering little people (myself included, although there is less of the 'little' about me in a wetsuit) lined up on the beach before him.

Fiona nods her head exuberantly like the swotty girl at school. All the other kids in Mac's Friday-morning cross-border lesson voice their yeses. I consider asking him to repeat the bits that came after the 'let's start at the beginning' part, but that was over an hour ago and I guess that request would make me hugely unpopular. These twelve-year-olds are hardly my peer group, but you know, I still don't want to be the thickie of the bunch.

I also nod my head, despite not having ingested a word of Mac's lesson. I have been here all week after all, so if I can just stop my brain quivering, I may be able to remember the essential details. I glance around and follow the lead of the children, picking up my foamy board and carrying it to the water's edge. I copy Patrick O'Connell beside me as he takes the end of the leash that is not attached to the surfboard and wraps it around his spaghetti-like ankle.

'Are ya natural or goofy?' he smiles, revealing a gob-stopper-sized lump of chewing gum in his mouth.

'Er, I think I'm fairly natural,' I stutter, self-consciously touching a hand to my hair as he blows a bubble of gum so large it could carry Richard Branson around the world. 'Just a bit of Sun-In and a few highlights here and there for shine and depth.'

My juvenile instructor sighs. 'Have ya learned nothing all week? Sure I mean do ya stand with yer right foot forward or yer left?'

'Oh yes, of course you do. I was just testing.'

I stare at my feet.

'And tell me, Pat, how exactly am I supposed to know which one I am again?'

'Well what about when yer out on yer skateboard?'

*Skateboard? Do I look like an extreme sports athlete?*

I feel like the uninvited old git at a teenage birthday bash.

'Feet together,' Mac says, appearing right in front of me.

'Feet together? But surely that will make balancing on the board even more difficult.'

'Ya big eejit, Milly,' he smirks. 'Stand here on the sand with your feet together.'

I do as I am told. Before I know what is happening, Mac raises a hand to my breastbone and shoves me firmly backwards. I lose my balance and stumble but manage to steady myself before I hit the ground.

'What the hell was that for?'

'You're goofy,' Mac replies with no hint of an apology.

'She certainly is,' Fi giggles behind me.

While I huff and puff and loudly complain, Mac quickly crouches down and attaches the Velcro strap of the surf-board leash to my left ankle.

'When I pushed you backwards,' he explains, 'you stepped back on your left automatically and your right one stayed in front. Sure it's just a crude way we use of seeing which way feels more natural for you. So now you'll be goofy.'

'OK, Pluto,' I grin, 'what's next?'

Mac points straight ahead.

'To the ocean.'

'Oh God, I was afraid you were going to say that.'

'Any final words before ya paddle out?' Dave asks.

He holds the video camera close to my face, the glinting red light indicating that it is recording the fear in my eyes. I squint at the lens.

'You wouldn't have a pair of water wings, would you? I'm not too good at floating.'

141

'You won't need them,' Mac assures me. 'We'll soon have you flying along those waves.'

I grimace at the camera.

'God bless this surfboard and all who sink on her.'

'Good on ya, Milly,' Dave grins, giving me a thumbs-up. 'Break a leg now.'

*It's not just my leg I'm worried about, Dave, I'm rather fond of this neck of mine too.*

I have never been so pleased to see Mac as when he appears beside me in the waist-high water, his confident stance indicating that he is as at home in this aqueous environment as I am in the January sales.

'Hey, Milly, how's the craic? Have you caught the bug yet?'

'Probably,' I sneeze. 'In fact I think I've inhaled enough water to catch most of the sea life in the area too. I'll be surprised if small whales don't come out of my nose later when I blow it.'

'I meant the surfing bug.'

'Oh, right.' I close my mouth as a wave rushes past, stopping only to smack me full in the face. 'Hmm, well I would be lying if I said I am positively overwhelmed by the sense of being at one with the ocean, but I'm trying my best.'

'Good girl,' he purrs, which sends an involuntary shiver down my spine. It is similar to the other shivers, caused by freezing water blasting in through the neck of my wetsuit, but is somehow different. I wobble as another wave slaps my legs while I am distracted. Mac grabs my arm and holds me steady. We remain that way until the set of three or four waves has passed and the sea becomes relatively still. Patting the top of my board, Mac gestures for me to mount the trusty steed.

'Come on then, plank yourself on here and let's get you a wave.'

I smile weakly and pull myself into a prone position on the surfboard. I am well aware that my neoprene-enrobed bottom is generously on view above the water level and is perilously close to Mac's hand, but I have no choice other than to swallow my inhibitions (along with several gallons of seawater) and allow him to turn the board and me around to face the beach. I hold on as if my life depends on it (which it largely does) and pray to every God I can think of that this goofy beginner won't drown in the few metres of water between here and dry land.

'When I shout "paddle", just go for it as hard as you can, OK?'

I nod stiffly, unable to converse because of the fear of what I am about to do.

'Then I'll give you a wee push, and when you feel the wave hit you . . .'

*Hit? Now that doesn't sound good.*

'. . . then try and jump up on to your feet, all right?'

I squeak a response only audible to dogs and squeeze my eyes shut to pray.

'Keep your eyes open all the time . . .'

*How did he know? He can't even see my eyes.*

'. . . and then you'll be able to see where you're going. You'll be grand, Milly, don't worry now.'

*Worried? Me? Oh no, I'm not worried; I'm about to have a bloody coronary!*

'Here you go,' Mac announces just seconds later. 'Now this looks like a wild good set so we'll get you on one of these.'

*Oh Mummy, help me.*

I almost eat my stomach from the inside out as the first wave arrives and the surfboard lurches like the boat about to come a cropper in *The Perfect Storm.*

'Don't panic like, I've still got you. Now get ready, Milly, this next wave is yours, hey.'

*But it doesn't have to be mine, does it? I mean, if someone else wants it I would be quite happy to let them have it. In fact, I'll pass if you don't mind.*

'OK, Milly, this is it,' Mac says excitedly.

'But . . .'

'This is the one.'

'But, but . . .'

'Get ready, Milly. Oh, it's a mighty one.'

*Mighty?!*

'Mac, I don't think—'

'Paddle, Milly, paddle!' he shouts.

I hear the wave approaching from behind like a watery avalanche. My stomach has now come out of my mouth and is floating in the water in front of me.

'Paddle, Milly, paddle!'

'Oh Jesus,' I wail, digging each hand deep into the water either side of the board the way Mac showed me.

I feel myself being propelled forward. The sound of the wave reverberates through my pounding eardrums.

'I'm going to die,' I cry out, although no one can hear me.

'GO!' Mac whoops, giving me a firm and final push.

I am hit from behind by something I imagine to feel like the force of a freight train, and a loud boom resounds against my eardrums. The surfboard catapults forwards, almost flinging my jelly-like body off the side, but I hold on so tight that my fingers carve holes into the foam. A blinding white froth engulfs both the board and me and hurls me around so wildly I briefly realise what it would be like to be on the spin cycle in a washing machine. I can't breathe, I can't see, I don't know where I am or where I am going. Am I under the wave or *in* it? Whether I am surfing or not is hard to tell; at this moment I am simply surviving.

The board charges onwards on a bumpy trajectory for what feels like minutes, but is probably only a couple of seconds. Just as I feel I can't possibly hold on any longer, I am thrust forward by an invisible force and catapulted free of the watery cave until I can see the beach fast approaching before my eyes. I hold on, pressing my belly against the top of the board and trying to keep my eyes open. I shoot past several surfers who are paddling back out to sea, one of whom I recognise as Fiona. Her mouth is open, her arms are punching the air and she is shouting something at me, but I can hear nothing except the overwhelming noise of the ocean.

Almost there, the beach is close now. I try to catch my breath but the speed I am travelling at and the spray from the water makes swallowing a lungful of air almost impossible. I then remember Mac's instruction to jump to my feet. I nearly forgot. How did the surfers do it in the movies we watched? Balancing on this wobbly watercraft cannot be possible, can it? Not even for Keanu Reeves. I grit my teeth, the taste of fear in my mouth. I glance up at the beach then down at the board.

*Come on, Milly, you can do it. At least give it a try, that's all Mac wants you to do. Put all that research to good use.*

With all the strength I have left, I push against my shaking hands. My arms lock straight, I lift my body in a press-up motion, and the board lurches precariously. I drag my legs underneath me into a crouch. My left knee hits the deck of the board and I make one last attempt to place my right leg in front of it. Whoosh! The wave smacks against my legs. I am thrown to one side and I fly through the air until I hit the water with so much force I feel my bones compress. I don't even have time to take a breath. I am under the water, being cartwheeled over and over. I don't know which way is up and I can't seem to right myself. I sense the panic begin to spread from my palpitating heart to my arms and legs, gripping them with fear and rendering them useless. Here I am again; Milly Armstrong, age six, at Bournemouth beach. Is this going to be the end? Have I done enough to be remembered?

I muster enough courage to open my eyes. After all, if this is the end I want to see what it looks like. The water is a murky wash of sand and seaweed, but through the foamy vortex I see a blue tunnel with what looks like a light at the end. I reach out to it, expecting to see the Pearly Gates at any second. The light grows brighter and I try to swim towards it. One final push and I gasp as my head pops out of the water and I suck in a lungful of air. My feet touch a hard surface, I take two or three precarious steps, the wave retreats and I collapse on to the beach.

'Are you OK, Milly?' shouts a voice that could belong to God but sounds suspiciously like Dave.

I open one eye and find myself peering into the lens of a video camera that is so close I swear I can see Dave's eye through the other side.

'That was fantastic, Milly,' he hoots in my face, 'quare fantastic. How did it feel? Did ya like it? Did ya know the ride would be that fast, like?'

I grimace and smile alternately for a moment as my brain tries to catch up with his questions while wishing Dave had opted for a shot other than the close-up. I don't need to look in a mirror to know that right now I am not looking my best. Waterproof mascara never does what it claims to do.

'Good effort trying to stand up, hey, Milly, especially as you're scared of the water. That was dead mighty.'

'I don't know about mighty,' I wheeze, 'but I was almost dead.'

I start to splutter and pull myself into a sitting position. With no warning, half a gallon of seawater gushes from my nostrils and rolls off my chin. Looking good, girl, looking good. I hastily wipe it away with my clammy hand and look out to sea. Still the waves roll into shore and hit the sand. Blimey, don't they ever get tired?

'Look at those waves,' says Dave, crouching on his haunches beside me. 'Ya caught one of those. Ya caught it all the way to the beach. You're a surfer now, Milly. Good on ya.'

I turn my head slowly and blink at Dave, then I look back at the ocean. A smile works its way across my lips, and before I know what I am doing, a laugh erupts from my aching lungs.

'I did catch one of those, didn't I?' I gasp, beaming at Dave through the video camera that is permanently glued to his right hand. '*I* caught one of *those*. Ha ha, and I can't even swim!'

I clasp my hands to my wet cheeks and giggle with disbelief and an overwhelming sudden sense of . . . what is it? Pride? Achievement? I grin so widely I feel my cheeks might burst. I faced my fear.

'I've done it, Dave, I've caught a wave. OK, so I wasn't exactly multiple champion Kelly Slater. I didn't fly through the air doing loop-de-loops or whatever it is you surfers do, but . . . but I got one, didn't I?'

Dave nods.

'And I didn't drown, did I?'

Another nod.

'Do you know what?' I giggle, looking back out to sea. 'I think I actually enjoyed it too.'

*Or at least now I am on dry land I can pretend I did.*

'Good on you yourself,' says Mac, striding towards us out of the water like the man in the Bounty advert only more Celtic. 'You're after catching a good one there, Milly. See, I said you could do it.'

He opens his arms as wide as his genuine smile. I race across the sand and throw myself into his embrace, squealing, 'Thank you, Mac, thank you so much. I did it, I did it. I'm not an April Fool. And I'm alive!'

We stay that way for a moment until my conscious inhibitions catch up with me and I nervously pull away.

'Ah right so, that's grand,' Mac coughs, the embarrassment visible through his tan.

'Yes, erm, thanks anyway,' I stammer, stepping gingerly back and nodding politely like an English businessman at a board meeting.

'Beautiful moment,' Dave laughs, at last lowering the

147

video camera from his eye and letting it hang on a cord around his neck.

He raises his hands in the shape of a movie clapperboard. 'Aaand . . . CUT!'

# CHAPTER FIFTEEN

## *Stepping Stones*

The feeling of euphoria I experience from not having drowned during my first real surf challenge is enough to carry me through a whole month of regular lessons. Not every day, you understand, as I find myself to be a fussy pupil. I like to surf only when the sea is blue, the waves are appealingly small, the sun is shining and there is little chance of rain. Which collectively is quite rare in Ireland in April, but not unheard of.

'But you'll be getting wet in the sea anyhow, for feck's sake,' Mac protests the first time I refuse to don my wetsuit in the rain.

'So?' I shrug. 'Is that any reason to do away with common sense altogether? Look at it, man, I could drown in that rain!'

I won't repeat his response.

I do make progress over the weeks, and even surprise myself. At the same time, however, I come to realise that surfing is a uniquely frustrating pursuit. While I try to concentrate on the basics of clambering to my feet (via one knee, then one knee/one foot, then two knees, etc.), Mother Nature seems to do all she can to scupper my chances by constantly changing the playing field. Obvious though it may be in hindsight, I had not considered how difficult it would be to master a technique when the conditions change every day. In fact every minute of every day. The sea is not like a running track where I could (if I wanted to, which I don't) practise my hurdling over and over again until I had perfected it. The ocean moves. It has tides and rips and swell directions. It crashes on the beach and against rocks, creating waves, each one different from the one before. I think I am getting somewhere one day, only to have the whole ocean change shape by the next day thanks to the cycle of the bloody moon. I mean, for goodness' sake, it is downright annoying, and quite frankly, the Hawaiians have a lot to answer for for introducing us to this sport in the first place. I honestly do not see how anyone can truly master surfing.

Nevertheless, as Mac repeatedly points out, I am not here to be the next world champion, so I just have to keep plugging away at the basics. I have to concentrate on getting the soles of both feet on the board simultaneously while balancing on top of the water on a piece of foam travelling at high speed. Easy!

It does not surprise me that Fi progresses quicker than me. By mid-April, she is springing to her feet on every wave and apparently balancing for at least two seconds. I say 'apparently', because the fact that I spend more time under the water than on top of it prevents me from actually witnessing Fi's skill. I have no doubt, however, that Fi can do it *and* look cute in the process. When Dave explains that small surfers like Fi have an advantage, as it is easier to balance with a low centre of gravity, I grab this excuse and run with it.

'I have a high centre of gravity,' I point out to whoever is listening after every one of my many wipeouts. 'I am at a mathematical disadvantage, you see.'

Most of the children just tell me to shut it.

Don't forget the fact (to continue my argument) that Fi also has the advantage of weighing less than most of the kids in the class. If I had the body of a matchstick man to work with, I would be leaping to my feet like a gazelle and positively floating along the wave. I, on the other hand, must fight the Earth's forces to haul myself upright like a fat seal attempting to walk on its hind flippers. No, I am neither graceful nor talented, but I am a try-hard and there is a place in the world of sport for us too.

As my fear of drowning lessens and my gritty determination grows, I succeed in dragging my feet nearer and nearer to their required position on the board. By the end of the month, all pride has been washed out of my waterlogged body by my efforts. My nails are brittle and broken, my hair is a straggly clump of saltwater and seaweed, and I have taken to wearing less daily make-up than most nuns. The point is, I don't care what I look like. I just want to be able to stand up on this bloody thing!

And I do. On the first day of May, as the sunshine glints off the last wave of our Sunday-afternoon lesson, I push my hands down on the deck of the board, I raise up my body and I jump to my feet. Just like that. It suddenly seems so easy. Like the first time you ride a bike without stabilisers and don't eat the pavement and you wonder what all the fuss was about. Just like that, I stand up and I am riding the wave. Unfortunately, I am so surprised by my own perform-ance that nerves get the better of me and I fall off before I have the chance to squeal 'Look at me!' But that does not take away from the fact that I did it. I surfed. Briefly, but still long enough to give me hope. And to be allowed to brag about it.

'Did you see me?' I ask the other kids in the class.

'Did you see me?' I loudly demand of Fiona.

'Did you see me?' I say to random strangers on the beach who just happen to be passing by walking their scraggy little windswept dogs.

I am a surfer and I am proud. Oh yes, on planet Milly, Mr Kelly Slater better watch his back, because a few more lessons and I could be calling for a coronation to snatch his surfing crown.

> *Dear Mum and Dad, Guinness-filled greetings from the fabulous west coast where I am researching my new, exciting film role. I thought you might like this postcard showing the view outside our cottage. You won't believe it but I actually surf in that ocean, which is fab. Check out those amazing waves! Work is brill, prospects are looking fabulous and vv excited about the film. Hope you are feeling better, Dad. Love from the leprechauns, xxx Milly*

'Jaysus,' Fi comments when she peers over my shoulder, 'how many feckin' fabs, brills and fabulouses do you need on one wee scrap of cardboard? Don't worry yourself, Milly, I reckon your folks will catch on to the giant hints about your new, successful life, like.' She punches me playfully on the shoulder. 'As well they should too.'

I shrug and repeatedly bend the postcard between my hands. Communicating with my parents is a necessity but always fraught with moments of self-doubt. I know it is only a postcard, for goodness' sake, but I want it to have meaning. To make them believe in me.

'Stop bending that thing, you're like Rolf bloody Harris playing his feckin' wobble board.' Fi shoves her card into my hand. 'Anyhow, what do you reckon to mine?'

'Dear absent parentals,' I read aloud, 'having a mighty time in the land you left behind with the relatives you don't give a flying shite about over Sligo way of all places. Hope it's a mouldy old day wherever yous are. Your loving daughter, me arse! Fi.'

The address reads, *Mr & Mrs O'Reilly, Somewhere Over the Rainbow, Shite Parentville, The World (perhaps).*

'Well, Fi, that's, er, very expressive.'

'Grand,' she beams, passing it over the post office counter

to the old man behind the glass screen. 'It is very therapeutic, I find, to be able to slag off my folks within the worldwide postal service, so it is.'

I place a stamp on the card to my parents and search for some euro cents.

'Good. Although it could be rather unfortunate for the people who do actually live at that address when they get a postcard from a mad Irish woman they've never heard of.'

'Ya big eejit,' Fi snorts.

'And her wee eejit friend,' pipes up a voice in the queue behind us.

'Dave, hi, I didn't see you there,' I smile.

'Too busy sending hate mail, hey,' he grins before kissing Fi on both cheeks despite the fact that we are not in France. Double the value, I suppose. I get one kiss.

'So no love lost between you and your folks then, Fiona?' he carries on. 'What's the story there so?'

Fi wrinkles her nose and hops from one foot to the other.

'Ah sure, it's nothing, just a family joke. My ma and da are a bit . . . mad, you know.'

'I don't doubt it,' Dave replies with a mischievous wink, 'to have produced a crazy little thing like you.'

Fi blushes and I raise my eyes to the ceiling as Dave steps between us to place his parcel on the counter, all the while glueing his gaze to Fi's face. I'm surprised men manage to cope with walking down the street in a straight line when there are good-looking women in the vicinity. Their eyes clearly work on a hormonal loop system.

'Give us first class to Dublin, would ya there, Jimmy?' Dave chirps to the postmaster, who is so old he looks almost transparent.

'Sure you are, David,' the old man croaks in a voice so rasping I can visualise the clouds of cigarette smoke that have curled their way down his throat over the years. He winks. 'More of those video tapes, is it now?'

'Video tapes?' I giggle, straining to look over Dave's shoulder.

153

'What video tapes? Don't tell me you're a dodgy porn peddler on the side, Dave Brennan?'

It is Dave's turn to blush.

'Don't be daft, Milly. Well, unless you would classify videos of yous two learning to surf as dodgy porn.'

'What?'

I try to snatch the parcel back but the postmaster moves with surprising swiftness for someone as ancient as Yoda.

'And give us recorded post, Jimmy. One that I can track further than Ballyshannon, unlike the last time.'

'What last time?' I frown.

'The last time David here sent away his videos,' Jimmy replies with a laugh in his voice. 'We put the trace on them, but sure didn't they just get lost after they left Ballyshannon just five miles round the corner there? Vanished they did, without a trace. 'Twas funny really, wasn't it, Dave?'

'Oh yes, hilarious,' I butt in. 'How uproariously amusing that there are video recordings of me in a wetsuit making an utter prat of myself out there in God knows whose possession for them to do whatever they like with. Mmm, that is so funny I feel quite hysterical.'

Dave laughs in the face of my embarrassment.

'Ah now, don't be so sensitive, Milly, you're getting on great with the surfing and we only lost the one tape, didn't we, Jimmy?'

Jimmy nods and smiles at me to reveal a set of yellow teeth like a row of condemned houses. A shiver runs down my spine when I consider that the lost tape may actually be in his bedroom, providing some late-night stimulation for his crusty old . . . Eugh, I almost said 'bones'. I scowl at Dave and turn to leave. He pays for his parcel and follows Fi and me out of the post office.

'Right then, maisies, I'm off to feck around in the surf shop in the name of work. What are you up to?'

'Nothing much,' Fi shrugs. 'We might watch *Point Break* for the hundredth time like.'

'I've got some bikini rep comin' in later if ya fancy modellin' the merchandise, so,' Dave winks.

'Feck off, ya cheeky gobshite.'

Fi giggles and tilts her head in an act of innocent seduction. A lock of her shiny red hair sparkles against her black coat like a length of tinsel. Dave's automatic response is to drop his jaw and gaze at Fi with sheer devotion. I get the feeling I am somewhat in the way. I am in fact a giant gooseberry baked in a gooseberry crumble, inside a gooseberry-shaped box on the gooseberry float at the gooseberry fair. I sniff the sniff of an uncomfortable gooseberry.

'OK, so I better be gettin' a bog on,' Dave whistles after they have stopped adoring each other in silence. 'Ah, but I almost forgot. Mac is getting four tickets from his uncle for the Frankie Doolan gig on Saturday night at the Tyrconnell Hotel.'

'Frankie Doolan, Jaysus, I didn't know he was still alive,' Fi shrieks.

'Alive and well and still charmin' the pants off every woman in Donegal over the age of forty. So how about it? Will yous both come?'

'Who's Frankie Doolan?' I ask.

'Isn't he just an Irish treasure in tight popstar pants,' Fi laughs.

'Now isn't that the truth,' Dave replies. 'So hows about it, Milly?'

'Sure,' I say, shrugging one shoulder. 'That sounds like fun, I suppose. Somehow I never expected popstars to play gigs in this town.'

'Frankie Doolan is not just a popstar, he's a legend so.'

I doubt he is anywhere near the same league as Dan Clancy, but I suppose a night of shaking my bootie to the sounds of a hunk in tight trousers will help me release some of the European hormone mountain my body has been building up of late during my extended (and involuntary) period of celibacy.

'All right then, Dave, if the man is a pop legend, count me in.'

'Dead on, hey,' Dave winks, 'me and Fi, you and Mac, Saturday night with Handsome Frankie Doolan. It's a date.'

'Well I didn't exactly say that,' I begin, but Dave has already gone.

# CHAPTER SIXTEEN

# *Fishing for Compliments*

'You have got to be kidding me.'

I stare open-mouthed at the life-size poster of Handsome Frankie Doolan in the hotel foyer.

'Let me guess, the "handsome" part is ironic, right?'

'Holy God, Milly, how can you say that about the godfather of Irish music?' Dave gasps theatrically.

'The grandfather of the ugly one from Westlife, more like.'

I peer at the photo and visibly shiver. Frankie Doolan definitely has something of the Engelbert Humperdinck about him. Imagine if you will Engelbert squeezed into one of Barry Manilow's tightest white suits and then dipped in grease to seal the look. The man is greasier than a trucker's café bacon sandwich. So much for my big night out on the town. Where is Dan Clancy when my hormones need him?

'Right, who's on for a pint?' asks Mac. 'I'm dying with the thirst.'

He leads the way across the highly polished floor of the reception into the hotel's Nolan Suite.

'Colleen Nolan won her first talent contest here,' Dave informs Fiona and me with more than a little pride.

'Wow,' Fi coos, 'that's amazing. I love the Nolans.'

She is not joking.

The Nolan Suite is a huge room with a high ceiling and

too many faux-crystal chandeliers. It is heaving with people, who are either racing to find a seat or jostling their way to one of the bars that line the three walls not occupied by the stage. Looking around, I note that ninety-eight per cent of the crowd would easily qualify for a SAGA holiday. Most disturbing is the riotous group of five hundred women in Scholl sandals and 'I Love Frankie' satin scarves in the 'mosh pit' next to the stage. Their excitement is audible as they prepare to throw their substantial granny knickers at a homosexual crooner in painfully tight trousers.

'OK, a pint and a small one for everyone, is it?' Dave asks when we reach the bar.

'Make that two. Of each,' I reply. 'Believe me, there is no way I am going to get through this night sober.'

'Feck, I'm bloating up like a dead cow in a river from all the alcohol and jumping about,' Fi hoots, stopping mid-dance to clutch her stomach. 'I'm desperate for a piss.'

'I need a shit-down. A *sit*-down. I meant a SIT-down,' I shout over Frankie's soft-rock rendition of 'Carrickfergus'. 'I'm knackered.'

'You're bladdered,' Dave laughs.

'I'm not. Ow, fuck, sorry. Fuck, that hurts.' I hop around on one foot, clutching the toes of the other foot that has been stamped on at least fifty times in the last half-hour by a jigging granny from Cork.

' 'Scuse us, Dave.' Fi grabs me by the arm and drags me through the mass of gyrating arthritic limbs towards the toilets.

I wait until our fellow gig-goers leave the room before I comment.

'Eugh, I've never been to a concert where people take their dentures out in the toilets before.'

'Me neither,' Fi snorts. 'It's a gas, isn't it? Speaking of

which' – she lets out a large burp, which blows her feathered fringe up in the air – 'Jaysus, I'm going to explode.'

'I'm going to be very hungover tomorrow.' I scowl at the girl in the mirror, who looks like me only her make-up is runny and sweaty, her hair is in complete disarray and she appears to be rather unironed (skin and clothes alike).

'Sure, those baby Guinnesses are lethal like, Milly. Tia Maria and Baileys might look inviting in the same glass but it's not a pretty sight the next morning in the toilet bowl.'

'What a lovely thought, Fi, thanks, but I'm not planning to be sick. I am just having a good night out. After all, we deserve it. How many times have you stood up on a surf-board this week?'

'I don't know, maybe like twenty times.'

'And how many times have I stood up on a surfboard this week?'

'Ehm, maybe like forty times?'

'Fi, you don't have to be polite.'

'OK then, ten at the most, so.' She wrinkles her nose. 'It's still an achievement, though, isn't it?'

'Absolutely, Milly,' Fi replies while rearranging her tight little red T-shirt above the waistband of her hipster black jeans. 'Especially when you consider how shite you were when we got here.'

'Er, yeah.' I pause to frown at her in the mirror before I continue attempting to apply my lip-gloss inside my lip line, which is not an easy task with blurred vision and four visible lips.

'Aye, you've done great, Milly.' Fi hugs me and knocks the lip brush halfway up my left cheek. 'And sure, you've still got weeks left to perfect the whole surf-chick thing. By the time we get back to Dublin they'll be begging you to be in every film going.'

I grin and hug her back and we stay silent for a moment until Fi pulls away, screws up her face and burps again.

'That'll be weird, won't it?'

'What?'

I pull myself up on to the sink shelf to give my aching feet a rest.

'Going back.' Fi shrugs. 'I love Dublin, and I love our flat, but I dunno, I like it here too.'

'I know what you mean,' I nod with a hiccup. 'I'm growing surprisingly fond of this strange little town. I like the fact that when you walk down the street complete strangers say hello, and the way every shopkeeper likes to chat even if there is a queue forming.'

'I love the people,' Fi agrees, 'and I love the scenery.'

'You're right, it's beautiful. I think I've even begun to take the open fields and the gorgeous mountains for granted. As for the ocean, how are we going to sit and watch the sunset when we're in a flat in the city?'

Fi sighs and pulls herself up on to the counter on the other side of the sink.

'Exactly. It's just a whole new life. And I like it.'

We sit quietly, Fi swinging her feet and me clutching the edge of the sink as my head spins from over-indulgence and too much thinking.

'I like having a new life,' Fi says eventually, her tone definite and humourless, 'I wouldn't miss my old one.'

I reach across the basin and take her hand. It is cold, but then it always is. Being so petite and fragile, Fi has the body temperature of a cryogenically frozen person. How she can stay alive in the Atlantic Ocean is beyond me. But then a lot of the things Fi has managed to survive are beyond me.

'As long as I'm in your new life.' I smile faintly. 'Don't go locking me up in a box with all your old memories.'

'Don't be thick.' Fi smiles back, 'I'm not letting you go. Sure, bumping into you that first day on Grafton Street is one of the few great things I've done in the last five years.'

I laugh as I remember that moment. There I was, the market research girl with the clipboard whom everyone swerves to avoid, desperately trying to get one more person to give me their views on PVC windows so that I could skulk back to my dreary bedsit and cry myself to sleep. Again. There she was, a tiny redhead with the smoothest pale skin, and the biggest boots on the end of her skinny little legs, tramping wearily up the street with her head bowed as if an invisible cloud was weighing her down. I approached her, she stopped, she politely answered my questions and then she burst into tears when I asked her opinion on replacement PVC doors. Ten minutes later, we were discussing our lives over tea and cakes in Bewley's tea room. One week later, I moved into Fi's flat and our friendship grew and grew.

'Jaysus, I was a mess,' Fi carries on, her eyes screwed tightly closed as she visualises herself. 'I used to cry at every bloody thing in the most stupid places. Remember the time I lost it in a-Wear because I wanted that pink leather coat and there were no size eights left in Ireland? Feck, I felt as if my life was over. What an eejit.'

I squeeze her hand. 'But now you hardly ever cry over little things, AND you are totally sociable and relaxed, AND you're here doing whatever you want to do and not going out and buying hula dancing lamps for no reason.'

Fi sniggers and turns to face me.

'And I haven't watched *Top Gun* for two months or more. And I am only taking one Prozac a day instead of two. Sure, I'm almost normal.'

'You're better than normal, Fi. Normal is boring, and no one could ever accuse you of being that. Everyone here thinks you're fab. Just look at Dave.'

'Where?' She jumps down off the counter and slips in a patch of water on the floor in her haste.

'Look out. Wow, I've never seen you move so fast. Does your body react like that every time I say DAVE?'

'Feck off.' Fi's cheeks have turned as red as her T-shirt.

'He's cute,' I wink, 'and he likes you.'

'He's only human.' Fi winks back.

'You make a lovely couple,' I sing.

'You're a feckin' gobshite,' Fi sings back.

I slide off the counter and groan when I realise I have been sitting in a pool of water. I wobble over to the hand-dryer, activate it and stick my bum out to dry my trousers.

'You seem very relaxed with him, though, Fi,' I shout over the noise of the dryer.

'I am, I've told you, he's grand. I mean, we can talk about stuff, and he's not really like other fellas. He knows about, you know, the depression and all, but, like, I haven't told him about my brother and all that stuff.'

'Why not?'

'Ah sure, I don't want to scare the boy off with my freaky family tales.'

I wiggle my bum and smile. 'Hmm-mm, so that means there might be a glimmer of a relationship there if you don't want to scare him off.'

Fi pouts comically and makes a clicking noise with her tongue.

'Don't keep speculating about my love life, lady,' she smirks, 'not when we can speculate about yours.'

I rub the seat of my trousers and follow her to the door.

'What about mine? I haven't spoken to Dan for ages and his texts are getting less frequent. I think it might be the old out-of-sight-out-of-mind phenomenon.'

'Jaysus, I'm not talking about that fecker,' Fi tuts, stopping to scowl at me. 'I'm talking about Mac.'

'Mac? What about him?'

My cheeks begin to heat up despite my silent orders to my body not to react to Fi's goading.

'What about him?' she giggles. 'You're full of shite, you, Milly. I see how you crack on with each other. And you've hugged him after you've caught your waves before. And he's a ride in that wetsuit of his, so don't pretend you haven't noticed like.'

I try to open the toilet door but Fi rests her foot against it to block my exit.

'We're just friends,' I groan.

'Oh yeah?'

'Oh yeah. And you should just be glad that we're not scratching each other's eyes out any more.'

'I am. But I reckon it's one of them love/hate things, like.'

'Do you now?'

Fi grins and rapidly blinks her eyes. I wrestle with the door handle.

'I think he likes you,' she continues in a girly voice, 'I think he wants to kiss you.'

I wrench open the door and stride proudly out into the hubbub of the Nolan Suite.

'Stop winding me up, Fiona,' I snap as we walk. 'Mac and I are just friends.'

She spots him over at the bar and nudges me in the ribs.

'Good friends?' she giggles, shoving me in his direction.

'No. Now shall we get back to boogeying with the blue-rinse brigade?'

'I need a drink first,' Fi replies, pulling me towards the bar. 'Come on.'

'But you're not supposed to drink with those tablets.'

'So? I'm not supposed to wear red with my colour hair either but I haven't been arrested so far. Now, what are you having?'

'Whiskey and Coke,' I reply as we reach Mac and my disobedient cheeks erupt into a volcanic display of embarrassment.

'No problem,' Mac replies, reaching for his wallet. 'Anything the lady desires.'

He turns to catch the barman's attention just in time to miss Fi's obvious wink in my direction. Damn my best friend, she certainly knows how to change the subject away from herself in spectacular fashion. Honestly, the idea of Mac and me being anything more than friendly with each other is ludicrous. The friendly part was hard

163

enough. The beyond friendly thing is just not going to happen. Ever. How can Fi get it so wrong? Mac didn't even like me to begin with, so he would never fancy me. Would he? And I could never fancy him in a million years. Could I?

# CHAPTER SEVENTEEN

# *Fresh*

Now, you know when you are out for a night and you begin to feel drunk and on the cusp of being out of control, so you recognise the danger and sensibly switch to mineral water? Well, I proceed to do all of the above . . . except for the sensible mineral water part. Instead of the water, as a matter of fact, I find myself necking whiskey and Cokes like a woman possessed. The extent of my predicament is clear when I attempt to crowd-surf to Frankie Doolan's rendition of 'If You Think I'm Sexy' and end up in a heap at Mac's feet thanks to the weak limbs of Jimmy the postmaster.

'Oops-a-daisy,' I mumble as I allow Mac to haul me on to the nearest bar stool.

A series of embarrassed nods of his head then informs me that my left boob has broken free from my Miss Selfridge bra and climbed out of the neckline of my top.

'Ooh, boob,' I giggle, shoving it back in.

'Very rock and roll, hey,' Mac comments nervously.

I have lost my composure and all sense of moderation. Granted, most people like to go a bit wild now and again and I haven't been drunk at all since we arrived, which is over two months ago now. The thing is, I could definitely do without being drunk right here, right now, in the middle of this mind-boggling OAP gig, in front of a very attractive-looking Mac, just after my friend has planted the seed in my head that Mac . . . well, that Mac may very well like to plant a seed in me. The very thought of it made me nervous, which led to the whole business of downing drinks to relax myself in the first place. Now I am in a pickle. In fact, now I am pickled.

'Are you OK there, Milly?' Mac asks.

He gently cups my elbow and bends closer to speak into my ear.

'Do you want me to take you home?'

*See? He does want me. Oh God, what should I do?*

'I could call us a taxi if you're ready.'

*Ready? Ready for what? Fi was right; her cousin wants to shag me. Damn, what pants have I got on?*

'Do you need anything, Milly?'

*Condoms, he means condoms.*

I attempt to cross my legs and almost fall off the stool in the process. Mac reaches out to catch me and succeeds in grabbing a handful of the aforementioned breast.

'Feck, shite, I'm sorry.'

'Don't worry about it,' I wink.

*I know it was no accident, you naughty boy you.*

I peer up at Mac and drag my dry lips back over my teeth to smile. Mac smiles back, his green eyes twinkling in the bright lights. A gasp escapes from my lungs, which could well be the gaseous product of too much alcohol but which could also be the fact that in this light and on this particular night there is something about Mac Heggarty. Somewhere between my waist and the cushion of the bar stool, a party popper explodes, sending streamers of blood racing around my veins. I giggle like an Essex girl on alcopops.

*Why shouldn't I take him up on his offer? After all, I haven't had any action for God knows how long; I don't want to get out of practice. And it would only be a bit of fun, wouldn't it?*

I lick my lips suggestively.

'Thirsty? Right, you want a drink . . . ehm, hold on a sec,' Mac stutters.

He is visibly nervous. He fiddles in his pockets for money and then spills his change all over the floor. When he bends down to pick it up, his head bumps against my knee and he stumbles.

*Blimey, I am driving the man wild. Be kind to him, Milly, let him have his fun. What harm could it do?*

'A glass of water,' says Mac to the waiter when he clambers to his feet.

'With whiskey in it,' I add with a wink.

'No, no whiskey,' Mac says hurriedly.

'Yes, yes whiskey,' I reply with a nod.

The barman looks from me to Mac and back again.

'In fact, hold the water,' I say decisively.

*Lord knows I need something to calm the fireworks in my groin.*

'Milly, are you sure now? You're looking pretty scuttered as it is.'

'Nonsense,' I grunt at Mac, almost sucking my tongue up the back of my nostril. 'I'm practically sober.'

I look both Macs straight in the eye.

*He wants to get me out of here as quickly as possible. He can't wait.*

I smile knowingly and attempt a seductive flick of my hair, but a split end catches me in the eye with a sharp whack.

'Ouch, shit,' I yelp.

'Oh dear, here, I'll look for Fi. Maybe she'll know what to do.' Mac coughs, looking around just as the barman places a tumbler of neat whiskey next to a hand that I presume to be my own despite its numbness.

'What do we need Fi for?' I ask, rubbing my eye with one hand and reaching for the glass with the other (which is no mean feat in my state, believe me).

*Oh God, the surf instructor's getting all kinky on me. He wants his cousin to join in.*

I take a deep breath and gulp back the whiskey to steady my nerves. The contents land in my stomach before my throat even has a chance to acknowledge their passage. The acidic after-shock of the substance races vertically through my body to my brain, as if a strong man has hit my feet with a hammer to ding the bell at the top of the sliding scale.

'Jaysus Christ,' I hear Mac shriek shortly before I hit the floor, 'she's after poisoning herself.'

What happens next is something of a blur. I feel myself being lifted off the floor by a pair of strong, familiar arms to the sound of cheers from Frankie's audience. I am then aware of being directed through the heavily lavender-scented crowd towards the neon exit sign.

'Ooh, what beautiful stars,' I swoon when I am finally outside. 'They're very bright, aren't they, Mac?'

'That's because they're feckin' car headlights. Now shift your arse before the both of us get killed.'

'Killed,' I repeat merrily, tripping over my eight pairs of feet until I come to rest against the cold wall of the hotel.

I breathe in the sea air gusting over the cliff on which we are standing. Instantly the nausea creeps up to just below my tonsils and the ground spins like the circular cars on a waltzer. I count to ten, kick off my shoes and sink my feet into the damp grass beneath them.

'It's OK, you don't have to hold me up, I'm fine.'

I shoo Mac's hand away and instantly topple over. Mac grabs me swiftly as I fail to locate which way is upright. He pulls me towards him. I grab his T-shirt and begin to climb up his body. He feels firm.

*Hmm, not bad. Not bad at all. At least my admirer has got the fittest body in town. Even if it is just a small town.*

I keep climbing. If only I had thought to bring crampons. I eventually come to rest with my chin on Mac's chest and my hands clinging to his elbows.

'Bloody hell, your boobs are bigger than mine.' I flit my eyes from one pectoral muscle to the other. 'And these biceps are chunky ones, aren't they? Must be all that paddling, mustn't it?'

I don't know if he nods but I carry on regardless.

'I said to Fi, I said, having a good body is part of the job description for a surfer. Especially one like you because you're really good, you are.'

I raise a hand to emphasise my point and slip towards his groin. Mac yanks me up again until I can see his face. I notice how the moon highlights the ends of his curls, making him look almost angelic.

'You must be really good,' I continue to slur "cos you, yes *you*, got me on a surfboard and you've helped me stand up on it. More than once too. And Dave has been there to film it all so no one can deny that I've done it. And now I am going to surf in a movie and so that film might be worth something some day and it is all down to you.'

I am overcome with an emotion that I do not recognise. I pull myself higher up Mac's body until I can feel his breath on my face. I gasp, sucking in more sea air and at the same time inhaling the smell of him. It is not a perfectly perfumed aroma. Not the aftershave that I always associate with Dan when I am passing through the toiletry department of Brown Thomas. No, this is a manly, natural scent with just a hint of salty seawater. I gulp it down and find myself drawn to its source. Mac and I are now so close we are almost balanced on the same blade of grass. I suddenly realise how good it feels to be in the arms of a man, and in the time it takes for another hormone to pop to the surface of my skin, I throw all my inhibitions to the wind.

*Why wait until we get home? Let him have it here, Milly.*

My tongue searches the desert that is my mouth for an oasis of saliva, and I raise my hand to brush it against his face. Mac jerks his head away but my hand pursues its target until I am stroking his cheek.

'Milly, I don't think . . .' he begins, his eyes wide in the moonlight.

I place a finger on his lips.

'Ssh, don't worry, I know. Fi told me.'

'Told you what?

'Ssh, Mac, you can take me home, but let me just give you a little taster. A little starter before the main course,' I say breathlessly.

I clasp my hands around his neck and yank myself sharply towards him. My own lips find moisture from within and slowly open in anticipation. I close my eyes and my breathing turns rapid.

'Mmm, yes,' I groan, 'I know this is what you want.'

I pucker my lips and prepare myself for the slow, lingering kiss.

'Right then, you feckers, who's fer a bag of chips from Abrakebabra?'

Dave's voice rings in my ears as the hotel door hits me in the arm. I open my eyes to see a sweaty Dave and Fi hopping up and down excitedly.

'I'm so hungry I could eat a scabby dog's arse!' Dave whoops.

Mac leaps away from me as if I am on fire, pushing me so sharply that I tumble backwards and sprawl on the wet grass like an upturned beetle. While I struggle to right myself and locate my shoes, the three of them march merrily off down the hotel driveway without me.

'Hold on,' I whimper, 'we were about to . . . We were going to . . . Mac? MAC! DOES THAT MEAN THE SHAG IS OFF THEN?'

# CHAPTER EIGHTEEN

## *Holy Water*

I gaze down into the chipped bowl of soggy Weetabix that is playing havoc with my hangover and I sigh. I then continue to sigh until my lungs have run out of sighs.

'I will never drink again,' I say to the carton of milk.

*Rubbish*, the orange juice replies mockingly, *you will and you know it.*

'OK smart-arse, I mean I will never drink and throw myself at a man again.'

*Holy God, did you really do that?* chorus the cornflakes

'Holy God, did I really do that?' I repeat.

I lower my head to the table and slam my forehead against the wood.

'Bloody hell, that's a first. I slept all night. I must have been wild knackered. Who are you talking to?' asks Fi.

She is so light I never hear her footsteps. She would make a great spy.

I sniff. 'Oh, just the breakfast things. I was after a bit of advice on how to deal with making a complete tit of myself by drinking more than George Best and then trying to shove my tongue down your cousin's throat.'

'And shag him.'

Fi's head disappears into the fridge.

'What?'

'Shag him,' she repeats as she sniffs an open pack of bacon. 'You shouted, IS THE SHAG OFF THEN? Or something very similar. Jaysus, it was hilarious.'

'Oh God.'

I slam my forehead a couple more times.

'Even in the dark I could see Mac going as red as a prostitute's knickers. He was mortified.'

'Well thank you, Fi, that makes me feel a whole lot better.'

'Grand, now do you want a fry-up?'

I wave my hand to reject the offer while keeping my head on the table and my eyes squeezed firmly shut. So it wasn't one of those dreams. The sort where you can feel, smell and taste it so vividly that you are sure it is real even after you wake up. I used to have a recurring dream that my father had bought me a white horse and put it in the back garden. I would wake up so convinced it was true that I would race downstairs in my pyjamas and bare feet to find my prize. Cute though my fat albino guinea pig was, I couldn't fail to be disappointed. Unfortunately, the image of Mac Heggarty staring at me with eyes as wide as those of my guinea pig shortly before the neighbour's cat chomped it is all too real.

His face was the first thing I saw this morning. And not, I might add, lying next to mine on the pillow. It was the face of fear as I grabbed the poor man and forced my drunken self upon him. How could I? I shake my head and wait for my shame to pass. I'm in no rush; I can wait here all day. Actually, I think I might well wait here all day because the prospect of showing my face in public is not a pleasant one. Oh why can't I just have full memory loss and go about my business in blissful ignorance?

Fi plonks a plate down on the table beside my head. I lift my chin and retch as I inhale the greasy aroma.

'I have to admit to feeling a bit off colour too, like,' she says as she folds a slice of buttered bread around a sausage and shoves half of it in her mouth. 'We were all knocking them back all right. Shite, I even remember having a couple of gin and tonics.'

'But you hate gin.'

'I know that. Sure, it's like bloody liquid suicide, that stuff.'

She wipes her mouth with the back of her hand and sniffs.

'But I was just doing my bit for medical science, you know. Testing whether a depressed person drinking a depressive drink is actually like two negatives making a positive. You know, like, whether it would make me perky. Gin, the depressive's drink of choice.'

'And did it?' I yawn.

Fi chews on a rind of bacon.

'Feck, I can't remember, I was wasted.'

She laughs and tucks in to the rest of her fry-up. Despite the telltale signs of the morning after the night before – Fi's dishevelled hair, the dark shadows around her eyes, the ghostly white of her skin and the enormous (even more than usual) appetite – I notice something different in her face. I can't put my finger on it exactly but there is a subtle sparkle about her. An inner sparkle. Fi is glowing with positivity from the inside out. Forgetting my own predicament for a moment, I smile and nudge her leg under the table.

'You and Dave looked like you were having fun last night.'

'Aye, we were, he's such a gas. Did you see the way he was flinging me round that dance floor? I felt like one of them couples on *Come Dancing*.'

'I didn't really notice,' I reply quietly.

*From my comatose position on the floor at Mac's feet.*

'So did you . . .?' I wink.

'Did I what?' Fi replies, spitting morsels of sausage sandwich across the tablecloth.

'You know. Did you . . .?'

'What are you doing that with your tongue for, ya big eejit? No, I did not give him a blowjob.'

173

'I meant a kiss, Fi! Did you kiss him?'

'Oh right. Of course I didn't, I'm shite at all that stuff.'

'You're just scared of getting too attached to men.'

'Well you're not,' she laughs, standing up to put the dirty plate in the sink. 'You had yourself well and truly attached to my cousin when Dave and I caught yous. Jaysus, I'm surprised the poor man could breathe, you were holding his neck that tight.'

I scowl at Fi, sharply push my chair back and stomp across to the sofa.

'It's all your fault, Fi. You were the one who went and put stupid ideas in my head when you knew fine well I was drunk and a bit—'

'Gagging?'

'No.'

'Horny like a dog on heat?'

'NO!'

Fi rests her bum on the single remaining arm of the sofa and tucks her knees up to her chest. She smiles at me until my hissy fit has subsided and I can look her in the eye.

'Don't worry about it, Milly. Sure, every person in this town will have made an eejit of themselves at some point or another. It's what the Irish do well, especially when we're on the drink.'

'But he's your cousin,' I groan, 'and he's my surf instructor, so I have to see him every day, and bloody hell I am so humiliated.'

'We were all just having a laugh. God knows, those Frankie Doolan nights can be a bit freaky with all the old ladies and their ancient hormones flinging about. It's no wonder you got yourself a bit drunk like. And I am sorry' – she places a hand on her heart like a Brownie swearing her oath – 'that I wound you up about Mac. I was just messing with you. I didn't know you'd go off and do that.'

'Oh God.'

'Not that he'll mind or anything. Sure, the man should be flattered.'

'Oh God.' I cover my face with my hands.

'You know what, that isn't a bad idea at all,' Fi says suddenly. She springs up from the sofa and claps her hands.

'What? What isn't a bad idea?' I groan fearfully.

'God,' Fi chirps.

'What about him?'

Fi searches under the armchair for her pink runners and sticks out her tongue as she yanks them on without untying the laces.

'We need cleansing, Milly.'

'Too right I do. A stomach pump and a lobotomy would do for starters.'

'Cleansing from the inside out, Milly, that's what we need today,' Fi says definitely. 'So that we can start this day with a new outlook on life.'

'What?' I sniff. 'What are you talking about?'

'We, my friend, are going to Mass,' she announces proudly, as if suggesting we spend the day eating ice-cream at the seaside.

'Mass? As in holy place Mass? But you never go to church. You're no more Catholic than I am Buddhist.'

'Well today I am.'

'But I haven't been to a church since Princess Diana died, and that was only because everyone else in Southampton appeared to be queuing up to go so I didn't want to miss out. I thought they must be giving away royal freebies.'

I duck as Fi throws my shoe, which narrowly misses my head.

'Milly Armstrong, I'm shocked. Now get to church before lightning strikes you.'

'I wish it would. That would be much more pleasurable than showing my face in public. What if people recognise me from last night? Shit, what if Mac's there? Fi,' I shout as she disappears out of the door, 'do you think if I pray hard enough, God could do me a quick miracle face and body transplant?'

The church is a bold grey structure that looms out of a car park so expansive I would, on another occasion, have thought that the architect overestimated the likely attendance figures. Today, however, every available space is filled with cars of all shapes and price ranges, as are the kerbsides of the main road that leads up to the iron gates and the grass verges.

'What's the big occasion?' I whisper to Fi as we shuffle through the doors behind tribes of people dressed in a super-abundance of sombre tones.

'It's Sunday,' she hisses back, before nudging me into one of the wooden pews.

I soon realise why most of the people in this place are so stony-faced. The prospect of sitting on this bench for an hour is already sending shock waves through my bum cheeks. Haven't they ever heard of cushions, for goodness' sake? Jesus lived in the land of eastern markets, didn't he? I bet he had rugs and cushions aplenty. My backside is far from bony but the unforgiving oak has already managed to make contact with my skeleton through the generous layers of flesh. Mind you, it certainly helps to take my mind off last night's events.

'Quit shifting about,' Fi mutters, her elbow digging into my ribs.

I pout in response and try to forget the penance my rear end is being forced to endure by concentrating on the people around me. I do love a good people-watching session. Especially one as intense as this.

I estimate that seventy per cent of the congregation were born back when nuns were in fashion. The other thirty per cent are either young children who have been buttoned and combed into their Sunday best, or young adults of around my age. I have to admit to being surprised by this, and even more so by the fact that they appear to be here willingly. In the next breath I am ashamed of my own narrow-mindedness. Of course, just because going to church isn't 'cool' these days, that is no reason to assume that people don't enjoy seeking solace in their Sunday ritual. I guess being a non-believer is easy in the noughties, given that it is no longer frowned upon to spend Sunday mornings drinking endless cups of coffee and eating chocolate muffins while watching children's television, rather than exercising one's religious beliefs. I just always seem to have something . . . I shan't say 'better', rather something other to do than spend my Sunday mornings in church. On reflection, though, I bet these people around me will be the ones laughing when we finally get to Judgement Day. The thought enters my mind that if Channel 4 invented an interactive reality TV show based on going to Mass, we would all want a part of it. Just think, the Church would be trendy again and reality TV might just be responsible for saving our souls.

I turn my attention to the goings-on at the altar. Most of my view is blocked by the feathered monstrosity of a hat that the woman in front of me obviously bought for a wedding and is trying to get as much use out of as she can. I tilt my head but can only see a nervous little altar boy who is fiddling incessantly with the rope belt of his oversized cassock while waiting for his next call to action. I follow Fi as much as I can with the standing-up-sitting-down-kneeling-on-a-hard-surface routine and try to sing along to the hymns despite recognising neither the tunes nor the words. I am aware that the majority of the people in our row appear to be finding me more fascinating than the Mass itself but I press on. I excitedly join in the 'Our Father' at top volume with the sheer delight of having recognised a prayer. I attempt the 'Hail Mary' and manage to remember most of the lines, just not in the right order. Smiling apologetically at the woman beside me, who has a face like an agitated crow, I suddenly dissolve into a fit of sneezing, probably brought on by Mrs

Big Hat's ridiculous plumage. This is closely followed by a coughing fit for no apparent reason other than my body apparently wanting to do its utmost to embarrass me in a confined space. This occurs during what I presume to be the climax of the service, judging by the looks I am being given by the good folk all around me. I can almost hear the crow woman praying to God for a very short but very fatal illness to strike me down some time in the next five minutes.

My role as Lucifer's fallen angel is finally confirmed when, having brought my coughing under control, I am sharply brought to attention by the noise emanating from somewhere about my person. The ringtone of my mobile, which has been sitting unnoticed in the pocket of my denim jacket, reverberates off the stained-glass windows like a giant gong. I grapple for the phone amid the tuts, gasps and 'Good Lord above's that join the chorus. I drop the phone and it clatters to the floor, still wailing at the top of its little phone voice. I fall to my hands and knees to retrieve it from underneath the pew in front, banging my head on the way back up, much to Fiona's amusement. I then stumble out of the row, tripping over worshippers and their dropped jaws as I go, until I can make a dash for the door and the noisy safety of the outside world.

'Shit, damn, fuck!' I curse, pressing every button in my anxious state.

'Well, that is a delightful way to answer the phone to your mother,' says the voice at the other end when I finally raise the mobile to my ear. 'Did you hear that, Frank?'

'I'm afraid I did, Georgina. It sounds like Amelia might need rescuing after all.'

'I think you could be quite right, Frank. It's a good job we were planning that holiday. Honestly, I've never heard anything like it. Have you?'

They carry on while I silently scream, *Hello, hello, Earth calling parents*. How two unquestionably intelligent adults can fail to understand the concept of having a telephone

178

conversation with the person they have chosen to call I will never know.

'Hello? Mum? Er, can I help you? Hellooo.'

I crouch on a smooth rock to the side of the church entrance and wait for my parents to remember I am here. This takes the best part of five minutes.

'Amelia, darling, good news this end,' my mother announces suddenly and with no reference to the delay.

*Tania's been run over by a bus?* I think to myself. *A very big bus driven by Ed?*

' 'Tis grand news altogether oo-ar oo-ar,' says my father, the plastic Paddy who has never been to Ireland in his life.

'I think that last bit was Somerset, Dad. Not bad though.'

*No, not bad. Absolutely bloody chronic.*

'So?' I prompt impatiently when no news is forthcoming.

My family always play this game; interspersing their tit-bits of information with meaningful pauses in the hope that I will be so overwhelmed with anticipation I will simply have to guess the punchline.

'Go on, guess,' says Mum.

You see what I mean?

I let out a sigh. 'Oh, I don't know. Ed's lost his job and Tania's left him for an impoverished tramp?'

'No. Why would that be good news, Amelia? Why would that be good news, Frank?'

Dad ignores the question.

'We're coming to find gold at the end of the rainbow,' he chirps.

'Pardon?'

'Where the leprechauns live, pudding. We're coming to visit the little folk, so we are bejaysus.'

Despite my father's unintelligible use of the vernacular and his overly active imagination, I get a sinking feeling in my stomach as my mind makes sense of what he is trying to say.

'You're what?' I croak.

Funny, I never knew my tongue could break into a cold sweat. Until now.

*Please don't mean . . .*

'We're coming to visit,' Mum announces, 'on a holiday.'

*Oh God, they do mean . . .*

'Your father has to take a holiday for his blood pressure, Amelia.'

'Oh, I see. How are you feeling, Dad? Have you built the gym yet? Are you OK?'

'I'm fine, I'm fine, Amelia, don't make a fuss.'

'But, Dad . . .'

'I knew you would be concerned, darling,' Mum butts in, 'which is why I came up with a perfectly perfect idea.'

'You did?'

'Yes. Your father doesn't want to travel too far, so we were trying to think of destinations when lo and behold we received your lovely postcard.'

'Oh, you did.'

'It looks absolutely fabulous where you are, dear, so we can't think of anywhere better than the land our daughter has decided to call home. How can we do better than a week in Ireland?'

*A week?*

'But . . .' I stutter, 'but I'm a long, long, *long* way away on the west coast. You wouldn't want to come that far, would you?'

'Of course we would,' my father replies.

*Of course you would.*

Now, don't get me wrong, I do miss my family, but Mum and Dad Armstrong coming to stay with me for a week sounds about as relaxing as being cross-examined in a witness box live on television. Some families are just not made to go on holiday together.

'That's all sorted then,' my mother concludes brightly.

*Is it?*

'We will put ourselves up in the nearest hotel, so don't go

worrying about us. Besides, then we can see what sort of research this acting lark of yours entails, can't we?' my father adds.

'Great,' I whine, 'I can't wait.'

'Donegal,' my father whistles, 'sounds "perfick". Now, where is that exactly, Amelia? And do they allow cars, or is it donkeys only?'

# CHAPTER NINETEEN

## *Hawaii Five-0*

'You're sitting on Father O'Hare,' Fi sniggers when she eventually emerges from saving her soul.

Realising my smooth rock is in fact a gravestone, I leap to my feet and hurry to the car park exit. I hear a chorus of disbelieving tuts in my wake. So much for being a good citizen and finding peace with God. I have never been so stressed in my life.

I don't reduce my pace until I reach the corner shop at the bottom of Main Street. Clattering through the door, I positively launch myself at the extensive pick 'n' mix sweet selection.

'Sugar's good for a shock, isn't it, Fi?' I mumble in between shovelling enough sweets into the bag to turn the whole town diabetic.

Fi screws up her face.

'Aye, I think so, but if you eat that lot there all your teeth will fall out and you'll probably explode, which will be quite a shock in itself, like.'

'Good.' I ladle several kilos of jelly bears into the bag. 'Then my parents won't recognise me when they come to stay. This could be my only hope of escape.'

I pay for the sweets. By *credit card*. Perhaps I overindulged; ten euros does seem quite steep for sweets.

'My parents are coming to stay,' I mutter to the assistant by way of explanation before leaving the shop and heading around the corner towards the headland.

Fi and I munch on sugar-coated strawberry laces while we walk. The May sun is shining and it would be warm in the shelter but a crisp coastal wind blows down our necks from the east. I pull my jacket collar up and duck my head.

'Ah now, it's gorgeous weather we're having today,' says Fi breezily.

'It's not exactly tropical,' I growl.

'Sure the sun won't burn us alive, but it's marvellous altogether and anyhow the wind is great for blowing away those cobwebs. I feel better already.'

'Never mind cobwebs, Fi, this wind could blow away polar bears . . .'

I squeal as I crash headfirst into a large rubbery obstacle on the pavement. My eyes move up its length, noting the sleek thighs, the trim waist, the six-pack visible through the neoprene and the surfboard tucked under the muscular arm. I cough as my strawberry lace disappears whole down the back of my throat. Apart, that is, from the tail end of it, that I soon realise is dangling from the side of my mouth.

'Mac, hi. I . . .'

My voice trails off for a second time when I lift my chin and my eyes meet his. His rabbit-caught-in-the-headlights look has now been replaced by narrowed eyes that dart swiftly away from contact with my own. I shove a handful of pink marshmallows in my mouth and shuffle behind Fi for protection from the man who probably wants to throw up at the sight of me. I feel so embarrassed and awkward. Like a thirteen-year-old the day after the school disco at which she was publicly knocked back by the cute guy. Not that I'm saying Mac is cute, you understand. I just mean . . . what do I mean? Well, whatever it is, I could die on the spot.

I know I could clear this all up in a second by being adult about the whole affair. I could apologise for my drunken behaviour, laugh about having been so forward and use my wit and charm to win back Mac's friendship. After all, I was adult enough last night to attempt to shove my tongue down his throat, so what's changed?

*Several pints of Guinness and half a bottle of whiskey, that's what.*

I squeeze my eyes shut and try to think of something appropriate to say that will clear the air between us. How should I put it?

*Sorry for throwing myself at you, please don't think I'm a desperate tart?*

Or, *I hope you didn't take me seriously last night, I was only pretending to come on to you?*

Or perhaps, *I don't remember a thing about last night. I hope I did nothing embarrassing. Please wipe all images from your mind and never mention it again?*

'So did you have fun last night with our Milly here?' says Fi before I can speak.

I choke, sending a globule of pink goo flying through the air. It lands on the shoulder of Mac's wetsuit and I stare in dismay as it slips slowly down his body. Mac lowers his head and silently watches the semi-ingested marshmallow until it eventually plops on to the pavement between us.

Now I really want to die. The man thinks I'm a lunatic. And right now I agree with him.

'Er, OK then.' Mac coughs, carefully avoiding my eye. 'I'd better be getting in the surf before the wind changes.'

'You're not going in there, are you?' Fi squawks. 'Those waves are feckin' massive.'

Mac taps the edge of the narrow, pointed surfboard that is resting under his right arm.

'Ah, but I've got the board for it, you see, Fi. The big wave gun.'

*Perfect. It wouldn't be loaded, would it? Put me out of my misery right now.*

'Well, have a good one,' Fi smiles, giving him a friendly

peck on the cheek, 'and you be careful now. But be sure to make it exciting 'cos we'll be watching.'

Mac smiles in the lopsided way that makes me think of Dan and causes my stomach to clench. He returns the peck with a tight hug before stepping towards me. I instantly panic, not knowing whether to peck, hug, or simply throw myself off the cliff. Instead, I shoot my arm out in the offer of a handshake. Mac accepts it with a bemused frown.

'Bye now,' he says, looking anywhere but into my eyes.

'Blubbub,' I reply, my mouth still full of marshmallow.

Mac gives me a wide berth as he heads for the cliff path, ignoring the *Danger! Cliff Edge* sign. Watching him walk away, I get a sinking feeling inside. Until last night, Mac and I had become friends. I was enjoying his company and I would go so far as to say that he was enjoying mine. I had broken the ice between us by taking part in the cross-border scheme and by taking the plunge into the ocean. I was at last getting to know the man who seems to let few people into his heart. Now, that ice has refrozen and metamorphosed into an impervious iceberg the size of the Great Wall of China.

Damn, why did I have to go getting so drunk? Why did I let Fi talk me into believing her cousin had a romantic interest in me? Why did I try to kiss him when the only person I have any desire to exchange bodily fluids of any kind with is back in Dublin being an irresistible movie star?

I kick myself, literally, and follow Fi to the carved stone bench on the headland overlooking the sea. As we sit in silence, a niggling thought taps away on my skull. What would it have been like to kiss those lips? Bloody hell, that tight neoprene suit has a lot to answer for.

Fi and I watch as Mac descends the cliff path and then picks his way over the flat black rocks towards the breaking waves. In my humiliated state, I feign disinterest. However, when he reaches the edge of the reef and pauses to attach the leash to his ankle, I realise the scale of the waves in relation to the man and I find myself drawn to the edge of the seat. If the waves I have been messing with were white horses, then these are like giant angry white buffalo stampeding full-pelt towards the land. They crash against the reef below, sending noticeable tremors up the cliff. They cascade over the town's sea defences that are visible to our left with such tremendous force that I swear I can see the Emerald Isle eroding before my very eyes.

'Lord help him if he plans to paddle out there,' says Fi, sucking in air between her teeth. 'He must be quare in the head.'

I chew silently on a giant cola bottle while I watch Mac stretch his body from side to side, lift his surfboard and finally plummet into the raging waters. Thank the Little Mermaid it's not me out there this time.

The next hour passes amazingly quickly as we become engrossed in watching the steadily building swell before us. It is the first time I have witnessed such a powerful swell at such close proximity and I am both impressed and shocked at how Mother Nature can turn something so beautiful into this ferocious, terrifying beast.

'It's like Hawaii,' Fi comments when another set of four or five mammoth waves thunders through.

'Only colder,' I shiver, wrapping my jacket tighter around my body to reduce the wind chill factor.

We do our best not to lose sight of Mac in the water, but this is no easy task. He frequently disappears from view with the rise and fall of the ocean. When he paddles out and dives his board beneath the waves, he resembles a duck looking for food below the surface. Now and again we animatedly point out a black object bobbing on the surface only to discover upon closer inspection that it is in fact driftwood or, on occasion, a seal. However, it is when Mac eventually reaches the right spot to turn towards the shore and catch the wave that his presence is unmistakable.

'There he goes,' I shout, squinting my eyes against the sea spray. 'Look over there, Fi, he's paddling for this one. Oh my God, that is definitely the biggest wave so far.'

'That's not a wave, it's a feckin' swimming pool standing vertical,' Fi gasps.

We ogle at the green wall of water rising up behind Mac as if the ocean has hit the shelf of land and has nowhere to send its gallons of fast-flowing water to but skywards. I am suddenly reminded of the man in the Guinness advert waiting, tick, tock, for his perfect monstrous wave. Mac doesn't wait. With a quick glance behind him, he digs his arms deep into the water and paddles. His speed increases to match the wave. Our mouths are open and silent, revealing semi-chewed globules of jelly sweets on our tongues. The sun that is trying its best to cut a hole through the persistent clouds above us glints off the black arms of Mac's wetsuit. He races the wave, thrusting the surfboard ahead by paddle power alone. Now he is at the top of the watery wall, looking like a tiny barrel about to be propelled over the edge of Niagara Falls. I clamp my teeth together and cannot help but marvel at a human being willingly taking on such a life-threatening rival. The wave surges higher still as it begins to break. At Mac's right shoulder, the peak crumbles into white-water and the wave starts to curl. He is pushed over the edge and we gasp aloud when it seems as if he will plunge headfirst down the countless feet to the surface of the ocean below. Suddenly he springs to his feet in one fluid movement and freefalls down the face of the wave as if his feet are glued to the deck of the surfboard. He continues to charge downwards, on and on, until he is almost at the bottom of the wave, when he turns the board effortlessly and begins to race along it at such a pace that I am sure he must have an engine on board.

'Jaysus, would you look at that!' Fi shrieks.

She points a shaking hand towards the wave that is curling spectacularly behind Mac to form a tube large enough to drive the Eurostar through. My eyes open wide, anticipating the moment when Mac will be swallowed up by the thundering gallons of water.

'Quick, quick!' I urge him. 'Get out of there.'

Mac, it seems, has other ideas. He places one hand in the wave and begins to reduce his speed along the face.

'Shit, he's stalled!' I cry out, still thinking of the imaginary engine.

'Ya big eejit,' Fi snorts, not taking her eyes off the spectacle for a second.

My eyes grow wider still as the entrance to the tube approaches at mind-boggling speed. One moment Mac and his board are in view and the next they are both gone, sucked into the watery vortex. We wait to catch a glimpse of him in the whitewater behind. I scan the ocean for any sign of a man overboard but don't know where to look. Without warning, a jet of water shoots out of the tube and with it comes Mac, still standing on the board with his arms in the air, celebrating his victory. The ride must only have lasted a matter of seconds but it was long enough for us to recognise the magnificence of the feat. Behind us a cheer erupts from a group of surfers I hadn't even realised were there.

'Bloody hell, did ya see that barrel?' Dave shouts. He races up to us with the video camera as ever attached to his hand. 'That was a feckin' mighty beast, that. I'd say that was almost twenty feet.'

Fi claps her hands with excitement. I let out the breath I realise I have been holding all along when I start to feel slightly dizzy.

'Amazing,' I agree, joining my hand against Dave's in a high-five.

'Bloody fantastic,' Fi shouts.

'So I guess that's how it's done then?'

Dave sits down beside me on the end of the bench and nods enthusiastically.

'Oh aye, that's how it's done, Milly, but you won't catch

many people around here surfin' like that so. Our Mac is one of the best. European champ he was just a few years ago.'

I stare at him in amazement. Mac Heggarty? European champion? I thought he'd never been further afield than the railway station to collect us off the train. I blush at my presumptions. Dave catches my puzzled expression and carries on.

'Yeah, Mac here is super-talented when it comes to surfin', so you're being taught by one of the best, so you are. He could have turned professional, hey. Got approached by loads of sponsors who were bloody desperate to fix him up and get him on the world circuit. He would have been wild famous, all over the TV and the like, but' – Dave shrugs and takes a breath – 'he didn't want any of it. Not at all.'

What? Am I hearing him right? Mac could have been a famous professional surfer, travelling the world in search of perfect waves and being paid to do so while appearing on TV and in movies and everything else that comes with a glamorous sport like surfing, and he chose to stay here? In County Donegal? With his mammy? To teach surfing to little kids? Gordon Bennett, the man needs his head read.

'Are you serious?'

'Ah yeah, 'course he is,' Fi pipes up. 'Did I not mention it before?'

I turn my stare on her.

'No, Fi, you didn't.'

Not that this surprises me in the slightest. Fi could have received a personal message from God warning her that the world was going to end at midnight and she wouldn't remember to tell me until eleven fifty-nine. And thirty seconds.

'But I thought he was just . . .'

How was it I summed him up when we went to the Heggartys' for dinner? That he was a homeboy who played it safe? That he had made no impact on the world and had no desire to be Nemo and explore the rest of the ocean? How wrong could I have been? Mac is not just a big fish in a little pond. He is a big fish who swam around the world and then came home.

'But I just assumed he was . . .' I begin again.

'You thought he was a small-town culchie with no ambition?' Dave laughs. 'Ah sure, lots of people think that about Mac because he keeps himself to himself and doesn't give much away until ya get to know him. Some people see it as arrogance, but he's just humble. You know, for a long time Mac has been careful not to let too many people get close to him. He's not unfriendly, sure, but he only concerns himself with the people that matter.'

I bite my lip and look out to sea, trying to catch a glimpse of the man I am learning more about every day. Over the weeks I have begun to realise that Mac has hidden depths. I just wasn't aware that his depths were so hidden they could be Taliban extremists. I have seen his softer side when he teaches the cross-border scheme, and until last night we had become comfortable as friends. He had let me in to that protected heart. Mind you, all along I have still been comparing Mac to Dan Clancy. Slotting him into second place as the unglamorous one. When all along he could have followed just as glamorous a career as Dan. Even more so. I tune in to Dave, who is still talking about his surfing mentor.

'He was even the first European to be invited to take part in the Eddie Aikau contest in Waimea Bay, Hawaii; the world's biggest big-wave comp. The guy's a total legend in big surf. Sure didn't lots of people think he was crazy to give it all up, but the thing was, Mac's best friend and surfing partner, Nicky, was killed in a bombin' just across the border. They used to go everywhere together to surf, you know, but one day when Mac was after winning the Europeans, Nicky found himself in the wrong place at the wrong time and that was it, bang, game over.'

I stare at the ground, my jaw dropping like the shovel on the front of a JCB digger.

'After that, Mac just didn't want to travel any more without Nicky and he decided he'd rather stay in Donegal to start the cross-border programme. You see, he thought he could do more good by bringing kids together from the North and the South and integratin' them through surfing. Of course, things have really improved now with the Troubles, as they call them, but Mac's scheme works like magic and it's more important to him than money and fame. Nicky's death is most of the reason he's so private and doesn't let people get close, I guess in case he gets hurt.'

I blink rapidly while I try to digest Dave's words. My God, poor Mac. Poor Nicky. Poor Mac. No wonder he comes across as somewhat cold and complicated. He lost his best friend to terrorism, something I cannot even begin to comprehend. No wonder he took a while to warm to me when I asked stupid questions about religion and called him a terrorist. Oh God, I am such an idiot, tramping over Mac's feelings in total oblivion. Mac hasn't had the easy life I imagined. He is damaged, and yet he has chosen to stand up and do something about the world. And he tried to tell me. The time he said he wasn't macho and that he had cried before. He was trying to let me in and tell me about Nicky I just didn't listen. Mac is far braver than I am. He is so much braver than Dan and he is making his mark in a much deeper way than flaunting himself in front of a camera. No wonder he treated my work as trivial. Right now it does seem trivial in comparison. Mac Heggarty is a bloody saint, for God's sake. No wonder he didn't want to kiss me. He's too good for me.

'Sorry for interrupting, like,' says Fi as Dave begins to launch into yet more tales, 'but has anyone seen Mac since he caught that massive wave?'

'No, I've been listening to . . .'

I catch the look of concern on Fi's face and whip my head around to look out to sea. Dave leans forwards, shielding his eyes from the wind and sea spray with one hand.

'He'll be grand,' Dave says with very little concern. 'Mac's been out in bigger waves than that before so.'

*Good. So let's all just relax and enjoy the show, shall we?* I sit back in my seat.

'Maybe,' Fi acknowledges, 'but isn't that his surfboard flapping about down there on the rocks like some sort of tombstone?'

I sit forwards with a sharp jerk.

Fi is right. On the reef below us, Mac's usually shiny white surfboard is standing upright, jammed between two large rocks and looking decidedly battered. I clasp a hand to my throat where a knot of fear the size of a tennis ball has jammed in my windpipe.

'Oh my God, Dave, that's Mac's surfboard,' I stammer. 'So where the hell is Mac?'

Dave stands up and steps closer to the sign warning of the edge of the cliff. Now he looks concerned. Fi does the same, with my own shaky steps close behind.

*Please let him be OK*, I think nervously, *please don't let him drown*.

Our eyes are almost on sticks, straining to see what is happening down below. Still the surfboard stands rigid, like the gravestone I was perched on just an hour before.

*If that was a disrespectful thing to do, I apologise*, I silently stress to God in case he happens to be listening. *Just don't take my church antics out on Mac.*

Suddenly a wave the size of a double-decker bus crashes down on to the reef. The cliff trembles and the surfboard springs free. It flies through the air and finally lands on the dry rocks below, where it smashes into pieces.

'Jaysus, Mary and Joseph!' Fi shouts. 'Where the Lord is my cousin?'

'Christ almighty,' Dave joins in, 'this doesn't look good, hey.'

'Fucking hell,' I shriek, unable to persist with the religious metaphor, 'he's drowned. Mac has bloody well drowned!'

We run as near to the edge of the cliff as we can and gaze helplessly out at the raging waves. A haze of spray carried on the wind stings my eyes. The ever-building whitewater stretches as far back as the horizon that bubbles ferociously to indicate yet more swell charging towards the land.

'Help him, Dave!' I cry, almost toppling off the cliff edge in my anxiety. 'Call the lifeguard.'

'He *is* the feckin' lifeguard.'

'Then call the lifeboat or the helicopter or the navy or something. Call Flipper the fucking dolphin. Just don't let him die.'

I start to cough as tears erupt from my eyes and stream down my face. I am shocked by the strength of my emotion, as is Fi, who looks at me strangely, her mouth wide open.

'It's all right, Milly,' she says with a mature calm. 'We'll find him.'

'But you don't understand,' I wail, 'I . . . I . . .'

The words catch in my throat and I start to sob, feelings of guilt and anger and something more profound that I don't quite recognise building up inside me like the waves as they thunder towards the shore. Dave pulls his mobile phone out of his back pocket and begins to dial frantically. Fi pulls me close and I hold on tight.

'I really LIKE HIM!'

The words blast out of my mouth and hang in the air despite the strong wind. Fi turns to stare at me. If I could stare at myself, I would.

'I really like him, Fi,' I wail. 'When you told me last night that he liked me, I felt so happy. And it wasn't just an alcohol thing. I knew he was special, I just never let myself realise how special. Damn, and I've never treated him right. I have never told him how much I appreciate his time and how great I think his scheme is with the kids and . . . and I've just realised that I really like him, Fi. I really care for him and not just because he's a surfing champion. I liked him before that. I just didn't realise because I'm so obsessed with DAN FUCKING CLANCY!'

I don't have to think about what I'm saying; it just comes from within.

'And now I realise that I've been using him for my own benefit to learn to surf and that I haven't been honest with myself and I haven't actually been that nice to him, and although he turned me down, I don't care because I really like him, Fi. He's amazing and' – I try to catch my breath – 'and now . . . oh God . . . now he's dead. He's gone, Fi. He's dead.'

'Who's dead?' says a voice behind us.

I wipe the tears and mucus away from my face with the back of my hand and turn around. Standing there, dripping wet but only slightly out of breath, is Mac. All of him. In one beautiful, toned piece.

'You . . .' I gasp and laugh and sob all at once. 'You . . .'

I feel faint with relief.

'Bloody hell, Mac, ya gave us quite a fright there, so you did yourself,' says Dave, lowering the mobile phone to race forward and pat his friend heartily on the shoulder.

'Aye, my feckin' leash snapped, didn't it,' Mac tuts. 'I got the whole set on the head and had to swim down the bloody river to get in. I'm knackered. But hey, it was worth it for that barrel. Did you see the size of it?'

They walk down the road towards the surf shop, carrying out a detailed post-mortem of the wave as they go. Fi and I stand together opening and closing our mouths like basking sharks scooping up plankton.

'Bloody hell, this surfing lark's a bit traumatic like,' Fi comments, tilting her head towards me.

I shrug nonchalantly.

'Yeah,' I sniff, 'I suppose it was pretty exciting, but that's what surfing's about, Fi. I knew that. I wasn't bothered at all.'

'Ah yeah,' she snorts, 'so how come you dropped ten euros' worth of pick 'n' mix over the edge of that cliff then?'

I look down at my empty hands and frown.

'And, Milly Armstrong, if you'd care to rewind just a second there, how come you just admitted to being in love with my cousin?'

Fi turns on her heel and begins to skip down the road.

'I did not!' I protest, half jogging along behind her. 'I did not say love, I said *like*. *Like*, I said. There's a big difference, you know.'

'Ah sure,' Fi calls over her shoulder. 'And I'm the feckin' Queen of England.'

# CHAPTER TWENTY

## *When the Boat Comes In*

Over the next fortnight the swell drops enough for the average humans among us to enter the water once again. With little more than a month of my stay left, I realise that time is short if I am to be surfing convincingly by the start of filming in July. I throw myself into my surfing lessons despite the fact that my instructor is as comfortable with me as I would be parading the beach in a shoestring thong. The drunken kiss was bad enough, but the declaration of affection seemingly tipped the balance. I know Dave told him. In fact, he probably caught the whole thing on tape. I can just imagine the two of them, feet up, beer in hand, crying with laughter as they watch me screaming 'I really like him' out to sea while Mac walked up behind me.

Mac and I are polite to each other and we are obviously still friends, but we are back to being visibly awkward together. Myself especially. Mind you, Mac's ability to teach me to surf and to pluck me from the froth in moments of peril without once looking me in the eye is quite astounding. I would love to clear the air between us, but I will be leaving here in a few weeks and right now I have more important matters to deal with.

The first of these is that although I am now at the stage where I can put my head under the water without screaming

'Help me, I'm dying!' I still cannot stand up and ride a wave like a legitimate surfer. Not to mention looking sexy for the camera in the process. I stand up perhaps one out of every five attempts, and even then not for long. If only I were like the kids in the class. They have no fear; I have *beaucoup* of fear. The kids are told to stand up and ride the wave and they just do it; I consider staying upright on this piece of foam and doing some sort of manoeuvre as likely as pulling off a back flip on a chopstick. Fi always emerges from the water with a smile on her face and a sporty glow to her cheeks, while I resemble a water rat that has been run over several times by a cross-Channel ferry. Not a good look for displaying my Hollywood starlet potential. I share my worries with Dave in the hope that he will reassure me that two weeks on Wednesday at precisely ten a.m. I will suddenly develop a natural talent for water sports and catch one of the best waves ever ridden in western Europe. Dave listens to my woes, records them on camera and then simply says, 'Mac can't work miracles, hey. Now are ya comin' for a pint or not?'

The second matter of great concern to me is easier to explain. My parents are arriving today.

I had secretly hoped that Frank and Georgina Armstrong would go off the idea of spending a week in Ireland in May and opt instead for a holiday in the Italian lakes or the Canary Islands. In truth, and I am ashamed (but only very slightly) to admit this, I even went to the trouble of calling as many travel agents in Southampton as I could find with a request to send holiday brochures to my parents' house. At one point they were almost swayed by a Disney cruise before Mum decided she didn't like boats. Shortly afterwards, she booked their ferry to Rosslare. The mind boggles.

I check my reflection again. My hair is pulled back into a tight ponytail, although this fails to hide the fact that daily surfs and salt water have done little for its condition. Exposure to the elements has changed it completely, and

197

my lack of a regular beauty routine means that, even though I may not perform like a surf chick, I am starting to look like one. My hair is lighter and now more bohemian than cat-walk chic. Make-up has also become a burden, as having to reapply it every time I come out of the surf is time-consuming, not to mention expensive. Since we arrived at the end of February, I have taken to using only a tinted moisturiser, a dab of bronze eyeshadow behind my double coat of mascara and a gold-effect lipstick to top it all off. As a matter of fact, I am pleased with my new, sporty, fresh-faced appearance. Fi says it makes me look younger. I say hallelujah to that. As for my once perfect manicured nails, I would cry every time I looked at them, if there were any-thing to look at that is. Seawater and regular collisions with everything from my surfboard to rocks and other surfing students are not kind to nails, and I just don't seem to have had the time (or the inclination) for manicures. My nails are so short I couldn't get dirt trapped underneath them even if I tried. Thank goodness my fingers are long or I would have hands like a bricklayer.

I pull on a loose grey jumper and tighten the thick pink belt on my frayed jeans. A genuine positive to come out of all this activity is my ever-reducing waistline, despite the fact that since living on the west coast I have had an appetite like a T-rex with a tapeworm and a thirst for the black stuff. I guess the fitness fanatics have been right all along; exercise is good for you. Then again, I can't believe I am saying this, but surfing no longer feels like exercise to me. It is totally exhausting, of course, but it is not like going for a run or slogging my guts out in a gym fitness factory. While I am surfing I can only think of catching that perfect wave. Oh, would you listen to me? I sound like a tie-dye-wearing hippie.

I clasp my hands together and peer at the mirror one final time before pulling on my shoes, grabbing my puffa jacket and leaving Pooh Corner to collect my parents. Please

God, let the next week fly by in the blink of an eye. And make it good. Or, if not good, at least bearable.

The drive from Rosslare is, according to Uncle Podraig, a good six hours by car because of the slow roads rather than the distance. I had expected my parents to do the journey in half the time considering the way my father wears out the accelerator of every car he owns. He is always in a rush. Largely because he is a stress-motivated barrister, but also because he is generally a *late* stress-motivated barrister. I have been worried about his health with all the talk of high blood pressure and bad hearts, but I am almost afraid to see him just in case he doesn't look like my big, invincible dad any more. The man who could do anything, just like my bloody brother.

Having been recently introduced to the wonders of mobile phones, my mum called en route to inform me of their progress.

'We're at the . . . where are we at, Frank?'

She held the phone in the direction of my father's mouth.

'We're coming up to Tullamore, Georgina.'

'We're coming up to Tullamore, Amelia.'

'Yes, I gathered that.'

'So we should be with you in about three hours. Isn't that right, Frank?'

'Yes, that's right, Georgina, ETA approximately three hours.'

'So you'll be waiting for us, won't you, Amelia? We don't want to get into any sort of trouble, you know, being strangers and being English and everything.'

'Mum, I really don't think that's a problem any—'

'Ooh, pull over, Frank, PULL OVER! I must take a picture of that thatched cottage.'

'Oh yes, and look, there's a donkey!'

Five miles later they remembered to hang up the phone.

The last call I received was to inform me that they were outside KFC only a few miles away and would be making

199

their entrance into town just as soon as my father had satisfied his curiosity as to whether Irish chicken tastes the same as English. Heaven help me.

I walk out to the end of Main Street and settle myself on the stone sea wall to wait. After five days of persistent rain, the sun is warm against my face. Irish sun always seems brighter after the rain, as if it has been washed and polished to its brightest by the raindrops. I close my eyes and hum a made-up tune to myself while I try to remember the last time I spent a holiday alone with my parents. The memory hits me in the stomach with the force of salmonella poisoning. I was sixteen and far too cool to want to go on holiday with my parents, but as Ed had been invited to go away to the Lake District with his best friend's family, I felt sorry for my lonely old mum and dad and agreed to a week in a rural hotel in the south of France. It was a disaster. The hotel was as welcoming as the horror house in *The Shining* and its inhabitants made Johnny look like a chirpy boy scout. Dad spent the entire trip practising some of the worst French I have heard since Inspector Clouseau and my mother insisted on asking every restaurant and café waiter whether we couldn't just have a 'nice bit of sliced Hovis' rather than the crispy baguettes that played havoc with her soft gums. To top it all off, it rained so hard that the mountain next to the hotel all but washed away and then the only cute French boy in the town turned out to be gay. I vowed never to holiday with my folks again if I could possibly help it. The problem is, once one reaches a certain age, it somehow becomes harder to say no to these things. This happens just after your twenty-fifth birthday. I think they call it an attack of conscience.

If I was worried about missing my father's car, I needn't have been. The honking horn is loud enough to rouse dead Father O'Hare up at the church. I whip my head around and gasp at the sight of the shiny new Lexus that, when compared to the cars around it in the street, looks nothing less than ostentatious. It is like an enormous black motorboat on gold (fake, I hope) alloy wheels sweeping through the town as if it owns the place. I blush upon blushes. We are not a rich family, but my father has always liked cars. By way of hard work and my parents' combined salaries my father has always (unfortunately) been able to pay for his tastes. Dad's ultimate car is a Bentley. I thank God his tax bills have kept that one at bay. If the car itself were not bad enough, it is when it pulls up to the kerbside, blocking most of the road, and my parents step out that I wonder whether I am too old to be adopted.

'Top o' the mornin' to ya,' Dad shouts, opening his arms wide to embrace me. 'Or should I say bottom o' the after-noon.'

I am yanked into the arms of a man who facially resem-bles the father I left back in Southampton, if a little heavier, but who appears to have raided the wardrobe of an Irish football fan with extremely poor taste.

'Dad, how are you? And what is that?'

He removes the two-foot-tall gold, green and white felt hat from his head and waggles it in the air with gusto. The bells on the rim sound a high-pitched jingle, and unless I am hearing things, 'Danny Boy' begins to play from somewhere in the hat's interior. My eyes move down to the top of my father's head.

'Did you smuggle in a ginger poodle, or is that thing a wig?'

'Is that not the funniest thing you have ever seen?' my father chortles, his rounded belly wobbling under the bright green I ♥ IRELAND V-neck sweater.

*Er, no.*

He ruffles his hand through the tangled orange wig and laughs his powerful laugh.

'We found all this great stuff on the ferry and I just could not resist.'

*I wish you had.*

'As for your mother,' he winks mischievously, 'she hasn't been able to keep her hands off me since we left Rosslare. It's the hair, you know, taking her back to my younger days.'

'Oh Frank, don't be so ridiculous,' my mother sniffs.

She pulls me into a hug, enveloping me in a cloud of Anaïs Anaïs perfume. The same perfume that she has worn for as long as I have had a sense of smell.

'How are you, darling?'

I smile and assure my mother that I am fine and all is well while her heavily kohl-lined eyes check me out from head to toe.

'You're very thin for a natural size twelve, Amelia,' she says, shaking her head.

Her coiffured hair doesn't move an inch, thanks to the hefty can of Elnette hairspray that I know I would find in her black leather bag – more hand luggage than handbag – if I looked.

'Are you eating properly? And if you need to buy some make-up, Amelia, I can help you choose. A good foundation can do wonders for those lines.'

I bite my tongue.

'Just as soon as we have settled in, we could have a wander to town. Where is it, by the way?'

She spins slowly on her neat black court shoes and surveys Main Street.

'You're in it, Mum. This is the town.'

'Ha ha, very amusing.'

'Um, yes, well I suppose it is a bit limited, but it's got everything you need really.'

'Just as long as there is an M&S it will be fine. There's always an M&S.'

I decide not to inform her that the nearest M&S is across the border in the North for fear that she will have a panic attack and force Dad to drive the six hours back to the ferry port. Although on second thoughts . . .

'Ah bejaysus, can you smell that, Georgina?' my father

202

shouts while I lead the way along the path to Pooh Corner. 'That's fresh air, that is, as fresh as it comes. Ah bejaysus, that doctor was right. I feel as fit as a fiddle already. Fit as a fiddle, that's apt now we're in Ireland, isn't it? Ha ha.' He stops beside the sea wall and pats his belly. 'Now, who's for a slap-up pub meal and a pint of Guinness? I'm parched.'

Before I let my parents loose on the local population, I manage to convince my father to remove the hat, wig, scarf and sweatbands. The pullover remains firmly stretched over his generous frame, but thankfully the rain has returned, so he is forced to cover the knitted fashion disaster with a waterproof jacket. I just hope it is raining inside the pub too.

By the time we meander along to Gallagher's Bar, my father having inexplicably felt the need to stop and exchange pleasantries with every single person we passed en route, they have finished serving lunch and have not yet started the dinner menu. I order two pints of Guinness for myself and my father and a half for my mother. She shakes her head at the dark substance, sniffs it in disgust and then proceeds to down the lot as if it were a slimline G&T. Dad licks the Guinness froth from his lips and lets out a satisfied sigh.

'So what is the story with your acting lark, pudding? This jaunt to the west coast is research, is it? Don't tell me we are to believe what you wrote on that postcard of yours about you actually going out in that water there.'

I look out of the arched window beside our table at the sea beyond while trying to ignore the flippancy of my father's tone.

'That's right, Dad, it is research,' I reply with as much confidence as I can muster. 'Every actor has to do a certain amount before assuming a role to help make their perform-ance as realistic as possible. My research is to learn about surfing and how to do it.'

'You see, it is the surfing bit I don't understand.' My mother frowns quizzically, as if I have just confessed to studying the art of voodoo. 'I thought actresses learned voice throwing and the like, not surfing.'

'No, that would be ventriloquists, Mum.'

'Don't be facetious, dear, you know what I mean. I just happen to come from the part of the human race who don't know the official terms for what actors and actresses get overpaid to do.'

I clear my throat.

*Patience, Milly, patience. This woman did give birth to you, after all.*

'Well, the film is based around a surf chick, Mum.'

'Chick?'

'Not of the feathered variety, a surfer girl. And as I have the lead role . . .'

I pause for the whoop of delight that never comes.

'. . . erm, that means I have to be able to surf.'

'Marvellous,' my father booms. 'Surfing, heh? I went surfing in the sixties, you know. I was bloody good too, I might add. Could have been a regular Beach Boy.'

*Yeah, if you lived by the sea and had a different body, perhaps.*

I smile pleasantly to entertain my father's fantasy.

'Shame we didn't get you into surfing earlier then, I suppose, Amelia. On our trips to Bournemouth.'

I shudder at the mention of the place.

'Bloody good those days out were, weren't they?'

'Oh yes, great, Dad, apart from when I almost drowned,' I mutter into my pint.

'Nonsense, you did not almost drown,' retorts my mother, the champion swimmer, 'you just swallowed a little bit of water. Goodness me, Amelia, you are so melodramatic at times.'

'Which is probably why she wants to follow the acting—'

'*Lark.*' I finish Dad's sentence for him.

'Actually,' I continue proudly, 'the acting lark is really taking off. This film could be massive when it comes out, and not that I like to brag, but the director totally begged me to take the lead role. He is paying all my expenses while I'm here in County Donegal and . . . and he has big plans for my future in the business. BIG plans. *HUGE* ones, in fact.'

I finish and inhale sharply. My mother smiles sweetly at me the way only mums can when you are seven years old and you swear you have just had a tea party with a fairy at the bottom of the garden. She tilts her head and murmurs, 'That's lovely, dear.'

With smoke blowing out of my ears like Ivor the Engine's funnel, I stomp across to the bar for more drinks.

'Two pints, a half, two bags of Taytos and a sharp knife for my wrists, please, barman.'

At what point in life does conversing with parents become an altogether painful experience? I don't remember. I do remember how I used to look up to them whatever they said or did and how I used to want to *be* like them even. How I used to glow whenever Dad called me pudding. Now I feel smothered by them and embarrassed by my pet name (for obvious reasons). I feel the need to assert my adulthood. To blatantly lie and exaggerate in order to prove that I can stand on my own two feet without their help or approval. Parents have that annoying habit of spotting a porky pie at twenty paces, especially my mother. Honestly, the way they look at me when I talk about my career just makes me want to scream.

*For heaven's sake, Milly, you're thirty-one years old. Get over it already.*

I load the drinks on to a tray and count to twenty (ten for each parent).

*They are here on holiday, your father is stressed up to the eyeballs and they want to relax as much as you do. Just chill out.*

With my self-help advice in my head and a friendly smile fixed to my lips, I thread my way through the ever-crowded pub back to the table.

'You know,' my father begins before I have even sat down, 'I read somewhere recently that that Juliet Robin woman gets twenty million dollars per film. Twenty million dollars. Can you believe that, Georgina?'

'It's Julia Roberts, dear, and yes I can, Frank, I can.'

'But that would be a damn sight more than a QC makes in a year, Georgina, and they do far more with their grey matter than some pretty girl who has had a few acting lessons. No offence, pudding.'

'None taken.'

*Bloody cheek.*

'Oh but she is jolly good, Frank,' says my mother, pointing a salt and vinegar crisp at my father for emphasis. 'I saw her in that *Pretty Woman* and she had me believing she was a prostitute.'

'Really?'

'Yes, but she's not, you know. Not a prostitute.'

I clamp the edge of the pint glass with my teeth.

'Well I suppose that would be the crux of the whole thing, Georgina. The crux of the acting—'

'Lark,' I hiss into the froth.

Mum delicately chews the single crisp about fifty times before she speaks again.

'So, darling, I take it from your level of accommodation that you will not be receiving twenty million for this film project of yours.'

'What's wrong with my level of accommodation?' I bristle.

My mother smiles faintly and says nothing, which is infinitely more annoying than if she had dissected Pooh Corner brick by brick and found fault with every one. Mind you, as attached as I have become to our sixties-throwback excuse for a cottage, I concede that she does have a point. You wouldn't exactly find Julia Roberts stepping her Jimmy Choos across the threshold. I change tack.

'I should point out that the accommodation was actually my own choice. Of course the director wanted to put me up in the best hotel in town, but then Fiona wanted to tag along and I just decided that' – I lower my voice to be sure no one is listening – 'it would help me get into the role by infiltrating the culture of the small town, as it were. To help me mix with the locals.'

'I see,' my father replies at double the volume. 'That's jolly clever, pudding. So you decided to stay in peasant quarters and mix with the natives. Brilliant.'

The conversation between the four burly men at the next table is immediately cut short. Dad's words hang in the stale pub air above our heads.

'Dad,' I hiss, instantly reddening, 'you can't say things like . . . like that any more. It's not PC.'

'PC rubbish. PC is what is getting the world in such a muddle, if you want my opinion.'

*I don't.*

'Honestly, one can hardly take a step forward in the legal profession these days without coming up against a brick wall of political correctness. It drives me mad.'

My father crosses his arms over the stomach that is a product of too many barrister–client lunches.

'There is just no common sense in the world any more. It is no wonder I am bloody stressed when we lawyers are forever having to make allowances for woofters and the like.'

I gasp and will him to keep his voice down. My mother moves my father's pint away from his hand and tuts.

'I think you have had just about enough of that for one afternoon, Frank Armstrong. Now hush and keep your opinions to yourself, we are trying to have a relaxing holiday drink.'

*You tell him, Mum.*

Dad raises both hands defensively.

'Oh, now don't get me wrong, I don't have anything against woofters. After all, I watch that Graham Norton fellow, don't I, Georgina?'

'Yes, you do, Frank.'

'And he is as whoopsy as they come.'

'Bloody hell, do you think we could change the subject?' I spit, removing my scarlet head from its retracted position in my neck.

My mother pats my hand across the table. The next-door conversation slowly starts up again.

'I understand, darling. Your father just gets a little carried away sometimes. I realise that we have to be careful what we say around these parts. I mean, one never knows what sort of scoundrel might be listening in. By the way, do we have to stay on the alert for suspicious packages? They do have a thing for bombs over here, don't they?'

I smack my forehead down on to the heavy oak table and groan while wondering whether it would be possible to keep two conspicuous adults like my parents hidden for a week.

'Milly, how's it goin'? And sure, this must be your folks. Hello there, Mr and Mrs Milly, nice to meet ya. I'm Kathleen.'

I look up and smile weakly at Mac's young sister, who is happily shaking hands with my parents as if she has known them for years. She flicks her long auburn hair behind her shoulders and pulls up a chair, oozing the kind of confidence that only a fourteen-year-old can.

'Fiona said you were arriving today, and then our Johnny is after seeing your car pull into town.'

*Who didn't?*

'So you're very welcome both, and aren't you blessed with gorgeous weather?'

I peer out at the rain and frown.

'We are indeed, Kathleen,' my father nevertheless agrees, thankfully choosing to ditch his Irish accent. 'Now, can I buy you a drink?'

'Sure, what harm will it do? I'll have a double Malibu and Coke, so.'

'But you're underage, Kathleen,' I say, feeling like her square older sister.

Kathleen's green eyes twinkle in the orange glow of the

pub's lights, instantly reminding me of her brother. I bite my bottom lip.

'So I am,' she grins mischievously, as if her age were news to her. 'Ah well, I'll be lovin' ya and leavin' ya. I've a few messages to get for Ma.'

She stands to leave with another flick of her hair.

'Now, Milly, Fi is still up at the house but will be back home to yous in a while. And Mac says if you want a surf lesson he can fit you in before dark if you can meet him at the main beach in a half-hour.'

She looks at her fingers to count the points.

'Oh aye, and Ma says yous are all to come for your dinner tonight up at the house.'

The words 'unbearable evening' flash in front of my eyes like a strobe light.

'Thanks, um, but Mum and Dad have had a long journey today and they're rather tired, so do you think we could leave it till another time?'

*Like never?*

'Not at all,' my mother responds immediately, smoothing the lapels of her black fitted jacket. 'We are always up for a social engagement. Aren't we, Frank?'

Dad slaps his hand on the table. 'We are that, Georgina.'

*Ooh hark at them, my parents the social butterflies.*

'We can quickly check into the hotel, Georgina, let Amelia have her splash-around in the sea, and hey presto. Dinner would be a pleasure, Kathleen. Thank your mother and we will see you there.'

'Dead on. No bother at all.' She skips towards the door and calls over her shoulder, 'See yous at eight thirty, then.'

My father gulps down the remainder of his Guinness and loudly smacks his lips together.

'What a marvellous holiday we're having, pudding. I'm having a whale of a time already and we've only been here a few hours.'

*Is that all?*

'Good Guinness as far as the eye can see,' he continues merrily, 'and on the menu tonight we have good company, good native food and good old-fashioned Oirish conversation.'

*Good grief.*

# CHAPTER TWENTY-ONE

## *Potty Training*

When, bedraggled and exhausted after my surf lesson, I arrive at the Heggartys' house with my mother and father, the door is ajar and the noise from within is already raising the roof.

'Goodness gracious,' my mother whispers, stepping carefully inside and eyeing the countless pairs of welly boots, 'what's the occasion?'

'Sunday dinner,' I shrug and lead the way to the sitting room.

In contrast to the crowd at the meal when I first arrived in town, today there seems to be just a selection of the family. Not that 'just' is an apt term when taking into account Mary, Podraig, Mac, Kathleen, Colleen, Barry, Johnny, the gorgeous Onya, Siobhan, Noel, Sinead, Danny and their befreckled children, who I swear have doubled in number since I last saw them. It is the Heggarty massive. All talking, laughing, shouting and drinking at once. Familial pandemonium.

Of course there is also Fi, who bounds up to my parents, her latest style of tight little pigtails making her look even younger than usual. She embraces Georgina and Frank and then draws them into the room, where she leaves them to become acquainted with every Heggarty and his dog (Eric, I do recall). Mum smiles and blinks in total bewilderment.

Dad works the room like a true lawyer, exchanging firm handshakes, memorising names and spending an inordinate amount of time discussing the weather with Onya. Men are so predictable. Content that my parents are in safe hands and will be (whether they like it or not) for some time yet, I accept a mug of coffee from Fi and collapse into the nearest armchair.

'Is it lovely to be having a holiday with your folks like?' Fi asks, balancing on the arm of the chair and crossing her legs.

'I don't know if lovely is the word for it, Fi. It's great to see them, of course, but I definitely feel in a state of high alert.'

I gulp my coffee, burning the tip of my tongue in the process. I constantly glance over at my father to make sure he is behaving himself.

'My dad has a tendency to pontificate in groups of people and he is rather an obvious tourist. He would be the one coming off a flight from Spain with a giant sombrero on his head and a straw donkey tucked under his arm.'

'Ah so, that explains the jumper,' Fi snorts. 'That's in wild poor taste is it not?'

'Hmm. Just pray to God that he doesn't start speaking in his Oirish accent, bejaysus.'

Fi laughs and peers at my father.

'But sure parents are allowed to be embarrassing, Milly; it's their prerogative. Straight up, I reckon they get instructions to bring up their cubs playing the role of proper responsible disciplinarian. Then when the kids are old enough to be their equal, like, and be socially aware, the parents go all mental and eccentric and embarrass the shite out of them. Being a parent must be a gas. Not that I'll ever be one.'

'You might. You and Dave would make great parents.'

Fi punches me on the arm.

'Feck off. Me and Dave will do no such thing. Anyhow, I would pity any cub of mine, being born with the O'Reilly mentalist genes.'

'Stop it, Fi, that's not true.'

Fi makes a funny face and laughs. The laugh is unnatural and forced, failing to conceal Fi's true feelings. She looks me in the eye and shrugs.

'My folks could only manage to raise one of us kids to adulthood before they fecked off to wherever it is they fecked off to. I don't want that responsibility.'

I sip my coffee in silence.

'What am I talking about? I do have some of that responsibility. Sure, didn't they blame me for what happened to my brother?'

'That was wrong.'

'No.' Fi shakes her head. Her ponytail bobbles clunk against her earrings. 'My ma and da were never wrong. Always right they were. Not that I can challenge their decisions now that I don't know where they are.'

'Have you thought about asking Mary? She might know where her sister is.'

'I have thought about it, but . . . but I don't know. I don't know if I want to know, if you know what I mean.'

Fi's eyes darken as she wrinkles her brow in thought. I watch her, wishing I were the sort of person who always knows the right thing to say. I am more relaxed with Fi than anyone else in my world but sometimes I don't know how best to deal with the depth of her emotions that I will never fully understand. I am not a trained Samaritan. But I can be a good friend.

I put my cup down and take Fi's cold hand in mine, squeezing it to reassure her. Fi turns towards me and wrinkles her nose in the trademark way she always does.

'Ah shite, how did I get on to this subject? I'm after depressing myself.'

'Don't be daft.'

'I can't help it, I am daft,' she grins. 'Now shall we get to the table? Mary has prepared thirty-five types of potato and I don't want to miss out on one.'

\*

Fi's eccentric parent theory is tested during dinner when my father begins to slip into his awful Irish accent, much to Kathleen's amusement. Onya eyes him as if he has just stepped out of a spaceship and said 'Take me to your leader, bejaysus', while Mac simply shakes his head. Sinead, Siobhan, their husbands and the noisy, freckly bunch leave after our gluttonous main course and a rhubarb pie with a crust as thick as a prison wall. The remaining tribe gather in the sitting room for after-dinner drinks.

My mother looks immaculate as ever in a knee-length navy pencil skirt, pale-blue twinset and court shoes, but as she lowers herself delicately next to Mac, I notice her cheeks are starting to disclose the effects of too many glasses of sherry. I watch her while she talks, listens and nods, acknowledging the various conversations careering around the room but not taking an active role in any. Something Mac says makes her throw her head back and laugh, a thing that my mother rarely does, and *oh my God*, was that a wink she just gave him or was it a trick of the light? I clamp my teeth together and continue to stare. Now she is smiling at him as if he has just presented her with a million-pound cheque. Now, *bloody hell*, she places her hand on his thigh . . . his mid-thigh.

'Like mother like daughter,' giggles Fi, who has also been watching the exchange.

I scowl and lean forward in my chair, straining my ears to eavesdrop their conversation.

'So you are the one teaching my daughter how to surf,' Mum gushes, leaning closer to Mac's left shoulder.

'That's right, Mrs Armstrong, I am that.'

'Ooh, do call me Georgina, Mac. After all, I'm still young. In my prime as they say, ha ha.'

She giggles and sips her sherry. Mac sucks his top lip behind his lower row of teeth.

'Right then, ehm, Georgina, that's grand.'

He returns his attention to a spot on the carpet in front of him. My mother leans closer.

'You must be very strong, Mac, to surf those powerful waves. Do you work out?'

*Eugh, what is this? A lesson in middle-aged chat-up lines?*

'Er, no, Mrs . . . Georgina. Just the surfing like, that's enough for me.'

'I work out,' Mum replies, leaning over at such an angle that I am surprised she doesn't just topple headfirst into his lap. 'Body of a thirty-year-old, they tell me at the gym.'

'Hormones of a pubescent teenager,' Fi chuckles with a loud snort.

I grind my teeth to stop myself either a) screaming or b) puking up the lead-weight portion of rhubarb pie all over the pair of them. My mother's hand slides higher on Mac's leg.

*Dad, are you watching this débâcle?*

But no, my father is engrossed in a debate with Podraig about the illegal properties of poteen. Mac focuses unblinking on the carpet, as if the meaning of life itself were written there.

'I was a swimmer myself, Mac,' my mother beams, 'a proper little water baby.'

'Were you, Mrs . . . Georgina?'

His voice is several octaves higher than usual.

'Ooh, I was, yes. So perhaps I could have a go at surfing while I am here, if you would care to give me a lesson?'

'Er, well . . .'

'I would probably be less of a liability than Amelia, to be truthful, Mac. Honestly, that girl and water are not a good combination. You won't believe it, but Amelia almost drowned in her *potty* of all places.'

My mother delivers the last sentence just as every other conversation in the room momentarily stops. I groan and realise I am in danger of grinding my back teeth to dust. I release my jaw and take a deep breath.

'Mum, I am sure Mac doesn't want to hear about that.'

215

'Ha ha, is that the potty story?' interrupts my father, whose nose is now as red as the port in his bottomless glass. 'Listen to this, Podraig, it's bloody hilarious this is, pardon my French.'

'Dad, I don't think—'

'Mary, Kathleen, Colleen, Barry . . .'

Trust him to remember their effing names.

'. . . Johnny, Onya, everyone listen to this, it is bloody brilliant. Oops, pardon my French. Go on, Georgina, tell us.'

'Aye, go on, Georgina, tell . . . *ow*, bloody hell, that hurt.'

I raise my eyebrows at the red spot on Fi's arm where I pinched it and sniff defiantly.

'Well . . .' my mother begins as if she is the storyteller on *Jackanory*.

I shift under Mac's intense gaze. I can't bring myself to look at him.

'Well, we were in the middle of the whole potty-training palaver,' my mother begins again when she has the undivided attention of the room. 'Amelia was, I have to say, a late developer in most things.'

*Do you have to say that? I don't think she has to say that, does she?*

'In fact, she was three before we could even think of getting her near a pair of pants.'

'Ah, it's a drama sure.' Mary nods in comprehension of the problem.

'Ed, our youngest, he took to the potty immediately, but then he did with everything. He always was a bright boy.'

'Bright arse more like,' I mutter under my breath, 'where the sun shines out of it.'

'Told you being a parent's a gas,' Fi whispers.

'Amelia was our first, you see, so we were learning as parents, and try as we might we just could not get her to go on that potty. Oh, she would sit on it all right, at home, in the car, even in the supermarket, but she just would not *go* on it, if you know what I mean. Anyway, to get to the good part of the story . . .'

*What, like there is a good part?*

'One glorious day we, Frank and I, heard the sound of tinkling coming from the sitting room when we were in the kitchen, and we just knew.'

'We whooped, "She's done it, she's done it", didn't we, Georgina?' my father announces so loudly he sounds like a town crier.

'We did indeed, Frank. She had gone wee-wee in the potty at last.'

'At LAST!' my father choruses.

'Oh, we were so proud.'

'The first and last time,' I grunt.

'Until, that was, we went into the sitting room to inspect the results and there she was, wasn't she, Frank? Face down in the damn thing. Face down in the potty.'

'Face down in her own wee-wee,' my father adds for clarification. 'Choking on the stuff.'

*Oh spare us the details, purrlease.*

'It seems she had put her head down to see what she had done and, bless her, Amelia never did have much natural balance. Would you believe it, she fell right in?'

A gasp races around the room, soon followed by a second wave of uncontrollable laughter. Even Fi is laughing and wiping tears – I'll give her bloody tears – from her eyes.

'Of course it wasn't funny at the time because we thought she might drown in the potty, and oh my, that would be an embarrassing one to have to explain.'

*Embarrassing? Embarrassing? How about downright tragic? This is my untimely death we are talking about here.*

'But now it always makes us chuckle when we think about it, doesn't it, Frank?'

'Oh, it does, Georgina.'

'And I must say it was an indication of what was to come, because as I said, Mac, she always was a liability in water.

Baths, swimming pools, the sea, she was about as buoyant as a giant boulder, the poor thing. Not like her mother at all.'

I gulp down what is left of my shattered pride and then wash it down with the rest of my scalding coffee until the temperature of my insides matches that of my crimson face. The laughter continues, somewhat uneasily on Fi's part, and it is now my turn to stare at the carpet.

What did they come here for anyway? To check up on their errant daughter? To put me down and mock me? To make sure I wouldn't have the confidence to carry off my lead role in case – heaven forbid – they would then be forced to be proud of my achievements? To flirt with *my* surf instructor who already thinks I am some sort of nympho and make him think I am an uncoordinated nympho with a wee-wee fetish? Parents. As Fi so rightly said, it is their prerogative to be embarrassing. Cringingly, toe-curlingly, kill-me-immediately so. I sigh and resign myself to the ritual humiliation.

'I *have to say*, Georgina,' says the one Irish male voice in the room I could not mistake, 'your story makes Milly's achievements while she's been here in County Donegal all the more impressive so.'

I look up at Mac and await the sarcastic put-down. Mac looks at me directly, maintaining eye contact for a brief but meaningful moment. The first eye contact we have shared since that night at the Frankie Doolan concert.

'When Milly first arrived she was fierce scared of the water and scared of it messing up her hair.'

Mac and Fi laugh. I find myself joining in, because I know he is speaking the truth.

'In fact I said to Dave, "Sham," I said, "I have got about as much chance of teaching this city maisie to surf as I have of teaching our dog Eric to do it. Less even. She's a nightmare. And a precious princess of a nightmare at that." That's what I said.'

I scratch my nose, which I can see is turning puce with

218

renewed embarrassment. Was there any need for that? I don't think there was any need for that. Mac runs a hand through his dishevelled curls and presses his lips together.

'Well didn't she just show me up to be the gobshite I am.'

Kathleen sniggers at Mac's use of the word gobshite in front of the guests.

'Milly has faced her fear and thrown herself right in at the deep end so. She doesn't give a feck about her hair and make-up any more . . .'

'I know, it's a shame letting oneself go like that,' my mother tuts.

'No, Georgina, it is not,' Mac replies with a firmness that surprises me. 'Milly has become so . . . so *real*, so *natural* since she got here three months ago. Now sure she is in there catching waves with the rest of my kids, who have been doing it a mighty sight longer. She is determined, enthusiastic, and by God she is high as a kite when she succeeds, which she does. Sure only tonight, Georgina, didn't she just catch a wave by herself, jump to her feet and ride it all the way to the beach like a true surfer.'

'You never did, ya bollix!' Fi shrieks, pulling me into a hug.

Mac rests his elbows on the torn knees of his jeans and nods. Through the locks of hair curling in front of his face, I see the now familiar vibrant green of his eyes that makes my stomach somersault.

'She did, no word of a lie, hey,' he grins, 'and Dave was there to film it all so we have proof. Stood up like a pro she did and turned the board to the left along the wave. I was hoarse from shouting congratulations. A real achievement for a girl who's got a history of drowning, I think you'll agree.'

He finishes with a wink in my direction. I stare at him agog, having just witnessed the longest speech I have ever heard Mac make in public.

'Glory be to God, well isn't that marvellous now,' Mary applauds. 'You must be so proud of your daughter.'

My mother glances at Mary to be sure the comment is aimed at her. I allow myself a victorious smile. 'Proud' and 'daughter' are two words that would not usually be found in the same sentence in our house.

'Erm, why, yes.'

My mother clears her throat and wrinkles her brow, first at Mary then at Mac, suitably chastened by his words and unsure how to deal with such a public bestowal of praise on her daughter.

I look directly at Mac, suddenly more comfortable in his company than I have ever been. I realise at once that despite my many faux pas and cock-ups and humiliating (of my own making) experiences, Mac and I share a connection. The ocean. It may be a liquid connection, but at this moment it feels solid. I mouth a thank you. Thank you for your compliment. Thank you for your patience as my surf teacher. Thank you for not telling them how you pushed me into that wave and how I stood up for all of three seconds before I fell backwards and swallowed half the sea due to overexcitement. No self-deprecation here, I am going to savour this moment for as long as I can.

Which is not long, it seems, as my mother is clearly desperate to change the subject.

'Speaking of daughters, Fiona, do your immediate family live in the town too?'

Fi coughs.

'Ah no, Mrs Armstrong, just Auntie Mary and Uncle Podraig here and my cousins galore. I used to come here on my holidays and remembered it as a wild good place, so I thought Milly would like it. Isn't it grand?'

Dad raises his half-empty glass in a toast, and Podraig promptly refills it.

'So where are the rest of your family? Are they in Dublin, or are yourself and Amelia left to your own devices as it were?'

'Haven't I explained this to you already, Mum?'

220

She shakes her head dismissively and focuses on Fi with her best questioning accountant expression. Fi twiddles a pigtail around her finger and coughs again.

'Well actually, Mrs Armstrong . . .'

I note how there is no instruction to call her Georgina.

'. . . I had a brother but he passed away like, and then my ma and da went abroad when I turned eighteen. They just decided to sell everything and buy a boat and then off they went like. Off to the Caribbean somewhere.'

'Bloody lovely job if you can get it,' my father comments with an admiring tut. 'Better than spending your life trying to solve the miseries and disasters I see in the legal profession day in and day out.'

No one responds, but several Heggartys nod politely. Fi turns to me quickly and grimaces.

'I see. I am sorry about your brother, dear. How did he die?'

'Mum!'

*Has the woman no tact?*

*What am I talking about? This is my mother; of course she has no tact.*

'It's OK, Milly,' says Fi, although I can tell from her face it is not OK. She never talks about her brother so directly.

'Was it an illness, dear?'

'Of a sort,' Fi nods. 'Yes, it was an illness of a sort, but my brother chose to die.'

'Oh,' says my mother, clearly baffled. 'And so you never see your parents, Fiona?'

*Who does she think she is, bloody Trisha?*

'Mum, I really don't think—'

'Amelia, darling, I am just trying to learn a little about your life over here and about your friends. We worry about you. Don't we, Frank?'

My father nods from behind his upturned glass of port.

'And I worry about you. Dad, if your health is not too good, perhaps you shouldn't be drinking so much.'

221

My father looks over at Podraig and raises his eyes to the ceiling, as if to say 'Huh, women, heh!' Podraig rolls his own eyes, which could either be by choice or as a result of the copious amounts of alcohol he is putting away.

'So whereabouts in the Caribbean are your parents, dear? Which island?' my mother continues unabashed.

Fi scratches her head. Her cheeks are reddening by the second.

'Ah well, they're on a boat, you see, so I don't know which island exactly.'

'Anyone for a coffee?' I ask to the air in the centre of the room.

'But roughly where?' my mother persists like a child who has just learned to say 'Why?'

'Tea then anyone?' I try again.

'Actually, Mrs Armstrong, I'm not entirely sure, like, because I don't hear from them that much right now.'

'Oh, really?'

'Yes, really, so I don't . . . I couldn't . . . well, I don't really know . . .'

Suddenly, Podraig strains to raise himself forward in his comfy chair, drinks his tumbler dry, lets out an uninhibited burp and announces, 'Fiona, sure isn't your one, your da, running a bar for air hostesses in Barbados? Aye, that's right, ever since your ma ran off with that pilot with the quare farty name and got herself pregnant. Isn't that so, Mary? A fierce mess it all was at the time, but sure that was ages ago now. What's that pilot bollix called again, Mary?'

The silence in the room settles around us like a heavy velvet cloak. We all stare at Podraig, who is now pouring himself another beaker of an unidentified clear substance in blissful ignorance of the loaded bombshell he has just dropped on his Sunday soirée. Our heads then turn to Mary, who for once in her life is stuck for words and has the sort of look on her face that suggests she would like to shove her husband piece by piece into the now empty bottle and hurl it out to sea.

'Auntie Mary,' Fi prompts, her voice faltering, 'what's he talking about? My ma hasn't had a baby, has she?'

Mary grimaces. Her silence speaks louder than words.

'Auntie Mary?' says Fi, her voice rising in tone and volume. 'Auntie Mary, tell me my ma hasn't had another baby. She's your sister, you must know.'

Mary's podgy hands fiddle with her apron.

'She's replaced me,' Fi gasps. 'She's gone and replaced our Sean and me. Hasn't she, Auntie Mary?'

Mary fights her facial muscles in an attempt to smile and then emits a laugh so fake it could be canned for a television sitcom.

'Hee, ha, hoo, hoo, no, Fiona love, 'course not. Podraig here's just got a wee bit confused.'

'No I flamin' well haven't, Mary,' Podraig splutters. 'What d'ya think I am, hey; thick as a jockey's bollix?'

'Now listen, Podraig . . .' Mary begins.

Our heads are whipping so quickly from side to side I wouldn't be surprised if they came unscrewed from our necks.

'No, I will not listen, Mary Heggarty. You are always the one who knows every bloody thing, aren't ya? Well, don't be goin' making out I'm wild stupid, because I know what I know and I do know that Fiona's ma is shacked up somewhere with that . . . oh, what's his name now?' He gulps his drink. 'Double-barrelled it was, the bollix. Sounds like he's related to the Queen, hey. And sure we've got a postcard from Barbados somewhere upstairs with her da's bar on it and the names of all his fancy women. I'll go and fetch it right now.'

'You will do no such thing, Podraig Heggarty. Now sit your arse on that chair and quit gabbing, would ya? Poor Fiona doesn't need to hear this now.'

She crosses her arms and casts a murderous look at her

husband. Kathleen's mouth is open so wide I can see her tonsils. The adults in the room all stare at the carpet, which has never received so much attention in its (probably lengthy) life.

'Auntie Mary,' Fi prompts again, her voice ever more distant, 'is Uncle Podraig having a joke with us?'

'Yes, Fiona, he's . . .' Mary begins, but her honest face discloses her discomfort. 'Well, in a way he's . . . well, what I mean is . . .'

Mary stops and whispers, 'Holy God.' She closes her eyes as if begging for divine inspiration. Or for a plague of locusts to drag her husband as far away from her wringing hands as possible. She sighs, and when she opens her eyes again, there are tears glistening on her eyelashes.

'Holy God, I can't lie to ya, child,' she says, shaking her head. 'Not any more. There have been enough lies in your family to last you a lifetime, you poor lassie.'

I hold my breath, dreading what is to come.

'No, Fiona, your Uncle Podraig is not after having a joke with ya. Your Uncle Podraig is a drunk bastard with a loose tongue, yes, but he is speaking the truth so.'

Fi's hand shoots up to her mouth and she wobbles on the arm of my chair. I place a hand on the small of her back and gently rub it, not knowing what to say for the second time tonight. My mother looks up and shakes her head in dismay or disgust, I never can tell. My father gulps back his glass of port as if it is a magic potion that will whisk him away to a less awkward domestic situation. Happy holidays.

Mary rubs her hands on her apron and tilts her head at Fiona, whose breathing is now the loudest sound in the room.

'I'm sorry, Fiona, I should have told ya,' Mary sighs, 'but I didn't know how. It wasn't something I could say on the phone and we hadn't been in touch with you at all. And since you got here, ah it's been so fantastic and it just was never the right time. Sure, your mother should have been the one to tell ya this, but she's a coward, Fiona, I'm sorry to say it. My sister has treated you wrong, but that's her business and she's too far away for me to give her a slap so. Maybe she was tryin' to protect her daughter. Maybe they didn't want to upset ya, love, and they didn't want ya to have to live with the shame of their divorce.'

'Divorce!' Fi repeats in a high pitch. 'But how long has this been going on for?'

'Ah, years,' Podraig nods sagely. 'They've been divorced a good five now. Since the baby.'

'WHAT?' Fi almost falls off her chair in shock.

'Podraig, will you button it?' Mary hisses.

'My parents have been divorced for five years, five feckin' years, and I didn't even know. And I have a half-brother or sister in the world who probably hasn't even been told I exist. Jaysus Christ, what kind of a situation is that? And here was I thinking my family couldn't get any more dysfunctional. Shite. They blame me for Sean's death, they leave me with that legacy and fear, and then they feck off and start all over again without me. Why? What did I do?' Fi screeches. 'Jaysus feckin' Christ, my da's a barman for trolley dollies, my ma's a ma for someone else, and shite, I can't believe this.'

She clasps her head in her hands and sobs.

'Fi,' I whisper, pulling her towards me, 'look at me, Fi.'

'Dear God, they're sending me as mad as Sean,' she cries. 'I'm losing it now.'

I hold my friend as tight as I can, feeling her body shake against mine.

'No you're not, Fi. You're stronger than them. You haven't run away from your problems. Hell, you're dealing with them so well you astound me.'

'What problems?' my mother hisses. 'Is she a drug abuser?'

'For heaven's sake, Mum, would you listen to yourself? Just shut up!'

Kathleen has stopped breathing and is chewing her lip so hard she is drawing blood. Mary shuffles across the room, looking defeated, pausing to slap her husband sharply across the top of his balding head.

'Ow, feck, woman, that hurt!'

'Good, ya bollix ya.'

She steps gingerly towards Fiona and attempts to cradle her like a mother would her injured child. Fi gives in for a moment but then I see her body stiffen. She brushes Mary's arms away and stumbles towards the door. She suddenly looks washed out and fragile, like a paper doll left out in the rain.

'It was the shame of it,' Mary tries to explain. 'The divorce and all with the Church, you know.'

'I don't give a flyin' shite about the Church.'

A gasp courses around the room, ending at Kathleen, who is now blue from holding her breath, her eyes as wide as an owl.

'Where was the Church when Sean needed help? I was only fifteen, I couldn't help him on my own, but he wouldn't let me talk to anyone about it. Where were they when we wanted to give him a beautiful funeral day but it was ruined by their bloody shame? They said it was a sin that he killed himself. They let his soul be tainted by their stupid rules and it tore our family apart. Stupid old-fashioned values.' Fi shakes her head. 'Better to forget your shameful family and run off and never come back to your responsibilities and have a mighty fling in the sun than have to admit you failed. Better to hide away and get divorced and have new babies to replace the old ones. Jaysus, this is the twenty-first century, everyone gets bloody divorced.'

'I wouldn't say everyone,' my mother begins before catching the look on my face.

I reach out for Fi's hand that hangs limply by her side. She sobs, a constant stream of tears washing away the glow that her cheeks have had over the past few weeks.

'Do you want to go, Fi? We could go and talk about this at home.'

Fi nods her head and smiles weakly at me with watery eyes.

'Aye, I think I'm going to have to.'

I stand to leave. She places a hand on my shoulder.

'No, Milly, you stay here with your folks. I need to be on my own.'

'But, Fi . . .'

I try to protest, but I can see her mind is made up, and Fi is nothing if not stubborn.

'Don't be letting my little problems ruin your night. I'm old enough to deal with this by myself. It's just, you know, a shock. I didn't know any of this. I have to sort it in my head, you know.'

She blinks slowly as if she has a headache.

'Parents, hey,' she whispers coldly, 'prerogative to embarrass.'

We all watch in silence as Fi turns robotically and walks away. It is several minutes, but feels like hours, before someone speaks again.

'I love your curtain material, Mary,' my mother says, employing the age-old English rule of brushing the subject under the carpet. 'Is it chintz?'

# CHAPTER TWENTY-TWO

## *Rain*

I try to bring the evening to a hasty conclusion, but it takes all my strength to drag my father away from the flowing river of alcohol at the Heggartys', despite the now sober atmosphere in the house. I deposit my parents at their hotel and make my way home, by which time it is raining cats and dogs. Big ones. With big teeth and claws. I race down Main Street, impressed by my raised level of fitness but cursing my decision not to wear a waterproof jacket. My mother advised me to wear one at the start of the evening, so of course I flatly refused. Which was rather mature of me.

By the time I reach Pooh Corner I look like an entrant for a wet T-shirt competition (only without the perfect silicone boobs) and my jeans are sticking to my legs like an extra layer of clammy skin. All the lights in the house are off so I position myself under the double row of tiles that are failing miserably as a porch, where I search for my keys. Not that this is a lengthy process considering the fact that I have no bag, no jacket and only four small pockets in my trousers. I also have prior knowledge of the fact that I didn't pick up my keys from where I left them on the table inside when I pulled the door shut in my haste to collect my parents. I search anyway. In vain.

Peering through the kitchen window, I spy my keys lying

in a bunch next to my snug waterproof jacket and my mobile phone. I wipe the window and look for Fi's runners, which would invariably be discarded somewhere in the middle of the room along with her coat. I see nothing except the Sunday papers scattered across the floor in Fi's usual haphazard manner. I wonder whether she spotted my keys on the table when she came home and whether she thought to leave me the spare. The house is eerily silent, which surprises me because Fi, being such an erratic sleeper, would not usually have fallen asleep in the time it has taken me to get home. She needs at least an hour or two to wind her mind down to normal speed. And then another hour to decide what she is going to dream about. I guess tonight is different. God knows I am exhausted by the events of the evening so it must be ten times worse for Fi. I feel a deep pang of regret that I did not accompany my friend home. I should have been there for her. She needed me more than my drunken mother and positively steaming father. Damn, hasn't she been there for me more than my parents ever have been? Why did I not walk her home? Am I a bad friend?

'Damn, where are you, bloody key?' I sneeze into the rain.

Not under the doormat. Not under the solitary brick positioned next to the front step. Not on top of the doorframe. Just call me the master of glaringly obvious hiding places. *Crimestoppers* would be appalled.

I sigh and rap lightly on the door, loath to wake Fi but also knowing that if I stay out in this downpour much longer the only role I will be playing will be a pneumonia case on *Casualty*. When there is no sound from inside the house I knock louder, then louder still. Finally I knock until my knuckles turn white and the wood creaks under the pressure but there is still no reply.

'Fi,' I call out, 'can you let me in?'

Nothing.

'Atishoo!'

I have to keep moving or this incessant shivering will

propel me into the ground like a pneumatic drill. How can it be so cold? It is May, for heaven's sake. Common sense informs me that as our bedroom is at the other side of the house facing the sea, it would be better to attract Fiona's attention from there.

*Good one, Einstein.*

I run down the side of Pooh Corner, gasping to catch my breath when the onshore wind blasts against my wet clothes. If only cagoules were still in fashion. A little orange number attached to my belt in its very own front pocket/carry pouch would be just the ticket right now. Listen to me, for goodness' sake, I'm becoming hysterical.

I hop up and down beside the railing on the sea wall, my boots splashing in the river of seawater that has made its way over the defences. The swell has picked up a little even since my lesson earlier and the tide is at its biggest because of the full moon that controls it. I have learned that since I came here. I allow myself a smile at my new knowledge and then strain my neck to peer up towards the bedroom window. The curtains are open, which hits me as strange because Fi has a phobia about sleeping when the moon can still see her. Frighteningly werewolfy, I know, but she has these peculiar notions. I holler, I yell, but the house remains as silent and dark as those along the rest of the small terrace, most of which are holiday rentals or weekend houses for people in the North who come on a Friday and will be well on their way back to Derry and Belfast by now. I give shouting one last try and then I decide to do what the star-crossed lovers do in the movies. Scooping up a handful of wet stones that will have been deposited over the wall by the waves, I toss them against the upstairs windowpane.

Well, I aim for a toss, but in my desperation I assume the strength of Fatima Whitbread's throwing arm and the toss becomes more of a bloody great chuck. Hence the hole in the window where a single stone penetrates and the network of cracks that is working its way across the surface like a map of the London Underground. That doesn't happen in the movies. Although I realise as I stand here with my mouth open that if I don't get out of the way quick those shards of broken glass are very likely to come raining down on top of me like one of the gruesome scenes in *The Omen*. I also realise that if Fi were inside, she would surely have woken up by now with all the racket I have been creating. Unless of course . . .

*No, Milly, don't even think that.*

Fi wouldn't do . . . that . . . would she? She knows how much it hurts the people left behind. She wouldn't. Would she? A shiver runs up my spine to collide with the many rivulets of chills gushing down it.

'She can't be in there,' I tell myself as I dodge the spray from a wave.

Biting my lip in thought, I begin to make my way back up the alleyway next to the house. I put my head down and march purposefully, trying to warm myself and leaving a trail of droplets from the end of my nose as I go.

'Bloody hell, why didn't I bring my mobile phone?' I curse out loud.

'Who is it ye need to call so?'

The solitary male voice makes me jump so high I practically have to peel myself off the roof. I squint into the darkness ahead of me, shaking with both fear and cold. My already icy limbs are suddenly frozen stiff and my heart thumps in my chest as loud as the heavy raindrops slapping on the ground around me.

'H . . . hello?' My voice is a whisper.

*Show no fear, Milly; don't let him know you're scared.*

'Hellooo, who's there?'

'The name's Billy.'

The man steps out of the shadows with an outstretched hand that, I am glad to deduce, is not holding an axe.

'I'm the Gárda,' he says politely, 'and I'm after comin' ta

check out the sound of breakin' glass. Now ye wouldn't be happenin' ta have anything to do with that, would ye, hey?'

A policeman! Praise the Lord, hallelujah and thank heavens I went to church two weeks ago. This must be my reward. I quickly scan the man's uniform before fervently shaking his hand. If I weren't still close to tears I would probably laugh.

'Oh, am I pleased to see you, Mr . . . Officer . . . Constable . . .?'

'Ah, 'tis just Billy.'

'Right. Billy. Goodness, you see I am locked out and I thought my friend was inside so I tried to get her attention and, whoops, smashed the window by mistake. Silly me, sorry.'

He eyes me suspiciously at first and then his gaunt face offers a half-smile. He extricates his hand from mine and massages his squashed palm with the other. I didn't even realise I was still holding it.

'Ah no, don't be sorry ta me, Miss . . .?'

'What? Oh, Armstrong, Milly Armstrong.'

'You're not from around here, are ye, I'd say?'

*Give the man a medal. Was it the plummy English accent that gave me away perhaps?*

I shake my head.

'OK now, Milly, just follow me.'

Billy leads the way back up the alleyway and towards the welcoming shelter of his slightly battered squad car. I slide into the front seat and quickly check my reflection in the sun visor mirror, wiping away mascara and rain before deciding to cut my losses and just avoid any reflective surfaces. I am not, I conclude, a natural beauty.

The car smells of coffee emanating from an open thermos flask next to the gear stick. A half-eaten jam doughnut tempts my taste buds from the dashboard and the warmth makes me aware of how cold and wet I feel. Billy settles himself in the seat beside me and reaches for a black-leather-covered notebook. He turns to a fresh page and – I didn't know people actually did this – licks the end of his pencil before posing his first question.

'So, Milly Armstrong, this wouldn't be your house now, would it?'

'No, it belongs to my friend Fiona's aunt and uncle. Mary and Podraig Heggarty,' I pronounce slowly.

'Ah sure Mary and Podraig. Me da is Podraig's first cousin. Or at least he was until he died.'

'Oh . . .'

'But Holy God,' Billy continues nonchalantly as if he has just informed me of the death of his budgie, 'it's a fierce wet 'n' dreary night for a maisie like yerself to be out on her own, Milly. Would you like me ta break the door down for ye?'

I glance at the Gárda's lean physique and think I would probably have more chance of bashing the door down than he would. Besides, the door has been there so long I wouldn't be surprised if it were a treasured artefact. I shake my head.

'No, it's fine honestly. If I could perhaps borrow a phone to call the Heggartys?'

He subconsciously places a hand on his radio as if to protect it from civilian intrusion.

'Um, OK then, what about if you help me track down my friend, that would be perfect. In fact, oh, she will probably hate me for telling you all this, but I am really worried about her. You see she got some bad news tonight and she was upset, so I don't like to think of her out on her own.'

'Bad news, ye say.' Billy nods, noting my words on his pad at a very slow pace. 'Did somebody die?'

'Pardon? No, nobody died. Well, not recently anyway.'

'Murdered?'

'Excuse me?'

'Badly wounded? Tortured?'

*The man's obsessed with death, for Christ's sake. He obviously doesn't get enough action around these parts.*

'Missin'?' Billy adds with somewhat less enthusiasm.

'Missing! Yes! My friend Fiona is missing, Billy. One hundred per cent missing.'

'Well, that's grand,' he beams, scribbling in his notebook.

I cough and glance uneasily at him out of the corner of my eye. I hope he is a real policeman. If not, I have to admit it is a bloody good disguise with the car and everything.

'So now, what does this friend of yours look like herself, Fiona?'

'I'm Milly, she's Fiona.'

'Right.'

'OK, well . . .'

I describe Fi in as much detail as I can while Billy meticulously notes it all down. He sticks his tongue between his teeth while he writes and concentrates intensely on the end of the pencil. His writing is the opposite of shorthand, painfully slow and laboured, and I am aware of the time ticking by on the dashboard clock. In fact, long after I finish talking, Billy is still making notes, his nose moving closer to the pad with every stroke. I feel a wave of impatience surging in my throat. If Fiona is out there somewhere then shouldn't we be out looking for her? Can't the paperwork wait until after we have done some groundwork? I drum my fingers on my knees and count to . . . gosh, I've lost count. The clock ticks and the radio crackles. The rain drums heavily on the car roof, resounding like Chinese torture in my head. Still he writes.

*Hurry up!* I want to scream. *What are you, a fucking retard?*

Of course I keep my thoughts to myself, but by the time the Gárda looks up from his notes and slowly licks the end of his pencil, I am on the verge of insanity.

'Well now,' he sighs, flicking through the pages and nodding his head, 'I am almost sure that I saw your woman just a half-hour ago standin' up there on the edge of the headland.'

My mouth slowly opens until my bottom jaw is almost resting on my wet knees.

'What? You saw Fiona, you say? Up on the cliff?'

'Aye, I did that. Sure I knew it was her from the moment ye started your description.'

*That was ages ago! Jesus Christ, the man is a lunatic.*

'Small, pretty thing with pigtails. Aye, that was her. Now I did stop and offer her a lift but she said she was grand.'

*Probably because she knew better than to get in a car with a death-obsessed fruit loop like you.*

'Mind ye' – he taps his nose – 'I knew she had been cryin', hey. I can tell these things from my trainin'. Nothin' gets by this brain.'

*Other than important electrical impulses and intelligence, you mean?*

'But what was she doing standing on the edge of a cliff crying, Billy?' I pronounce each word slowly. 'Was she OK? She didn't look like' – I swallow before I can continue – 'like she was going to *jump*, did she?'

The policeman laughs.

'Ah don't be daft, Milly, nothin' that exciting happens around here.'

I swear if he weren't a policeman I would smash his stupid face in.

A mixture of my building impatience, trepidation, disbelief and helplessness threatens to blow the top of my head off. I am just trying to put these feelings into appropriate words when the radio crackles into life calling for immediate assistance to a death. My eyes freeze into wide spheres. I am unable to speak or move or breathe. Despite my silence, Billy shushes me with a raised palm and springs (a very slow spring) into action.

'Ah, Jaysus,' he sighs a moment later, a look of both excitement and mock-distress on his pale face, 'that's wild bad news that is.'

*WHAT? WHAT?*

I feel as if I am about to hyperventilate.

'We've got a dead one all right,' he nods, failing to conceal the smile on his lips.

My hand flies to my mouth and I whimper.

'Sure isn't a dog after bein' run over on the Sligo road by some eejit tinker in a van. I'll bet ye that's wee Dervla O'Neill's puppy now and I'll have to go scrapin' all the bits off the road.' His eyes sparkle at the thought. 'Feck it, Dervla only got the poor wee thing a while back. I noted it down. When was it now?'

Billy begins to flick through the dreaded notebook to recount the life history of Dervla O'Neill's dog in, I imagine, very slow, very irritating detail, but I am already away. Out of the car and into the drenching rain. Now I am running past Pooh Corner and along the waterfront towards the headland.

*I haven't got time for Dervla's dead dog, Billy, I have to find Fiona. I have to find her now.*

# CHAPTER TWENTY-THREE

# *Undercurrent*

The full moon lights my path as I run, the refraction of the light making the raindrops look like glittering crystals. My feet are soon heavy and sodden, my footsteps drowned out by the thundering orchestra of the waves, the wind and a downpour. Mother Nature can be bloody noisy when she wants to be. I race on along the waterfront to the bottom of Main Street, where I turn left and urge my legs on up towards the headland. I am breathless but still able to call Fi's name into the night. My attempts are in vain, however, as my voice is swept away in the storm, which is growing in its intensity. I charge on.

When I reach the top of the headland, the rain surrounds me like panes of glass. I pass the bench from where Fi and I watched Mac catch his twenty-foot tube. I look frantically around me and then, ignoring the faded *Danger! Cliff Edge* sign, clamber over the low fence that lines the path and make my way out to the last few inches of rock. My heart is beating rapidly, afraid of what I may find when I peer over the edge. I am also aware that a sudden strong gust of wind could blow me off the cliff and smash me to smithereens on the rocks below, just like Mac's surfboard. Crouching down on my haunches, I grasp a few long blades of grass as a safety precaution and cautiously look down. The reef is almost covered by the high tide, just a sliver of shiny black rock left below to inform me that any fall would be a hard one. The waves are not huge, but look messy and cold, a visual depiction of the wind itself. I call Fi's name again and scan the grassy cliff. I pat the ground, feeling for footprints or some sort of clue as to where she could have gone.

'Where are you, Fi?' I cry out, but there is still no response.

My stomach lurches when I stand to stretch my legs and my left foot slips on a patch of mud. I am dangerously close to the steep drop but my mind is focused solely on my best friend. Why was she standing up here on her own in the rain? Why did that bloody Gárda not pull her back from danger? What was going through Fi's mind? I kick myself for letting her go home alone. I should not have let her get her own way so easily. She may act tough and wear the mask of a happy-go-lucky person, but inside she is fragile and scared. Scared of life in general and scared of being alone.

'I'm sorry, Fi,' I shout into the wind. 'I should have come with you tonight. I'm so sorry!'

As if in a mocking response, a gust of wind forces my limp, tired body off balance. I gasp and reach out but find nothing except rain and air to hold on to. I slip and slide and finally fall, my legs splayed out in front of me. One foot comes to rest in mid-air over the edge of the headland. My hands sink into the mud and I collapse backwards, my head hitting the wet ground in relief.

'God Almighty, Milly, what the Jaysus are you doing? You nearly had yourself over that cliff, for feck's sake!'

Mac's strong voice is music to my ears, blasting out of the darkness like the voice of the Angel Gabriel. I lie still and hear his footsteps thump towards me. Now he is above me, reaching out to me, but I cannot move. My whole body is numb.

'It's Fi,' I croak over and over again, 'we have to help her.'

'Maybe so, but first we have to help you, so come on now.'

He pulls me up and leads me to his car that is parked on the kerb with the engine running and the heating on. He bundles me into the front seat and, ever the organised lifeguard, wraps a thick tartan blanket tightly around me. The wool itches my face but encourages limited sensation to return to my limbs. Mac explains how he was on his way to meet Dave in Gallagher's to let him know what had happened to Fi at dinner. As he talks, my eyes flit towards the clock. It is a quarter past twelve.

'You just have to know the right knock on the pub door,' Mac smiles softly.

Imagine. A lock-in at a cosy pub. What a welcoming thought. Fi, Dave, Mac and me warming ourselves beside a real peat fire and lining our chilled stomachs with a meal of frothy Guinness. The thought makes a perfect picture in my mind. How I would love to be in that picture right now, not out in the rain in the middle of the night wondering if I will ever see my best friend again.

I squeeze my eyes shut and only open them again when I feel a hand squeeze mine. Mac and I exchange weighted glances before I in turn explain to him what has just happened, from the smashing of the window to Billy the Gárda and my race to the headland.

'Ach, the man's a quare eejit, so he is,' Mac tuts in annoyance. 'Sure he wanted to join the army but they didn't trust the man with a gun.'

*Thank God.*

Mac is attentive and reassuringly calm. He quickly assimilates all the information, tells me not to panic and assures me that we will find Fi. As if he in fact *were* the Angel Gabriel, I believe him. I suppose in the same way that his fit body is part of his job description, his capacity to take emergencies in his stride must be too. Mac turns the car heater up to full blast and dials Dave's number on his mobile.

'Check the main beach as you're close so,' he politely orders his friend after swiftly summarising the crisis, 'and we'll head up to the Strand. Meet us there, Dave, if you don't . . . if you don't find . . . you know. Thanks a million.'

Mac distractedly pats my knee before shifting the four-wheel-drive into gear and pulling away. His presence is so comforting. I feel myself slowly drifting into a daze while we drive, my eyes blurring as I stare at the repetitive swish, swish of the windscreen wipers. My stomach is knotted by the fear that comes with the thought of losing someone as precious as Fi. Of course I knew she was special before this, but this moment makes me realise just how special. Day to day she is my family and I am hers. We help to fill the gaps left by our own families that have somehow failed us, even, in the case of my own family, in small, seemingly insignificant ways. I just wish I hadn't failed her tonight.

We reach the Strand in no time at all. Mac pulls into a parking space at the end of the beach on the top of the cliff and kills the engine while leaving the lights on full beam.

'Wait here,' he tells me before hopping out of the car and striding purposefully forwards in the headlights, his head dipped against the wind. I cough, I sneeze and I shake my head all at once.

'No,' I tell the empty inside of the car, 'I'm coming too.'

The Strand is a sandy beach at the north end of the town, separated from the main beach by another thirty-foot-tall headland where the coastline turns at a ninety-degree angle. We stand on the cliff at one end and stare out at the two miles of golden sand stretching ahead of us up to the next town. This could almost be a tropical paradise were the weather not quite so Arctic. And the circumstances not so tragic.

'Sure I told you to wait in the car,' says Mac firmly before reaching an arm around my shoulder and pulling me into the warm crook of his elbow. I numbly let myself be hugged.

'You maisies,' he sighs, 'nothing but trouble, hey.'

240

I smile weakly and follow Mac's eyeline as he turns to scan the expansive beach below. The rain is almost horizontal now, blasting into our eyes with the full force of the wind, but I am so wet and exhausted already, it does not seem to bother me any longer. I must be like a waterlogged sponge, unable to absorb any more moisture.

'Can you see anything, Mac? Can you see her?'

Mac gives a noncommittal shrug.

'I think we're gonna have to go down on the beach, it's too dark to see. Come on, let's keep 'er lit.'

I frown.

'I mean let's get a move on, it's feckin' pissing down.'

We turn our backs to the wind to make our way back to the car, just as another set of headlights appears beside Mac's four-wheel-drive.

'Dave!' I cry out, releasing myself from Mac's grasp and quickening my pace. 'Was she there? Did you find anything?'

Dave jogs up to us, pulling a jacket on over his head.

'Nothin' at all, Milly,' he replies grimly, 'and sure this weather is desperate. It's hard to see anythin', especially in the dark. Any joy here?'

His face is pale and set into a worried frown. His lips form a firm straight line when Mac informs him that we can't see anything from the cliff and will have to make our way down on to the beach. As Dave sprints back to his car to grab his rucksack, I realise that he is as worried about Fi as I am. He has strong feelings for her, that much is obvious.

We bypass the safe beach path that winds down the hillside, opting instead for the sharp drop that is the fastest route from A to B. Dave lights the way with a torch he retrieves from his car and we slip and slide downwards, taking care to avoid the large eroded holes in the rock that show the sea down below and that are quaintly termed the Fairy Bridges. We don't say a word the whole way down but I know that in each of our heads, silent prayers are occupying our thoughts.

Once on the sand, we begin to run down the beach, all the time looking left out to sea and right towards the adjacent sand dunes. We work well as a team, keeping each other calm and reassured, despite the desperation we all feel inside. We carefully check every inch of the Strand and I am immeasurably grateful for the presence of my two new friends. We call out Fi's name, and Dave sweeps the area with the torch beam like a lighthouse scanning for distressed ships. Mac is tall and can see further than I can, so I keep my head down in the rain and look at the ground. It is then that I find Fi's shoe.

'Oh my God, her runner!' I wheeze, grasping the familiar shoe to my chest and feeling tears of confusion and distress bursting from my eyes to mix with the raindrops.

'Are you sure?' Mac asks.

'Of course I'm sure.' I am almost shouting. 'These are her favourite, Mac. Her favourite glittery pink Diesel ones. She would never leave this behind, Mac, she loves these shoes. Oh God, she can't have . . .'

Dave takes the shoe and nods.

'It's hers all right.'

He stares at it intently, as if trying to speak to the spirit within.

'But no, she can't have,' Dave carries on, his voice quavering. 'She has no reason to do . . . *that*. She wouldn't. Not my Fi. Why would she?'

I gasp as a single heavy tear rolls down Dave's cheek. I want to hold him, to tell him everything will be all right. That his Fi will be fine. But I can't, because I don't know that everything will be OK, and if I hug Dave now I know I will lose control of my own emotions that are threatening to tear my heart in two.

'Milly,' says Dave, looking at me with hurt in his eyes, 'why do ya think Fi would kill herself? I don't understand.'

We stare at each other for a moment. I can hear Mac's heavy breaths above the wind. I blink in the darkness and

242

concentrate my focus on the shoe that seems to have lost its usual sparkle. I begin slowly.

'It's just everything Fi found out tonight, about her parents being divorced and her mother's new baby and everything. It would be enough to destroy a much stronger person than Fi.'

Mac wraps his arms around my shoulders from behind. I am shaking from cold, fear and adrenalin. He says nothing but I hear a silent reassurance. Even the storm seems to have lowered its volume in respect as we gather around Fi's lost shoe. The moon is trying to brighten the night but all I can feel is the darkness closing in around us.

'Fi always had this unrealistic view of her family,' I continue in a whisper, 'that one day it would be back together like the Heggartys, full of fun and the usual family ups and downs. I know deep down she knew it would never happen, but while her parents were away somewhere unknown, I think it was just easier for her to pretend that they would come back and then so would Sean and they would live happily ever after.'

'She's such a dreamer,' Dave remarks lovingly, 'like a cub with a magical imagination.'

'Daydreaming is safer for Fi than real life,' I shrug. I clear my throat before saying the next words. 'Sean, her brother, he committed suicide when Fi was fifteen.'

Dave grips the runner so tight I can see the white bones of his knuckles through the skin. I plough on, never daring to look into Dave's eyes as I speak.

'He was a year older than Fi and had been bullied for years about his red hair and other stupid, unimportant things. He was clever and got high grades and he was always a bit different.'

'Unique,' Dave corrects me, 'like my Fi.'

I nod. 'He told Fi about the bullying but he made her promise not to tell anyone. So, true to her word, she didn't, but then she came home from school one day and when herself and Sean were alone in the house he hung himself. She found him.'

'Dear God,' Mac breathes.

Dave takes a sharp inhalation of breath.

'Fi tried to save Sean but he was already dead. Of course she blamed herself, and when her parents found out about the bullying, they hit out and blamed her too. They were all angry, I guess, and needed someone to blame. So the family fell apart and Fi found herself alone most of the time. She told me she would lie awake worrying about it happening to her. She thought the depression and the suicide would run in the family, that it would happen to her too eventually. As if it was a foregone conclusion.'

'But that's so wrong,' Dave cries. 'The poor girl just needed help and support. Shite, it's no wonder she was depressed going through all that on her own. Jaysus, why didn't she explain it to me? I would have helped.'

'She's scared of getting close to men in case . . . well, in case you go away too.'

'I can understand that,' says Mac very close to my right ear.

I rub his arm gently. He has not confided in me about his best friend's death, but his words let me know how he has felt since Nicky died so out of the blue. Bloody hell, why does no one ever tell us when we are young how frightening and complicated life can become if we don't learn how to share our burdens?

I wipe wet locks of hair from my eyes and peer at Dave through the rain. His face is as pale as Jimmy the postmaster's. His shoulders are slumped and he is hugging Fi's shoe as if it is a winning Lotto ticket.

'I just thought you should know it all,' I end meekly, wondering whether I have done the right thing or just made things worse.

'Thanks,' says Dave, looking directly at me.

I feel suddenly very close to my two Donegal friends.

'She didn't deserve this, Milly,' Dave murmurs weakly, 'my Fi didn't deserve any of this.'

I place my hand over his and leave it there for a moment, but Dave suddenly lifts his arm and hurls Fi's shoe into the sand. He clasps his hands around his head as if to protect himself. Mac lets me go and races to his friend's side. He bends down to console Dave, but as he does so, his head whips up and he peers towards the horizon.

'What is it, Mac?' I ask when he doesn't move. He is still, like a preying hawk waiting to dive.

Keeping his eyes on the ocean, Mac slowly straightens up and then races towards the waterline. There is a moment of total silence.

'I SEE HER!' he shouts suddenly. 'I SEE HER. SHE'S OUT THERE!'

Dave and I try to run, but our emotional exhaustion is evident as our legs give way in the soft sand. By the time we reach Mac, he has already removed his jumper and shoes. He assumes the role of lifeguard naturally. His eyes never once leave the point he has identified out at sea. I look at him for a brief moment and then start to remove my shoes too.

'What are you doing, Milly?'

His eyes don't leave their target.

'I'm bloody well coming with you, what does it look like?'

'No way, maisie,' he shouts over the wind. 'This is my job. Now I don't want to be saving the both of yous.'

We are in the water now, the biting cold water stinging my ankles.

'She's my friend,' I gasp, 'I have to be here for her. So can we stop bloody debating and just get on with it?'

Mac curses into mid-air, tells Dave to wait for Fi on the beach in case he needs back-up and charges ahead. He dives into the water and powers away from me like a torpedo set on its course to destruction.

'But Milly, you're scared of the water,' Dave pleads from the beach behind me.

'I'm not scared,' I say, my voice lost somewhere in my tightening throat. 'I am not scared.'

'Milly,' Dave calls helplessly, but I am now up to my waist, my arms raised high to subconsciously delay the moment I have to plunge them beneath the surface.

I plough on, straining my eyes in the moonlight to catch a glimpse of my friend. Finally I see her, a small, desperate-looking figure, struggling in the chest-deep froth.

'FI!' I shout. 'It's me, Milly. Oh God, Fi, come back. Don't do it. We need you. Please, Fi, we love you. Don't kill your-self!'

# CHAPTER TWENTY-FOUR

## *Water Rescue*

'I'm not gonna feckin' kill myself, ya big eejit,' Fi splutters as I drag myself within earshot, 'but if you pair of useless bollix don't hurry up and help I might be ending up killed at this rate.'

'It's all right, sham,' Mac shouts back to an anxious Dave, 'she's fine. It's a dolphin!'

'A what?' I shriek as I fight the whitewater that so obviously wants to send me back to land with a bump. 'Let me see it. Where is it?'

'In my bloody arms,' Fi calls back. Her features are now clear in the moonlight and I see the look of weariness mixed with excitement in her eyes.

My friend. Thank God.

I reach them through a combination of heaving myself over the smaller waves, diving under the larger ones and occasionally performing a kind of doggy paddle/front crawl when there is a section of flatter water. Exhausted and out of breath, I grab Mac's arm and pull myself upright, glancing at his face and then at my best friend's.

'Fucking hell, Fi, you gave me a fright. I was really worried about you. What were you doing standing on a cliff in the rain?'

'Watching this little fella and his family,' she replies with a broad grin.

I glance down as the dark object in Fi's arms emits a sound that is somewhere between a squeal and a cackle.

'Oh my God!' I gasp, amazed that I didn't notice it before. 'It's a dolphin.'

My voice becomes quiet with the awe of seeing such a magical creature at such close proximity. I cover my mouth and stare through the raindrops dripping from my eyelashes.

I wouldn't profess to being a specialist in estimating marine mammal ages, but this dolphin looks like a baby of the species. He appears big enough in Fi's arms, but I imagine he could fit in most household baths with a little room to spare. His coat – is that what it is called, or would it be his skin? Well, he is predominantly grey in colour, the moonlight glistening off his rounded back, making patterns of the water droplets settling there. I notice how on closer inspection he is marked with small scratches and grooves. Hardly surprising really, considering he has to deal with the rough and tumble of the ocean every day. I have had more bumps and bruises in the last three months than I managed to accumulate throughout my childhood (even with Ed constantly whacking me around the head with heavy objects like Swingball racquets just to be annoying). I gaze at the dolphin's curved dorsal fin that stands proud on his back, and the smooth rounded tip of his nose. He is perfect. Almost too beautiful to be real.

'He's amazing,' I coo while the rain lashes down around our open sea party.

'He's dying,' Fi answers matter-of-factly, 'unless we can help the poor wee thing. Here, Mac, will you hold him for a minute. Jaysus, thanks a million, my arms are dead tired.'

I watch as Mac slowly takes the baby dolphin in his arms and supports it in the water. It makes a vain attempt to struggle but then lies still, producing what I interpret as a whimpering sound in dolphin language. I frown and reach out one hand to touch him while wiping my stinging eyes with the other. My fingers run over his coat, which is both silky and rough in patches. He doesn't protest. My hand stops when my fingertips reach the hard object that is alien to the dolphin's texture.

'What is that?' I ask Mac.

'A fishing net, or what's left of one. The poor thing's got it all wrapped around him, so he has. He must have swum into it and got a bit tangled so.'

Fi nods sadly, steadying herself as a wave crashes against her side.

'I was watching the whole pod from the cliff path there,' she explains over the wind. 'I walked all the way round from Pooh Corner, I just didn't want to let them out of my sight like. They were so fantastic, Milly. A whole family of them swimming along together, and the moon was so bright that I could see them even in this desperate weather. I know it was probably daft, but I felt so miserable and there was something magical about them that cheered me up. They made my worries seem miles away. But then we got round here and I saw a bit of a commotion and some splashing and then this little thing was struggling. Jaysus, I didn't know what to do, but I ran down on to the beach, and then, would you believe it, he got washed up on the bloody shore. He couldn't swim at all for the net around his fins and he was just lying there staring at me with his little black eyes. I nearly had kittens so I did. I just looked at him and then thought, feck, I've got to get him back in the water. His family left him and there was just me here. I've been here for bloody ages just trying to sort him out. Thank God yous came to find me.'

I reach out and stroke Fi's arm. I can feel she is shivering under her wet clothes, which are becoming wetter still the longer we stay out here in the sea.

'Right then, let's sort little Flipper out,' I say determinedly, happy to be turning my attention to the welfare of a baby mammal rather than the life and death of my best friend. I can deal with this.

'Just tell us what to do, Mac, and we'll do it,' I continue firmly. 'Let's save him and send him home.'

We listen to our instructions from Mac the water man and then spring into action, each of us assuming a role. Despite the lead weight of my legs, I make my way back to shore, where I update Dave. His relief is visible when I tell him Fi is OK. It may just be the rain, but I swear I see tears in his eyes and he lets out a breath so long he must have been holding it since we arrived. Dave lowers his torch, unhooks his backpack from his shoulders and delves inside.

'I always keep this bag in the car,' he says, producing a Leatherman tool and his trusty video camera. 'Sure, ya never know when it'll come in handy round these parts.'

'Not another dodgy video for postmaster Jimmy,' I laugh, relieved to have an excuse for humour after tonight's events. 'What is it this time, *Flipper* the porno version? *Slippery When Wet*?'

'Something like that so,' Dave smirks.

He takes off the lens cap and raises the tiny camera to his eye.

'You and that bloody video camera,' I tut, slipping the Leatherman into my pocket. 'You must be good at filming by now, the amount of practice you get. It's never out of your hands.'

'Ah, I'm not bad at all. And I can't be goin' missin' this moment, now can I? Now, Milly Armstrong, would ya like to give us a quick summary of the mission?'

Back out to sea, we work to cut the net from Flipper's body, taking care not to damage him any more than he already has been by man's carelessness. The rain eases while we work and the tide drops back until we are standing comfortably in the water. The moon and stars provide our torch. It is as if Mother Nature is playing her part in saving one of her children. The atmosphere between us all is electric. Thankfully metaphorically so, considering we are waist deep in water. Mac's composure, however, is a calming influence and we follow all his politely given instructions. At last I cut the final string of the net and Fi drags the tangled mess away from the dolphin. It cackles appreciatively but softly, obviously weakened by the unnerving and I imagine painful experience of being tied up and beached. Mac strokes the dolphin with a tenderness that surprises me. I watch him through the spray carried on the wind. His incredibly green eyes focus on the little creature without distraction. Beneath the wet curls that hang over his forehead, his brow is wrinkled with concern. He bites his bottom lip while he concentrates and cradles one strong arm around the dolphin's back the way he cradled my shoulders earlier. He rolls the dolphin tenderly in the water to ease its battered body, then begins to softly massage its fins and holds it under its belly while slowly propelling it through the water as if teaching it to swim.

Fi and I watch, entranced by Mac's patience and control of the situation and by his gentle side, which in the intensity of the moment he does not try to conceal. My stomach churns, but not because of the hunger and cold that will undoubtedly soon grip me from the inside out. It churns at the thought of how wonderful this man is. He may be confusing at times, and weathered by both the elements and the things he has experienced in life, but he is also able and genuine, patient and caring, and he never ceases to amaze me. What was it he once said to me? That saving people was his job? Mac could not save Nicky and has been making up for it ever since. And not content with saving humans, he has now moved on to sea life. I doubt Dan Clancy would be out here in the cold, wet dead of night trying to help a baby dolphin fight its way back to health, never mind to help me search for Fi in the first place. No, Dan would be tucked up in bed with a generous lathering of beauty products on his undoubtedly beautiful face, learning the lines of his latest film project and gazing at studio pictures of himself in glossy magazines. Mac, on the other hand, is here, and he is making a difference. I am overwhelmed with a sudden urge to kiss those lips he bites in concentration, but I have been there before and I am not going to make that mistake again.

I follow Mac into slightly deeper water while Fi, who is now shivering so much I can hear her teeth clanking together, makes her way back to the beach and to Dave. I manoeuvre myself around Flipper's desperately flailing tail and position myself on the opposite side from Mac. I glance up at him. Our eyes momentarily connect and our fingers touch under the dolphin's belly. Mac releases his lip and turns his mouth up in a gentle smile. I return the smile, and without a word we cradle the dolphin together and turn its nose towards the horizon. I stroke its back and crouch to whisper reassurances that I am sure Flipper does not understand but which I hope will help to calm him. We slowly stride deeper into the water. Up to my ribs. Now as far as my chest. Now the water is chilling my shoulders.

'Are you all right, Milly?' Mac asks repeatedly.

I nod and smile, gasping occasionally as the icy water moves higher up my body. Mac is still standing with ease, clearly comfortable in the depth. I, however, reach the point where I have to let my feet leave the sandy bottom of the ocean. I am no longer in my depth. I am treading water, kicking, breathing hard and telling myself not to panic. Beside me, the dolphin wriggles as if telling himself the same. Mac also lifts his feet and lies horizontal in the water. Now we are swimming together, just the three of us, Mac, Flipper and me. We are picking up speed, charging through the waves. Behind us we can hear calls of support from the beach. The rain is clearing and the moon reassuringly lights the water around us.

I shudder when a shadow appears in front of us, even darker than the already murky water. My hand slips but Mac catches my wrist in time and efficiently nudges it back up towards the dolphin's dorsal fin. I squeeze my mouth shut to stop any water getting in and stare straight ahead. Beneath the surface, my legs manically tread water as if I am trying to ride a bike up a Pyrenean col in the Tour de France.

*Do you get sharks in Ireland? Well I'm about to find out.*

Just twenty feet away, a sharp-edged fin rises out of the water. I almost wet myself and stiffly turn my head to raise my eyebrows at Mac. My jaw is frozen shut. Mac's face is still the image of calmness. He tips his head at me in a single nod and then turns to look forward again. I do the same, clutching the quivering little dolphin to my side. The moment I turn my head, the menacing fin is joined by another and then another until we are almost surrounded by a circle of fins, jutting out of the water like the bars of a prison. I don't feel panic but a strange sense of resolute calm. Nevertheless my heart is in my mouth, apparently about to become my last meal before I am torn to shreds by a pack of hungry sharks.

It is only when the first fin rises higher out of the water that I see the shape of the body attached to it. Not pointed and deadly looking the way I imagine a shark to be, but a curved head tipped by a rounded snout. The line of the mouth that curves into an alarmingly human smile. The jet-black eyes set into opposing sides of the body but which somehow fix on us, acknowledging our presence. It doesn't take long for me to realise that we are treading water in the centre of a pod of dolphins. Dolphins of all shapes and sizes who all gaze at the young man and woman cradling one of their own.

'Is this a good thing or a bad thing?' I whisper to Mac, wondering whether a dolphin has ever actually been known to eat a human being.

'What do you think?' he whispers back, and I instantly know what he means.

This is a wonderful thing, an amazing thing. A gob-smackingly beautiful thing that I never in my wildest dreams thought someone like me would ever experience. There is something fascinatingly peaceful about dolphins. These dolphins are gorgeous and they are so close I can smell them and hear them chattering amongst themselves. I have a baby dolphin in my arms, a family of dolphin friends and a beautiful man by my side. Wow, what more could a girl ask for? How far I have come from my days as a Captain Chicken padded chicken nugget.

I draw in a sharp breath when the pod suddenly moves en masse towards us. I let go of Flipper and flap my arms as I try to keep my head above the water. Unperturbed by my splashings, the dolphins swim nearer until they are touching me, nudging me with their noses as if to say 'What are you, then? We haven't met you out here before.'

'They like you,' Mac laughs, reaching out and holding my hand.

I squeeze it tight and I laugh too. My laugh grows louder when one of the larger dolphins glides beneath me and almost lifts me out of the water as if trying to help me swim.

'We've helped their baby and now they're helping you,' Mac chuckles.

'Oh my God,' I giggle, 'they know I'm a rubbish swimmer, Mac. How do they know that? This is amazing!'

The big dolphin nudges me until I am facing the beach and begins to swim alongside me. Mac turns too and we swim towards the shore – him in his usual effortless front crawl, me in a Women's Institute style dry-hair breaststroke. We are surrounded by dolphins, swimming, rolling, leaping over the waves in front and behind us. My eyes can't take it all in, my brain tries to imprint every scene on my memory for posterity. We are swimming with wild dolphins in the ocean, under the stars. I never thought I would say this about this funky little west coast town, but I think I must be in paradise.

When we have swum far enough, Mac and I both stand and shake ourselves. I wave at Fi and Dave, who are watching the spectacle from the beach, Dave with one arm holding his video camera and the other around the waist of my grinning best friend. I wave before turning to watch the dolphins, which are still enjoying the surf.

'They're better surfers than we'll ever be,' says Mac, clapping one lithe dolphin who races down the face of a wave before hurling itself into the air, its body glistening in the moonlight.

Suddenly, as if the playtime bell has been rung and it is time to return to class, the frolicking stops and the pod come together in a group not far from us. In the centre is the smallest dolphin, our baby Flipper, who wriggles happily and, I want to believe, smiles over at Mac and me. A loud cackle rises up from the dolphins, all of them shaking their noses at us as if to say thank you. Overcome by emotion, I feel a tear roll down my cheek. I then feel a manly hand wipe it away and pull me to his side. With one more wave of their snouts, the pod glides away with the baby tucked safely in their midst. Their tails are the last thing to dip under the water, and they are gone.

'I don't know what to say,' I stutter, staring happily out to sea.

'Then don't say anything.'

Mac guides me slowly towards the beach. I see Fi's smiling face and Dave holding her tight as if he will never let her go. I feel a wave of relief that the evening has ended in a much more pleasant way than I originally feared. I shiver when a gust of wind blows and my nose erupts into an almighty sneeze.

'Come on, girls, let's get you home,' says Mac firmly.

'Mighty,' Fi grins, clapping her hands. 'Hot chocolate and munchies back at ours then. Now who can build a good fire?'

Our celebration continues well into the early hours of the morning after we leave the cold dampness of the beach and all return to Pooh Corner for a welcome hot drink. I make hot chocolate, which Mac helps to whip to a froth. Dave first passes by the surf shop to collect dry clothes for all of us and then stops off at his cousin's pub, which is shuttered and lifeless from the outside but still a den of alcohol-fuelled merriment inside. If you know the right knock, that is. He buys a bottle of whiskey and scrounges some cloves, which he and Fi then turn into tasty hot toddies with the addition of sugar, lemon and water. The soothing liquid slips down the back of my throat, which has been showing signs of a chill ever since I left the beach. Mac builds a peat fire that warms the room and our bodies. The comfortingly smoky aroma gives our impromptu party the atmosphere of a camping adventure. We are relaxed and natural in each other's company; more so than we have ever been during the time Fi and I have been in town. Tonight we shared rare experiences. Not only Fi's distress, which indeed led to the whole night's events, but also the fear Mac, Dave and I silently shared that we were never going to see Fi again. Never forgetting the magic that then unfolded with the injured baby dolphin and its family pod. It has brought us closer together. So close in fact that Fi is now sitting on the floor in the protective embrace of Dave's long, slim legs. Occasionally Dave affectionately strokes her arms as if checking she is still here. They share biscuits, exchanging relaxed smiles every time their eyes collide. Fi looks happier than I ever remember. At first I feel a surprising hint of jealousy that it is Dave and not me, her best friend, who has made her this happy, but I soon kick myself for being so childish. These feelings vanish entirely when Fi pads up behind me in the kitchenette while I go in search of more munchies. She reaches her arms around my waist, hugging me like a child.

'I'm sorry I worried you, Milly,' she says quietly. 'I didn't mean to scare you, like.'

'It's OK, Fi.'

'No it's not. I should have been more thoughtful and left you a note when I wandered off, though mind you I didn't think I'd be off saving dolphins on my walk. There I was drifting on like a string of misery and there they were out of the blue. It just goes to show, Milly, you never know what's round the corner.'

I peek over her shoulder at Dave, who is eyeing Fi adoringly from across the room.

'Oh, I know what's round the corner for you, young lady,' I whisper. 'A lovestruck young man who is missing you even though you are only a few feet away.'

Her cheeks blush the same colour as her fiery pigtails and she lifts her shoulders up to almost touch her ears.

'OK, I admit it, I like him.'

'And he likes you.'

'Ah well, the fella's only human, like,' she giggles mischievously. 'You know he told me he was so worried about me he was nearly sick.'

'He was very worried,' I reply, deciding to spare Fi the details of Dave's tears. Heaven knows, she doesn't need any more guilt loaded on those bony little shoulders.

Fi nibbles the end of her fingernail, glances briefly around at Dave and then leans closer to me.

'I'm gonna give it a go, Milly,' she whispers.

'What, you and Dave?'

'No, me and Bertie feckin' Ahern, who do you think?'

I rub my hands conspiratorially.

'That's great, Fi, I am really pleased for you. He's lush and I think you will be very happy together.'

'Hold on now, lady, don't go getting me married off already. I only said I would give it a go, not have the poor fella's babies.'

'Well, that's a start.'

Fi places her hands on her hips, looking at once vulnerable yet determined.

'Aye, it is a start. It's a start towards me getting pleasure out of the bits of life I've been missing out on. You know, tonight was so shite and then it turned into a fairy tale just like that.' She clicks her fingers. 'It was a feckin' cold fairy tale but it was one all the same and who would have seen that coming?'

I shake my head and let her continue.

'So I thought, well, why can't I do that with my life? Depression is curable these days, like, and I reckon I can beat it. I reckon if I give up that arsey fantasy I had of my family being back together again like in a bloody Disney movie I can start moving on. Jaysus, haven't I already got a family that cares enough about me to go drowning themselves in the middle of a storm just to make sure I'm OK?'

She gently pinches my arm.

'You, Mac and Dave, you mad bastards, and the rest of the Heggartys, sure you're all a better family than the one God gave me. And besides, I am an adult, you know, and why should I let Sean and my da rob me of the right to be happy with a man and trust him? I mean, shite, have you ever seen a nun with pigtails this bloody colour before? It just wouldn't work, like.'

I laugh out loud along with Fi.

'No, Fi, you are definitely not nun material, that's for sure.'

We hug each other tightly.

'Ah Mac, would ya look, girl on girl action,' Dave hoots from his sprawled position on the floor. 'What are yous two busy gassin' about?'

Fi turns towards them and places her hands on her heart.

'Oprah,' she announces sarcastically, 'I am ready. I am stepping out of a bad place and walking into a good place.'

Dave purses his lips together and pretends to be perplexed, although I know he understands what Fi means.

'Aye well, that's grand, but first would you mind stepping over to the place called the fridge and bringing a man a beer?'

'Ya cheeky wee fecker,' Fi gasps before doing exactly that

and delivering herself and a four-pack into Dave's out-stretched arms.

'What happened to this?' Mac asks, lifting up the arm of the sofa that now lives on the floor.

I plonk myself down next to him on the ancient sofa cushions and hungrily nibble on a chocolate digestive.

'Fi sat on it,' I say through a mouthful of crumbs, 'the fat cow.'

'Yeah, she does need to lose a bit of weight like,' Dave winks, patting Fi's toned thigh.

She punches him teasingly and they begin to play-fight. Mac turns to me and raises his eyebrows, a smirk playing on his lips.

'I think we might be intruding,' he whispers, flicking his eyes towards Fi and Dave, who are obviously desperate to rip each other's clothes off but are somehow maintaining a certain decorum. 'Here, I've got an idea.'

'It doesn't involve going out in the rain again, does it? Because I really think I would die this time.'

'We can't have you dying,' he says, motioning for me to copy him and collect the Sunday newspapers from the floor. He turns to me after retrieving a roll of tape from underneath the kitchen sink and adds, 'I'd miss you.'

My legs feel strangely weak as I follow Mac out of the room – totally unnoticed by Fi and Dave – and climb the stairs behind him.

*Where are we going? What's with the newspaper and tape? And why does he have to walk in front of me? I can't help but look at that bum in those jeans!*

At the top of the landing, Mac turns to me and says, 'So where's your bedroom then?'

*Excusez-bloody-moi?*

'Umm, erm, ooh, that one there,' I whimper and point at the door, totally taken aback by his directness.

Not that I should be surprised, I suppose. I mean, Mac Heggarty is not one to beat around the bush.

*Er, so to speak.*

I cross my legs and hop nervously into the room behind him.

Now, I am not saying I am disappointed when Mac places a hand on my shoulder, pushes me to a sitting position on one of the twin beds, takes the newspapers from my hands and then turns his attention to the window I broke earlier. No, I am not saying I am disappointed. After all, the window needs to be fixed if Fi and I are going to get any sleep tonight, doesn't it? Not that sleep is high on Fi's agenda, judging from the high-pitched shrieks and giggles now emanating from downstairs. No, I am not disappointed, it is jolly nice of him to remember and to be so chivalrous and manly and . . . Oh fuck, of course I am disappointed. Totally hormonally wretched, in fact. This attractive, muscled, strong yet gentle champion surfer is in my bedroom and we are alone, both of us single and both of us more aware of each other's qualities after tonight. Why doesn't he want to kiss me as much as I do him? Why doesn't he want to lie on this bed with me and explore the parts of me he would never otherwise get to see? Why is he so intent on taping up that sodding window rather than jumping on top of me and just letting me have him?

'Pardon? Sorry, Mac, did you say something? I was miles away.'

*Very close to your private parts, but miles away all the same.*

'I said are you OK, Milly? You're looking a bit anxious there.'

*Anxious? Me? God no, I'm positively yogi-like in my chilledness.*

My ovaries scream out for action.

'No, I'm fine,' I sniff, 'just a bit . . .'

*A bit what? On heat? Gagging? In lo . . . I mean, in lust?*

Mac finishes taping the thick layers of newspaper to the small hole in the window and its, I now realise, relatively minor cracks. He turns to me, steps closer, bends down and places a warm palm on my forehead. Unable to control my reactions, I shiver under his touch.

'Ach, I shouldn't have let you come out in that water,' he tuts, peering so deep into my eyes I feel as if he is staring straight into my soul.

*Please God, don't let him be able to read minds too.*

'It was fierce chilly out there and now I wouldn't be surprised if you wake up smothered with the cold. It was thick of me not to make you stay in the car.'

I lower my eyes under his gaze, feeling my cheeks turn crimson with both embarrassment and longing.

'But I wouldn't have missed it for the world. Those dolphins were just incredible.'

I feel the mattress beside me sink as Mac sits himself down. His shoulder and leg are touching mine. He is tantalisingly, painfully close. I visibly jump when he reaches into my lap and takes my hand, pressing it between both his palms. My mouth is dry and any words I want to utter are trapped behind the hormones racing up to my lips, desperate to be released.

'You were incredible too tonight, Milly,' he breathes.

I force myself to turn my head. My eyes rest on his broad chest. I gulp and work my eyeline up to his neck, then to his jaw, his tanned lips, that lightly freckled nose and finally to his sparkling eyes. Bloody hell, it is no wonder I threw myself at him the night of the Frankie Doolan concert. Who have I been trying to kid? The man is gorgeous. Stunning in fact, and not just on the outside. At the risk of sounding as if I am in psychotherapy, the inside, his soul, shines out at me from those green eyes, as beautiful and peaceful as the dolphin I held in my arms tonight. I shiver again. Mac clasps my hand tighter.

'I meant what I said up at the house tonight in front of your folks. About your achievements since you came here.'

I blink. 'Thank you so much for that. I didn't know what to say. Especially,' I grimace, 'after my mum had been flirting with you and after the horrible potty story.'

Mac grins. 'Yeah, that was a bit grim, but I mean it, you've done great, Milly, with the surfing and all that. You've shown real fighting spirit and even more so tonight. I thought you'd be wild terrified going out in that water in the dark.'

'I was,' I grin. 'I was totally shitting myself.'

We laugh together at my bluntness, all our inhibitions and pretensions now gone. Mac lets go of my hand and reaches up to move a stray lock of hair back behind my ear.

'You know you're beautiful when you look natural like this,' he says in a near whisper.

I self-consciously touch a hand to my face, suddenly aware that I have no make-up on and my features have been ravaged by several heavens-worth of torrential rain. Funny though, right now I feel more beautiful than I have felt in a long time.

'Thank you,' I whisper back, knowing that it is more gracious to accept a compliment than dismiss it.

*Just kiss me*, I want to add, *please just kiss me, Mac*, but I can't say the words. I feel suddenly shy, unnerved by my own feelings and embarrassed in case he can see the longing in my eyes, the dilating of my pupils. My cheeks flame redder still. Mac frowns and presses his hand against my burning skin.

'Jaysus, Milly, are you sure you're all right so? I really think you're sickening for something.'

*Love? Lust? You?*

I bite my tongue and frantically shake my head.

'No, Mac, I'm fine. Honest.'

I stumble over my words and cough. I then feel a sneeze racing up my spine until it explodes out of my nostrils at such a speed that it almost sends me flying backwards. Mac leaps to his feet, grabs my hand and pulls me to the head of the bed.

'Bed for you, maisie,' he says firmly.

*Yes please, oh yes please.*

I oblige and hop under the covers still fully clothed.

Better to let him take them off, I tell myself. I prepare myself for what is to come, but before I can protest, Mac has covered me in the duvet and tucked it so tight around me I feel like the stuffing inside a sausage roll. Which is not exactly what I would call sexually stimulating.

'Bed and no complaints,' he says, bustling around me like a doctor on call. 'We can't have the film star dying with the flu, now can we?'

I nod and shake my head in quick succession.

*Wait a minute. What about . . .?*

'Now you stay there until that cold is long gone, you hear, and I'll have Fiona bring you up another hot toddy.'

He bends over me and gently strokes my forehead. I gaze up at him, not wanting him to leave, wanting him to get in here beside me and warm my body with his. I don't want a hot toddy, I want a hot Mac Heggarty. I hold my breath when, without warning, he leans close and places his lips on my forehead, kissing me gently.

'Well done for tonight, Milly,' he whispers. 'You did all that for your friend and I'm proud.'

He moves as if to walk away but then turns to speak again.

'Milly?'

'Yes, Mac,' I croak.

'You know . . . you do know I like you, don't you?'

I nod stiffly, unable to respond. My head becomes instantly dizzy.

'I always have, but I can be a bit awkward sometimes with girls, I mean women, you know.'

My heart is overcome with fondness for his sudden vulnerability.

'And the thing is, I have always liked you, I just don't like to get too close, but I couldn't help it, much as I tried. Jaysus, the minute I saw you back in Sligo, you blew me away.'

*I would have done if only you had asked!*

I squeeze my lips tight to stop any words coming out that

263

will ruin this moment. I want him to keep saying these things, to make me feel special. Above all, I want him. I squeeze my eyes shut as tight as my lips to fully absorb his words.

'Ah look, you're tired and sick and here am I droning on while you're dying with the cold.'

'What? No, Mac . . .'

'See, I told you I'm not very good at this stuff.'

'It's fine, honestly . . .'

'Ssh now, we'll maybe talk more tomorrow, but now you have to have a good sleep. Good night, Milly, God bless.'

With that he turns and walks away. He actually walks away, closing the door softly behind him. No snog, no nothing. Bloody hell, Mac has the willpower of a monk.

I feel frustrated for a moment until I allow my eyes to close and I realise how exhausted I really am after tonight's efforts. And there was I thinking my parents' arrival would be the focal point for any drama. Gosh, they were a breeze in comparison. I smile. Although I may have the beginnings of a chill, I am very warm inside.

'Good night, Mac,' I whisper to the dark, empty room. 'Thank you for everything. Tonight I can dream about you. Tomorrow, though, is another matter altogether.'

I can't wait.

# CHAPTER TWENTY-FIVE

## *Point Break*

It is already Monday afternoon by the time my body drags itself back from revelling in its dreamtime to consciousness. Early afternoon, but late enough for my mother to raise a judgemental eyebrow when I trip downstairs looking like a blurry photo from *America's Most Wanted*.

'Top o' the—'

'Afternoon, Dad,' I yawn, 'how are you both today?'

I give Fi's shoulder a squeeze in an effort to transmit the message *Your bed wasn't slept in, Miss O'Reilly, so just where did you lay that weary head of yours?* I steal a piece of buttered toast from her plate and plonk myself down at the kitchenette table.

'We have already had a brisk walk, haven't we, Frank?'

'We have, Georgina,' my father replies, flicking his eyes towards the ceiling when my mother is not looking, which causes Fi to giggle.

'Your mother doesn't believe in hangovers, do you, Georgina?' he continues, clasping his head in both hands and making a face.

'All in the mind, Frank, hangovers are all in the mind.'

'They certainly are, Georgina, and right now my mind could do with a good old-fashioned fry-up and a hair of the dog.'

'Honestly, these Irish people are a very bad influence on your father, with their penchant for whiskey and whatever it was you and the old Irish drunk were poisoning your bodies with. No offence, Fiona dear.'

Fi laughs into her cup of tea and gives my father a surreptitious wink.

Was it only last night that my father and Podraig were heartily knocking back their drinks? So much has happened since then I feel as if a week has passed since I last saw my parents. I scratch my head through the tangled mess that has appeared overnight and clasp my other hand to my face to block the plotted trajectory of my sneeze.

'Oh dear,' my mother tuts, rummaging in her hand luggage for a tissue, 'that doesn't sound too promising, Amelia, and those bags under your eyes make you look absolutely dreadful.'

'Thanks,' I cough, accepting the tissue with a grimace, 'that makes me feel so much better.'

My mother cocks her head to one side and frowns, as if she is a vet pondering whether to put a small domestic animal out of its misery.

'Of course we have been hearing about your midnight adventures from Fiona here. I don't know what you expect if you go gallivanting around in the sea at all hours like a fishwife.'

*Like a what?*

'We weren't exactly "gallivanting", Mum, it was a search-and-rescue mission, not a skinny-dip.'

*Although whether Fi and Dave did a bit of naked gallivanting after I went to bed I would not like to speculate.*

'And it sounds like a very successful search-and-rescue mission, pudding,' my father concludes. 'That dolphin was lucky Fiona spotted him or he would have been caught, fried and served up by the natives in our hotel restaurant this lunchtime. Ha ha.'

I discard my piece of toast and breathe in deeply. I am too

tired to make polite conversation, regardless of the fact that I have just slept until one o'clock. My body is, as Mac rightly predicted, gripped with a chill and I feel as if there is so much mucus forming in my sinuses I am going to have to grow another nose to cope with it all. I am a physical wreck but emotionally, in the part of my brain dedicated to matters of the heart, I have renewed hope and definite flutterings. Like the first flutterings of a butterfly emerging from its cocoon. I have Mac. Or at least I hope I will.

'It's a lovely day,' I say to change the subject, glancing out of the window at the sun glistening off the now calm ocean.

'It's a glorious one, so it is,' Fi agrees, giving my leg a nudge under the table to let me know that she is not just talking about the weather.

'And, Milly Armstrong, surf chick and dolphin rescuer,' she continues, standing up and walking towards the hallway, 'your day is about to get better. Are you not after seeing what Mac left for you at the bottom of the stairs this morning?'

I feel an adolescent flush travel across my cheeks at the mention of his name. I shake my head fervently to disguise my embarrassment and watch in anticipation as Fi nips out of the door while my mother and father exchange a knowing glance.

'I don't know how you missed it, ya big eejit, it's feckin' massive.' I hear her grunt and groan as she struggles to drag the surprise into the room. 'Ta daa!'

I stare open-mouthed at the brown paper parcel. Over six foot tall, tied with a red bow and a shape that only an over-zealous Body Shop gift-box wrapper could hope to disguise.

'Bloody hell, it's an aeroplane wing!' my father guffaws.

'I rather think it could be a coffin,' my mother adds, delighted with her own joke.

My legs buckle every other step I take as I walk over to Fi and take the parcel in my shaking hands.

'Can you tell what it is yet?' Fi smirks, doing her best impression of Rolf Harris. 'Come on, Milly, open it. I want to see the fecker. Oops, pardon me, Mr and Mrs A.'

Everyone, including my mother, is silent while I rest the flat end of the parcel on the floor and begin to untie the red ribbon. A small white envelope flutters to the floor, which I quickly scoop up and shove into the back pocket of my jeans. That is mine for later, not for prying parental eyes. Although I promise myself I will not get my hopes up about its content. After all, nothing really happened last night apart from an affectionate kiss on the forehead and Mac admitting that I blew him away. I smile dreamily at the memory.

'Hurry up, hurry up,' Fi squeals, hopping up and down beside me.

'Yes, do hurry up, darling, we haven't got all day,' says my mother, trying to disguise the excitement in her voice.

I pull off the ribbon and hold the object upright with one hand while tearing away the brown paper with the other. Each of us gasps in turn as we stare at Mac's present. It is gorgeous, far too gorgeous. I don't know what to say.

'Golly, is that a surfboard?' my mother asks.

'I rather think it might be, you know, Mrs A,' Fi giggles. 'Not an aeroplane wing after all. Ah well, never mind.'

Yes it is a surfboard, but it is a perfect, stunning surfboard. More stunning than Fi's even and a hundred times more attractive than the lump of sponge I have been dragging to the beach with my head lowered in shame whenever I pass a real surfer with a real board. This surfboard is a colour wash flowing from a deep blue at the nose into light blue, then purple and finally into pink at the tail end. Silver stars adorn each rail of the board where I will place my hands, and across the deck more stars mingle with leaping dolphins. It is amazing.

'That's jolly nice of him, Amelia,' my mother comments, crossing her arms and legs simultaneously. 'What exactly did you do to deserve that?'

She raises one eyebrow to express *You shagged him, didn't you, you little slapper? There is no way you earned that without sexual favours.*

'It wasn't one thing in particular like,' Fi interrupts. 'She's just tried so hard, you know. She didn't have to *ride* him or anything.'

'Thanks for clearing that up, Fi,' I groan, my face now scarlet. As is my father's.

I turn away and give the glossy surfboard a stroke. I lay it gently on the floor, picturing myself paddling it out to sea where it will propel me into the wave of my life. While Fi busies herself fetching fresh cups of tea for my parents, I sneak over to one of the windows and slide the little envelope out of my pocket. I stare at it for a moment, clasping it tightly in my hands the way I did when I received my A-level results in the post, as if wishful thinking could change what was already written inside. Turning to check that the others are preoccupied, I open the envelope, sniff away the drip from the end of my nose and begin to read.

> *Dear Milly, I'm not very good at writing letters so this is just to say I thought it was time my star pupil had a board of her own. Dave and I planned this for your surfing graduation but I want you to have it now, you have earned it after your bravery last night. Thank you for helping me and for making it a magical moment. I hope this helps to bring you everything you want. God bless,*
> *Mac x*

I speed-read the letter over and over as if I am memorising a script. *Dear Milly*, he wrote. *Dear*. But then doesn't everyone when they are trying to write a polite letter? It doesn't mean I am *dear* to him necessarily, but then again it could mean that. And he does call me his *star pupil*. That has to mean something. I am the first to admit that I am hardly the greatest talent when it comes to riding waves, so he has to be referring to me being his *favourite* pupil, the one who brightens his classes. The way the stars and the moon eventually brightened the sky last night. Last night during our *magical moment*. So he felt it too. Then just the one '*x*' but a kiss all the same. It is a definite *x*, not just an ink smudge on the paper or a squashed fly. Now that is promising. Perhaps a promise of what is to come?

Tell me, do women ever grow out of over-analysing romantic correspondence?

'What does he say then?' asks Fi, appearing suddenly behind me and peeking at the note over my shoulder.

I clasp it between my hands so that she cannot see the words.

'Oh, you know, just . . . er, the usual,' I reply, shrugging the shoulder she is resting her chin on.

'What d'you mean, "the usual", ya bollix? I don't exactly think it's "usual" to get a feckin' great surfboard delivered out of the blue all fancied up like in red ribbon and with a love letter attached.'

'It's not a love letter, Fi, it's just a note. It's nothing really.'

*Nothing except the thing that is causing my heart to beat like the bass of a dance track at a rave. Nothing except the thing that promises I am going to have a very good day.*

Fi clicks her tongue against the roof of her mouth.

'Ah, I think it's great,' she whispers, wrinkling her nose. 'Yourself and Mac, me and Dave.'

I bite my lip, longing to ask her all the details about last night after I went to bed, but my parents are in the room and I am suddenly aware that a telephone is ringing.

'Phone, phone, phone!' my mother shrieks, the way she always does when a telephone rings, as if it is likely to be the Queen inviting her and my father round for a bit of lunch with herself and Philip.

I locate my mobile down the side of one of the sofa cushions and glance at the screen. *Gerald Agent* the display warns. Looking for an update on my progress, no doubt.

Well for once I have the upper hand, what with my midnight ocean adventures and my very own board. Have I got news for him!

'Amelia? Gerald,' my agent barks before I have a chance to say hello. 'Are you sitting down? Have I got some news for you!'

'Call Mac,' Fi instructs me ten minutes later while attempting to peel my fingers from the mobile phone and lift me up off the floor.

'Call him,' she repeats into my stunned face.

Fi dials Mac's number but waits to press the call button.

'He's the fella in an emergency. Mac will know what to do, like.'

'Well I think it is rather exciting myself,' my mother pipes up with a delighted expression on her face. 'A film director coming here to this place to see our daughter in action and to plan a film. I think that's jolly exciting actually. Don't you, Frank?'

'I rather do, Georgina, yes.'

'At least we know now that you weren't just making this whole thing up to impress us. There is a real film after all. Not that we ever doubted that fact, of course.'

My mother pats the solid layer of spray on her hair-do while steam erupts silently from my ears.

'So what is the problem with it, Amelia? I don't see a problem with it.'

'The problem, Mother,' I seethe through teeth so gritted they could stop road accidents in the snow, 'is that the film director just happens to be arriving here tomorrow. *Tomorrow*. When not only do I have snotty sinuses and a nose like an ageing alcoholic, I also do not yet have the ability to display the kind of action he is looking for. I told the man I could surf, for goodness' sake, and I was supposed to have another month to perfect my lie. And now this. What am I going to do? I am doomed.'

My mother ignores my self-pitying wail and picks imaginary dust from the ironed-in crease of her navy slacks.

'I won't say that's what happens to girls who tell fibs, Amelia.'

*You just did.*

'Look on the bright side, pudding,' my father chirps, 'at least you will look like a professional with that jazzy new board of yours, so that is bloody good timing. Pardon my French.'

I glance from the board to my father and smile falteringly.

'Thanks, Dad,' I sniff.

'Not at all, pudding. So,' he continues heartily, 'we just have to hope that the swanky board distracts your audience if you make a total pig's ear of the actual surfing lark. Don't we, Georgina?'

'Spot on, Frank.'

'OK then, come on now, Mr and Mrs A,' Fi interrupts before I have a chance to hurl myself across the room and bang my parents' tactless heads together. 'Why don't we leave Milly here in peace like to sort out her wee dilemma and we can hop in your car and go off for a bit of sightseeing and shopping? Sligo town is grand for shops, like, and I'm keen to get myself some new knickers.'

My father is out of his chair and at the door, car keys jangling excitedly in his hand, before my mother even lets out a gasp. Fi ushers them both out of the room, turning to wink at me before she ducks out of the door.

'You can do it, Milly,' she nods. 'Just look on it as a bit of last-minute research. Now call Mac so. Himself would give his right arm to help you. And very likely the rest of his body too.'

After trying in vain to contact Mac by telephone, I finally track him down at Dave's surf shop. His mobile, he explains, is switched off and in his pocket, defeating its purpose entirely.

'I need your help,' I wheeze, grasping on to a plastic palm tree leaf while I struggle to catch my breath. I sneeze and cough simultaneously.

'It bloody looks like it,' Dave laughs, hopping up on to the counter. (He has a definite spring in his step today, I note.) 'What's with the hair?'

'What? Oh.'

I glance in the nearest mirror and realise that in my haste to leave the house I failed to tame the nest of noodles that is masquerading as my hair. It is currently defying gravity, which when combined with my cold symptoms of red eyes and runny nose makes me look horribly unattractive. I flap my hands impatiently.

'I haven't got bloody time for that shit right now, I need to talk about surfing.'

Mac pushes his hands deep into the front pockets of his loose jeans and leans back against the counter with an amused smile.

'Wow, you've changed, Milly Armstrong, so you have. No time for a beauty regime? Wants to talk about surfing. Holy God, it's a miracle.'

Mac smiles warmly and I can't help but smile back.

'Well now, how can I help?'

*You can help by not looking so bloody gorgeous in that relaxed T-shirt-and-faded jeans way you have of looking bloody gorgeous. It is very distracting.*

I place my hands on my hips and take a deep breath, trying to ignore the look of delight in Mac's startling green eyes. I dreamed about him last night, for God's sake, how embarrassing is that? Does he know? Can he tell?

'Look,' I say matter-of-factly, 'this crash course I am having in how to surf and be a surfer. Do you think it could, erm, crash any quicker?'

Mac folds his arms while he considers my admittedly ridiculous question.

'Like how quick would you want it to, er, crash?'

'Like really quick?'

I shuffle my feet and toss a fake coconut from the counter from one hand to the other. Dave and Mac eye each other warily.

'Well, you know, Milly' – Mac brushes a wayward curl from his forehead – 'four months is already wild quick to be trying to master the ancient sport of Hawaiian kings. It's not easy, you know.'

'I know it's not easy, thank you very much, Mac, but something has come up and I just need my progress to be a teensy bit quicker than I originally planned.'

'How much is a teensy bit?' he frowns.

'Um, like twenty-four hours?'

'How much like twenty-four hours?'

'Very like it. In fact exactly like twenty-four hours. Twenty-four hours and counting as we speak.'

'Jaysus feckin' Christ,' they say in unison.

Dave sucks air between his teeth as if he is trying to inflate himself, and Mac places his hands on his head. He looks like a soldier trying to surrender his lost cause. I grimace apologetically at them both and then explain the call from Gerald.

'Gerald,' Dave hoots. 'The man just sounds like an eejit.'

'Perhaps, but that "eejit" is rather important to my career, and it is my own fault for telling the director I have been surfing since the age of two.' I blush at my own lies as Mac and Dave fall about laughing. 'So you see, I really need to be convincing or this whole thing has been a complete waste of time.'

'I wouldn't say that,' Mac says with a mischievous grin.

'You don't want much, do ya, Milly?' Dave snorts.

'What do you reckon?' I ask Mac pleadingly.

'I reckon,' Mac begins slowly, exhaling while he speaks, 'I reckon that this is gonna be one feckin' long night.'

And not at all in the way I had planned, I think sourly.

'But, Milly, if you're up for it then, hey, how can I refuse?

I am your surf instructor after all. Come with me, maisie, we've got work to do.'

He walks towards me and squeezes my shoulder.

'It will be my duty and my pleasure to help you.'

I could kiss him. In fact I think I will. Just as soon as I pluck up the courage.


'Gosh, did you decorate this yourself?' I ask somewhat patronisingly as I glance around Mac's immaculately tidy front room.

His decor is minimalist but comfortable. A tasteful combination of wooden floors, a cream leather sofa, a rug of knotted suede, and furniture carved in unvarnished oak. Silk wall hangings adorn three of the four walls, with framed pictures covering the fourth. Above the open grate, various artefacts that look as if they have been collected from around the world are displayed on the single beam that forms the mantelpiece. If Mary and Podraig's cluttered, fussily decorated house were the North Pole then Mac's would be the South. The complete antithesis and yet another thing to surprise me about the man. I walk towards the mantelpiece and pick up a small carving of an angry-looking creature, turning it over in my hands.

'You never told me you had a house, Mac.'

'You never asked.'

He stands beside me and leans against the mantelpiece beam.

'I guess I just presumed that you still lived at Mary and Podraig's.'

'I guess you did.'

I glance up at his face and wonder if Mac really does not care about how people perceive him. He does not seem to. After all, he never felt the need to crow about his surfing successes or his crusade to unite kids across the border. He never cared that I thought he was a live-at-home mummy's boy. Is it really possible these days not to care about image?

'He is Kanaloa, a Hawaiian Tiki god,' Mac says, nodding at the wooden object in my hands. 'He's the god of the sea, so I brought him back with me from Hawaii years ago, you know, for good luck. Do you like it?'

'I do,' I nod, gurning at the Tiki's ugly face. 'He reminds me of you.'

Mac laughs and traipses off to the kitchen in search of refreshment.

'So you've been to Hawaii then?' I ask rather obviously to fill the silence in the house.

I raise a giant shell to my ear, listening for the ocean that, as a small girl, I used to believe was trapped inside.

'Yeah, a few times,' Mac calls back. 'There's a photo on the wall over there of my friend and me at Waimea Bay on the north shore of Oahu a while back. That's the total surfing Mecca over there. In the world, in fact, 'cos Hawaii's where the whole surfing thing began, like. It's grand. It's a paradise really, you know, especially for surfers, with gorgeous beaches and loads of wild good waves. I love it.'

I locate the photograph and peer at the two young men. Their toned arms are linked across each other's bare shoulders and both of them are grinning as if they haven't a care in the world, their teeth blindingly white against their bronzed skin. The one on the left is definitely Mac, but he is younger, much more boyish in his appearance. Still broad-chested, but skinny with it. His hair, although characteristically dishevelled, is streaked with strands of prominent blond.

'Highlights?' I ask, accepting a glass of orange juice.

'Don't be daft, Hawaiian sun more like. I tell you, that sun is so feckin' hot you could fry eggs on your back if you sat out in it long enough. That's where I got this leathery look from.'

He touches a hand to his cheek. I pause and admire the faint creases around his eyes and mouth that give his face so much character.

'It suits you.'

I turn back to the photo.

'So who's the other beach boy with you?'

Mac slowly sips his drink as if deep in thought.

'Ah now, that would be me and Nicky at the Eddie, the big-wave comp.'

*Nicky.* Mac's best friend who was killed in a bombing in the North. I kick myself for my nosiness but Mac laughs distractedly beside me and continues to talk.

'Nicky, ha, what a gas he was, man. Always messing around and having a laugh. I missed some important contest heats when I was off with him, but sure I got through a damn sight more with him there too. He was always grand at inspiring me to surf better, you know, and at telling me off when I was surfing like a feckin' eejit.'

I laugh along with him and tilt my head at the picture. Mac's young friend's smile is fixed on his face for eternity. His speckled blue eyes shine with innocence and hope. His perfect beach boy features could have made him a fortune in Hollywood. Tears press against the back of my eyes at the thought of this promising life wiped out in an instant. I say a silent thank you that my worst fears for Fi were never realised.

'He looks lovely,' I comment quietly.

Mac sighs and laughs simultaneously.

'He was lovely, and always better-looking than me, the bastard.'

The words catch in his throat.

'Yeah, Nicky was a great mate, the best. Dave's grand too, you know, a fantastic friend, but Nicky and me, we went back a long way. We shared so many surf trips. He . . . he—'

'I know,' I interrupt softly, hearing the emotion in Mac's voice. 'Dave told me what happened. I'm sorry.'

I reach out my hand and place it on his shoulder, just happy to be close to him, physically and now emotionally. He places his own hand over mine and we maintain a comfortable silence before he speaks again.

'Right now, enough of this chit-chat. I believe you've got work to do.'

The strong, unflappable Mac is back again, his softness hidden behind the barrier forming in those emerald eyes. I smile sadly and follow him to the study.


'So from this internet weather chart here we can tell that the swell will be dropping by tomorrow and there will be light winds for the next couple of days, you see?'

Mac points at a web page depicting isobars and things that only Michael Fish would have a hope in hell of understanding. I peer at the screen and make a vague agreeing sound.

'In other words,' Mac continues, 'this weather pattern lets us know that the waves will be small at the main beach and God willing our Milly will have a chance to impress your one from the film world.'

I grin and breathe easier.

'Great! Yeah, that's what I thought it said.'

'Right. Now back to this diagram of the break you'll be surfing. Show me where you'll be wanting to position yourself.'

I stare at the scribbled drawing in front of me and exhale. We have been at this for two hours now and my brain feels as if it has swelled to twice its normal size with all the information Mac thinks I need in order to be fully researched in the art of surfing. The problem is, it has all gone in somewhere but I am having trouble locating it again at will. Why does it have to be so bloody complicated? Surely I could just strut around with my shiny new surfboard, paddle up and down a bit and catch a wave when Mac tells me to. Why do I need all this scientific stuff just to be allowed out in the water on my own? Why am I bothered about isobars and rips and wave priority and off-the-lips? Science never was my strong point. In fact *learning* was never my strong point, unless it was a script for the school play.

'Can't you just paddle out in the same wetsuit as me and then pretend to be me on a wave?' I groan as I grow anxious and tired.

'I'm hardly your size now, and besides, that would be cheating.'

'And the problem is?'

After all, what is one more lie to add to all the others?

'Ah, come on now, if you just concentrate on what I'm telling you about where to paddle out and where to catch the wave you will be grand. Then all you do is catch it, stand up, ride it in. You've done it before.'

'For about a millisecond. And without an audience with the power to decide my whole future.'

'No one has that power, that's up to you,' Mac says firmly. 'But you've done this before and you can do it again, I know it. Just be cool but not too cool. If you go talking all *Baywatch* when they arrive and shite like that I will drown you myself.'

'You may as well,' I sigh theatrically, slouching in my chair with a pout. 'I am never going to do this.'

'Well sure, that's the spirit.' Mac shakes his head.

'But the director is going to expect me to paddle out like it is the most natural thing in the world and for me to pick a wave and ride it like a professional. I've never even been out in the water without you, Mac. What if I just drift out to sea and never come back?'

Mac laughs, turns to face me and rests his head on one hand.

'Don't fret, Milly. Sure you'll wash up somewhere in America eventually.'

I whimper. He shakes his head and takes my hand, giving it a reassuring squeeze.

'I'm only messin', you'll be grand so you will. I can come and watch and show you where to sit and then all you have to do is exactly what I've shown you in the lessons. You can do it. In fact' – he glances at his watch and peers out of the window – 'there's still some hours of daylight left, so let's leave the theory and get out in the water for the practical lesson. That'll bring it all together in that head of yours.'

He ruffles my hair as I nod sadly and trudge out to the sitting room. A warmth moves down through my body from where he touched me like the warmth from a hot shower. As if to emphasise the metaphor, my nose decides to start dripping like a leaky showerhead. I grab a tissue from my pocket and blow hard, aware that in the silence of Mac's front room I sound like a trumpeting elephant. Not exactly the sexy image I had of myself in my romantic dreams last night.

'Are you OK for this surf lesson now, Milly?'

Mac appears beside me and bends down to look at my streaming face.

'I don't want you getting even more sick after last night's shenanigans.'

I shake my head and shove the moist tissue back into my pocket.

'No, I'm fine, just a bit of a sniffle.'

My nose throbs in front of my eyes like Rudolph's, lighting the way for Santa's sleigh. Mac turns me slowly towards him and places both hands on my shoulders. I bite my bottom lip and lift my eyes to meet his. They are full of concern, which makes me feel suddenly cared for.

'You're fierce determined, Milly,' he smiles, still clasping my shoulders, 'and I think no matter what a girl like you puts her mind to she can achieve it. That's why I thought you deserved that surfboard. I knew you would see this through to the end.'

My hands fly up to my cheeks and I gasp.

'Oh God, Mac, I can't believe I didn't even thank you for it. Oh no, how awful of me. I was so overcome with panic about the director coming that I totally forgot.'

My toes curl at my own ungratefulness.

'I really, really love it, you shouldn't have. Honestly, it is the nicest present anyone has ever given me and I didn't even thank you. You must think I'm a right cow.'

'I don't think that at all.'

His face is so close I can feel his breath hot on my skin.

'Actually, I think you're fantastic.'

We pause and stare at each other, each waiting for the other one to speak. I let him continue.

'Last night you didn't even think of your fear of the water, so that just shows you what you can achieve when you put your mind to it.'

'That was different,' I reply nervously. 'I was on a mission to find Fi and then that poor dolphin. I had to help.'

His eyes burn into mine. I am caught in their beam.

'And now you're on a mission to do something for yourself and I know you'll do it. Like I said, Milly, you're my star pupil.'

I blush and think of the note that is still concealed in my back pocket. His *star pupil*. He hoped it would bring me *everything you want*. I gaze deeper into those eyes and know instantly what I want. I want to kiss those lips. I want to pull Mac Heggarty as close to me as I can and break down his barriers once and for all. My eyes flit to the wall behind Mac where Nicky smiles directly at us from the photograph as if giving his approval. All that hurt Mac has suffered, all the time he has given to those children across the border in an attempt to make the world a better place. His actions move me. His eyes melt me. His lips . . .

A small gasp stirs in my throat as Mac pulls me gently towards him and our lips touch. He tastes salty from the seawater he spends every day in, but at the same time his mouth tastes sweet. Our lips press tightly together and then slowly part, our tongues exploring each other tentatively at first and then with more urgency. I hear myself groan. Mac returns the sound. His hands are firm yet gentle, caressing the base of my neck and then moving searchingly over my shoulder blades. I kiss him harder; I can't get enough. I suck his lip and run my tongue along his teeth. I should stop. I might give him my germs. But I don't want to stop, and what is the small matter of a cold between friends? Or lovers?

At last, I think to myself, my mind whirling as if detached from my body.

At last what? At last I am being kissed by someone, anyone, after so long without male contact? Or at last I am being kissed by Mac Heggarty?

*The latter, of course.*

I pull him nearer still, my hands pressed against the small of his back.

It feels too soon when Mac pulls away from me, a broad smile playing on his lips and his eyes dancing with mine. His chest moves up and down beneath the cotton of his T-shirt, tempting me to touch it.

'I've been waiting for the right moment to do that,' he blushes. 'That time at the Frankie Doolan concert I so wanted to, but you were drunk and I didn't want to take advantage, you know. I wasn't even sure you liked me.'

'I like you,' I reply softly.

'Well that's grand. Fantastic. That makes things a fierce lot easier. Now come on, my star pupil,' Mac beams with laughter in his voice, 'we better get your surf lesson done before it gets dark.'

He threads his fingers through mine and leads me towards the door. I am too breathless to resist.

'Come on, Milly, time to get wet.'

*I already am, Mac, I already am.*

# CHAPTER TWENTY-SIX

## *Stirrings*

I emerge from the water at dusk, utterly exhausted but with my confidence suitably bolstered after having wobbled enough waves to the beach to justify labelling my pursuit as surfing. No matter where I was in the water, on it or (more frequently) *under* it, Mac was always nearby calling out instructions and cheering encouragement. With my inhibitions wiped away by the events of the past twenty-four hours and especially by Mac having recently had his tongue in my mouth, I feel natural and at ease, which made the surfing all the more pleasurable. Now out of the water and on dry land I don't know what is expected of me. Do I ask him back to Pooh Corner for coffee? Do I invite myself to his exquisite house for a nightcap? Or do I start kissing him again right here, right now, in the middle of the beach? Gosh, the early throes of passion are so confusing and I am ashamedly out of practice.

I rest my lovely new board on the sand with the wax facing upwards to keep it clean and peer at Mac out of the corner of my eye. He is already out of his wetsuit, a towel wrapped around his waist to hide the good bits while he pulls on his jeans. I copy him, hurrying to extricate myself from the cold, wet neoprene and rushing to put on my clothes that I left in a pile on the beach.

*Towel around waist, that's it, now where are my knickers?*
*Oh sod them, oops, it's slipping, quick, get my jeans on. Yikes,*
*my nipples are showing.*

Blimey, I am the epitome of a typical city-dwelling tourist at the beach. Trying to dress with the help of just a towel while hopping and floundering and showing all the parts I am trying to conceal in the first place. How does Mac do it? He looks so cool.

*He looks so hot.*

I hurriedly pull on my jumper, wrench my dripping wet hair back into a ponytail and slip my feet into my shoes.

'Ready?' Mac asks, the picture of post-surf perfection.

'Ready,' I reply with a sneeze.

'Your jumper's inside out,' Mac grins, walking towards me and tugging on the label at my waist.

'Er, I know, it's the new cool thing to do in the city.'

'Is it now? Right, well, I'll be sure to do that tomorrow when your big director one gets here.'

I beam up at him, noting how good he looks when he is wet. Locks of hair hang down past his ears and caress his glistening eyebrows. His skin glows healthily in the dusky light, his adorable freckles just visible across his nose. My stomach churns.

'And so would I be right in thinking,' he smiles, moving closer, 'that it is also cool to wear your knickers outside the bottom of your trouser leg?'

'Huh? Oh shit, damn.' I scramble to yank out the blue thong that is protruding from the left leg of my jeans and quickly shove it into my pocket. 'Bollocks, I am such an arse.'

Mac laughs and pulls me towards him, placing a gentle kiss on my forehead.

'You have a great arse, Milly,' he grins, 'and I love it when you blush. It makes you look cute.'

Right on cue, my blushing mechanism goes into over-drive. Mac moves his hands up to my cheeks and presses them gently, tilting my head up towards his.

*Kiss me again, kiss me again*, I want to beg. *Take me home and ravish me!*

'Do you mind if I kiss you again, Milly?' he asks quietly.

'Er, no, not at all, actually that would be rather ni—'

His lips envelop my words and I give in to the kiss. This time we are both salty. This time the kiss is even sweeter, more passionate, more sure of itself. Just right.

'Cooo-eeeee, Amelia, are you there?'

The voice jolts us both back to reality. I whip my head around to see my mother standing behind the low wall at the back of the beach, her unmistakable coiffured hair outlined from behind by the flickering lights of the fairground. Mac and I step apart but I notice how his palm still rests on the small of my back. My mother places a flat hand across her forehead like a sailor lost at sea and peers into the rapidly descending darkness.

'Amelia, darling, is that you down there?'

'Ye . . . yes,' I croak back, my mouth still numb from the kiss.

'Fiona said you would be here. We thought you might like to join us for dinner, your father, Fiona and I. We're going to the next village and I am not exactly sure of the level of cuisine on offer, but by the look of the figures around these parts I get the feeling they like their food, so with any luck we will find something.'

Mac chuckles and gives me a nudge when I am mid-cringe. I shake my head and mouth 'sorry'.

'Amelia, do you want to come, dear?'

*Do I? No, not really, Mother. I want to stay here and kiss this very kissable man.*

'Yes, Mum,' I call back, 'that would be lovely. Just a sec.'

I turn to Mac and run my hand down his bicep. It is tantalisingly firm under his clothes.

'Come with us?' I ask hopefully.

He shakes his head and kisses me gently on the lips, leaving me wanting more.

'No, I'll leave you to it, Milly. I've got stuff to do, and anyway you should spend time with your folks. I have been kinda monopolising you since they arrived.'

I nod resignedly.

'I guess I should spend the evening with them. My dad has been a bit stressed lately.'

'He certainly wasn't stressed last night so,' Mac grins, 'not after my da's help with the devil's drink. Now,' he smiles, bending down to lift up my surfboard, which he then places under my arm, 'you make sure you get lots of sleep, 'cos you've got a big day tomorrow and I can't have my star pupil on poor form, now can I? Not when you have your one to impress. Good night, God bless and good luck for tomorrow in advance.'

'Thank you,' I sigh, finding it hard to repel his magnetism and drag myself away. 'You will be there tomorrow, won't you?'

'Of course,' Mac winks, 'you can count on me. I wouldn't miss it for the world.'

I catch his blown kiss on the wind and walk away.

The hotel is the best in the county, occupying a vast castle that towers majestically above the harbour at the south end of the town. I have never been inside before as, to be frank, it is not the type of place Mac and Dave would frequent on a night out. There are way more airs and graces than at Gallagher's Bar, I find myself thinking as I arrive for the meeting ten minutes early. It also crosses my mind that I would probably not even have thought that thought a couple of months ago. Perhaps my tastes have changed since I came here?

The director, Matthew, is much smarter than I remember from the audition, and also younger. His scruffy, almost student-like attire from the audition day has been replaced by the very thespian get-up of black woollen polo neck and black slacks. His ginger goatee beard is gone, along with the

286

remnants of food that dwelled within. He is freshly shaven, his hair is closely cropped and he exudes such confidence I fear his head might just topple off his shoulders with the weight of it. He arrives ten minutes late.

'Milly Armstrong, *enchanté*,' he gushes, despite neither being French nor, in all honesty, looking genuinely enchanted to see me.

I take his hand, shake it vigorously and just stop my knees from bending into a curtsey. This man holds the key to my future success. The big bunch of keys, in fact, that may just open those impassable heavy doors that have kept me out of the inner circle of 'the business' for so long.

'You're looking delightfully *surfy*, I must say, darling,' he smiles, leading me to an entire herd of cows-worth of leather sofas in the centre of the hotel bar.

I sneak a glimpse at myself in the full-length mirrors that line the far wall, creating an optical illusion that the bar stretches on for miles, which wouldn't surprise me in a hotel like this. I am indeed 'surfy', as Matthew chose to define my look. Not naturally so, of course, although that was what I was aiming for during the intense styling session with Fi, Dave and my mother this morning. We were the first people in Dave's surf shop at the ridiculous hour of seven o'clock. A full two hours (or even four if Dave has a morning surf session) before the usual opening hour. Fi took charge of Dave, making him race back and forth to the stockroom like one of the Olympic relay team in search of colours and sizes. He is clearly a man in the early stages of infatuation – eager to please and always with a smile on his face despite the demands. My mother assumed the role of both Susannah and Trinny, telling me what not to wear and detailing the reasons exactly why not. If such makeovers are becoming common, I envisage much higher suicide rates in those of us not blessed with perfect bodies and tastes. Honestly, I was informed I had body shape oddities I did not even know were possible. By mid-way through the session I had resigned myself to the fact that I would only be able to wear one cut of trouser and two tops for the rest of my life.

Nevertheless, I am pleased with the finished look – a pair of bubblegum-pink hipster flares emblazoned with the words *Roxy Life* across the bum. (They could probably have fitted *Roxy Life is a Really Fabulous Life* across *my* bum but the designers have been kind and used large lettering.) A belt made of shells interwoven with pink beads is slung across my hips. On top I have a T-shirt embroidered on the chest with a shiny pink hibiscus flower. Shell jewellery adorns my neck and wrists. Fi was very keen for me to wear glittery pink flip-flops to match the ensemble and so talked my mother into painting my toenails silver to make me look extra 'beachy'. I eventually convinced Fi that pretty though the flip-flops were, I would probably not perform well in the sea this afternoon if all my toes had fallen off due to frostbite. I chose a pair of black suede pumps instead and quietly advised Dave to put the flip-flops away until the next Irish heatwave. My mother, who has always been a perfectionist when it comes to appearance, painted my fingernails silver too and then kindly styled my hair into natural-looking soft waves for the effortless beach look. This took almost two hours. And much effort. The curl emphasises the different tones that my once-chestnut mane now sports and adds a spring to my step with its bounce.

My mother also became my make-up artist, laughing and joking with Fi and me while she concentrated on my look and surprisingly not irritating me much at all. Other than with the odd peculiar phrase of hers like 'Oh Amelia, you have the wrinkles of a Portuguese woman' and 'I wish you hadn't become Irish, dear, Celtic skins are finicky when it comes to foundation shades.' I declined to comment and just let my mother get on with the task in the hope that we would bond through it. She was clearly in her element and enthused by Fi's regular compliments. I have to admit, the tinted moisturiser, the deftly dusted bronzing powder and the light pink eyeshadow to tone with my pinky lip-gloss really do the trick. My snotty nose has thankfully improved, so I look and feel radiant. I *am* a surf chick. As Matthew said, I look delightfully surfy.

'Thank you, Matthew,' I say, accepting the compliment with a smile as I lower myself into the magnificent leather sofa and pray that my snug hipsters don't rip. 'Well, you know me, Matthew, surf surf surf when the waves are . . .'

*What was the word Mac taught me? Ripping? Pumping?*

'. . . er, waving.'

'I bet. Holy God, how fantastic, waving waves. Ooh, I feel the shivers of pleasure already.'

Matthew flaps his hands theatrically before ordering a sparkling mineral water from our hovering, bowing waiter. I ask for the same and then cross my legs when I realise my nerves are already getting the better of me and I am desperate for the toilet.

'So, Matthew,' I begin breezily, 'I trust you had a good journey, Matthew.'

*Stop saying his name, you sound like a desperate creep.*

Matthew nods and jangles the heavy silver chain bracelet on his wrist.

'Not bad, Milly, not bad at all. The landing was a wee bit bumpy, you know, but I got through it with a boiled travel sweet and the hand of a glorious man to grip on to.'

'Right.' I cough nervously. 'You said the landing?'

'In Sligo airport. Sure didn't we come over from Dublin in the funniest little plane.'

*Sure you did. Plane indeed. While your leading lady came by a boneshaker that once upon a time used to be a train. Who's the star of this show anyway?*

I smile sweetly to disguise the bitter taste in my mouth. Swanky hotels, planes here, there and everywhere. That is 'the business' that Dan Clancy knows. That is 'the business' that I want to know. Not Pooh Corners and rickety trains.

*Hang in there, Milly, this man will lead you to all that.*

I fix my best sparkling eyes on Matthew while the waiter delivers our drinks.

'So who are you with, Matthew?' I ask, cringing as I hear myself say his name again. 'You said "we" came by plane.'

'I did, I did, you are absolutely right, Milly. Well, that is the great news so it is.'

I sit forward in my seat and sparkle even more.

*Steven Spielberg? Brad Pitt? Who?*

'You see now,' he continues, 'events with the project have really moved on in the past few weeks, Milly. Gerald may have explained this already to you . . .'

I try not to convey a negative response and remain silent.

'. . . but we received some rather fantastic financial assistance from a private backer in the business in Ireland. And you know, I do mean fantastically fantastic.'

Images fill my mind of my first pay cheque having to be one of those huge cardboard ones presented at charity events to accommodate all the zeros on the end of my salary. Of cruising into Cannes on my luxury yacht to attend the film festival in my dress of precious rubies, of sipping Cristal champagne with my friends George Clooney, Cameron Diaz and Puff. (That's Puff as in Daddy, not as in the Magic Dragon.) Not that I am allowing myself to get carried away with it all.

'Well that is fabulous news,' I beam, hoping the euro signs aren't visible in my eyes. 'And who is this backer?'

'Ooh now, nosy nose, I can't divulge that information at the moment, darling, but he loved the project pitch and all I can say is that he has been very generous. Very generous indeed.'

Matthew fans his face and jangles his silver-clad wrist again. I suddenly understand the reason for his new image. Generous sponsor obviously means generous amounts of jewellery and clothes for our esteemed director. Noting the satisfied grin on his face, the words 'cat' and 'cream' immediately spring to mind.

Running a hand glistening with chunky silver rings over his closely cropped hair, Matthew leans forward conspiratorially.

'Now come here, Milly darling, I am sure I don't have to explain to a woman like yourself that this backing changes everything, absolutely everything.'

He sweeps his arms around dramatically, attracting bemused glances from the other groups of people in the bar. So much for being conspiratorial.

'You see now suddenly, darling, we have all the funds we need to make the film I so so sooo want to make. We have the opportunity at our tingling fingertips to, you know, push the project forward, choose our locations, attract the best actors . . .'

My head expands with pride.

'We can find the most experienced extras, the most wonderfully fantastic crew. Suddenly, Milly, this project is bigger than itself and growing by the minute. We can afford to have the script rewritten by someone fabulous, we can afford a marvellously marvellous wardrobe full of the most gorgeous clothes and we can purchase all the equipment we need. Then we can go out, sure, and bloody well promote this movie until the bloody cows come marching home. Until the names on everyone's lips out there in the land of Joe Public are our names. Our names, Milly Armstrong!'

He punches his chest victoriously. I gasp and find my hands clapping with the sheer magnitude of it all. Where once I thought I had been offered the lead in a small Irish film that could perhaps perform well if we gave it a heart with our sheer determination, now it sounds as if I am Kate bloody Winslet in the money-making epic that *Titanic* became. I am the king of the world! And despite Matthew's dramatic personality, I believe every word. He is passionate about the project and clearly thrilled. As am I to be part of it. A big part of it. I cross my legs even tighter in case I wet myself with excitement.

'Gosh, wow, well that is just amazing,' I gasp, still applauding. 'I can't believe it.'

'Neither could I, Milly darling, neither could I,' Matthew says so emotively that I fear he is going to cry. 'But you know, it *has* happened, and that is why I am here with my leading man to recce our location out here in Donegal and to touch base with anyone and everyone of importance to my film. Then I can return to Dublin with the green light to go, go, GO.'

'And here was I thinking you were just checking up on me,' I say, forcing a laugh.

'Ha ha, not at all, not at all. As if that would be top of my agenda, darling. Ooh, dear God, no. I have much too much to think about now, like.'

A frown slips on to my brow as I struggle to interpret the last sentence.

'Now, darling, I must say that time is tight, tight, tight' – I actually see him clench his buttocks during this statement – 'so today may be a little hectic. Basically, Milly, I want to check out the location with your help, see a little surfing action from yourself to get my brain into this whole surfing thing and the logistics of it all, and then go from there. Is that fine and dandy with you?'

'Fine and dandy,' I repeat, my stomach cramping at the mention of my surfing action, 'fine and dandy.'

'That's grand, and I am so glad that you understand about the importance of our backer and how his presence changes the whole emphasis of the project.'

I try to nod enthusiastically while feeling slightly worn out from trying to sparkle for so long.

'And, you know, how his presence has brought us the lead man I could only have dreamed about in my bed at night. Never did I think this fantastic boy would be ours.'

I snort at this admission and then quietly sip my mineral water while Matthew manically fans himself. A lead man. A lead man to the leading lady. Film stars. Co-stars. I smile into the bubbles of my drink and wriggle deeper into the sumptuous soft leather. I try to picture my co-star and wonder what he will be like. Will we have that chemistry to make our performances leap off the screen? Will we have to kiss? Will we be heralded as the greatest romantic performance to come out of Ireland since . . . well since for ever? I lick my lips and tilt my head at Matthew.

'Does he have a name? Our headlining actor?'

Matthew smoothes his almost nonexistent hair again and titters delightedly.

'Ooh he does, Milly, he certainly does, darling. He has a fabulous name and a perfectly fantastic body and face to match. In fact he is up in his suite right now grooming that body of his before he greets us. God, the thought just sends me all like that.'

He shakes himself vigorously like a hyperactive octopus.

I grimace at Matthew's obviously sexual enthusiasm and pray that his trousers do not begin to display any tent-like structures while he drools on.

'Our actor,' Matthew continues, 'is one of a kind. God knows he can carry any film, just by his looks alone. But then that talent and that voice . . . oooh.'

My eyes flit anxiously to his groin. No erection yet, thank the Lord.

'What can I say about him, Milly?'

*Quite a lot by the sound of it.*

'The boy is an absolute darling. I would do anything for him.'

*Spare me the details.*

'And oooh, Holy God, speak of the devil, if it isn't himself coming over now.'

Before I turn my head in the direction of Matthew's yearning gaze, I take a deep breath and prepare myself to meet the actor I will be working very closely with over the next few months. I smooth down the front of my gorgeous new trousers, push the waves of my hair gently behind my ears and squeeze my lips together to redistribute the remaining lip-gloss. I rise up from the sofa, turn to greet him and offer my cheek to be kissed in an as self-assured-thespian way as I can possibly muster.

'Bloody hell, Mimi! You're a dark horse. Look at you, babe. I never knew you were a bona fide Hawaiian surfer girl. Lovely shells, darling. What, no chicken nugget suit?'

I freeze in an air-kiss, my lips pouted at the ready, my eyes half shut, my body leaning precariously across the back of the sofa. I want to open my eyes and see for myself but I am suddenly incapable of movement. He kisses both my cheeks before patronisingly ruffling my hair. I open my eyes, flicking them downwards.

He is unmistakable even from the feet (clad in Gucci shoes) up. Those long legs and that slim body clothed in what are obviously such expensive designer labels they need show no logos. Those slim hands with their elegant piano-player fingers. I cautiously lift my gaze. There it is; that pretty, boyish face. Those pink lips too perfect and soft to be intended for a man. That dark, almost black hair that is shorter than usual but still framing his face in regular tamed curls. Those big, beautiful eyes. Oh. My. God.

I feel my styled bravado drain from my head to my body and out through the soles of my stiff new shoes, which probably still have the price on the bottom. I shuffle on the spot, suddenly uncomfortable in my new styled image. After all, he knows me. He once knew every part of me. He has seen me naked and been privy to my innermost thoughts. He has even seen me as a chicken nugget, for fuck's sake.

'Hello, Dan,' I croak, blushing beneath my bronzing powder, 'what a lovely surprise.'

My mouth is dry. My brain even drier, sucked clean of anything witty or meaningful to say. Dan Clancy winks at me and smiles his trademark lopsided smile. He breezes around the sofa in a cloud of 212 Men aftershave, aware that every woman in the bar is watching him with awestruck admiration and every man with sheer jealousy. He lowers himself into the centre of the largest chocolate leather sofa, stretches his arms across the back and slowly exhales. Matthew almost has an orgasm on the armchair to my right.

'Milly Armstrong,' Dan says, clicking his perfect tongue against the roof of his perfect mouth, 'how could I not have put two and two together? You and I on the same film project. How uncanny.'

He fixes a white smile on me, which I try to nonchalantly return. A flick of Dan's elegant wrist informs the scurrying waiter that he would like attention, which he will undoubtedly receive by the silver-plated bucketload.

'Well this is going to be fabulous, Matthew,' Dan Clancy announces with a wink at the giggling director. He clasps his hands behind his head and clicks his tongue again. 'Yes, Matthew, I definitely have good feelings about our location, and with my Mimi here in County Donegal as our tour guide we can surely do no wrong. We are off to a flying start.'

# CHAPTER TWENTY-SEVEN

## *Feeling Swell*

'He said what?' Fi splutters when I finally return to Pooh Corner with my tail between my legs and my head in utter turmoil.

'Tour guide,' I repeat, unenthusiastically rubbing wax on to my surfboard.

'I'll give him feckin' tour guide, the cheeky bollix. You are not a feckin' tour guide, Milly; you are his feckin' co-star, the stupid gobshite. And I'll give him flying start. I'll kick the stupid bastard flyin' into next week if he treats you like that so I will. Ignorant arse. I always told you he was a gobshite, Milly.'

*Perhaps, but a totally adorable gobshite all the same.*

I sniff, sneeze and concentrate on waxing my board. Fi bangs around in the kitchenette muttering strings of obscenities under her breath. Thank God my mother and father just left to freshen themselves up; my mother has never been one for enthusiastic swearing. Or pigeon French, as she likes to call it.

Who would have thought it; Dan Clancy playing my co-star in my first ever film role? We used to allow ourselves to fantasise about working together, back in the days when we would lie in the sun on St Stephen's Green reading scripts before castings. Not that we ever auditioned for roles together, because whenever I went up for a job and begged Dan to read for the male role, he would always find a reason not to. Fi said this was because Dan Clancy always thought he was better than me. That he aspired to bigger and better things and so if a play or a film was good enough for Milly Armstrong to audition for, it was definitely not good enough for Dan Clancy. She was wrong, of course. He was obviously just waiting for the right role and the right moment to establish us as an electric on-screen couple. Dan knows best. I allow myself a proud smile as I rub the block of wax in a therapeutic circular motion across the surfboard. Dan Clancy may have sprinted on up the ladder while I slid down the snake to chicken nugget suit territory, but all of a sudden we find ourselves on the same square. Although Dan pretended in front of Matthew that he did not know I would be here, I know differently. Dan was well aware I was here because I told him so myself in great detail when we spoke on the phone as I sat on the sea wall outside Pooh Corner. So Dan knew who his co-star would be if he accepted the role and clearly thought the time was right for us to become a team again. Here we are. I love the clandestine nature of his plan, and Dan need not worry; I can keep a secret.

Who would have thought that, despite everything, Dan Clancy and his doe-like eyes would still have the same effect on me as they always have? I tried to ignore the butterflies in my stomach but, and this is strictly between you and me, for the duration of our meeting in the hotel bar this morning I found myself gazing longingly at him, wishing he were mine. I know, I know, I kissed another man several times yesterday and with passion, but how can I control the flutterings in my heart? Dan may be arrogant and vainly groomed while Mac is humble and as natural as the ocean, but Dan is Dan. He was my big Irish love back when he was a nobody and now he is a somebody, the love of a nation and soon to be the love of the entire worldwide female movie-going population no doubt. He has a presence, and that presence is impossible to

297

ignore. Do I still love him? I can't be sure, but I just can't help myself.

'Well, Milly,' Fi mutters, stomping across the sitting room collecting her shoes and jacket on the way, 'I hope you've got over the stupid eejit once and for all.'

I clear my throat and nervously increase my waxing speed. Fi carries on.

'The man is a bollix, Milly, and I don't care how many shite TV shows he's in or how many arsey Hollywood parties he goes to, he is still a bollix. He thinks he's too good for all his old friends now he's moved on.'

I mumble a forced agreement, keeping my head down for fear that my best friend will read the look in my eyes.

'Here now, you just go out there and you show that Dan feckin' nancy-boy what you're made of, right? Show the both of them that you are a surf chick and that you're a bloody good actress who can do exactly what they ask, no bother at all. OK?

'I said, OK, Milly?'

'What? Oh yes, right.'

'Milly' – Fi crouches down on the floor and takes my hand – 'I think if you go rubbing any more wax on that surf-board, like, it's gonna bloody sink as soon as you put it in the water. Sure you've got more than enough.'

I look from Fiona to the board (which is beginning to look decidedly candle-like) and back again.

'You might be right.'

'I'm always right,' she giggles, slowly helping me to my feet.

We stand in the front room of Pooh Corner, our very brown but now very homely dwelling of the past three months, and clasp each other's hands. Fi looks up at me and smiles so warmly I can't help but grin back. I feel a knot of tension easing in my shoulders.

'OK, my bestest friend Milly,' Fi says firmly, 'this is it. Now, you've done your research. We watched every feckin' surf movie ever made hundreds of times. You've near exhausted yourself with your efforts and you've even saved a dolphin like. You've come a long way for a city mott with a fear of water, so you have.'

I press my lips together and nod tentatively.

'Sure and haven't you got the mightiest surfboard in the land? Not to mention the best instructor, and you've got your friends there to cheer you on. So all you have to do is catch a wave. All you have to do is wait for that curtain to go up and give your audience the only performance you can – a bloody fantastic one. You can do this, Milly, you're the best.'

Fi's tone is utterly sincere and full of encouragement. I hug her to me, tears of fear, excitement and anticipation welling up in my eyes.

'Thanks, Fi.'

'Not at all, I'm your biggest fan. Anyhow, let's get on. Are you ready to go and show those feckers what you can do?'

'I'm ready,' I say, taking the deepest breath I have ever inhaled. 'Let's show them.'

Now I know how that poor Kelly Slater must feel when he rocks up at one of his world championship contests with the weight of expectation on his broad, muscular, bronzed (you get my drift) shoulders. Granted, the crowd forming on the beach to watch my display is small, but it is a significant one by the characters contained within it.

There is Fiona, my best friend and greatest support, who has championed my career from the moment we met, never once doubting my talent despite the crap jobs she has witnessed me undertake. Fi is waving two giant red pompoms from goodness knows where, ever the cheerleader. I don't want to let her down.

Beside Fi are my parents; Fiona's antithesis when it comes to their attitude towards what I am doing with my life. They have never supported my acting 'lark', but they are bewildered yet visibly excited by the day's events. The presence of Dan Clancy on the same beach has clearly had a profound effect on my mother. She has not said a word since we got here, which is definitely a first. I want to prove to them this is not a pipe dream. I want to make my parents proud of me. I want to be better than darling, perfect Ed for once. I want my dad to take off that ridiculous tartan flat cap and shamrock-embroidered fleece.

Next there is Matthew, the rather smarmy director who started my career hurtling down this path to the waters of Donegal in the first place. Unbeknown to Matthew, I lied to him about my ability in the water, but he saw my potential as an actress and he gave me this opportunity. I just have to make this work.

Much to my mother's disappointment, Matthew stands between her and the man who is responsible for the rest of the crowd forming in a giggling female gaggle behind him. Which I see includes Kathleen and her posse of friends, in skirts so mini they could be naked from the waist down and cause just as much of a stir. The skirts, I suspect, were not purchased at Joyce's Fashion Emporium. The man responsible for such displays of bare flesh is, of course, the one and only Dan Clancy. Dan knows me. He knows how much I have wanted this dream to become reality and for how long. He chose to become my co-star in this film. I want to show him . . . to show him I can do it and that I am worthy of the part. To show him (and I hate to admit it) what he has been missing out on for the last year.

Which leaves Mac and Dave, my intrepid surfing instructors. Mac stands to my right at the water's edge, swathed in neoprene as ever, tall and confident as he discreetly points out the currents to me, explaining where I should paddle out and where I should sit when I am out there. Dave stands to my left with his faithful video camera trained on my profile, recording the anxious expression on my face. Dave has been a good friend to me and an even better friend to Fi. He is making Fi happy, which makes me happy. I want to thank him by surfing well.

And Mac . . . well, what can I say? From the moment we met, Mac Heggarty has been gorgeous, confusing, infuriating, supportive, encouraging, modest, patient and a whole other thesaurus of emotions. He has amazed me every day with the things I find out about him and he is the one who has pushed and guided this waterphobe to where I am now. He has let down his defences and explained his feelings for me. He kissed me with a gentle passion I have never experienced before and he bought me the beautiful board I will ride today just because he thought I had earned it. I have not kissed Mac today; I couldn't in front of Dan. In fact I am terribly unsettled by the presence here on the same beach of the two men who have stirred my heart since I moved to Ireland, perhaps both to witness me fail. I owe Mac so much, but Dan and I have a history that has become part of me. Can knowing Mac for three months really produce feelings to rival those I have for Dan, or is it just an instructor crush? I don't know right now and I cannot dwell on such matters. I have to deal with the job in hand and be professional. I have to succeed. I owe Mac that much for definite. I can try and live up to his expectations as the wonderfully kind surf instructor he is. I must succeed. For Mac and of course for myself. For Milly Armstrong, the one this crowd is here to watch.

'If you need me I am right here, Milly,' Mac says at the end of his practical coaching instructions. 'Don't go getting yourself in a position where you feel uncomfortable just for these city bastards; they don't know what it's like to be out there in that water.'

I nod and fiercely chew my top lip.

'Just give me a sign and I can be out the back in a shot, OK?'

I nod again and chew harder. My eyes flit to the audience and to the bemused expression on Dan Clancy's face. *Nice wetsuit, babe*, he mouths, making a gesture with his hands as if tracing my hips. I squirm and wish I could have fitted a full body corset under this thing. I have got used to exposing my curves in skin-tight rubber since those first excruciatingly embarrassing days. After all, a wetsuit is both functional and essential. The surfers in town do not mock me when they see me walk past in my neoprene suit. Far from it, in fact, they eye me with a certain respect. I am one of them. However, Dan, Matthew and my parents are outsiders to our surfing world. All they see is a pair of size twelve hips in a ludicrously tight costume. My self-consciousness returns. I want to cry.

I suddenly feel Mac's hand lightly cup my chin and move my head away from Dan's direction.

'Focus, Milly,' he says with such firmness it jolts me. 'Don't go getting distracted by eejits.'

'He's Dan Clancy. He's not an eejit, he's a star, and you're just jealous,' I reply petulantly. The words hang in the air between us like a cloud of smog.

*Why did I say that?*

Mac's brow creases into a frown and he regards me silently as if deciding how to respond. I see a flicker of hurt in his eyes and lower my own to stare helplessly at my neoprene boots.

'Well, whatever,' Mac says with a quiet cough. 'Let's just get on with this thing, hey.

'Then we can all get back to living our feckin' lives,' he adds under his breath but loud enough for me to hear.

Mac walks away to the edge of the water, turns to me and taps his watch.

'Have ya got anythin' to say to the camera before your big performance, Milly?' asks Dave, moving the lens closer.

I blink and look out to sea before turning to look at Dave.

'I feel like a five-year-old going into her first ballet exam,' I say with a flicker of a smile. 'I feel scared and unprepared, but this is it, this is the moment. I came here at the end of February not able to paddle my feet in the sea and now I am

302

going to go out there and try to catch a wave on my very own board. Some of these people are cheering me on, some of them probably want me to fail, but all I can do is give it my best shot. Oh God, I am nervous, I am so nervous, but wish me luck. And don't say break a leg!'

Once I am out in the water alone it is no longer about my acting career but simply about catching a wave; that is my focus. I manage to paddle out the back without too much drama, shivering as I duck my head under the water for the first of many ice-cream headaches. Remembering Mac's coaching yesterday, I paddle out close to the cliff at the north end of the beach where the current rushes the water back out to sea. That way it is like hopping on to a moving conveyor belt and stepping off once I have travelled as far out as I need. The waves are apparently two feet high at their biggest, although this will still mean they reach my chest *if* and *when* I stand up. I will never understand how surfers estimate the size of waves. Safe to say they always *under*estimate, so two feet to a surfer would be double that in real terms. It must be a psychological trick to make one think it is small and rid the mind of fear. It doesn't work for me; my fear is still here and very real. However, I understand well enough to appreciate that today I have been blessed with favourable conditions for my task. Relatively small surf, blown smooth by the light offshore breeze, and spirit-lifting May sunshine. My wetsuit is keeping out the chill of the Atlantic water and I am comfortable on my new board, which glistens delightfully in the sunlight.

I sit up on the board with my legs straddling the sides and peer at the beach. My audience is nothing more than an inaudible blur of moving colours and shapes in the distance. A rippling stretch of water separates us but it could just as well be an entire ocean, as I feel completely detached sitting here out to sea by myself. It is a rare opportunity to sit here peacefully and look back at the land. To be able to view the town from this angle. To see the beach and the rusty fair-ground and the colourful buildings of the town flanked by the majestic flat-topped mountains behind. It is as if I am in my own little bubble, calmed by the lapping of the water around me and observing civilisation from afar. Suddenly I feel like a real surfer. I am sitting patiently waiting for the ocean to bring me a wave that has travelled all the way from America, the nearest landmass to the west, just to be ridden by me before it is broken apart by the Irish shores.

I want to feel the wave push me from behind, committing me to the ride ahead. I want to jump to my feet and cruise to the shore while the wind races through my hair. I want to be a surfer. Of course my ability may fall short of *jumping* and *cruising* but I can but dream. According to my parents, I have been dreaming my whole adult life. So why stop now?

I come around from my reverie when I detect movement on the beach. I can make out Dave and Mac standing knee-deep in the water. Dave has the video camera trained on me so I give him a wave from afar. Mac is hopping up and down at Dave's side, waving his arms in the air. I wave back. Mac waves again. I give him a double thumbs-up. He gesticulates wildly.

*Mac, would you quit the waving and let me concentrate? I've got a job to do here.*

My eyes are drawn back to Mac's frantic movements. I frown, trying to pull the wits about me that have begun to drift out to sea. I remember now, that wave means some-thing. I just don't quite remember what.

With the offshore wind I don't hear the thunderous noise approaching until it is too late. Fearing I am about to be run over by a passenger hovercraft at full speed, I whip my head around from Mac's semaphore and peer behind me. In fact I don't even manage a full peer. *Pee* would be more apt a description for what I do when I witness the white-topped mountain of water bearing down on top of me.

'Shit, that's what Mac's signal meant,' I yell to no one, as there is of course no one here to help me.

The first wave in the set; there may be four more behind it and I am right in their path. In the 'impact zone' as it is known. I am history. The lip of the breaking wave curls above me like an open jaw. I whimper pathetically and prepare myself for impact while trying in vain to paddle through it and out to sea. My reactions are too slow. A shadow looms above me like the grim reaper himself rising up and spreading the arms of his black cloak. I know what is about to happen and I fear it but I am helpless. The jaws of the wave close on their prey, the lip crashes down on the backs of my legs. I am thrown violently from the board, hurled over the falls and pushed under the water to a murky depth, spiralling as I am churned over in the mouth of the watery beast. I hold my breath and try to stifle the scream of terror that is ringing in my head. What do I do now? What can I do now?

*If you wipe out, just relax. Conserve energy, count to ten and be calm. You will come up eventually. Trust me.*

Mac's words from our intensive coaching session yesterday reach my ears as clearly as if he is beside me under the water. Calm is the last thing I am feeling right now but I begin to count slowly.

*One . . . two . . .*

My lungs relax.

*Three . . . four . . .*

I wonder how much longer.

*Five . . . six . . .*

*Help me, Mac.*

I am pushed upwards by an invisible force and gasp as I see the sky above me.

'Thank Christ for that,' I wheeze while tugging on the end of my leash to locate my surfboard on the surface of the water.

I am alive. *Thank you, Mac.*

I glance quickly around me to check that Mac is not out here with me, so real was his voice, but I see him standing on the beach gazing anxiously towards me. The man is in my head. Either that or he would make a very successful ventriloquist. I have to concentrate now; there will be more waves behind. Sure enough, my eyes locate the second beast rapidly approaching. I bale out from the surfboard again, take as deep a breath as I possibly can and dive beneath the wave. I hear the rumble as the powerful whitewater races over me, thankfully leaving me untouched this time. I do this twice more, diving for cover in the calm waters below until the set has passed and there is a lull. I survived, but as they say, this is the calm before the storm. I clamber back on to the board and prepare myself for the next set of waves. I am exhausted and somewhat bedraggled, with tears of frustration in my eyes, but I will not give up. Every good surfer wipes out, even Mac Heggarty, so it doesn't mean I have failed. I give Mac a thumbs-up and position myself out of the impact zone. When the next wave comes I will be ready.

It is not long before the calm of the ocean is broken again. I hear the now familiar rumble of something brewing on the horizon. The sound builds as the wave grows. I paddle in a circle and face the nose of the board towards the beach like a dart aiming for the bull's-eye. I then face my fear and glance behind me. Here it comes; a wall of water topped with a white cap that lets me know the wave is about to break. I am momentarily startled when I see a dark shadow in the body of the wave that is illuminated from behind by the late afternoon sun. I blink to rid my mind of images of big sharks with even bigger teeth and I begin to paddle. My arms pull through the water and propel the board forwards, taking me up to speed with the travelling wave. Another glance. The shadow is there again, moving through the water beneath the surface, growing bigger and more defined. If it is a shark, this should certainly win Dave a few bob on *You've*

*Been Framed.* All I can do is paddle and hope for the best. I am already committed. I dig deep with my hands and even deeper with my self-belief. One more stroke and the wave hits. I feel it pick me up, lifting the tail of the board and pushing me into the air. The drop looks steep between where I am and the bottom of the wave. With wide eyes, I push down on the board with my shaking hands and somehow locate my feet. They slap on to the deck, my toes clinging on for dear life through the thick neoprene of my boots. I am upright, I am standing up. Fuck me, I am bloody well surfing!

The board flies down the face of the wave, which must only be chest height but which feels like the descent on a freefall parachute jump. I crouch for balance and position my bent arms above my knees. The surfer's stance. I am smiling and laughing as I hurtle towards the beach and I hear the cheers erupting from my audience. I only have a split second to acknowledge the menacing dark shadow beside my board before it blasts out of the water and becomes suddenly real. I gasp aloud and wobble precariously when the grey shape leaps into the air before plunging back into the sea.

'Flipper!' I cry when he leaps again and I see the familiar shape of a baby dolphin.

This time he is more confident, hurdling the nose of my moving board like a trained circus performer. The wave pushes me on towards the beach while my baby dolphin friend surfs along beside me, toying with the whitewater and prancing over my board with ease. The moment is pure magic. Who needs a *Titanic*-sized production? For a few seconds at least I am the king of the world.

When I reach the shore the wave runs out of energy and I topple off the board into the shallows. I open my eyes beneath the surface just in time to see the dolphin wriggle happily, spin around and disappear towards the horizon with a flick of his tail. When I emerge I am already smiling.

'Bloody hell, Milly, you were feckin' brilliant!' Fi cries with tears glistening on the tips of her long eyelashes.

She throws herself fully clothed into the water and flings her arms around me.

'You did it, my friend,' she whispers into my neck.

'I did, didn't I?'

'Amazing, Milly, that was a mighty wave all right,' Dave hoots. 'Ah shite, I'm getting the bloody camera wet.'

I follow him as he retreats on to the sand and I deposit my board on the beach. I squeeze my eyes shut to stop the sting of the saltwater and smile inside and out. I feel like the world champion emerging from a contest final to claim my trophy, such is the triumphant thrill racing through my whole body. My audience claps and cheers.

'Wonderful, pudding,' my father exclaims with a broad smile. 'Wasn't that just wonderful, Georgina?'

I turn to my mother. Is that a tear I see on her cheek? She self-consciously brushes the droplet away before I can ascertain its origin.

'I . . . I didn't know you had it in you, Amelia, truly I didn't,' my mother gulps. 'I am . . . we are . . . I am so proud.'

Tears spring to my eyes at the sound of these words. I smile and slowly wipe them away with the back of my hand. I may be thirty-one years old, but making my parents proud means a lot to me. For once I am not second best to Ed, and it feels bloody great.

'Fantastic, darling, fantastico.' Matthew congratulates me with a slap on the back and a hearty cheer. 'Ooh, I can so picture the climax of my film already. I am so thrilled I could burst. Holy God, this is great stuff, and the big screen will adore this type of surfing action, you know.' He winks. 'Bloody great touch with the dolphin too, darling. I am totally loving that, like.'

'Er, thanks,' I snigger, wondering whether he honestly believes I have the power to set something like that up.

Honestly, these creative people, their reality/fantasy line can become rather blurred.

I move on down the group, shaking hands with strangers, hugging a very giggly Kathleen and lapping up the compliments. I could get used to this. At the end of the line, I reach the two tallest figures, both of whom are unsurprisingly attracting the most female attention. I am suddenly as breathless as when I was being churned beneath the first wave as I struggle with the decision about who to approach first. Dan stands to my left, his arms folded across the slim front of his elegant wool coat. He is as immaculate as ever in smart black trousers and a dark woollen polo neck that is just visible below his freshly shaven jawline. He flicks his head, causing his rich dark locks to fly backwards before they settle again in their precisely gelled style. His huge brown eyes are fixed on me. I think he looks impressed. I glance quickly at Mac to my right. He is taller than Dan and much broader. He does not have Dan's *Vogue* model looks but his features are strong and rugged. His glowing complexion reflects his outdoor lifestyle and his hair is, as ever, an unruly mass of curls. His arms too are crossed but across the chest of his superhero-style Quiksilver wetsuit rather than a designer coat. I look into his breathtakingly verdant eyes, which burn right into me as if they can see my soul. Dan and Mac. Mac and Dan. Two gorgeous men, so utterly different yet both with the ability to raise my heart rate and make me squirm with pleasure. What suits me best, chalk or cheese?

'So . . .' I begin, unable to decide which name to say first.

'So . . .' Dan purrs.

'So . . .' Mac repeats gruffly.

Dan of course chooses to speak first, forever willing to take centre stage.

'Well done, Milly old girl, that was bloody thrilling, I have to say. My acting should complement that surfing thing perfectly.'

*I could do without the 'old girl' stuff, but overall I'm happy with that.*

I shuffle my feet and smile coyly up at Dan, blushing at having his undivided attention. There is a heavy pause before Mac coughs and steps forward. He touches my arm softly and smiles so warmly I feel the chill of the ocean leave my body.

'You were great, maisie,' he says quietly, 'and this is one of the proudest moments of my life.'

'Thank you, Mac,' I beam, feeling the urge to throw my arms around my instructor's neck and to tell him how his words were in my head when I wiped out, as if he were right there with me. I don't. In fact, when Mac bends down to kiss me in front of Dan I feel myself pull away. It is not a conscious decision, it just happens. Dan smiles victoriously while Mac's cheeks turn puce. I look around to see the video camera capturing my discomfort.

'S . . . sorry, Mac,' I begin in a whisper.

'Don't be,' he shrugs coldly, 'I'm not.'

Matthew appears suddenly between us, the theatrical waving of his arms breaking our eye contact.

'Well now, I will give you a couple of hours to compose yourself, Milly, while himself and I do a recce of the town, all right? Then tonight I'd like to convene a meeting at our hotel bar, if that is fine and dandy with you?'

'Fine and dandy,' I croak, still reeling from Mac's dismissal of me.

'Anything to get me off this awful beach,' Dan scoffs. 'My Guccis are going to be ruined.'

If looks could kill, Mac would be a weapon of mass destruction with his sideways glance at Dan.

'Away and stick your Guccis up your hole,' Mac comments under his breath.

'I'm surprised you even know what Gucci is, country boy,' Dan retorts with equal indiscretion. 'I can't imagine it has been seen in this dump before.'

Fi steps in to take charge of the situation.

'Whoa there, macho men,' she says, placing her tiny self in between Dan and Mac. 'Any more testosterone flying around and we'll all be getting pregnant just by breathing in. What's the problem, like?'

Mac shakes his head.

'No problem,' Dan pouts. 'Just a little poor-boy jealousy, I suspect.'

'Ah, stop blowing shite out of your word hole,' says Mac with a scowl.

'Stop it now, the both of yous. This is Milly's moment, so just cool it, ya pair of bollixes.'

Fi shakes her head like an angry schoolteacher and then takes my arm to lead me up the beach.

'Men,' she tuts loudly.

'Men,' I repeat, flicking my head around to glance behind me.

*Beautiful, gorgeous, sexy men. Both of them. Damn. Who the hell am I going to kiss tonight?*

# CHAPTER TWENTY-EIGHT

## A Storm Brews

I spend longer than usual in the shower, using each beauty product twice and conditioning every hair on my body until I feel like a preened poodle emerging from a pet salon. I then pluck and shave most of the aforementioned hairs before moisturising so thoroughly I am surprised my skin does not simply slide off my bones. I slip on the dress chosen by my 'stylists' at Dave's shop just this morning, step into my favourite kitten heels and give my reflection the once-over. The dress is a swirl of sunset colours, draping loosely and flatteringly from the diagonal neckline, pulling in just below my waist and lightly hugging my hips to stop at mid-thigh length. I haven't worn a dress since my arrival in County Donegal and I suddenly feel more feminine than I have for weeks. I dry my hair very straight to show off its blonde lights and slip on my new shell bracelets. One more dab of lip-gloss for luck and I am ready. At the risk of sounding egotistical, I am rather pleased with the results.

'Jaysus, would you look at you,' Fi grins when I elegantly descend the stairs and sway my hips into the sitting room. 'Anyone would think you're off on a date tonight with that rig-out.'

I tut and flap my hand. I do have a date of sorts. With Dan . . . and (unfortunately) Matthew.

'Just trying to make a good impression, Fi, that's all.'

'Hmm,' she whistles pensively as I reach for my coat, 'but on whom?'

I avoid her eyes when I kiss her cheek and tell her I will see her later.

'I hope your man Matthew offers you millions of euros for the role,' Fi tells my retreating back. 'You deserve it after the work you've put in.'

'Thanks, Fi, fingers crossed.'

'But . . .'

*Shit, I knew there would be a 'but'.* My shoulders stiffen and I focus on the door.

'. . . you just be careful of your one.'

'Who?' I croak.

'You bloody well know who, ya big eejit. Dan up his own arse Clancy, that's who. I wouldn't trust that fecker as far as I could throw him. Not that I'd want to throw him because that would mean touching the stupid gobshite. He's full of it, Milly, so you just be careful now.'

'I will.'

My feet urge me to sprint for the door.

'And . . .'

*Fuck, I could have guessed there would be an 'and'.*

Fi pauses as if deciding how to phrase her sentence, which is rare for the girl who could chat for Ireland.

'. . . and you just mind out for Mac in all this, Milly Armstrong. He's a good fella, one of the best, and he's my cousin, so don't you go hurting him now, you hear me?'

Yes, I hear her. I hear the words and I know how loaded they are but I do not want to dwell on them. Not right now. I murmur an acknowledgement and hurry out of the room with my coat flapping open as if any second the magic spell will break and I will revert from the beautiful Princess Cinderella to plain old Cinders. I charge out of the car park from Pooh Corner as fast as I can possibly charge on kitten heels and turn right towards Dan's hotel. The further I walk, the more I push Fi's words to the back of my mind, where my guilt also quivers. I try to plaster over them with dreamy thoughts of my day. Of rising to one of the biggest challenges of my life by catching that wave. Of seeing the genuine pride on the faces of my parents, who did not stop talking about it until the sun went down and my father succumbed to the call of Gallagher's Bar. I shudder with excitement at the prospect of what lies ahead. Months of filming, which will be a hard slog but which will also be everything I have ever dreamed of. I am not scared of hard work; I welcome it in fact. Especially, and this is just between you and me, if that work involves starring opposite Dan Clancy. I close my eyes while I skip along the pavement and savour the thrill of my own success. I promised myself back in February that I would change my life. Well here I am. Today is a new beginning and I am a new woman.

*But what about Mac? Where does he fit in?*

'Shush,' I scold myself out loud, 'don't complicate matters.'

Of course Mac fits in. He definitely fits in somewhere. After all, he is fantastic and . . . well, you know *who* and *what* he is by now. He is the reason I can be here tonight, celebrating the fact that I learned to surf sufficiently to pull off my original bluff. He has been my guiding light. Yes, he fits in somewhere. I just don't know where.

'Which is why I left the beach as quickly as possible without putting my lips anywhere near his,' I mutter.

'Talking to yourself is the first sign of lunacy,' says a voice up ahead. 'Skippin' with your eyes shut is the second.'

I open my eyes to see Dave and Mac filling the pavement just ahead of me. I skid to a halt and run my hands quickly through my hair.

'Hiya, surfer girl, how's the form?' Dave smiles, approaching me with a kiss and a quick hug. 'We were just after decidin' to pop round and take yous girls for a celebratory pint. Or maybe something a bit fancier if you're lucky, hey.'

I look hastily from one to the other and clamp my teeth into a smile.

'Oh, that's very thoughtful of you both, but, er, I'm actually just on my way to see . . .' I clear my throat, aware of Mac's eyes burning into my consciousness, 'to, er, meet the director of the movie. We have to discuss business, you know, *sigh*, really boring stuff. You know.'

My faltering answer would not convince a judge.

'Ah, shite, have ya not been there yet?' Dave tuts. 'We thought you'd have been done with all that long ago. Sure it's ages now since we left the beach. What have ya been doing like?'

Mac, who up until this point has been silently and steadily fixing an icy gaze on my reddening face, looks down to my shimmering shoes and slowly back up my body. I sharply pull my coat shut but not before he takes in the full length (and that would be 'full' in the shortest sense) of my dress.

'Getting ready, by the looks of it,' Mac comments when I fail to offer an explanation. 'That's a wild sexy outfit for a business meeting.'

'Well, we are having dinner too,' I retort, annoyed that Mac appears to want to burst my bubble by insinuating that I am overdressed. After all, I bought the dress in his friend's shop; it is hardly Vera Wang. 'Image is important in my business. This is who I am.'

'Is it now?' Mac says sharply while Dave inspects the sky with such concentration one would think a UFO was about to land.

'Yes,' I reply with equal acidity. 'It. Is.'

Mac flicks his head back. I notice how it causes his hair to stick out at disjointed angles. It does not slide obediently back into place like Dan's shiny mane.

'So you scrub the sea salt away, get as far away from that *awful beach* as you can and run from the image of the surf chick for the night. Hey presto, we suddenly see the real Milly Armstrong. Is that it?'

I smart at Mac's words and flick my own hair like an agitated horse. Dave stares up at the sky so hard I am surprised Scotty doesn't beam him up.

'No, Mac, that is not it, and who do you think you are, talking to me like that?' I growl. 'I am supposed to be celebrating my achievements here.'

Mac's eyes narrow and darken to a smouldering olive green. He stands tall, his broad shoulders almost blocking the moon behind him. I try not to imagine my arms around that muscular neck and my lips on that mouth that is now fixed in a solid line. I continue.

'This is my career and this is a business meeting, not some post-surf pub piss-up.'

He raises an eyebrow.

'I appreciate everything you've done for me, both of you, and I would like to see you later if my meeting is over quickly, but right now I have important matters to attend to. All right? Do you understand?'

Mac bites his top lip and pauses for a moment. Dave starts to whistle nervously. Finally Mac nods as if in resignation.

'Oh sure I understand, Milly, I totally and completely understand.'

'Right, er, well that's great then, sorted.'

'Aye, sorted. So we'll go off and find your best friend and we'll take her out for the night.'

'Um, yes, great. Thanks.'

I frown at his confusing tone.

'Sure we'll leave you to your business.'

'Thanks.'

'And if you're at a loose end later maybe, and your one has fecked you off for some tart and you can't think of anything better to do, then maybe you could honour us with your presence.'

My jaw drops open in mortification. Mac steps around me on the pavement and motions for Dave to follow. I turn to

316

watch him slowly walking away, a ball of humiliation form-ing in my throat.

*How dare you, Mac Heggarty? How could I ever have thought you were wonderful?*

'You look beautiful, by the way, Milly,' says Mac's voice the second I spin on my heel to leave.

I stop in my tracks and stare at the pavement.

'Your dress is gorgeous.'

I don't move.

'And if you value my opinion at all, you're too good for that bastard.'

I spin around but they are already walking away towards Pooh Corner.

'It's a business meeting, Mac,' I whisper tearfully as if trying to convince myself. 'It is just a business meeting.'

Composed after ten minutes of staring at myself in the mirror of the opulent ladies' toilets, I take a deep breath and enter the bar. I am sexy and I am a successful actress. I am totally confused. I tell myself to forget it, that I can't dwell on injured relationships right now. I know I have been unfair today after kissing Mac yesterday, but I was under pressure, and having Dan Clancy in the same town just knocked me for six. Seven even. Granted, Mac may have deserved more respect, but today is about me. It is not about Mac and me. I am on the first rung of that ladder and tonight will take me higher. I just have to be professional; the show must go on. I can deal with Mac later, he will understand. This is just a business meeting.

The fact that Dan Clancy is bending to kiss my hand is purely coincidental.

'Darling Mimi, you look fabulous,' he purrs. 'Much better than in that nasty wetsuit.'

'Thanks,' I say with a giggle that I can't control.

*Get a grip, girl*, I warn myself while following Dan's neat bottom through the bar and up to a table laid with so much sparkling silver cutlery I am surprised the legs don't buckle under the weight.

'Matthew thought dinner would be a good idea,' says Dan, indicating my place with a flowing gesture. 'A perk of the job as it were.'

'Lovely,' I gush while I settle myself to Dan's left.

'He'll just be a moment.'

Silence descends on us as the waiter scurries into action, expertly filling slender crystal flutes with golden champagne, placing tiny knotted bread rolls on each of our side plates and presenting us both with elaborate menus. I handle mine like an original Picasso, scanning the poetic description of the dishes for anything that sounds remotely familiar.

*What is a morel when it's at home? Is confit stuffed goose, or is that foie gras? Has anyone ever heard of quenelles? Bouillabaisse?*

I gulp some champagne and smile at Dan.

'It's French cuisine,' he explains, 'and not bad by all accounts. Do you need me to translate or shall we just forget the food and eat each other instead?'

'Pardon?' I splutter, hastily wiping champagne from my chin.

Dan strokes my hand and winks.

'Just joking with you, Mimi. Although you are looking fantastically edible in that dress, and I have been on a rather long rain check for that dinner date you promised me. I am positively starving.'

Dan slides his tongue quickly over his bottom lip.

*He's flirting with me. But of course he is, Dan is a flirt right to the bone. Oh God, don't think 'bone'.*

'You always did have great curves, babe. I remember running my youthfully hormonal hands over them, just desperate to rip your clothes off.'

*Flirting with me? Now he is practically shagging me on the table.*

'The way you say "youthfully hormonal", anyone would

318

think it was years since we . . . well, since we were . . . together.'

He strokes my hand again, moving gently up to my wrist. I feel my toes curl with pleasure inside my kitten heels.

'Not years, Mimi baby, but long enough. Too long. Seeing you in Grafton Street that day, and being in touch with you since, has just reminded me of how well we fitted. We were great together, you and I.'

The pleasurable sensation shoots up my legs and races up my spine, missing no important parts along the way. God, this is quick; we haven't even ordered our starters yet and already I feel as if we have jumped to the coffee. I sensed there might be chemistry after Dan's show of masculinity on the beach with Mac. In all honesty I hoped for that chemistry to still be there, sizzling away in the test tubes, ready to explode. I just didn't think it would be so soon and so blatant. I briefly consider asking about Roma but I stop myself by raising the champagne glass to my trembling lips. What about Roma? Who cares? Fuck her, I'm here now.

I try to control the shivers in my arm as Dan moves his fingers higher. I order the tiny hairs on my skin to stay lying down, to not show him how much I am enjoying this. His hand swirls up my arm, glides across my shoulder and briefly sizzles on the bare skin of my neck before he clasps a lock of my hair and twists it around his finger, gently pulling my face closer to his. I stop breathing when I am so close I can see every colour in the iris of his eyes.

'Do you think,' Dan breathes, 'we could ever fit that well again?'

'Well I . . . gosh, Dan. Possibly, maybe . . .'

*I am willing to try for perfect tesselation right now, in fact.*

Dan smiles at my flustered response and moves as close as he can without actually having his tongue down my throat.

'Possibly? Maybe? I think most definitely, Mimi. Just

wait till I slip that dress off, I know just how to fit us together.'

I stare at him transfixed until he slides so near I can feel my eyes begin to cross. Without paying too much attention, I am already aware that every female eye in the room is looking in my direction, all of them green with envy even if they were previously brown or blue. I am the woman they would trade places with at whatever cost. To be this close to Dan Clancy's beautiful lips is something these women can only dream of. My head grows bigger knowing that I am the centre of attention. To say I do not enjoy the thrill would be a lie. I am flattered and happy that my plan worked. I showed Dan what he has been missing and now he wants me.

I want him.

Right now, nobody else matters.

'Er . . . so when were you thinking of exactly?' I say, as if trying to slot an appointment into my diary.

Dan blinks slowly, fanning my face with his long eyelashes that most transvestites would die for. I am drawn into the spell of his beautiful eyes, remembering how I used to gaze into them when I first came to Ireland, marvelling at how I had managed to find this stunning man and make him mine. Images race through my mind of our first kiss, of the first time we made love, of the tears flooding my face on the day we decided to . . . on the day he dumped me.

'I was thinking tonight after dinner,' Dan replies in a throaty, wanting voice. 'Mimi my baby, will you be mine again?'

My head spins and Mac is whirled away by the hurricane of emotion. My resistance is gone. I give in to the feelings that have been with me for the past year. I have missed him and now I have the chance to be with Dan again. I succumb and let myself be kissed. Our lips touch.

Now I am not saying the moment is an anticlimax, of

course it isn't; it is just a quick kiss, that's all. I suppose I am just too overwhelmed to be communicating fully with my senses, and we are in a public place, and I did just kiss another man yesterday.

*This one wasn't as good.*

Shush, I tell myself, shocked by my own thoughts, don't be ridiculous. Of course it was.

*That test tube must have gone off the boil.*

But chemistry can take time, it can be slow and sizzling, I argue.

My conflicting opinions are interrupted when I realise Dan is frowning at me, obviously awaiting my reaction.

'Oh gosh, that was lovely,' I murmur, sounding like I have just opened a Christmas present from a relative with extremely poor taste.

*What is wrong with me, for goodness' sake?*

Dan runs his tongue along his lips as if to moisturise them, and winks.

'There's more where that came from, darling, just you wait.'

I smile, unable to think of a suitable response. Dan repeatedly strokes my hand. I squirm in my chair and gulp down a mouthful of champagne to wash away the taste of the kiss.

*Fuck me, did I just think that? Was I really trying to wash the taste away?* I lower my head to catch up with my dropping jaw and place my free hand on my thumping heart. The heart that is trying to tell me what my head already knows. That it was a kiss. A kiss I have waited so long for. A kiss I dreamed would be a fairytale re-ignition of love. A kiss that was OK as far as kisses go . . . except for one thing. It was not a kiss from Mac.

'Bloody hell,' I breathe quietly.

'Oh, don't be too overwhelmed,' Dan murmurs in my ear.

I press my heart harder.

*It is Mac I want. I am in love with Mac.*

'It's Mac,' I say aloud.

'I know,' says Dan. 'The freak has been standing there ogling us for bloody ages. Does he want an autograph, or does he just like watching other people snogging?'

'What?' I reply impatiently, so taken aback by the clarity of my own feelings that I cannot be bothered to listen to Dan. 'What are you talking about?'

Dan points across the room at the man standing at the entrance to the restaurant. I am almost afraid to move my eyes and focus on the dumbstruck figure. I already know who it is. I already feel the damage I have done to his heart. The man who just witnessed me kissing Dan Clancy is the one man whose kiss made Dan's fade into insignificance. Oh God, please do not do this to me.

'Mac,' I whisper as my eyes register the pain and disbelief in his fiery eyes.

'MAC,' I call out as he looks at me for one final moment before whipping his head away and making for the door.

I jump to my feet, panic gripping my chest as I realise what I have done.

'MAC!' I shout again, trying to extricate my legs from the excessive folds of the tablecloth.

'Milly, for God's sake, would you sit down and quit causing a scene,' Dan hisses, grabbing my hand.

I strain to release myself from his grip, but he holds my wrist tight.

'Let me go, Dan,' I cry out as Mac disappears from view.

'I will not. Here comes Matthew, so sit yourself down and let's get on with business.' He flaps his other hand. 'Less important things will have to wait.'

I look anxiously at Dan, and then back to where Mac stood, but he has already gone. A grinning Matthew, his hand outstretched to shake mine, fills my view.

'Glad you could join us, Milly. Now let's enjoy ourselves, shall we? Ooh, I am like totally buzzing with creativity after today, so I am. I could explode.'

I look from Dan to Matthew and back again. I try to smile, but a rumbling thundercloud has settled over my head. All I can think about is Mac and the pained expression on his beautiful face. Mac, my Mac, will he ever forgive me?

# CHAPTER TWENTY-NINE

## *Blurred*

Dinner is an extravagant affair of six courses which cumulatively would only add up to the size of a kid's meal portion at McDonald's. Having managed to order without understanding the majority of the menu, I am still no clearer as to the ingredients of each dish even after eating them. Nevertheless, whatever I consume has little effect on my depressed taste buds despite the fact that the price would buy me a whole winter wardrobe. Thank goodness I am not paying. We wash whatever it is down with sumptuous red wine and several more flutes of champagne until my cloud thins a little. Matthew indulges in an inordinate amount of gossip about names and faces in the acting business while Dan enthrals Matthew with tales of life as the darling of the film industry. I listen and join in when I can but often find my mind wandering to the kiss and the expression on Mac's face. I feel wretched sitting here listening to all this showbiz talk but I know how important this meeting is for bonding with my director and co-star. Mind you, perhaps we bonded a little too closely, and in haste. I also find myself being irritated by a persistent dog begging underneath the table by rubbing up and down against my leg. Glancing under the tablecloth, however, I realise that the dog is in fact Dan Clancy's hand, rubbing away as if trying to set fire to my dress by friction alone. I brush his hand away discreetly several times but it immediately returns, refusing to be interrupted. I do not want his attention any more and, quite frankly, I find his affections annoying. I try to relax but there is nothing erotic about being rubbed like a cat scratch pole.

Finally our personal canteens of cutlery are cleared away and we are left with tiny silver spoons for our espresso coffees and a plate of handcrafted chocolates. I am still starving after the day's exertions and the cordon bleu cuisine, so I dive into the delicate treats with gusto. Dan refuses for fear of love handles and Matthew follows Dan's lead. Creep.

'You know, Milly, body image is very important for actresses these days,' says Dan as I munch on my fourth morsel of rich dark chocolate.

I nod agreeably and continue to chew. Dan scans my figure with his eyes. I wait for the conversation to continue and reach for another chocolate.

'What I am saying is, Mimi, curvy girls are not so sought after.'

'Really? Right.'

'So,' Dan continues, 'if you are serious about this business, perhaps you should . . .' He reaches for the hand that is about to pop the chocolate into my mouth and lowers it to the table. I immediately redden.

'You mean me?'

I almost choke at his insinuation. Dan pats my hand condescendingly.

'Just doing what is best for you, Milly darling. Roma doesn't have your ability but neither does she have an ounce of fat.'

*Or an ounce of grey matter.*

'You are serious about being an actress, are you not?'

I don't know whether to reply or whether to smack him in the face with my coffee cup.

'Of course I'm serious about it, Dan,' I say icily. 'It's my dream, you know that.'

'Then you won't mind me giving you a little advice along the way, will you, darling? There's a good girl.'

He returns the chocolate to the plate and pats my hip beneath the table. If the waiter hadn't just cleared all the knives away I swear I would cut his bloody hand off. God, he is driving me crazy all of a sudden. And not in the way I expected.

I stew for a while, concerned by my own feelings of animosity towards my gorgeous co-star. After all, it is not his fault I kissed Mac yesterday and that now I find myself juggling their affections. Perhaps I am just tired from today's efforts. The pummelling I received in the surf, not to mention actually riding the wave, really took it out of me. And dealing with my parents, making sure they are having fun and that my father is careful of his stress levels. My own stress levels, however, are another matter. I could currently steam vegetables with my blood pressure. Perhaps the alcohol was a bad idea. I take deep breaths and a few gulps of water before attempting to return to the conversation. My mind is in utter turmoil.

'. . . and so now I do agree with you, Dan, that this is the best direction to take for everyone. Are you all right with that, Milly?'

I look at Matthew and grimace.

'Sorry, Matthew, I missed that bit.'

'Which bit?'

'Er . . . from the, um, the . . . all of it.'

Dan groans in harmony with Matthew's sigh.

'Sorry, I'm just a bit tired after the surf.'

*And I'm wondering where Mac is and when I can get away to find him.*

'Of course you are, darling, of course you are.' Matthew tilts his head and beams at me across the table. 'Holy God, which is exactly why I don't think our leading lady should actually do the surfing now. You know it is fantastically dangerous and exhausting, and to be honest we just cannot risk damaging any of our precious cargo and having them looking like bedraggled rodents on the screen, you know.'

I frown.

'Ooh, not that you looked like one today at all.'

I smile.

'Well, perhaps just a little bit, which is why I am so pleased we can rely on you to be our fantastic action stunt double. Then, you know, we can leave the pretty parts to someone more suited to the close-ups.'

I now have no idea what he is talking about.

'I'm sorry, Matthew, I don't quite understand. Action stunt double?'

Matthew rubs his hands together and nods excitedly.

'Why yes, Milly, you will be absolutely fantastically perfect, I just know it. Dan talked me into it, you know, and I have to take his advice. I see I can rely on you to perform the action scenes without too much difficulty. The odd wipeout will simply add to the drama and danger. So what if I have to find the face somewhere else, as Dan said.'

'I beg your pardon?' I gasp.

I shift uncomfortably in my chair as I try my best to grasp the meaning of Matthew's words. I cannot be hearing him right. Did he just say 'find the face somewhere else'? What is wrong with my face? Noticing my confusion, Matthew reaches across the table and dishes out a condescending pat on my hand.

'Ooh, you *are* tired, darling. Now let me explain the conclusion Dan and I have come to today.'

I glance quickly at Dan, who winks at me with a mischievous grin.

'Now in my opinion, the location for the film is totally perfect as far as the ocean scenes are concerned. God knows the town is a little twee and shabby perhaps, but we can do wonders with special effects and fantastic cut-aways and the like, you know.'

I briefly consider how Mac would react to such a statement but don't allow my mind to wander further than it already has. Matthew continues.

'The surfing is fantastic, Milly, and will be great on the big screen, so well done you.'

'Thank you.'

'And well done for understanding that now our big financial backer has allowed us to bring in an actor of Dan's calibre, the casting obviously has to be altered a little to balance the roles.'

*Does it?*

'Yes, of course,' I cough nervously.

'By which I mean we need a leading lady who can match Dan's star performance. Do you see where I'm coming from?'

*I can see where you're coming from. I am just a bit concerned about where you are going.*

'Er, yes,' I reply to their questioning glances.

'Marvellous.' Matthew claps. 'So, Milly, a lovely lovely little actress though I am sure you are, you are just a little too surfy to be our leading lady here. Dan and I both agree that we need someone of a more ... how can I say this? ... a more classy nature. You know, someone in Dan's league, although obviously not his equal, dear God. Nobody could be, could they?' He caresses Dan with his eyes. 'But we have discussed it and we both agree that Roma Chantelle is the girl for the role, with yourself as the stuntwoman and extra. That is what Dan wants, and ooh we want him, so that is the way the cookie crumbles. Anyway, that is how we will be operating from this point on. Don't worry, like, you will still get your name on the credits, but not your face on the screen, which Dan and I think is better all round, you know. Is that fine and dandy with you?'

By this time I have almost swallowed my tongue in shock. My whole body is trembling and my mouth is as dry as if I have been dead for a week. I stare at the bottle of wine in front of me and wonder whether someone has laced it with hallucinogenic drugs. I can't be hearing him right. Can I? I open my mouth to speak, but no sound comes out except the pitiful whimper that manages to circumnavigate the ball of tears clogging my throat. My eyes flit from Matthew to Dan and back again, looking for their expressions of mirth, waiting for the punchline to this oh so hilarious joke. Their expressions say it all. This is real, they are not laughing. Neither do they seem at all moved by the earth-shattering news they have just packaged and delivered to me with the impact of a semtex letter bomb.

What was it he said? *A lovely little actress . . . too surfy . . . more classy . . . in Dan's league . . . Roma Chantelle.* Roma Chantelle? Where have I heard that name before? My hand shoots to my throat as I realise who is swiping my role from right under my nose. Roma Chantelle, the pasta sauce girl! Oh my God, not only am I being replaced in my dream role, but I am being replaced by Dan's plastic straw of a girlfriend who probably can't even spell *actress*, never mind be one. How can she be more classy than me? She's not even real, is she? I am lost for words. Tears, though, tears are plentiful, and are threatening to wash the table away if I allow the floodgates to open.

'But . . . but I'm . . . I'm not surfy,' I stutter, reaching for a glass of water to steady my nerves. The shell bangles jangle argumentatively on my wrist.

'Ooh, of course you are, Milly,' Matthew guffaws. 'You're the perfect little surfer girl, and you know, that is nothing to be ashamed of, it is actually rather cute. Only, you know, our focus has changed so you don't quite fit the bill of the main female role. The business is tough out there.'

'But I have to fit the bill,' I wail. 'It's my role.'

'Not any more,' Dan states firmly.

'It is, it has to be,' I carry on with an audible sob, my voice steadily rising. 'This was all just research to get me into the character. I'm not really like this; I can be anything you want me to be. Please.'

Granted, my words may smack of desperation, but I have no choice; I am desperate.

'Ooh, we wouldn't want you to change, darling,' Matthew smiles. 'Not at all now, you're fantastically cute as you are.'

*Stop saying* cute, *I want to scream. What do you think, I am a bloody Yorkshire terrier?*

'You understand, don't you, Mimi?' Dan asks with yet another pat of my hand.

I snatch it away as if he is poisonous.

'No. No, quite frankly I do not understand. This is my job, this is my career, and I earned this chance. You can't take it away from me and you can't treat me like this.' A solitary tear of mammoth proportions rolls heavily down my cheek. 'This is my role and Matthew knew what my face looked like when he offered it to me.'

Dan sighs as if I am making a scene over nothing more important than the flavours of ice-cream on the dessert menu. (Which I am not, because this place is so bloody pretentious I couldn't even find ice-cream on the dessert menu.)

'Oh, come on, old thing, don't take it personally. It's just that you are hardly a strong enough actress to play opposite me. I mean, how many roles have you had? Other than the cheese ones in your lunchbox at your little promo jobs, that is.'

He throws his head back and laughs. I suddenly wish Mac were here to wipe the smile off that pretty-boy face. Mind you, I am up to the job myself. Just how much damage could a kitten heel do?

*Help me, I'm turning into a psychopath.*

The solitary tear has now been joined by its brothers, sisters, first, second and third cousins. My face is awash with visible distress.

'Please, Matthew,' I cry, 'you can't give my part to Roma. She . . . she can't even say her "L"s properly. How can you have a script with no "L"s in it?'

(I am clutching at any straw, no matter how small.)

My shoulders heave and my eyes are so blurred I have to hold on to the edge of the table for support. The eyes that were previously on me in the restaurant are on me still, but for a very different reason. Gasps and whispered comments drift around the room. Dan rubs my leg and urges me to keep the noise down.

'Get your bloody hands off me!' I yell, slapping away the hand that I have longed to touch me for the past year.

'Now come on, darling . . .'

'And I am most certainly not your darling,' I hiss, smearing mascara across my face with a very expensive embroidered napkin. 'If you knew Matthew was about to give my job to that poor excuse for a woman that you call your girlfriend, then what exactly were you doing asking me out, *Pumpkin*?'

'Of course Matthew is giving Roma the part, Milly, she is a lady and a very good actress, actually, and much better-looking than you. The "L"s aren't an issue here.'

'Ooh, and her fantastically wealthy father also just happens to be our financial backer,' Matthew beams.

Now I understand.

'And pardon me,' Dan interrupts haughtily, 'but Roma is my girlfriend, so when exactly are you insinuating I asked you out, Milly, or was that in your dreams?'

I turn on him, eyes blazing.

'This evening, Dan, at this very table, and don't try to deny it.'

Dan glances at me, raises a plucked eyebrow and laughs until his shoulders shake.

'Asking you out?' he says. 'Dear God, I wasn't asking you out, Milly. I was asking you for a shag.' He leans closer but maintains his volume. 'And from the signals you gave me, I think I am on to a sure thing. You always were crazy about me.'

'Ooh, Dan,' Matthew giggles with just a hint of jealousy, 'you are awful.'

The rage inside my trembling body is now engulfed by a tidal wave of humiliation and defeat. I stare at the two men through my watery eyes, watching as they chortle and joke together with no thought as to how my world is imploding. How could I have trusted their moral make-up? How could I have let Dan Clancy kiss me? He is such a snake. I want to press the rewind button and go back to yesterday. Yesterday I had everything; I just didn't know it. I swallow a fresh ball of tears and smear more mascara on to the napkin before gathering my belongings together and standing to leave.

'Ooh, are we off so?' Matthew says with a clap. 'Fantastic. Now, you're the local in this one-horse town, Milly. What bar will suit us best for a few little nightcaps?'

'None of them will suit you, Matthew,' I say drily. 'The people in this "one-horse town" are far too decent to be forced to drink with the likes of you two.'

Matthew clasps his chest as if mortally wounded. I wish.

'In fact, if I were you I would leave before the locals get to hear about the way you treat people. You see' – I lean across the table – 'in this town, people earn their respect. They couldn't give a fuck whether you are famous or whether you wear Gucci shoes or how many contacts you have in the celebrity world. These people are real. And do you know what? Every single one of them is worth more than the two of you put together.'

Matthew's jaw drops. Dan runs his hands through his perfect hair and sniffs nonchalantly.

'Well, you know, I don't think that's a very good way to speak to me if you want a part in my film,' Matthew huffs. 'I can't have my extras disrespecting me like that. Don't you know how important I am?'

'You're not,' I answer firmly. 'Not in the real world, where some people are working hard to make a real difference to people's lives.'

*Like Mac Heggarty*, my mind prompts.

'Bloody hell, would you listen to her,' Dan snorts, 'the

332

proper little surf hippy. Away and hug a tree and leave us to our Bollinger.'

I smooth down the front of my beautiful new dress that was bought in advance of a celebration, lowering my eyes to hide my disappointment that the day has not ended in the way I had dreamed. I want to break down right here in the middle of the restaurant, but I dig deep to maintain my composure. I slip on the coat that the waiter discreetly brings to the table and button it around me like a cloak of confidence. I then reach for the newly opened bottle of champagne and shakily pour myself a glass while standing.

'You are right, Dan, I was crazy about you. At least I was crazy. Crazy to have ever thought you were the man I imagined. Fi was right all along about you; you are an untrustworthy fecker. You let me tell you all about my dream role and then you snatched it from me, buying yourself and your little plastic eye-candy the role without the slightest twinge of guilt. You are heartless, Dan, and you know, you won't always be the nation's darling. Not once *they* have used *you* up and spat you out. Mac was spot on too; you are a bastard. I am just glad I know that now so I don't have to waste any more of my life on a pathetic egotistical wimp like you.' I silently raise the glass to shoulder height and force a smile. 'To you, gentlemen, and thank you for a truly horrendous evening in every way. You deserve each other.'

I then tip the glass with a swift movement of my wrist and pour the contents over Dan Clancy's immaculate hair.

'Jesus Christ, Milly!' He leaps out of his chair, frantically brushing his shirt. 'Do you know how much this cost, you crazy bitch?'

He stumbles backwards as I saunter confidently past. I touch his shoulder just as our waiter moves behind him with the dessert trolley. Dan Clancy, the vainest man I have ever met, falls to the floor in a heap. A rich chocolate torte lands in his Armani-clad lap and a bowl of Chantilly comes to rest on his head. The room erupts in hoots of uncontrollable laughter. Dan shrieks in horror and Matthew slips on a chocolate eclair while racing to his star's rescue.

'You bitch!' Dan hollers as I stride towards the door, ice-cool on the outside but burning with emotion on the inside. 'You always were a no-hoper. You will never work in this business again. Never!'

I don't doubt the truth of his statement, but if I stop to dwell on what that means for my future I will never make it to the door, I will surely collapse. I keep walking, my head held high, and I don't look back until the cold evening air hits my face. Then I run.

I run to the end of the hotel driveway, my kitten heels scratching and breaking with every heavy step on the gravel path. On reaching the gates, I race across the dimly lit main road and turn right towards Pooh Corner. The wind stings my face, icy cold against my fresh tears. I am crying now, my sobs being carried away on the wind towards the hills of Donegal. By the time I reach Pooh Corner, my legs are aching with the exertion and my lungs are begging for a rest. The house is dark and I know I cannot face sitting alone to concentrate on the cruel twist that has turned my dream into a nightmare. Everything I have worked for over the last few years. All the crappy jobs to get me to this point. All the surf lessons and all the effort from Fi, Mac and Dave since we came to Donegal. Even the help of my parents. All in vain. Somehow I have failed them all, Mac especially, in every way. How could I have thought Dan was a better man than Mac? Gorgeous, talented Mac who has been so patient with me. Who cares about more than just himself. Who cares about his family, his friends and the kids he integrates across the border for the greater good of the world. How could I have forsaken all that for a man as self-obsessed as Dan Clancy?

'I've ruined everything,' I cry out to the darkness as I begin to run again. 'Mac, where are you?'

I half run, half limp now along the seafront and up to Main Street until I reach Gallagher's Bar. The doors are locked and the lights are low but I hear sounds of music and revelry coming from the inside. I bang on the door but I don't know the right knock. Inside my friends will either be celebrating my success or cursing my blatant infidelity, while here I am excluded from the lock-in and unable to explain or share my feelings.

'Hello? Mac?' I whimper, but the door remains steadfastly shut.

I am still an outsider and will be even more so after tonight when word spreads of what I did to Mac, one of their own. One of their best.

I drag myself up from my half-slumped position against the pub door and run on to my parents' hotel.

'Ah sure, they went out hours ago with Fiona O'Reilly and Dave Brennan,' the receptionist informs me. 'Now don't they make a lovely couple, those two?'

I nod but am incapable of speech.

'Are you all right there?'

I turn away, crashing against the doors and running out to the street. I run and cry until I reach the headland, where I collapse on to the carved stone bench, gasping for air. There I sit, staring out to sea, the tears running silently down my face as my mind continues to run, churning what just happened over and over in my head.

I don't have a leading role. I am not a real actress. The last three months have all been for nothing. Which is exactly what I have now . . . nothing. No job, no prospects, and above all no Mac.

I hold my head in my hands and let the emotion flow out of my exhausted body. Not even Flipper the dolphin comes to rescue me tonight. I have never felt so alone.

# CHAPTER THIRTY

# *Driftwood*

I say goodbye to my parents on the railway station platform, our hugs awkward for more reasons other than the suitcase placed between us. I check my watch for the umpteenth time in the same minute and glance at the platform entrance.

'You know, Amelia, we really are sorry it didn't work out for you,' says my mother, her eyes focused on the dust swirling along the floor in the strong wind. 'Aren't we, Frank?' Her voice is quiet, her tone uncharacteristically unsure.

My father sorrowfully waves the Irish flag on a stick he thought would be a nice touch for my send-off. He nods sagely.

'We are, pudding. It is a bloody shame.'

I shove my hands into the pockets of my black combat trousers and shrug.

'It's OK.'

'No, it's not OK, pudding. You deserved that job. You showed them exactly what you could do and' – he raises one palm like a witness swearing the oath in court – 'I know we were never the greatest supporters of the acting la . . . of your acting career . . .'

My eyes fail to hide their surprise.

'. . . but being here with you we could see how much you

wanted this to happen and we are just proud that you put so much effort into trying to achieve your dream. Aren't we, Georgina?'

'We are, we really are, dear.'

I smile weakly, pleasantly surprised by just how much difference spending the past few days in County Donegal with my parents has made to my relationship with them. They have noticeably chilled, probably due to all the Guinness, and they are willingly showing me their support. So I failed in front of them, so what? They have not judged me. I underestimated them and I know now that I will miss them. If only all my other relationships were going so well.

'Shame about Mac too,' my father continues, blowing his nose on a shamrock handkerchief. 'He's a bloody nice lad that one, pardon my French.'

My mother nudges him somewhere around the ribs, clearly trying to tell him to keep out of my romantic affairs.

'If you put your mind to it, Amelia, I am sure you can get an even better acting job in the near future,' she interrupts, swiftly changing the subject.

I laugh weakly and look briefly up and down the platform.

'Thanks, Mum, but I think perhaps you and Dad knew what was best for me in the first place. I'm thirty-one and I promised myself this would be my last attempt to make acting my career. I think I will be hanging up my Equity card and looking for a proper job in Dublin from now on.'

'You feckin' will not,' says Fi's voice to my right. She shuffles along the platform against the wind with Dave's arm linked through hers. 'Excuse my swearing, Mr and Mrs A, but there is no way I am going to let your one give up everything she has worked for now just because of that bastard Dan bloody Clancy.'

'I'm glad to hear it,' my mother pipes up, sweeping a proud hand across her solid hair-do. 'I never did like him anyway.'

'See, your mother has great taste,' my father quips as he heaves my suitcase on to the waiting train.

I hug them both again, breathing in the comforting aroma of my mother's Anaïs Anaïs perfume, before turning to Fi and Dave. They make a handsome couple. Fi fits snugly under Dave's arm and he is visibly proud to be seen in public with this petite redhead in the tight jeans who effortlessly succeeds in turning heads.

'I think you should stay,' Fi says with watery eyes. 'Don't leave so soon.'

I bite my lip and glance once more along the platform.

'No, I have to go. Gerald has summoned me to his office tomorrow, and anyway, I think it would be best if I got back to Dublin and sorted things out.' We link hands. 'I need to work out what I'm going to do next. Staying here would only remind me of what I nearly achieved.'

*Staying here would only make me want Mac more.*

Dave steps forward and gives me a warm hug, which surprises me after the pain I caused his friend yesterday.

'Don't give up, surfer girl,' he says softly into my ear. 'You've got talent.'

'Thanks,' I sniff, and turn to hug my best friend.

Fi is staying behind at my insistence to make a go of things with Dave and spend time with the family that can't replace her own parents but that can, along with Dave, do a much better job of making Fi feel part of something special. She is happy here. Of course she may not be completely cured of her depression, who knows what will happen down the line? The main thing is that she is happy and the sea air is definitely doing her good. Why should I drag her back to Dublin to watch me mope around until I find a new focus? It wouldn't be fair, and besides, I need some time alone to reflect. My mother and father have decided to spend the next few days travelling through Ireland, visiting Galway, Kerry and Waterford on their way back to the ferry on Sunday. The holiday is doing my father's health the world of good. I don't want to stay around and stress him out. Despite my failure to become an actress, drama seems to follow me wherever I go. My parents know I lied about Matthew initially begging me to play the part in the film, but they have not mocked me for it. I am not so much embarrassed about being rejected for the film as I am disappointed that my parents, Fi, Dave and Mac will never see me acting and surfing on the big screen. I wanted to do it for them as much as I did for myself. Anyway, my dream has now returned to the pipeline, which will soon be sealed and forgotten about. Or perhaps not forgotten. Now I can get on with making something of my life. I see it as a fresh challenge, starting today. I can't stay here in Donegal, the point of my trip has snapped off like the end of a soft lead pencil and I would only be wasting time. Besides, where would the fun be in surfing without Mac?

At the thought of his name, my eyes drift from my watch to the platform entrance one more time. An old man with an even older dog struggles to board the train. A young couple dressed as punks have their belt chains and tongues interlinked as they trip towards the train. Several smartly dressed men and women are engrossed in business talk as they locate the first-class compartment. There are men, women, children, dogs and baggage but no tall, muscular surf instructor and lifeguard. No one matching the description of the mouth-watering, rugged Celtic man who met myself and Fi at this very station back in February. The day I blew him away, as he described it. Fi and Dave recognise the look in my eyes.

'There's still time,' Fi reassures me quietly.

'He'll be here, unless he's working,' Dave adds, subtly qualifying the statement.

I shrug as if Mac's presence means nothing and busy myself checking that I have my wallet and ticket. I am well aware of the loaded looks being exchanged between the four members of my farewell party, despite the fact that my pride keeps my eyes focused on the ground.

Where is he? I tried to find him this morning and Fi told me that he knows I am leaving this afternoon. Why doesn't he come and let me explain what happened? Let me explain that yes, I was a sucker for Dan Clancy, but that I soon realised that what I felt for him was all in the past and should remain there. Granted, I wasn't over Dan when he rocked into town all famous and preened. Truthfully, I wanted to show Dan what he was missing, and yes, I thought I would take him back in a shot. But that was before ... before I realised. As soon as I let Dan kiss me I knew it felt wrong. Mac made my whole body explode. With Dan it felt as thrilling as snogging my own pillow as a teenager. It was all fantasy, and the reality was a squib left out in an Irish rainstorm, more drowned than damp. I know, I know, I should never have been comparing the two men in the first place. I mean, who do I think I am behaving like an Arab prince taking his pick from a harem? I was weak, I was foolish and I treated Mac terribly after everything he did for me, but now that I have been able to make the comparison between the two men, I know that Mac Heggarty wins on every count. I was crazy dwelling on what had been with Dan and now I am crazy about Mac, but I am too late.

If only it were like in the movies and Mac would come running along the platform at the last minute to scoop me into his arms. In reality, though, no matter how many times I stare at the station entrance, Mac Heggarty is not going to come. He is too proud for that. He knew I was willing to give him up for Dan and he was deeply hurt by it. He saw me kissing Dan, for God's sake. In fact, I don't think I could face the condemning expression in those deep green eyes if he did appear, which is why I have to leave now. I can't face up to what I did. If I know Mac at all, I know that he only opens himself up to a few people in his life, and those people he would do anything for and they would do the same for him. As a lifeguard, Mac is willing to risk his own life to save someone else. I believe he would have died for Nicky if he could have, the few friendships he has are that strong. Mac would have come to my rescue at any moment without a second thought and did so on several occasions. I trusted that, which is why I had the confidence to start surfing. Mac trusted me and I betrayed that trust. I blew my chance and now I am running away.

'Maybe he got held up in traffic,' Fi offers quietly.

'Yes, that's it, those tractors on single-lane roads are a bugger to get round,' says my father.

'Or perhaps there was an emergency at the beach,' my mother kindly suggests.

'Could be,' Dave nods, 'and I did see a coachload of kids from Belfast truckin' into town, so they might be booked in for a surf lesson.'

I smile at them all and clamber on to the train as a small female guard with masses of curly hair skips past happily blowing the whistle.

'All aboard for Dublin,' she announces. 'Let's get this show on the road.'

I yank the heavy rusted door closed and lean my elbows on the open window.

'Don't worry, I'll be fine,' I tell their worried faces, 'and thank you all so much for your support.'

'Nae bother.' Dave bows.

'Glad to be of service,' my father announces.

'I'll call you every day,' says Fi, 'twice a day even.'

'Me too,' says my mother, which is a frightening prospect, however well we have been getting along for the past few days.

The train emits a painful screeching sound like fingernails on a blackboard and shudders forward an inch as if waking from hibernation.

'Jaysus, I hope it goes faster than that or you'll not be getting home till Dublin has eroded into the sea,' Dave hoots.

I force a laugh and wave as we progress a further three inches and then begin to gather speed. (Speed being a relative term in this instance.)

'Goodbye everyone,' I call out, 'and thank you. Dad, you look after your health now, and Dave, please say thank you to Mac. I could never have done it without him.'

'I will.' He waves back. 'He'll be sorry he missed ya.'

'I don't think so,' I say sadly to myself as we pass the end of the platform and embark on the boneshaking journey to Dublin. 'But I am sorry, Mac. One day perhaps I will tell you myself.'

My heart is broken.

# CHAPTER THIRTY-ONE

## *Snow Business*

'Hotpants?' I screech, holding the miniature red shorts up to the light. 'I can't wear hotpants outdoors in November, I'll die of overexposure.'

'Overexposure is just the look we're after,' says my sleazy employer for the day, almost foaming at the mouth. 'But sure you've got tights to wear underneath, and a lovely pair of legwarmers. Look it, they light up. Ach, but you'll make a lovely elf so you will.'

*I despair.*

'Now away with yeh and get yerself changed before Christmas gets here. Here's your Jingle Gin drink samples, and if any Gárdai bug you about a licence to flog them in public, then you know, just make somethin' up.'

*God help me, I am masquerading as a criminal elf.*

Half an hour and much grumbling later, I stand shivering in the unpredicted snow falling on Grafton Street. I stare dumbly at my reflection in the window of Brown Thomas department store. The hotpants cover my hips thanks to a not insignificant amount of physical exertion on the part of the Lycra. The jagged hem of the green felt tunic top points mockingly at the shorts, toning with the opaque mushy-pea-green tights that do nothing to distract from my exposed thighs. Thankfully I have managed to maintain my new surf-fit figure since returning to Dublin six months ago. (Is it really that long? It feels like much longer since I last saw Mac.) My diet has not been a result of willpower, but simply a distinct lack of funds. Comfort eating is just not the same with economy beans and cheap white bread. Nevertheless, no amount of dieting can disguise the fact that my calves are sporting not only a pair of eighties pixie boots but also red legwarmers with flashing fairy lights. The ensemble is completed by an oversized felt pixie hat, which plays an off-key rendition of 'Jingle Bells' whenever I tilt my head. Many more choruses of that bloody carol and I swear I will be jingling all the way to the mental health ward. If my cheeks were not already caked with circles of red face paint, I would blush.

All around me, elegantly dressed shoppers bustle in and out of Brown Thomas. With one month to go until Christmas Day, the purchasing frenzy is already in full flow. I gaze morosely from my own reflection to them and back again, marvelling at how Christmas, a time for goodwill and peace to all men, blah de blah, only serves to emphasise our inadequacies. I don't have a lover to buy presents for, and even if I did, my bank account could just about stretch to a pair of tacky novelty boxer shorts. My family are not big on the whole present-giving thing, and my best friend is holed up on the opposite coast of Ireland, busily being in love. I hate Christmas this year. Why does the run-up have to begin so bloody early? Just to prolong the pain? Listen to me, bah humbug, I am Scrooge. Although to be Scrooge suggests that I have money to be scroogey with in the first place. Bloody hell, I can't even be Scrooge when I want to be.

I have come full circle since my last promotional job as a chicken nugget in Grafton Street. Like a lump of driftwood floating out to sea and then being dumped back on the land, weathered and disorientated. Since February, I have reached out and touched my dream, not to mention the man of my dreams, and been left with nothing. I am back where I started. In actual fact, this is worse. I would actually welcome a chicken nugget suit right now. I am freezing to death out here.

I did of course try to get a so-called 'proper job' on returning to Dublin. However, a very rusty English degree and the ability to paddle out in three-foot surf do not constitute essential office experience.

'How narrow-minded is that?' I whined at the young recruitment consultant during my third successive week of unemployment.

'Narrow enough to make us the most prestigious recruitment agency in Europe,' replied her cantankerous female boss, 'Now get yourself off to a dishwashing job and stop wasting our time.'

I suspect she moonlights as a life coach in her spare time.

Gerald, my loyal agent, and I also parted company after he received a heated telephone call from Matthew. As the director of Ireland's most eagerly awaited movie, Matthew, it transpires, could ask Gerald to pluck his bikini line with his teeth and Gerald would happily oblige. In this instance, Matthew simply ranted about my lack of professionalism in creating a hideous scene in public and asked that I be blackballed by the agency. He then faxed through an invoice for Dan's dry-cleaning and emergency haircut due to champagne damage, which Gerald ordered me to pay. Judging from the total amount, I could only conclude that a million miniature Vidal Sassoons performed the haircut, each tending to one individual hair. I told Gerald to inform Dan Clancy exactly where he could shove the invoice, shortly before Gerald told me where I could shove my agency contract. Well, at least we were even.

My only option, therefore, was Truly Scrumptious, my promotions agent, who assured me there would be lots of work in the run-up to Christmas and who has since proceeded to stay true to her word while signing me up for the worst jobs of a very bad bunch. I think it is payback for leaving her in the lurch with my boasts of acting success. Crap jobs and hotpants notwithstanding, I need the money, and pride stops me calling on my parents or Fi for help. I reassure my mother every time she calls that I am fine and coping and working in a publishing house as an editorial assistant. (I find lying is very effective in a long-distance parent–daughter relationship.) I reassure Fi that I am coping and that she does not have to drag herself away from Dave to check up on me. At times I wish she would, though.

'Ah, would you look it, Brian,' burps a lunchtime reveller in an Ireland football jersey. 'Santy cannot be paying his elves too well, like. That one's got a face on her like a wet weekend in Navan.'

'Hey, elfie,' hoots his equally legless friend, 'come over here, will yeh, and sit on my knee, and I'll give yeh somethin' ta smile about.'

I growl and plod on up the street towards Bewley's tea rooms, the place where Fi and I shared cakes and gossip on the very first day we met. The snow is falling more heavily now, the moisture making my musical hat more tuneless with every step of my waterlogged pixie boots. I offer the miniature red bottles of Jingle Gin to passers-by, but the only takers are a couple of students celebrating the fact that it is Friday (as they probably do every day of the week) and a red-nosed tramp. I am beginning to suspect that my depressed expression is doing a good job of advertising the perils of gin indulgence, or, as Fi calls it, liquid suicide, rather than promoting its fun qualities.

'It's *free*,' I hiss at a hoity-toity middle-aged woman who looks as if I have just begged for money rather than offered her something for nothing. 'It's a *gift*, Christmas spirit and all that? Never look a gift horse in the mouth?'

She mutters something about market researchers being an evil infliction and shuffles off down the street with her nose pointing skywards.

'Bah humbug, you old trout,' I mutter while she is still in

earshot, before taking cover in the doorway of Bewley's. 'Bloody hell, will somebody take some of this sodding stuff so I can go home and get out of these stupid hotpants? I am getting frostbite in places I would rather not mention.'

'I'll have some,' says a high-pitched voice from below my tray of drinks.

I peer over the edge and see a small boy with the face of an angel and the torn clothes of a skater punk gazing up at me with an outstretched hand.

'Er, sorry, kid,' I shrug, 'but this is alcohol, and I'm only guessing, but I think you might be underage.'

*By about eight years.*

'I'm small for my age,' he pouts, tilting his head so that his yellow-blond hair covers one eye. 'I'm actually nineteen.'

'May I see some ID?' I laugh at his young bravado. 'Perhaps your pilot's licence, or an FBI badge?'

'Don't be daft,' he giggles, shoving his hand back into the pocket of his oversized parka. 'Ya can't be a pilot when you're eleven.'

'Oh, but I thought you were nineteen.'

'Ah, shite.'

My new little friend leans against the wall beside me and crosses both graffiti Converse boots at the ankles. He only reaches as high as my ribs, but the expression on his face when he glances up at me is that of a wizened old man.

'I think you're feeling sad,' he says with a sigh.

I place the tray of bottles on the slush-covered ground and also lean against the wall, crossing flashing legwarmer over flashing legwarmer.

'Do you now?' I reply, enjoying this break from monotony. 'So what makes you say that?'

'Because your face is all like this' – he pulls his mouth down at both sides with his fingers – 'and ya keep growlin' at strangers in the street, like.'

I grimace.

'And to be straight with ya . . .'

'Please do, er . . .'

'Joe, me name's Joe.'

'And mine's Milly.'

'Milly, right, that's excellent. Well, Milly, if I had to wear a stupid costume like that in public I'd be feeling like a right eejit. I mean, that hat is just sad, like, totally shite.'

I self-consciously slide the hat off my head. The batteries are running low, so that 'Jingle Bells' sounds out from the wet felt like the final chords of a funeral dirge. He is right, it is sad. My whole sorry get-up is *sad*. In fact, I could go as far as to conclude that my whole life is *sad*. With a capital S. The problem is, I don't know what to do about it.

'You're right, Joe, I am a bit unhappy. You see, I'm thirty-one years old and I don't have a purpose. My talents haven't blossomed yet, so to speak, and I guess I feel like I'm running out of time.'

Joe shakes his gorgeous blond head.

'You've still got time to blossom, like,' he replies maturely. 'Did you know oak trees only produce acorns when they're fifty years old? So that's pretty late to be blossomin'. And you've got a while till you're fifty, haven't ya?'

I laugh. 'I didn't know that, no, and I suppose I have got a while till I'm fifty. Where did you find that out?'

'Ah, just in school. We learn loads of shite like that.'

I like Joe's company, it is so refreshing.

'So, my new friend Joe, what do you suggest I do about my being sad then?'

He scratches his head and then grins.

'Get out a bit, enjoy yerself. After all, it is nearly Christmas, like.'

'Yes, I know that, but I have to work to make money to buy Christmas presents.'

Joe's expression becomes one of concern and he digs into the elbow-deep pockets of his coat as if searching for something.

'But you don't have to work tonight, though, do ya?'

He produces a white envelope along with a handful of crumpled sweet wrappers. I shake my head and watch him, intrigued.

'So you're free to go out and have fun?'

I nod.

'Well then that's grand, so I can give ya this.'

Joe hands me the envelope, which is sticky with the remnants of whatever sweets melted into his coat lining.

'What is it?'

'It's an invitation to a party and ya have to come.'

I smile and press the envelope between my cold palms.

'Well thank you very much for that, Joe, but I think I might be a bit old to come to a party with you. Thanks all the same.'

'Don't be thick,' he laughs, showing two rows of sparkling white teeth. 'It's not my party. Ha ha, you'd be way too ancient for the parties I go to.'

'Thanks.'

'There you go with that growlin' again.'

Joe pushes himself off the wall and hops to the middle of the street. He turns to face me, jumping excitedly up and down on the spot.

'It's me uncle's party,' he chirps happily, 'and ya have to go 'cos he really wants ya to.'

'What? How does your uncle know me?'

Joe ignores the question.

'It's a big party and there'll be champagne there and all sorts, so ya have to go, and if you do I get more money for delivering the invitation and then I can buy a new skateboard 'cos mine's broke.'

'Oh, I see.'

I turn the blank envelope over in my hands and scan it for clues. When I look up again Joe has already hopped off to the other side of the pedestrian precinct.

'Wait, Joe!' I call out.

'Just make sure ya go!' he shouts back. 'Then I can get

me skateboard. Me uncle says you're a special guest. See ya.'

By the time I have replaced my hat and gathered together my tray of drinks, Joe has disappeared into the mêlée of shoppers. I stand still in the middle of Grafton Street until the snow begins to settle on my elf tunic epaulettes. I try to catch a glimpse of the blond mini skater boy, but with no luck.

'Party,' I wonder to myself, looking distrustfully at the envelope lying between the bottles of Jingle Gin.

It is as I glance at the bottles that I realise I am being as narrow-minded as the people refusing my free product. Perhaps good things do come for free now and again. Not that I really think Jingle Gin is good as such, but this party . . . who knows?

I rest the tray on top of the nearest litterbin and lean against it while I open the envelope. Inside there is a single piece of aqua-coloured shiny cardboard with a message written in silver-embossed calligraphy. Only two words are scribed by hand, at the top of the invitation. *Milly Armstrong.* Joe did know who I was. I read on.

> *You are cordially invited to the premiere screening and after-show party to celebrate the release of the documentary* WATER WINGS *at this year's Irish Documentary Film Festival on 25 November. The film screens at 8.30 p.m. with champagne reception preceding. Dress smart.*

I turn the card over and read the details of the evening's events along with the map of where the premiere is taking place. I re-read the invitation countless times, scanning the street around me in between reads for a glimpse of my young delivery boy.

'Who are you?' I whisper aloud to the invitation. 'Why did you send him to find me?'

350

I glance up and down the street one more time before my gaze focuses once more on my own reflection in the nearest shop window. *If I had to wear a stupid costume like that in public I'd be feeling like a right eejit. I mean, that hat is just sad, like, totally shite.* Joe's voiced observations echo in my head and I start to giggle. I then start to laugh, feeling the pressure of the past year releasing from my tight shoulders. He is right, I do look like an eejit, and I am very glad he told me so. A thrill of rebellion races up from my pixie boots and I grasp the envelope between my now numb fingers. Joe, the invitation, the film festival, they are all part of a mystery that has just presented itself to me when I was in danger of sinking into a rut. Hey, it may amount to nothing, but heaven knows I need a bit of fun. After all, it is nearly Christmas. I glance quickly around me and then tip the contents of my Jingle Gin tray into the bin, closely followed by the tray itself and my now defunct singing hat.

'Jingle all the way,' I whistle aloud.

I then turn on my pixie heels and skip off down snow-covered Grafton Street with the invitation firmly clenched in both hands.

# CHAPTER THIRTY-TWO

## *Go With the Flow*

By the time I reach the flat, my bravado has dwindled somewhat, especially after having experienced the wrath of my Jingle Gin boss. He wanted me to explain exactly how I was mugged for both my product and my musical hat in broad daylight in Dublin's busiest shopping street during the Christmas shopping season.

'Personally, I blame the parents,' I tutted in response before legging it out of the door, miraculously with my pay packet intact.

I pour myself a glass of warm red wine from Fi's collection, find a bar of half-eaten chocolate in the fridge and relax into the sumptuous sofa with the invitation resting on the cushion beside me. I read it again several times and wonder how Joe could have possibly known where I would be today. How did he find me in the centre of Dublin? Granted, there were not many hotpant-wearing elves in Grafton Street as far as I could see, but how would he have known what job I was doing? I didn't even know myself until I got there this morning. I peer at the clock. Six thirty. I have two hours until the party starts if I am planning to attend. I would have to decide what to wear and how to get there, and of course then there is the whole issue of whether I look like a loser going to a film launch party without a date. Jumping out of a scabby taxi with my best high-street outfit on and nothing but fresh air on my arm as my chaperon is not exactly how I dreamed of attending my first premiere. Then again, it is not *my* premiere, it is just *a* premiere to which I have been invited, and it probably beats sitting at home watching reruns of Christmas comedies that weren't funny the first time around, never mind twenty Christmases later. I call Fi's mobile; she will know what to do.

'Go,' Fi says immediately when I explain about the invitation. 'Jaysus knows you need a bit of a gas, Milly, and anyhow, you've not got any work tomorrow from the sounds of it.'

'True,' I giggle, glugging back a second glass of wine. 'I think I've well and truly blown it on that front.'

'Ah, feck'em, Milly, it's nearly Christmas.'

'So people keep telling me.'

'And you deserve a good time. This party definitely sounds intriguing, like.'

'But what if it turns out to be Dan Clancy playing a trick on me?'

'What? That eejit is too thick to come up with something like that, and to be honest, I don't think you're on top of his list of party invites. Sure his film won't be out for ages, so it can't be that.'

'You're right,' I reply slowly, 'and this does specifically say it is a documentary festival not a movie festival.'

'So now you should get yourself there. I'd be there before you could say free bubbly if I could, it'll be deadly.'

'Where are you, by the way, Fi? It sounds really noisy in the background.'

'Ah, nowhere special. I'm just out with Dave and Mac and some of the lads, you know.'

A flash of self-pity tugs at my heart as I picture them all chatting over smooth pints of Guinness around a roaring peat fire in Gallagher's Bar. The strongest pull on my heartstrings is the thought of Mac, whom I have had no contact with since I left County Donegal. I suddenly feel lonelier than I have done since the night Dan and Matthew broke the news to me about the movie. I break off a chunk of chocolate and quietly nibble it.

'Go to the premiere, Milly,' Fi says firmly as if sensing my feelings. 'I don't want to hear that you sat there all night alone watching shite TV. Get yourself all done up, wear that wild sexy dress you wore on your last night here and go and have a ball. You deserve it.'

I make agreeable noises down the phone.

'I'll be up in a day or two and you can tell me all about it,' Fi continues. 'Go to the party, Milly, you won't regret it.'

I step out of the taxi at Temple Bar and stand in the middle of the cobbled street smoothing down the folds of my dress. The bright oranges and pinks of the fabric look suddenly out of place on a dreary, slushy night in the centre of Dublin, and I am, after all, no longer a surf chick. I am regretting my decision already.

'I should have worn black,' I tell myself, glancing forlornly at my pink shoes and matching pink bag.

I feel self-conscious and glaringly conspicuous standing out here alone. Like a solitary Christmas cracker with no one around to pull it. I peer up and down the street but the taxi has already sped off to pick up the next extortionate Christmas-season fare, and my chances of hailing another from here range between rare and impossible. Staring at the glass entrance to the Irish Film Centre, I summon all the self-confidence I have ever possessed and yank open the door. I try hard to dispel all stereotypes of lone cinema-goers from my mind. I am not sad, I am just . . . a film buff.

The sign above the ticket desk in the spaciously trendy reception area reads *Water Wings SOLD OUT*. I grimace at the young man behind the counter and explain that I did not realise I had to purchase a ticket before the showing.

'No bother at all,' he smiles, nodding as I flash the shiny

invitation. 'You won't be needin' a ticket with that thing there, you're a special guest.'

My invisible peacock feathers are sufficiently smoothed by this treatment.

'It's a mighty film,' he adds conspiratorially. 'I'm after seeing some of it at the sound check. I love the part when . . . ah, but you probably know already.'

'No, I haven't . . .'

'Well, I'll just let you enjoy the showing. You must be dead excited like.'

'Mmm.'

I feign dead excitement and drift away to the busy bar area of the reception in confusion. Are people staring at me, or is it just my paranoia as a singleton at a party? Is it just me, or is everyone else in this crowd dressed in various shades of black while my own colour scheme screams loudly for attention? Should I mingle or should I just grab a drink and play the wallflower? Not a discreet-blend-into-the-background wallflower in my case, of course, but a bloody great bouquet of Birds of Paradise. I shouldn't have come. I should have stayed at home with crap TV and chocolate and wine. That is far preferable to standing alone in a crowd of people who all have things to say to one another while waiting to see a documentary I have absolutely no interest in. Honestly, I don't think there is even a popcorn machine.

'Champagne, madam?' asks a stunningly attractive young waiter with a skilled flourish of a silver tray.

'Ooh yes, thanks.'

I enthusiastically grab a flute of champagne that is even pinker than my shoes.

'Pink champagne, how cool,' I smile, holding the glass up to the light.

The young man smiles and leans his head towards me.

'Down that one quick and I'll let you have another one, they're free.'

I start to gulp and return his mischievous grin when he hands me a second flute.

'I loved the film, by the way,' he adds before returning his gorgeous self to the throng of party-goers.

'Shame,' I sigh quietly, 'I wouldn't have minded being a wallflower if he wanted to join me.'

I sip my champagne and cast my eye around the bar. The crowd is not an average cinema audience. There are no rowdy, excitable children or casual young people slurping from oversized plastic cups of Pepsi. Everyone here looks smart and self-assured, as if they are here for a purpose. The majority I would estimate are aged between twenty-five and fifty, and most are engaged in intense conversations that I can tell from the body language are more in-depth than whether Johnny Depp (who I doubt is in it, of course) gets his kit off in the film or whether they should go for a curry after the showing. The bar has the aura of one big business meeting, with tongues and probably wallets loosened by the free-flowing champagne and pints of Guinness. So this is what a film festival looks like. At last I get to see one from the inside. I only wish they were interested in me.

Just as I am beginning to lose myself in a reverie I have enjoyed many times before about this being my film pre-miere, a bell sounds from the far corner of the reception and we are all informed that the first ever showing of the long-awaited documentary *Water Wings* will begin as soon as we have taken our seats. I suppose I would not classify this afternoon as sufficiently long to make the film 'long awaited' from my point of view, but I am nevertheless tingling with anticipation as I am swept up by the crowd. No longer con-spicuous by my lack of friends, I exchange smiles with strangers as we mount the stairs to the auditorium.

'Your seat is here, madam,' bows the man from the ticket desk, suddenly appearing at my side.

I thank him and slip into the wide, comfortable seat next to the stairs that sweep down to the front of the cinema. The chatter of voices continues for a few minutes until the lights dim and we are plunged into darkness. The sound system is crisp and clear and I feel as if I am in the ocean when the unmistakable rumble of breaking waves blasts out from the concealed speakers. There is the high-pitched sound of a dolphin and the whistle of a swirling wind before the opening credits appear on the screen.

*Water Wings*, I mouth in the darkness, *a unique surfing documentary . . . by Dave Brennan.*

# CHAPTER THIRTY-THREE

## *Floating*

'*You wouldn't have a pair of water wings, would you? I'm not too good at floating,*' says the girl in the opening scene, who is shivering nervously at the water's edge.

'You won't need them,' her instructor smiles reassuringly. 'We'll soon have you flying along those waves.'

I stare at the screen. The images reach out and draw me into the film like one of those 3D movies in a theme park only without the need for the ridiculous plastic glasses. In fact, these images are more than 3D. They reach through my brain and touch my soul. I instantly recognise the characters and I know that beach. I remember the fear gripping the girl as she took to the water for the first time. I even know the next line.

'God bless this surfboard and all who sink on her.'

The girl in the film is me.

The next hour passes in a blur as I witness three of the most memorable months of my life unravelling on the big screen before my eyes. There is the first wave I ever caught, which is visually nothing more than a few seconds of gripping on to the rails of the board for dear life before tumbling into the whitewater but which I remember as a moment of euphoria at having conquered my fear. Tears stream silently down my face when the camera zooms in on Mac sweeping me into his arms on the beach, a triumphant smile on his handsome face. Our first hug, the first of many. Our self-consciousness immediately after our public display of the affection we had not yet admitted to. There is the night with the injured dolphin, which causes most of the audience to gasp and cheer. The discreet sniffs around the auditorium are evidence that some are moved to tears. The camera pierces the darkness, showing Mac and me struggling to free the dolphin before we stroke and coax him back to his family. It is strange looking at my own actions through another person's eyes. I hear my voice but hardly recognise it. I become aware of facial expressions and hand movements that I never knew were part of my character. Most strange of all, I see how people see me. I especially see how Mac sees me, his emerald eyes following my movements intensely from scene to scene. Time after time, the camera witnesses our interaction – how we smile at each other, how Mac encourages me, and how we hug and touch at every celebratory moment. I never knew that was how we looked when we were together. Bloody hell, our love and affection for each other was so obvious. Just not from the inside . . . until it was too late. My heart pounds so loudly in my chest at our visible chemistry that I begin to fear I will be asked to leave the cinema for causing a disturbance. I then realise that I know the ending. I know how things turn sour between us and how we have not spoken since, and my heartbeat becomes a dull thud. My tears continue to flow.

The documentary is so beautifully filmed that I can hardly believe it is the product of Dave's trusty little video camera. County Donegal is shown in all its rich green glory, with the images of the cliffs and beaches perfectly complemented by powerful shots of the mountains at sunset. There are flashbacks to the history of surfing in Ireland, bringing the sport to the present day where it is still regarded as out of the ordinary.

'People don't surf in Ireland, do they?' says one Dublin man questioned on camera.

'No, no, no, you have to go to California to do that,' comments another.

'And girls can't surf anyway, it's only for boys,' adds the first, raising a laugh from the audience.

Fi and Mac are interviewed seated on the familiar stone bench on the headland where I sat many a time to watch the ocean. Fi talks about how and why we came to learn to surf. Mac explains the learning curve for the girl who almost drowned as a child and has a fear of water, trying to become a surfer in only a few weeks. (Thankfully, he has the decency to leave out the potty story.) We then see brief images of the children taking part in the cross-border surfing scheme, and incredible footage of Mac surfing his twenty-foot barrel on the day I thought I had lost him for ever. Of course, in the end I did not need the ocean to do that job for me; I managed to lose him all by myself.

Suddenly we are pulled into the climax of the film. The day I stood on the beach alone with my shiny new surfboard, preparing to paddle out and catch the wave that will prove what I have managed to achieve. I feel nervous all over again, almost wondering whether this time I will drown or whether I will catch that wave.

*'I feel like a five-year-old going into her first ballet exam,'* I whisper along with my own words coming out of the speakers. *'I feel scared and unprepared, but this is it, this is the moment.'*

'Do you think she'll do it?' whispers the elegant white-haired man sitting beside me.

'I hope so,' I whisper back, a smile playing on my lips.

'God, so do I, so do I. I'll die if she doesn't do it.'

I settle happily into my seat and immerse myself in the final scene. I watch it as though the girl is a stranger, willing her to succeed. She paddles, she wipes out, and the audience gasps en masse in genuine dismay. Gosh, that looked painful. Did I really emerge unscathed from underneath that mountain of water? She paddles back out and gives the thumbs-up. On the beach, her instructor Cormac Heggarty prays that she will be OK.

'Bring her back to me, Kanaloa,' he whispers to his Hawaiian god of the sea, his emotion audible.

I did not know he said that. That he had prayed to the Tiki god he and Nicky brought back from Hawaii. The one I held in my hands the day we kissed. I am really crying now. Sniffs and sobs fill the auditorium, some even sounding too masculine to be coming from the women. The orchestral soundtrack by the Irish band Kila is infectious, helping to create the already explosive atmosphere and making my skin tingle. On the screen, the girl turns and paddles for the wave; she takes off, the board almost in freefall. I knew it was bigger than two feet on the day. The wave looks enormous against me. She makes it, she is up and riding. The music builds, the tension is almost tangible. At the last moment a dolphin leaps into the air and plunges over the board and back into the water. The scene is purely magical. The audience cheer and jump to their feet all around me. A standing ovation! They love it, they really love it.

*Water Wings,* the screen proudly declares, *the story of an ordinary girl who reached for the stars . . . and flew to them . . . THE END . . .*

The lights flood the auditorium, and without knowing it I also find myself on my feet, applauding and cheering with the rest of the crowd.

'Fantastic!' my neighbour shouts, pulling me into an impromptu hug. 'Jaysus, my heart was going like a train. Glory be to God, it's you. It's YOU!'

I laugh as he clasps both hands to his lightly wrinkled cheeks in surprise.

'I was sitting next to the star all along. Look, everyone, it's Milly!'

Hundreds of pairs of searching eyes turn on me and I am

suddenly being hugged, patted, kissed and applauded from all sides.

'Well done!'

'Dead on!'

'Great job!'

'That was deadly!'

'Here's my card.'

I look down to see business cards of identical shape and size but of differing colour and font being thrust into my hands.

'Call me, I can find you work no bother,' says a voice to my right.

'I'm from the Discovery Channel, we could use you,' calls another anonymous voice to my left.

My head is whirling. Is this another of my actress dreams that I promised to give up when I returned from Donegal? But it feels so real. I want this to be real.

'Come on now, people, don't crowd the star,' laughs a very familiar voice from somewhere in the throng.

The crowd parts like the Red Sea, revealing in its centre my very favourite redhead. She might not be as statuesque as Moses, but heaven knows she has his presence.

'Fi,' I cry, 'what are you doing here? How did this happen? Did you know about this all along?'

'Stop, stop,' Fi giggles, 'or I'll be getting you a job as a quizmaster.'

We hug tightly and I feel a sense of relief and happiness at being with my best friend once more. When we pull apart, both of us have tears in our eyes.

'I've missed you, Fi,' I sniff.

'Ah, ya big eejit, I've missed you too,' she sniffs in response. 'Now away you go and stop messing up my make-up.'

Fi takes my hand, makes our excuses to the crowd and leads me down the stairs to a group of people gathered at the front of the auditorium. I immediately recognise Dave, who is engrossed in a conversation with two people who look suspiciously like the Men in Black, except one is a woman.

'I don't think we should interrupt,' I whisper to Fi.

'Don't be daft, they're gagging to meet you.'

Dave greets his petite girlfriend with an uninhibited kiss on her freckled nose before they all turn to face me.

'Ladies and gentlemen,' Fi announces dramatically, 'may I present Miss Milly Armstrong.'

I nudge her and self-consciously step forward to shake hands with the couple, whose suits are so sharp their collars could cut through glass. They introduce themselves as the directors of a prestigious film production company based in Dublin.

'The best film production company in the country,' Fi adds out of the corner of her mouth.

'We loved the documentary, Miss Armstrong,' the woman begins.

'Oh, call me Milly, please. But honestly, I had nothing to do with the making of this, it was all down to Dave here.'

Dave grins proudly at me but remains silent.

'We are well aware of Mr Brennan's creative skills,' the woman continues. 'We have been for quite some time.'

'Really? I thought he was just playing around,' I hear myself say.

The people around me titter in amusement.

'Not at all, Milly. Dave here is a very promising young filmmaker. His work has soul, you know, which is why we have just entered negotiations with him to produce a film for us. For a fee, of course.'

'Well that's great,' I reply, wondering what all this has to do with me.

The man then takes the speaking role.

'We have had our ears to the grapevine and have been eagerly awaiting *Water Wings*, and what we see is even better than we expected. We would now like to go into production of a film about the cross-border surfing scheme featuring Mr Heggarty, and also with yourself as the presenter.'

'You have incredible presence on screen, Milly,' the woman says sincerely.

'And you are even more beautiful in the flesh,' the man adds without a hint of sleaziness.

My eyes are jumping from one to the other, trying to absorb their compliments and to make sense of all this information.

'We also have many other commissions from television networks which would be perfect for you,' says the woman in black, 'but we would of course go through your agent.'

'Oh,' I groan, images of a furious-faced Gerald rushing through my mind, 'I don't think—'

'Who I must say,' she continues, 'is doing a grand job tonight.'

My head whips around to follow her gaze. Dear God, tell me Gerald isn't here. The only person I can see is Fi, who has now moved on to talk to yet another suited and booted gentleman.

'We will have no qualms in dealing with Miss O'Reilly,' the man smiles. 'She is very professional.'

A smile plays on the corners of my mouth. Fiona, my agent? Well why ever not? She certainly has the gift of the gab, and if anyone knows me well it is Fi. As for being supportive, Fi makes me believe in myself more than I ever imagined I could. I press my lips together and turn back to the conversation.

'Delighted to meet you, Milly,' the woman, who is clearly the one in charge, concludes, 'and don't worry, we will be in touch. We think you will all make a wonderful team, travelling the world together and making documentaries for us.'

I shake their hands and stare in awe as they sweep away through the now dispersing audience. Commissions? Presenting? Films? Travelling the world together?

'Have I just got myself a job?'

'Ya most certainly have,' says Dave, resting his arm on my trembling shoulders.

'Have I just got myself a job travelling around the world with you lot making films?'

'Sounds about right, Milly. After Ireland I say we make a big-wave tow-in surfing film in Hawaii, and then we could stop in Barbados for smaller waves, and you know we could maybe drop in on Fi's da if she fancies it.'

I smile, overcome by the thrill of it all.

'It's deadly you'll be with us, and if you ask me it's about bloody time you got a break.'

'I'll second that,' Fi grins, popping up beside me. 'You've got far too much talent to waste on flogging shite drinks to people in Grafton Street.'

I place my hands on my hips and grin at them both.

'Now just a minute, you two, how did you pull all this together?'

They go on to explain how Dave had been planning the film since the day he heard of our trip to County Donegal. He had been dabbling in filmmaking for years and had even had short documentaries shown on RTE television, but this was to be his greatest work yet and he was determined to have the documentary showcased at the prestigious film festival.

'I couldn't exactly fail with all the adventures yous two put us through, could I?' Dave laughs, giving me what must be my hundredth hug of the night.

'Gosh, and I just thought you were playing around with the camera, Dave,' I reply apologetically. 'I'm afraid I didn't even take you seriously.'

Dave shrugs. 'And Fi thought we should keep it quiet as a surprise for ya after the last film fuck-up, so we've been workin' away to get it done and make it good. It's taken a long time but I think it was worth the wait.'

'Absolutely. It is not just good, it's fantastic. Amazing.

Oh, and thank God you left out the scene from the swimming pool. I would have had to kill you otherwise.'

'I guessed that,' Fi giggles. 'So then we employed little Joe to deliver the invite. He's Dave's brother Michael's son from here in Dublin. You know when we caught Dave sending those tapes from the post office? Well, that was who he was sending them to.'

'Little Joe, the yellow-blond hair,' I whistle, pointing at Dave's own sleek blond locks. 'I knew it looked familiar.'

'And I knew you were working in town, so I took a chance on you being easy to spot like.'

I chuckle and raise my eyes to the ceiling.

'I suppose little Joe told you about—'

'The hotpants,' they hoot in unison.

'Jaysus, what a feckin' shocker,' Fi adds with a snort. 'You're well out of that.'

Once they have finished splitting their sides at the thought of my humiliating daywear, I reach for one of Fi's hands and then squeeze one of Dave's.

'Thank you both,' I say with complete sincerity. 'You are the best friends anyone could have.'

'Ah, don't go getting all soppy now, Milly, I'll start weeping again.'

I wink at Fi, whose eyes radiate a deep happiness. She smiles back.

'Thank you,' I say again, 'and well done, Dave, you should be very proud. This is going to make you a star.'

'I am proud,' Dave nods, blushing slightly, 'but I couldn't have done it without you and Mac. The pair of you were electric.'

The sound of Mac's name makes my smile instantly disappear. My heart quickens from a trot to a fast run.

'How is Mac?' I ask, my voice breaking.

Dave lifts his eyes and looks behind me.

'Why don't ya ask him yourself? After all, he'll be a big part of our world-travellin' team too.'

The fast run becomes a gallop until I feel as if my heart is charging around my chest trying to break free. My whole body stiffens so that I cannot even turn my neck independently of my shoulders. I glance nervously at Fi, who nods, takes Dave's hand and silently walks away. I gulp and inhale the slightly musty aroma of the dimly lit auditorium. As I slowly turn, the smell softens when I breathe in the familiar scent of a man I once kissed who carries the wonderful fresh aroma of the ocean with him wherever he goes. I squeeze my eyes shut, silently wishing, but also not knowing what to do if my wishes come true. I open my eyes.

Mac stands just inches from me, his body for once clothed in smart city wear. I lift my chin. He looks uncomfortable, probably because of the uncharacteristic crisp shirt and tie as much as because he is looking down at the girl who strutted into his life and asked for his help before taking his heart and stamping on it. What was it Dave said? *Mac only concerns himself with the people that matter.* He concerned himself with me, so I must have mattered, but that was before . . .

'Mac,' I breathe, hardly able to speak.

'Milly,' he replies, his mouth not displaying any hint of a smile.

What am I supposed to say now? *How are you? I am sorry I dumped you at a shot for a wanker called Dan Clancy? Looks like we're going to be working together so let's just get along? I have dreamt about you every night since I got home and also most days when I am not even asleep?* My nails dig nervously into my own palms and the euphoria I felt at being adored by the cinema audience melts away under the heat of his gaze. In an instant I realise that, ego-boosting though that kind of public adoration is, it is not worth nearly as much as the adoration I crave from this one man. I want him to adore me the way I now know I adore him. I would give up all the fame and fortune I dreamed of for this one man. For Mac Heggarty.

'I . . .' I begin, but my voice box is unresponsive. A tear drips out of the corner of my eye.

*I don't know how to make this better. I don't know how to make you love me.*

Mac continues to look at me, but his eyes soften and I see a brief flash of the real man beneath the hard exterior.

'I . . .' I try again, but I can only manage an inaudible squeak.

Mac runs his hands through his hair and clasps them around the back of his muscular neck. He tilts his head from side to side as if warming up for intensive exercise. He appears stressed and suddenly unsure of himself. He places his fingers inside his shirt collar and runs them along towards the buttons. I smile faintly. Mac must be the only man I know who is more at home in neoprene than normal clothes.

'You don't like that suit, do you?' I say in an attempt to break the ice.

'Feckin' hate it,' he tuts. 'Give me a wetsuit any day.'

*Give me you in a wetsuit any day.*

'You look very attractive, though,' I add, my eyes shooting towards the floor in embarrassment.

There is a pause before I hear Mac reply.

'And you look more beautiful than I remember, Milly. Even more beautiful than in my dreams.'

I whip my head up and find his eyes with mine. I rapidly search them for his true feelings, for how he truly feels about me. They are so overpowering, I have never seen eyes so green. Mac steps closer, our eye contact never breaking. I gasp as I feel him take my hand in his, but I don't want to look away in case when I look back he has retreated into himself again.

'I'm sorry, Mac,' I say almost in a whisper, but he is so close now the words sound loud between us. 'You were so good to me and I let Dan . . . you know, after he had already dumped me once.'

*There, I have said it.*

'And he didn't champion me to be in that film at all, and if you must know, he hasn't even got a big pe—'

With the other hand, Mac places a finger on my lips. I swallow and fall silent. My lips sizzle under his touch.

'Don't,' he urges me, 'let's leave him in the past.'

I blink.

'God, I've missed you, Milly,' he continues, his words drowning out all other sounds in the auditorium. 'Nothing is the same without you now. The town seems so quiet and pointless. I don't have the same adventures I had when you were around. Even the ocean seems different. I can't surf without thinking about you and it drives me mad. Unbelievable, I tell myself. No one has ever interrupted my thoughts when I'm surfing before, it just doesn't happen. But you, Milly, you are everywhere. I can't stop thinking about you and hearing you and feeling you inside my head.'

I stare at him, the man who is usually so economical with words, especially when those words are to express his feelings. The tears are now streaming down my face but I don't try to wipe them away. I take a chance and slide my arms around Mac's firm waist, pulling myself into his warm body. I pray that he won't push me away. Mac sighs as if battling with his own emotions. He places a hand on my head and runs it down the back of my hair to the nape of my neck.

'And that,' he whispers, 'is how I know.'

I lift my head, his hand still cupping the back of my neck, and look up at him with a frown.

'How you know what, Mac?'

'How I know,' he begins before stopping to inhale, 'how I know that you mean more to me than anything else in this world, even more than the entire ocean. That is how I know . . . that I am in love with you, Milly Armstrong.'

Our kiss is even more electric than the first time. I kiss

him passionately as if this will be the last time. I know it won't be. My body melts into his and my tears metamorphose into tears of happiness rather than of sadness and fear.

*Merry Christmas, Milly!* my heart whoops.

'At feckin' last!' I hear from the crowd around us.

We pull apart, both of us laughing, and I scan the faces of the people still left in the auditorium. The suits have gone and the people who remain are all as familiar to me as if they were family. There is of course Fi and Dave, looking very much the couple in love. Beside them are two people who look like my parents, but no, they couldn't possibly be. I race forward and throw my arms around my mother and father, who are both crying in public. A rarity for a barrister and an accountant, believe me.

'Mum, Dad, what are you doing here?'

'You know,' my father grins, 'just checking up on that publishing house job of yours, pudding.'

'Oh,' I cringe, 'I lied.'

'We know.' He winks.

'And we don't care,' says my mother with a quivering voice, 'because you've done it, Milly. You've really done it. Hasn't she, Frank?'

'She bloody well has, Georgina,' my father cries proudly, 'she bloody well has.'

I hug them again before stepping back and trying to regain my composure. Mac grasps my hand tight and I wipe my blurred vision with the other. I see Podraig and Mary, Colleen and Barry, Johnny and the beautiful Onya, Kathleen (who is giggling helplessly at the sight of her eldest brother snogging in public), Siobhan and Danny or it could be Noel, Sinead and Noel or that might be Danny, Adam, Malachi and . . . goodness, how can I be expected to remember the names of all the others? Even Joyce from Joyce's Fashion Emporium stands happily at the end of the line, a vision in knitted peach.

Mary steps forward, for once without a floral print in sight, and crosses her arms across her ample bosom.

'Well now,' she tuts, 'I'd say it's about time you two cubs got together.'

I squeeze Mac's hand behind my back, amused by how Mary can still consider her strapping lifeguard son to be a cub.

'I was about ready to bang your heads together for yous so I was, and as for our Mac mopin' about the place . . . Holy God, I'm glad this film came out when it did, or he would have forgotten how to smile.'

'Good on ya,' Podraig cheers. 'Let's have a whiskey ta celebrate.'

'Good call, Podraig,' my father chirps loudly.

'Kiss her again!' Kathleen hoots.

'Aye, kiss her again,' Mary joins in.

I turn to Mac, the ice between us now totally melted by the warmth of such a wonderful family. He strokes a hand gently down my cheek.

'You're still crying, Milly. Are you sad?'

'No,' I reply quickly, thinking back to my conversation with little Joe earlier in the day that led me here in the first place. 'I'm not sad. Not any more.'

I have my man, I have great friends, and it looks as though I at last have a job in the film industry. Not the job I thought I would have, but, you know, this one sounds even more of a challenge. No, I am not sad. I just blossomed late, like that oak tree Joe told me about.

Mac bends down and kisses my tears with his soft lips.

'Any more of those,' he smiles, 'and you'll drown us all.'

'Good job there's a lifeguard in the building then.'

I shiver with pleasure as he kisses my other cheek.

'I would rescue you any day, Milly.'

'You already have, Mac.'

The next time we kiss, I am smiling inside and out and I allow myself to relax into my feeling of utter contentment.

Just when I thought my life was in danger of becoming a treacherous sea, tonight came along to turn the tide. Nine months ago, when I auditioned for that film, I did reach for my star, and at last I have grasped it with both hands. I guess all I really needed to help me get there was wings. In this case, water wings.

**Other bestselling Time Warner Paperbacks titles available by mail:**